THE BUTTERFLY WITCH

A STANDALONE ETHEREAL WORLD NOVEL

E. L. WILLIAMS

Bramble Leaf
BOOKS

ISBN: 978-1-0686673-3-6

For my mum, Joy

ALSO BY E. L. WILLIAMS

The Ethereal World Duology

The First Ethereal

The Blessing of Crows

Standalone Ethereal World Novels

The Magic Keepers

The Butterfly Witch

"Time is too slow for those who wait,
Too swift for those who fear,
Too long for those who grieve,
Too short for those who rejoice;
But for those who love, time is not."

— HENRY VAN DYKE

PART I

1612

CHAPTER 1

GWEN, 1ST SEPTEMBER 1612

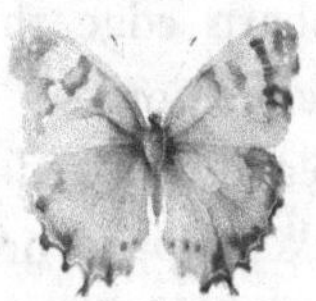

Tân planted his feet a heartbeat before I twitched the reins. I sighed, my breath misting in the crisp morning air before drifting lazily into the still-waking sky.

'Right again,' I laughed, letting the reins slip from my fingers. 'Don't you ever get bored of being so clever?'

I leaned forward in my saddle and wrapped my arms around his wide neck. He was the colour of midnight. Coal black but for two hidden white stars – one under his forelock, the other tucked under the breastplate on his chest.

We always stopped somewhere along this stretch of the mountain, and granted, the top meadow was my favourite, but despite never choosing the same spot twice, he always guessed.

I rubbed lazy circles on his chest as I drank in the rich, musky scent that was earth and sky, fire and water and, above all else, spirit. Who needed flower waters; this was the best perfume in the world.

I gazed at the Nefoedd valley. It looked like the Goddess herself had thrown down an enormous picnic blanket and filled it with delights for our eyes to feast on. The silver ribbon of the Usk meandered through a patchwork of thick emerald forests, rolling green hills and golden fields under the watchful gaze of the Black Mountains in the distance. And Tân and I had explored every glorious inch.

The day was new, only an hour old if you counted from sunrise. There was a chill in the air, a reminder that the dawn had also delivered a new month. September was here, benign for now but with a sharp edge that reminded me that summer would soon be a memory.

How different the meadow looked now, the heather faded to soft mauve, the bracken tipped bronze and curling, and even the grasses fading to gold. The wildflowers, save for a few determined harebells, all spent – their seeds long scattered to the earth, waiting patiently for the spring.

I sat up and glanced over my shoulder to make sure my cloak was still covering Tân's flanks. The cold did cruel things to old bones, and he would be nineteen this year.

Satisfied, I turned and watched a thin, ethereal mist swirl across the valley floor. Nain called it dragon's breath, and it was easy to believe, such was the magic of this place. The pink light of dawn streaked a fragile cornflower-blue sky as wisps of clouds drifted like half-remembered dreams.

The moth-white quarter moon had not yet retired, as if it too wanted to linger and marvel at this new day. As I watched, a white-tailed eagle swooped into view, then dived to the valley floor, disappearing into the mist. Was she looking for dragons too?

This was my home. The place I'd taken my first breath and the place I'd take my last, although I hoped that wouldn't be for a long time yet. My father's family came from over the border in England, but my mother's line went all the way back to the Welsh kings. According to my grandmother, Nain, the Llewellyns were as much of this place as the river and mountains in the distance.

I drank in the beauty before me, imagined the power of it coursing through my veins and settling in my bones, delivering my long-awaited magic. This had been my mother's land, and sometimes, when the wind was soft and willing to be generous, I could almost hear her voice – or at least, what I imagined it might have been.

I cleared my throat, trying to dispel the emotion pebbled there. The dragon's breath had me in its thrall. Nain called it Hiraeth: a tangle of love, grief and longing that had the power to all but close my throat whenever I thought about my connection to this land.

The eagle's sharp, high-pitched cry pierced the air as she emerged from the mist. *Klee-klee-klee.* I took a deep breath, glad of the distraction.

Tân turned his head and fixed me with a look I knew all too well.

I groaned. 'Aww, not yet, please. She's already going to have my hide for not practising that floating spell.'

Tân didn't so much as blink.

I tried another tack. 'You don't understand, Tân. It'll be, "Gwenllian Llewellyn, this is in your blood, child. Stop thinking yourself out of the magic you were born to."'

I parroted the words, doing what I thought was a passably good impression of my grandmother's imperious tone. 'Honestly, I'm almost as old as you, Tân, and she still speaks to me like I'm a babe in arms.'

Tân remained unmoved.

I sighed and felt the resistance drain out of me. He was right. He was always right, annoying as that was. Oh, to be as wise as a horse.

The saddle creaked as I leaned forward and wrapped my arms around him. He was my everything. The rock that held me firm. The shoulder I wailed into when the world seemed set against me. From the time I could walk, his stall was the first place I ran to when I needed to hide.

How many times had Nain found me like a nestling in Tân's straw bed, his enormous head and neck encircling my tiny body and as powerful to me as any castle's keep? I still remembered my furious sobs and pounding fists as she carried me back to my bed.

Tân turned slowly, without my needing to say a word. His pace was unhurried. Deliberate. He'd deliver me home, but there'd be no rush about it.

'Maybe we can sneak out later and catch the sunset,' I said as my body rocked with the motion of his steps. I tied up the reins and let them rest on his withers. Tân's ears twitched back. We both knew the chances of that happening were almost non-existent, but the possibility of it, no matter how slim, gave me an ember of hope to see me through another day I'd fill with failing. My mother would be turning in her early grave if she could see me now.

I suppose it was no wonder Nain's patience wore thin sometimes. She'd raised me since the day I was born, but I could no more float a feather with a spell than fly to the moon. And yet, still she persisted. Every. Single. Endless day.

I tried. I really did. But the truth was, I had no magic. Horses didn't always breed true, so maybe magic was the same, or perhaps my mother snatched it back on the birthing bed that she'd never leave.

Tân bucked. Not enough to unseat me – that had never happened – but enough to make his point clear. I caught my breath and steadied myself, bracing my arms against his neck. He snorted, long and loud, as if emptying his huge lungs of a bad smell.

'Well, stop reading my mind then,' I grumbled.

We left the meadow, retracing our steps though the wood and following the path back down the mountain to my father's house. The air was much colder here in the shade of the trees, so I leaned back to rearrange my cloak over Tân's haunches.

Tân was just a yearling when I was born. Wild, untouchable and full of fire and fury. According to my father, the new arrival was good only for feeding to the hounds, and that might have been his fate had it not been for my mother.

It was one of the few stories my grandmother could sometimes be coaxed to retell. I loved hearing how my mother sat for hours, day after day, with the furious colt who refused to be touched. Then one day, he'd come trotting to the fence to greet her. She'd whispered to him, shown him the first swell of her belly that was me and offered to teach him how to control his fire so that it didn't consume him.

He'd accepted her help along with her love and the name Tân, 'fire' in Welsh. When she died and left me in the world as a poor substitute, he loved me, too.

I felt tears prick my eyes. Tân stopped and turned to look at me. How horses could say so much without ever uttering a word would always be a mystery to me.

'I know,' I croaked. 'My mother loved me with all her heart, or so Nain tells me.'

I swallowed hard, swiping at the tears that had escaped down my cheeks. Nothing good ever came from self-pity.

'And you're as strong as an ox and will likely outlive us all.'

Tân watched me for a moment and then nibbled the toe of my boot. 'And you're as flexible as a foal too,' I added with a little laugh.

We fell back into an easy rhythm, Tân picking his way down the steep, tree-covered path as surefooted as a mountain goat. I rocked in the saddle, listening to the wind stirring the leaves above us and watching the shadows dance across my closed eyelids as the sun found gaps in the canopy and threw us occasional sunbeams.

I opened my eyes when I felt Tân tense beneath me – a flicker of warning in his withers, though he didn't break his slow, steady pace. A stag stood frozen just a few feet away, a thin strip of velvet hanging from his impressive antlers. I dipped my head in greeting, and the stag went back to his polishing work.

At the foot of the mountain, we left the cover of the wood and joined the dirt road that connected my father's grand farmhouse and my grandmother's modest cottage. One a house, the other a home.

Reluctantly, I turned left, away from home and towards my father's house.

I could hear the yard before I saw it. The blacksmith was here. The sound of his hammer on iron was enough to wake the dead. My father's horses would take the best part of the day to get through, so with any luck, the stables would be in a state of organised chaos and I could slip in and out again without being noticed.

I heard the carter's booming voice over the clang of iron. Even better! With any luck, Cook would have invented an excuse to storm out there and complain about something ordered and not delivered for the kitchen. The hammer fell silent.

'You will not!' Right on cue, Cook's voice, stuffed full of indignation, barrelled down the lane. I smirked. She needed to work a bit harder if she really wanted everyone to believe she hated the man. Anyone with eyes could see how perfectly suited they were. Both in their middling years, alone in the world after losing their spouses – Cook's husband to the pox, and the carter's wife went the same way as my mother while delivering their tenth child.

I sighed. Maybe one day they'd drop the pretence and

take a chance on being happy again, but at this precise moment in time, their bickering would be another useful distraction.

As we turned off the lane into the yard, the picture I'd imagined in my mind crystallised into reality. My father's four hunters stood in front of the stable block, some being groomed while others dutifully lifted their feet for the stable-boys to inspect.

Cook, red-faced and flustered, was gesticulating wildly, her words lost to me under the renewed hammering, but the carter was clearly getting a dressing-down about something. By the look on his face, though, she might have been reciting love poems.

There were two things missing from the mental image I'd conjured from the sounds alone. The first was little Bryn, one of the youngest stable-boys, throwing anxious looks at Cook as he tried to shoo the geese back into the adjoining paddock.

The second was my grandmother, Mary Llewellyn, standing like a heron waiting to spear an unsuspecting fish, which would, I realised, be me. I groaned whilst trying to organise my face into a smile. She raised an eyebrow and inclined her head towards us.

Dressed head to toe in widow's black, her hands clasped serenely in front of her chest, she was everything we were told women were meant to be. Elegant. Poised. Dignified. Until she opened her mouth and you realised that she had a will of iron and, when the situation demanded it, a tongue like a lash.

She was both my tormentor and my protector, and after Tân, the person I loved most in the world.

'I see you have been leading my one and only grand-daughter astray again, Tân,' Nain said to the horse as she rubbed the white star hidden under his forelock. He snorted appreciatively and leaned into her hand.

'It was me leading him astray, Nain,' I said, sliding reluctantly from his back. I felt the blood rush into my thighs and rump, making them tingle, already aching to be back in the saddle.

Nain stepped forward and cupped my chin in her long fingers, turning my head gently from side to side.

'All that sunshine and still as pale as milk,' she tutted, shaking her head. 'Perhaps if you slowed down once in a while, you might give the sun a chance to catch you.'

I tried not to grin as I made to tuck a long strand of hair behind my ear, found a twig instead and flicked it away. The morning's gallop had been worth whatever little gifts the forest had left in my hair.

Nain raised an eyebrow, but I caught a twitch at the corner of her mouth. 'Come. Let this fine horse have his rest before it's his turn with the farrier. You can tell me all about what you saw before we start our lessons,' she said, touching me lightly on the back.

Mal, the stable-boy, appeared as if bidden, and I laughed as Tân's ears pitched forward. Everyone, especially the horses, knew Mal had a mysterious and almost endless supply of apples, no matter the season. A few years younger than me, he was a kind boy with gentle ways, and I trusted Tân to him without a second thought.

'Thank you,' I whispered, kissing the horse on the neck and pulling him into a quick hug. I sucked in a deep breath, then, as an afterthought, quickly rubbed the edge of my cloak against his cheek, hoping his scent might linger and see me through the day.

Mal giggled in the way only young boys can and pulled an apple from his pocket. Tân whickered, and I smiled as I watched him follow the boy into the barn.

'Now then. Gwenllian Llewellyn ...' Nain began.

Here it comes, I thought. *Lecture time.*

The sight of a stray, waddling goose caught Nain's attention, and she stopped.

'Back to the paddock, please. You don't want to get stepped on or kicked by a horse, do you,' she said softly.

The goose tilted its head and considered her for a moment before turning around and ambling back to the paddock, its flock mates following behind. At the gate, little Bryn beamed in relief.

'I thought we might try something new today, Gwen,' Nain continued as she steered me out of the yard, her hand still on the small of my back as if I, like the errant goose, needed shepherding.

I stifled a sigh and gritted my teeth as I felt my freedom slip from my fingers for another day.

CHAPTER 2

GWEN, 1ST SEPTEMBER 1612

'You're not concentrating, that's all,' Nain said as she pushed back her chair from the table. 'I'll make you some camomile,' she added, already reaching for mugs.

I let out a long breath and rolled my aching shoulders. Despite my best efforts over the last few hours, the hen's feather remained stubbornly table-bound.

The cottage, cooler than the day outside when we'd first arrived from the yard, had grown hot as the sun grew in strength, baking the fat stone walls like loaves in an oven.

I longed to go outside, to walk up to the meadow or down to the river that meandered past the lower reaches of the orchard, but those trips were for the days when my learning was listening, reciting spells and answering Nain's quick-fire questions.

On days like today, when learning meant doing things – or in my case, not doing things – that others would think impossible, we had to remain indoors, away from prying eyes and wagging tongues.

'Could we go into the garden, at least?' I ventured.

Nain shot me a withering look and went back to her tea-making.

The world has never been kind to witches, child. You'd do well to remember that. Nain hadn't spoken, but she'd said it so many times over the years that the words buzzed in my mind like late-summer wasps.

I'd never really believed the horror stories. What would they do, these people who supposedly hated witches so much? Hunt us down? Throw us out of the village? My father owned half the county, so I'd like to see them try.

People came from miles around seeking Nain's herbs and ointments. She delivered half the village into the world, and it was always Nain's door that the desperate turned to when their loved ones were beyond healing and struggling to leave it. They begged for a draught and a gentle, dignified goodbye, and no matter the hour or the weather, she'd pull her cloak from the peg, collect her bag and follow them.

I asked her once why she didn't just give them the tincture, and she said it was because in the long nights of grieving that would follow, she wanted the bereaved to have someone to blame other than themselves. Not that anyone ever had.

It's not like we were the only people with magic here, either. By my reckoning, around a tenth of Pont Nefoedd were from a magical family. Did these magic-haters intend to lock us all up? It was ridiculous.

Nain set down the mug of tea on the table in front of me. The camomile was fresh, picked at dawn no doubt to prepare for the trial of the day ahead.

I watched the steam rise, twisting and coiling in the air like a serpent. 'Maybe it's time to admit that I just don't have what you and my mother had.' I mumbled the words without thinking and instantly regretted it.

Nain spun around so quickly that the feather I'd been

trying and failing to move sailed into the air on the draught from her skirts.

Here we go, I thought, lowering my head.

'You,' Nain said, pointing at me, her eyes blazing like an angry cat's, 'have the Llewellyn bloodline. Same as me. Same as your mother, Goddess keep her. The Llewellyns have always been witches, and you are no different, my girl.'

I knew better than to argue, but I had heard this speech so many times I could recite it by heart. I was just so tired of feeling like a failure. If she would only admit the reality, then I could focus on something I was good at, like the herbs, or tending the garden.

If I'd been a boy, I'd be able to work in the stables, but I already knew that would be out of the question, which was ridiculous. I was a better rider than any boy in the village and showed more care for the horses. I felt my anger rise at the injustice, and the words came tumbling out of my mouth before I could stop them.

'But what if I'm the exception? Not all horses breed true – what if the Llewellyn magic skipped a generation?' I hated the whine in my voice and how it made me sound like a complaining child, but I needed to say this or the weight of these endless days of failure would crush me.

Nain stood staring at me, her expression caught somewhere between fury and pity. I didn't know which one I hated more. She took a deep breath and pulled out the chair opposite me.

She studied me for a long moment, her expression shifting as if caught between a smile and a frown. She looked tired, and it didn't sit well on her. Like a poorly fitted smock that gaped and pinched in all the wrong places. My anger snuffed out at the sight, and I shivered as a draught slid over my skin.

'You're exactly like her, you know. Your mother. The

raven's-wing hair and those eyes. Honey stirred with smoke, your grandfather used to say. And just as wild.' Nain smiled at that, but the sadness in her eyes brought tears to my own. I gritted my teeth. I preferred it when she shouted at me.

'Your mother's magic didn't come in until she was sixteen,' Nain said, dropping her eyes to the table between us. 'You're a bit older than she was, granted, but not everyone is born with it.'

I held my breath. In the stories I'd been told, it seemed as if my mother had been born to the craft. I bit back my question, not wanting to stem the flow of whatever new information Nain might be about to share.

'She doubted herself, just like you,' she said as a ghost of a smile pulled on her lips.

My heart picked up, fluttering like a desperate bird. I'd heard people remark on my physical resemblance, of course. 'Oh, she's the image of Catrin, isn't she?' And the way my father seemed to flinch whenever he laid eyes on me was evidence enough of that, but this new information felt like a new jewel. I tucked it into the vast, hollow space in my chest, barely daring to breathe as I willed Nain to continue.

When she stood up abruptly, I bit back my disappointment and lifted my eyes to the ceiling to ward off tears. In all my eighteen years, I had not once seen Nain cry. I'd seen her comfort the sick and the dying enough times to see how much it pained her, but throughout, her eyes remained as dry as sand. I wondered if she'd used up her store the day fate delivered her a granddaughter and took a daughter in payment.

The entire coven had attended my birth, although nobody would tell me why. When I asked, the aunts would smile sadly and tell the same part of the story. The part where Nain pulled the cord from around my neck and rubbed my back until I finally took a breath. They always stopped there, because the next part we all knew. The part where even the magic of a full coven could not save my mother as she bled to death. I will never understand what would make someone so determined to die that she couldn't even wait to hold her newborn child.

Nain cleared her throat and brushed imaginary cat hairs from her skirt. 'Magic has its own time, Gwenllian. It can be like a bolting horse one day and a timid doe the next. No amount of coaxing or pleading will make it come any quicker. But it will never arrive if you turn your back on it. You must never give up. Do you hear me?'

I nodded without looking up, my eyes tracking my finger as I traced the deep grooves in the old table. I felt something flicker into life within my chest. A tiny, fragile spark of hope that maybe she was right. Maybe I just needed to be patient. My mother waited, so maybe I could too.

When I looked up, Nain was frowning at me, but her expression was more concern than irritation.

'Let's get some air, child. You look like a wild thing caged,' she said, her tone returned to its usual briskness.

I felt a weight slip from my shoulders the moment I stepped out into the midday sunshine. I hurried to catch up to my grandmother, who was already striding down the lane towards the forest path.

Ahead, a small brown kit darted across the dusty road, and I caught up just in time to see Nain's lips move in a quiet blessing for the creature.

We usually spoke of domestic things or my so-called schooling when we walked anywhere we might be overheard. I thought it a nonsense, really, another rule invented to tie me down and keep me afraid of a wolf that had never been at the door and would likely never come calling.

Once we reached the top meadow, we would speak freely about all the things that Nain told me must stay secret, even from my father. I found that part of the rule the most ridiculous. Why couldn't we speak of magic when he himself was married to a witch and entrusted with the knowledge on their betrothal? But on that topic, Nain was resolute.

Not that it was a difficult promise to keep. My father and I barely exchanged a dozen words a week. Perhaps he might have forgiven me for killing my mother if I'd been a boy. My older brother, Thomas Llewellyn the second, was just eleven months old when he died of a fever six months before my mother.

They were buried together in the churchyard, and on my worst days, I wondered what it would be like to trade places with the brother I never knew – or give myself to the Goddess so that she could return my mother to the world and all the people who loved her so much.

Before we reached the forest path at the foot of the hill, Nain stopped abruptly.

'Wait,' she said, turning.

'Is that Cook?' I asked, squinting at the figure hurrying down the lane from the big house.

She was trying to run but was clearly struggling to catch her breath. She gave an exhausted-looking wave in our direction and then bent double, bracing her large forearms on her knees.

Nain hurried up the lane, moving at a pace my father would think unbecoming for a woman, not that he'd have dared say as much to her.

'Wenda. What happened?' Nain asked once we'd reached her.

Cook's face was even more flushed than usual, and her breaths looked hard won. There were tears in her eyes and her expression reminded me of a frightened heifer. She opened and closed her mouth, but whether to breathe or speak, I wasn't sure.

Nain placed a hand lightly on Cook's shoulder. I felt the offer of the spell like a thickening of the surrounding air, and even before she nodded, I felt her energy grab for the magic in the way a drowning man might clutch at a rescuer.

Cook's cheeks returned to their usual colour, and with her eyes closed, she sucked in a series of slow, deep breaths, making her ample bosom swell beneath the confines of her straining dress. When she opened her eyes, she looked a little less frantic than before.

'Let's have tea,' Nain said.

I stifled a groan at the thought of heading back to the cottage after only just escaping it, but Cook was in no state to climb up through the forest path to reach the meadow, and the low fields were too high with crops to see anyone approaching. Cursing Nain's paranoia, I followed them back to the cottage, my dragging feet scuffing in the dirt.

I lingered for a moment in the garden, bending down to stroke Sage, our cat, who lay lounging in the middle of the path, her white fur covered in dust and dried petals. She rolled on her back, blinking at me with the one and only eye she'd been born with.

Cook was already at the table, a mug of tea in her hands, when I entered.

'Dafydd brought news,' she said, her voice unusually tremulous. 'Terrible news.'

I slipped into the chair beside Nain.

Cook sniffed, her face crumpling and her chest heaving again.

'Take your time, Wenda,' Nain said, placing her hand on Cook's arm.

Cook took a handkerchief from her sleeve and blew her nose loudly.

'He said a messenger arrived from England. He's been travelling for weeks. He was there when they did it,' Cook said, speaking to her untouched mug, which was trembling slightly in her hands.

'Did what, Wenda?' Nain prompted gently.

When Cook looked up, her round brown eyes were wide with fear, and I felt something cold slide down my spine.

'When they hung them,' Wenda cried, before slopping down the mug and then burying her face in her hands.

'Who did they hang?' Nain asked.

When Wenda continued, her words came between hiccupping sobs.

'Twelve was accused. One poor soul died in prison before her trial, one was acquitted, but ten,' Wenda said, a sob escaping her, 'eight women and two men was hanged for witchcraft up in England, in a place called Pendle.'

CHAPTER 3

GWEN, 8TH SEPTEMBER 1612

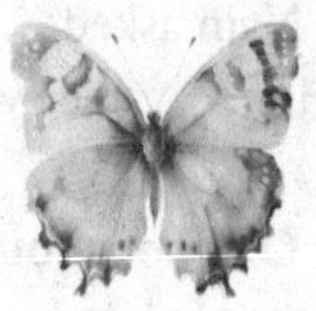

A soft, questing paw on my cheek roused me from a deep and dreamless sleep. There was a comforting weight on my chest, and as I smiled into the darkness, I felt the purr even before the sound reached my ears. Nain said a cat's purr was healing, and I didn't doubt it for a second.

'Morning, Sage,' I breathed, reaching out to stroke her head. I cracked open an eye and frowned. It was still dark – and not the waning darkness that precedes the dawn but the type still building to its peak. Sage crept closer, and the purring intensified as long whiskers tickled my chin.

I opened my eyes and reached for the thick curtain that covered the small round window above my bed. Moonlight slipped, quick as a darting fish, into the small room. Sage's purr intensified as she turned her one green saucer of an eye to the window, her paws kneading the blanket.

I heard movement downstairs and groaned. It was still two days until the full moon and our usual coven meet, which meant that Nain had something else planned.

Sage bumped her head into my cheek a few times, which I knew she meant as a sort of feline pep talk. I mumbled my thanks as I redoubled my efforts on the stroking.

When Nain sprang things like this on me, it was usually a magical test of some kind. A test I would, of course, fail miserably. I gave Sage a double ear tickle before reluctantly pulling back the blanket.

Nain's voice floated up the stairs. 'Gwenllian Llewellyn. I know you're awake, child. Rouse yourself, quickly. I'll wait outside.'

'Yes, Nain.'

I swung my legs from the warm bed and shivered. A few minutes later, still fastening my cloak around my shoulders, I stepped out into the moonlight and the smell of damp earth.

I cast about, searching for my grandmother.

'Here, child.'

I turned towards the sound and, squinting, saw Nain standing across the lane beneath an old oak tree. Had she not spoken, I would never have seen her.

She insisted the skill was invaluable and subjected me to long hours of training in the art of going unnoticed, though I never saw the point.

Nain took off towards the woods without waiting for me, her stride long and her head bowed inside her dark cloak. I followed, trying to keep my footsteps light and silent, but a dry stick cracked under my boot after just a few steps. I winced. I knew better than to ask her to slow her pace as we climbed up the wooded incline, but it was even harder than usual to keep up with her today.

Nain hadn't been herself this last week. Not since the day we met Cook in the lane. I felt awful for the people involved, but despite Nain's lengthy explanations, I still didn't see what it had to do with us. It had happened in England, and this was Wales. Things were different here. Besides, my grandmother had powerful magic, as did the other coven members, although nowhere near the same strength. Nobody would be fool enough to threaten us.

My argument had fallen on furious ears and earned me bone-achingly long lectures, so I'd taken to just nodding and agreeing with her for the sake of a quiet life.

The situation had delivered a silver lining, though, as Nain had cancelled my lessons. She spent three days away on what she'd only say was 'coven business', and on her return, she barely moved from the kitchen table, writing by candle-light long into the night, her fingers ink-stained and her brow frozen into a perpetual scowl. I didn't dare ask her about her task in case she invented a reason for me to help her with it.

As we broke from the tree-line and entered the clearing, I had to swallow the gasp that rose in my throat. If this was a coven meet, it was like nothing I'd ever witnessed before. Our usual number was just eight, but tonight, I counted close to twenty cloaked and hooded figures standing around the small fire. Whether it was the presence of strangers or something else, the atmosphere was nothing like our usual light-hearted gatherings. This felt more like a wake. I shivered and pulled my cloak around me.

Nain wasted no time. She strode into the middle of the circle and threw off her hood. I shuffled into a space between the cloaked figures, my heart pounding and my mouth dry as ashes.

'Friends,' Nain said as she prowled around the fire. 'We have come together at a time of great danger. A fever is grip-ping the world. A madness driving the murder of innocents by those who seek to either possess or destroy what they do not understand.

'These men, consumed by their lust for power or right-eousness, victimise ordinary people, sometimes just for the crime of being a woman. And now, our kind are being swept up in it too.

'I shall not defile the sanctity of our circle by naming the evils that prey on all that is sacred, but we have all sworn to protect the magic of the world – and protect it we must.

'We have already lost so much. Witches and cunning folk, just like us, forced to take their magic to the grave. Forced to break ancient vows of lineage, not out of betrayal but out of love. Love for those they sought to protect from tyranny and persecution.'

I heard someone close by sniff back tears. Opposite, two people reached simultaneously for the comfort of the other's hand. My breath hitched as the true gravity of the situation landed hard and jagged as a freshly split flint in my heart.

'It is my dearest wish that all people be spared from this madness. There is work afoot to protect the innocents, to encourage those that prey upon us to see reason, but our work here tonight is to protect the magic of the world. The spell we cast under the light of the waxing moon will enable our kin to send their magic to us for safekeeping. They, or should they not survive, one of their line, will then recall it once the danger is past. We are none of us above corruption, so as custodians of this orphaned magic we can never wield it …'

Nain's words flew past me, like leaves on the wind, snatched from my grasp. My vision blurred, and I blinked hard, but it only made it worse. Three versions of my grandmother now stalked around the fire, her words drowned out by a raging river thundering inside my head.

Suddenly unbearably hot, I fumbled with the fastening of my cloak, desperate to feel cool air on my skin, but my fingers wouldn't obey me.

Sweat erupted from every pore, and I tried to focus on my breath as panic crept its way up my throat. I felt the fastening yield, and my cloak slipped from my shoulders. Blessedly, the wind quickened, sweeping away the heat from my skin and clearing my vision.

Nain must have started the spell as the coven had begun their low, murmuring chant. I didn't know what they were saying, so just bowed my head and hoped that Nain wouldn't look my way. This was the most important coven meeting I'd ever attended, and I'd already messed it up.

I saw Nain open her arms to the sky, her lips moving furiously as a tiny thread of silver light mingled with her breath and drifted up above her head. As she spoke, the thread grew as if feeding on her words, twisting and coiling around itself until it was a shimmering orb large enough to swallow us all.

I gasped as a dazzling streak of silver burst from the chest of one of the hooded figures, shooting arrow-like into the pulsating orb. A second later, the process repeated with the next in the circle, then the next. My stomach lurched as I realised she meant us all to take part.

Why hadn't she warned me? Why had she even brought me here? I had no magic! When my turn came, there would be no silver arrow, or whatever the hell it was, for me to contribute. Everyone would know what a failure I was.

Unless … Hope burst like an eager sapling from somewhere in my core. Had she found a way to call in my magic? Was that the coven business she'd been so preoccupied with?

My blood thundered once again in my ears as I watched the spell inch ever closer. Five people away. Four. Three. Two. I would be next. This was it. My moment was finally here. I bit my lip.

The next thing I knew, I was falling.

CHAPTER 4

GWEN, 8TH SEPTEMBER 1612

I tried to scream, but the sound died in my throat, muffled by the hand pressed firmly across my mouth. A circle of faceless, hooded figures crowded around me as I lay prone on the damp forest floor. The wind picked up, rattling the trees and herding the clouds across the moon, snuffing out the light. Panic surged through me, and I thrashed against the hand at my mouth, and the second one now pressing down on my chest, pinning me in place. I tried to scream again, desperate now. Someone tutted, and I felt a spell slip around my throat, silencing me. I flailed, wide-eyed and helpless in the darkness.

'Be still, cariad,' a familiar voice whispered, her breath warm against my ear.

My body went limp as relief flooded through me. Morvith. One of the coven elders and Nain's closest friend. The spell slipped from my throat just as the hands released me.

'There were strange men in the woods, but you can get up now. Can you stand?'

'Yes,' I said, gagging on the word and the idea that the silencing spell still lingered like a slug's oily trail.

Morvith grunted, then leaned on her stick and pushed herself to standing with a stifled groan.

The circle of figures stepped back, releasing me. I lay on the ground, pulling in great lungfuls of cool night air and willing my heart to return to a normal rhythm. The strengthening wind sent clouds, thick as winter blankets, barrelling across the night sky. The leaves rattled in the trees, and those already fallen swirled around me, dancing with the ash from the extinguished fire.

The dampness of the forest floor seeped through my cloak and dress, cold fingers searching for warm skin. I didn't care. Grateful for the chill, even as it seeped into my bones, I tried to imagine it sucking away the heat of shame that was searing through me. Had I really believed this might be the moment my magic arrived? Worse, that Nain had nothing better to do than spend her time looking for ways to call in magic that clearly wanted nothing to do with me? My cheeks burned.

Nain was trying to save the magic of persecuted witches – murdered witches, I corrected myself – and I had ruined everything. She would have every right to be truly ashamed of me now.

On balance, the terror of waking surrounded by faceless, cloaked figures was preferable to this.

I heard a whispered conversation beyond the circle, too far away for me to make out the words, but moments later, Nain strode into view. She held out her hand and I took it, her grip like a vice as she hauled me to my feet.

'I'm sorry, Nain,' I mumbled, the threat of tears thickening my words.

'Nonsense, child. Come. We must leave quickly.'

She ushered me out of the clearing, her hand on the small

of my back. The rest of the coven was already slipping away into the shadows.

Before we reached the trees, a hooded figure stepped out of the wood.

'Wait here,' Nain instructed.

I planted my feet, too tired and ashamed to do anything but obey. My legs still felt as shaky as a newborn foal's.

Something shifted above me, and I stepped back, heart pounding, but it was just a barn owl, drifting, silent as a ghost, through the clearing.

Some said owls were bad omens, but I had always thought seeing such beautiful birds to be a blessing. Right now, I felt anything but blessed.

A vast and endless loneliness reared up inside me, its jaws yawning wide as if it were about to pierce me in its bloodied maw. Tears stung my eyes, but then Nain was at my side again and the feeling vanished, leaving only my shame.

'The men are headed east, but they might return. We need to get home.'

My weak, miserable legs obeyed, and I stumbled through the woods, catching my feet on tree roots and tussling with the brambles as they snatched at my skirts, leaving them and the silence in tatters.

If ever I needed a sign that the magical path wasn't mine to tread, this had been it.

CHAPTER 5

GWEN, 8TH SEPTEMBER 1612

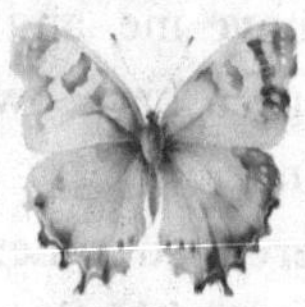

I trailed Nain into the cottage. After hanging up my cloak, I paused at the foot of the narrow stairs. Sage was curled up on a chair by the fire in the kitchen. She acknowledged our return by opening her eye, yawning and then returning to her slumber.

Tiredness hit me like a wave. 'I'll say goodnight, Nain,' I mumbled, my foot already on the first tread. I hoped the cat might follow me – I didn't want to be alone tonight – but she didn't stir.

'No,' Nain replied, not taking her eyes off the fire she was stoking under the kettle. 'I have things I need to tell you, and you have questions to ask of me.'

I let my head fall to my chest, the weight of it suddenly too much to hold upright. For a moment, I considered just telling her again it was time to stop the charade. Time to admit that I was not, in fact, like my mother, or her, or any of the other Llewellyn women before us, that no amount of waiting would ever be enough. But my words would not come, and my legs betrayed my mind by walking me to the table. I slumped into a chair and rested my head in my hands.

The touch of petal-soft fur on my cheek made me smile despite my misery. I looked up to see Sage standing in front of me. I leaned back in my chair, and she stepped into my lap, turning twice before curling up and resuming her nap. I stroked her back; her soft fur was still hot from where she'd been basking in front of the fire. My touch ignited her purr, which vibrated through my legs. I might not have magic, but I could make a cat happy, and I supposed that was something.

Nain busied herself while the kettle boiled. She moved silently between the dresser, the hearth and the small forest of herbs that hung from the beam in the far corner. She pulled pots from the dresser shelves, pinched off the ends of herbs left drying and stripped leaves from stalks with deft fingers.

I turned my attention back to Sage. The cat's feet were flexing back and forth, revealing delicate pink toes the colour of cherry blossom. *Oh, to be a cat.*

Nain placed the mug of tea on the table and took her seat opposite me. I lifted my nose to catch the scents drifting in the still-steaming brew. Rosemary, camomile, lavender and lemon balm. I sniffed again, trying to identify the other, less familiar ingredients. Nothing came to mind. I let my fingers drift over the steam, felt them tingle as I sensed the spells Nain had whispered into it. One for soothing, one for alertness and a third for remembering.

When I lifted my eyes to Nain's, she gave a nod, as if she'd read my mind, marked my homework and found it correct. Sensing magic was something, at least. I should be content with that. Horsewoman. Friend to animals. Passable herbalist. Sensor of magic. That would have to be enough.

'I don't want you to worry about the fainting,' Nain said, interrupting my train of thought. 'I can't tell you why it happened, but it is no weakness on your part. Hear that,

Gwenllian, and do not doubt it. Is that clear?' Her tone was even more brisk than usual.

I nodded, but I didn't believe it for a second.

'With your voice, child. A nod lacks the power of a word.'

'Yes, Nain,' I said, feeling the lie on my lips like a nettle's touch.

Nain studied my face for a few moments before continuing. I tried to hold her gaze, but couldn't, so turned my attention back to Sage.

'Tonight's spell did not go as planned because we were almost discovered. Had you not fainted, Owain wouldn't have noticed the lights down the hill that warned of the danger. We don't know who the men were, but the owl told us they were strangers. We all of us owe you a debt of thanks, Gwenllian.'

I felt a strange lightness bubble in my chest and smiled. I didn't know what to say, so lowered my head back to the sleeping cat.

'That we were not discovered is a blessing from the Goddess herself, but the interruption has left us with a complication that will need to be rectified at the next moon.'

Nain pushed herself to standing and crossed to the dresser, busying herself by turning jars and sweeping spilled herbs into her palm.

The lightness in my chest evaporated like a thin mist in bright sunshine.

'What sort of complication?'

Nain's shoulders tensed, suggesting that whatever it was, and whatever she might say to the contrary, it was troubling her. She walked to the fire and tipped the herbs onto it. I heard them spit as the flames consumed them.

When Nain replied, her voice had lost some of its crispness.

'There have always been those who desire power, Gwen,

those who want what we were born with, but never on this scale. Their envy has curdled into something hideous and cruel, and it is spreading like the pox.' Nain shook her head.

'The people hanged at Pendle weren't of our kind,' she continued, sinking back into her seat. 'They had no magic, and yet all it took was a peddler's complaint and then the testimony of a nine-year-old child, one of the accused's own, would you believe.' Nain stabbed her finger into the table for emphasis. 'That was enough to see them hang for witchcraft.'

Shame caught in my throat like thorns when I remembered how dismissive I'd been when Cook first delivered the news. I swallowed and tried to think of a sensible question.

'And what of our kind in Pendle?'

Nain sighed. 'They are terrified. One or two have left, those that have plausible excuses, but most have just stopped their covens and are no longer teaching their children for fear of them being accused or—' She flung her hands in the air and seemed to lose the words.

Nain sighed and rested her head in her hand.

'Imagine being so afraid that you don't raise your children with the gifts that should have been their birthrights.' She spoke the words to the table, her voice weary.

When Nain looked up, she waved her finger towards my untouched mug. I sipped my tea and felt my muscles soften and my heart slow to a gentler rhythm.

She watched me for a moment before continuing. 'What do you remember of the ritual?'

Images flashed into my mind. 'I remember the fire. The coven was much larger than usual. The owl.'

I caught my breath as the image of the great silver orb crystallised in my memory.

'There was a huge glowing light above you, and the coven members were sending their magic into it!'

'Not their magic, Gwen, their oaths. Those strands of silver were solemn promises to protect magic.'

I nodded and made an 'Oh' sound, but I felt foolish for getting it wrong – again. I licked my lips before I spoke, my voice quieter now.

'I fainted before it was my turn,' I mumbled, dropping my head.

Nain let the silence stretch until I looked up and met her eye.

'The orb of light was our beacon – an invitation to witches everywhere to send us their magic for safekeeping if they found themselves imperilled.'

She looked to be choosing her words even more carefully than usual.

'The spell was intended to share the burden of any magic others sent to us. One soul's magic would be sent to me, the next would go to Morvith, then Ann, and so on, in order of our service to the coven. I would only receive a second soul's magic once everyone else in the coven had received their charge, although we hope that there will never be more than twenty-two souls in such desperate need.'

'But that didn't happen,' I ventured.

Nain looked pale in the lamplight. My breath hitched as a chill slid down my back, like unseen fingers brushing my spine.

She shook her head. 'As the initiator of the spell, it was my duty to cast it and then offer it up for each member to accept a share, but that is not what happened.'

I felt for a second as if I were falling. The memory of the time that, had it not been for Nain's swift hand around my tiny arm, I might have been lost as the loose rocks on the edge of the mountain path slid from beneath my feet. I must have swayed, because Sage's claws in my leg brought me painfully back to the moment.

'What are you saying, Nain?' I asked carefully.

'I'm saying that I made a mistake, child.'

Nain stood abruptly, knocking over her chair. It hovered an inch above the flagstones before righting itself, and I tasted her magic on the air, bright and coppery.

Bracing her hands on the back of the chair, she said, 'I should have crafted the spell so that had we been interrupted, it would have failed. That would have been the safer option.'

'Safer?' My heart was pounding now.

Nain waved her hands in the air as if my concern were woodsmoke to be wafted away, but the skin around her eyes was tense, her lips flattened and her jaw tight as a trap.

'Don't look so worried, child. It just means that until we can reconvene at the next moon, any magic sent to us will come only to me.'

She turned away abruptly, her long skirts swirling behind her as if they too had been unprepared for the move and needed to hurry to catch up. Nain went again to the dresser but, finding nothing to occupy her, shook out the blanket Sage had been sleeping on before re-folding it.

'But what does that mean for you?' I asked, my tongue stuttering around words that felt like ash in my mouth. 'You are the most powerful witch in the coven, but how much of this magic can one person bear?'

Nain glowered at me before turning her attention back to the blanket. She didn't know. I wanted to scream. This wasn't fair. So much for the coven owing me a debt of gratitude. My fainting might have saved the coven from these so-called witch hunters, but what if they had merely been poachers? And what if this ruined spell … I couldn't finish the thought.

'Don't look so horrified, child. We'll convene again at the next moon, finish the spell and share the burden. Owain has it, so it is safe till then. And I seriously doubt that I will be inundated with orphaned magic between now and then.'

'But, Nain,' I spluttered, 'if the spell wasn't meant for just one, won't that—'

She raised her hand, cutting me off, the folded blanket clasped to her chest.

'It is only until the next moon, Gwenllian. I am plenty strong enough to hold whatever comes my way until then, which may very well be nothing at all.'

'But …' I said, no longer caring about the wail in my voice. I felt sick to my stomach. 'What if—'

'Let that be an end to it for now, child,' she said, the sharpness in her tone returning as she threw the blanket onto the chair.

She walked slowly back to the table and touched her hand to my cheek. 'Get some sleep, cariad. You're as pale as the cat.'

Lacking the strength to argue, I lifted Sage from my lap and cradled her against my shoulder. I mumbled a goodnight and made for the stairs, turning at the first step. Nain sat at the table, her fingers tracing the pattern in the old wood.

She glanced up, and I glimpsed not just fear but something close to terror in her grey eyes. It was gone again in a heartbeat, but my hands were still shaking as I reached for the handle of the bedroom door.

CHAPTER 6

GWEN, 18TH SEPTEMBER 1612

I slid into the wide, panelled hallway with seconds to spare. I'd heard the squeak of my father's bedchamber door just as I'd bolted out of mine, which gave me exactly nine seconds to take my place at the foot of the stairs. I'd done it in five before now. By the time I heard the first tap of his cane on the landing, I was halfway there.

I would have been all the quicker had I not been required to wear my ridiculous formal dress for this charade of a dinner. I only used the room in my father's house to keep the dresses he insisted upon for occasions like this one. Nain had raised me since the day I was born, and she had flatly refused to live under my father's roof, so the cottage had always been home.

For the last two hours, I'd had to endure the indignity of Olwen, my father's house maid, raking, twisting and pinning my unruly mane into some monstrosity that was, she told me, fashionable for young ladies.

That was bad enough, but the dress was the ultimate indignity, the same delicate shade of pink as the dog rose that clambered over the kitchen garden wall. Olwen had huffed and broken into a sweat as she laced me into a bodice so tight there was barely room for air in my lungs.

The lace scratched at my neck and wrists, and given the choice, I'd have rather taken my chances wrapped from chin to toe in the dog rose.

I tried to ignore my prickling neck and screaming lungs as I stood in the hallway, a dutiful smile plastered across my face, trying to look like the picture of patience.

My father took an age to descend the stairs, his gnarled hand clutching the banister while he manoeuvred his stick with the other, tapping at the step below him before committing his weight to the movement.

I hoped Nain would arrive soon. She'd be in Father's bad books for not being here already, lined up and waiting like a pliant horse, not that he'd be fool enough to say so.

It had been ten days since the incident at the coven, and Nain had been away for nine of them, returning only this afternoon.

I'd spent the time enjoying the last of the summer, riding through the woods with Tân, stopping here and there to collect wildflower seeds. I filled a bag with wild hazelnuts from the grove in the east valley and hunted with little success for some early chestnuts. I tended the garden, picking apples, damsons and plums for preserving. I pulled onions from the vegetable beds, and once I'd tucked Tân into his stable for the night, sat at the kitchen table, plaiting their long green stems by candlelight before hanging them from the beams.

In the mornings, once the dew was past, I gathered the last of the yarrow and meadowsweet for drying, and shook the seeds from the fennel and dill, making sure to scatter enough on the soil for new plants to take root in the spring.

The bees I left for Nain to see to. I wasn't afraid of them, not really, but I just sensed that they preferred her company, and so I respected that. I checked on the hives each time I went to the orchard, greeted them, as was polite, but I left them to their business, and they left me to mine.

Nain's return had delighted the bees. In fact, I only knew she was back when I saw them swarming around the orchard, my grandmother the centre of an aerial display designed for an audience of one.

She refused to tell me where she'd been, but that wasn't what worried me. She looked more angular than normal, her face drawn, and her eyes, usually so sharp and bright, seemed dulled. There was a weariness that clung to her like an ill-fitting cloak, and while she insisted that, so far, no witch had sent her magic for safekeeping, I couldn't help but wonder if the spell had taken a toll on her. It had never occurred to me to worry about Nain before – and I wondered why. The answer was as bitter as wormwood – I had never needed to.

She had barely removed her travelling cloak when Mal, the stable lad, arrived at the cottage with a message from my father. The cousins were coming to dinner. It was a thunder-cloud in the blue sky of Nain's return, but at least I wouldn't have to suffer them alone.

Now, hours later, my skin crawling beneath lace and my scalp screaming under the weight of pins, I stood resigned to an evening lost to unimaginable boredom and breathing through my mouth to limit the stench of old sweat from Cousin Prudence's and Cousin Charles's malodorous feet.

'Daughter,' my father said by way of greeting when he at last reached me. His eyes slid past me to where, I suspect, he expected to see Nain. He flattened his lips into a thin line of disapproval, but just then, the front door swung open, delivering a gust of chill wind, a flurry of autumn leaves and, amongst them, my grandmother, looking polished and imperious in her best black dress, her dark hair swept into its usual tight bun.

Beside me, my father made a noise that might have been a grunt of approval or an exasperated tut. Taylor, my father's servant, hurried into the hallway and dropped to the floor to collect the invading leaves. The staff would be on high alert after receiving news of dinner guests. I wasn't alone in detesting the cousins, and I could just picture Cook's buttoned lips as she prepared the meal while trying to keep her opinions to herself.

'Mary,' Father said tightly. 'Good of you to join us. Charles and Prudence will be pleased to see you, I'm sure.'

Nain arched an eyebrow. 'I very much doubt that, Thomas, but thank you for the invitation to your table,' she said with a fractional nod of her head. 'Gwen, please remind Cook that I will need honey for my tea.' It was an instruction delivered in a tone that would reassure my father of my obedience, but the hitch at the corner of her mouth told me she was gifting me a few more precious moments of freedom before the performance began.

'Yes, Nain,' I said, already backing towards the kitchen.

I lingered there as long as I dared, enjoying the smells of roasting food and warming breads but trying not to get in the way of Cook and the scullery maids who were rushing around like soldiers preparing to ward off an invading army.

I heard the cousins arrive, but then again, they were loud enough to be heard in the next county. When Taylor rushed in, pink-cheeked and flustered, I knew I could delay the moment no longer. Cook threw me a sympathetic smile. I waved from the door and mouthed 'thank you' as I pointed to the table laden with food.

Back in the hallway, I plastered on a smile and pushed open the door. The dining hall was brighter than usual. There were always extra candles when we had guests, but from the sweetness in the honeyed air, these were the beeswax ones, not the vile tallow variety that left a greasy, rancid smell hanging in the air like spoiled meat.

My father sat at the head of the table, his cousin, Charles Parry, to his left. Opposite him, in the place that, by rights, should have been left empty for his wife, Prudence, was my grandmother.

I fancied that Nain looked more herself in the candlelight, or maybe it was the serene expression that had cast off the years. Nobody would guess by looking at her how much she hated Charles or the woman sitting next to him, who she referred to as 'the viper'. I didn't need to see Charles's face to know that it would be contorted into a scowl.

Nain lifted her chin as I entered. 'Good evening, grand-daughter,' she said pleasantly, her face breaking into a generous smile. 'Perfect timing as ever.'

'Good evening, cousins,' I said, trying to match my grand-mother's tone as I took my place next to her and tried not to notice the fetid smell that snaked beneath the table from Charles. No amount of beeswax could smother that stink.

Prudence nodded, flattening her thin lips into the approximation of what might look to the uninitiated to be a polite smile. I knew better.

Charles pretended not to have heard me, which was typical.

The conversation continued as if I'd not spoken.

'Cousin Charles, tell me, how is business?' my father rasped. His voice was thin and just as insubstantial as he was these days. His clothes hung around his diminished frame, making him look like he was wearing someone else's.

Charles's eyes narrowed for a moment, and his mouth tightened before he recovered himself. He looked like a man busy burying the truth and digging frantically for some more palatable lie to offer in its place. When he'd unearthed something of use, he smiled, revealing yellow teeth, and launched into his story.

'We are blessed, cousin. The good Lord continues to provide for us, even though the land is far from sufficient to meet all our earthly needs.'

This old chestnut again, I thought. I wished that, just once, my father would suggest that not selling off parcels of land to fund gambling debts might be a good way of meeting their earthly needs.

When Charles's eye flicked towards me, I dropped my gaze from the sweating lump of a man with a turkey's neck, the complexion of a salted ham and the wispy, pale curls of a sickly child pulled from his fever bed. Had his character redeemed him, his unfortunate looks might have gone unnoticed, but I struggled to think of anyone who was more unlikeable than Charles Parry, although Prudence was a close second.

They fell into an awkward, stilted conversation, and I was glad when Taylor re-entered the room, shepherding in the serving staff and the platters of mouthwatering food.

I spent the rest of the meal listening to my father answering what felt like an endless list of questions from Charles on the running of the estate. Which crops were doing well, which tenants were the best farmers, what did he plan to do with the meadow. I felt my hackles rise at that. The meadow was perfectly capable of taking care of itself. I opened my mouth to say as much, but Nain cleared her throat in warning.

Eventually, my father sighed and held up his hand to halt the inquisition. He looked even more exhausted than normal. I wondered vaguely if he was eating enough. He was as thin as the reeds in the lower pond, and by the mound of uneaten food on his plate, maybe that was the trouble.

'How is your health, Mary?' Prudence asked, her voice as high and pinched as her narrow face.

'I am in fine health, thank you, Prudence. I trust you are?' Nain replied, her voice low and smooth as a silken robe.

My cousin's disappointment lay thinly veiled behind that flat, barren smile. When she turned her gaze on me, the smile vanished entirely.

'The child looks to be robust. Although, many her age are married with babes of their own.'

I clenched my jaw. I didn't know what was worse – being called a child, being criticised for not already being some kind of brood mare or being spoken about as if I weren't sitting just feet away. Nain's foot nudged into mine. I plastered a thin smile onto my face that was as wooden as the tabletop.

Nain stared at Prudence until the other woman lowered her eyes.

Always remember the power of silence, Gwen. Nain didn't need to speak for the memory of her words to play in my mind.

As the servants cleared the plates, Charles inclined his head towards my father and lowered his voice. 'I wonder if we could speak in confidence for a few moments about business matters. In your study, perhaps?'

His eyes flicked in my direction, but as he had done throughout the meal, he studiously avoided looking at my grandmother.

'Let us withdraw,' Nain said smoothly to Prudence. 'Gwen has chores to complete so will bid you good evening now,' she added, her foot finding mine under the table. When I looked at her, she gave me a slow nod, her head angled to the left, her eyes wide and fixed on whatever silent instruction she was trying to give me.

My father and Charles were already on their feet.

Think! Nain clearly had a plan, but what?

Rising, I forced a smile. 'Good night, cousins. Safe journey.'

Prudence nodded, but Charles ignored me completely as he waddled from the room after my father, simpering like a lapdog. Nain had a plan, I just needed to understand what it was – and quickly!

CHAPTER 7
GWEN, 18TH SEPTEMBER 1612

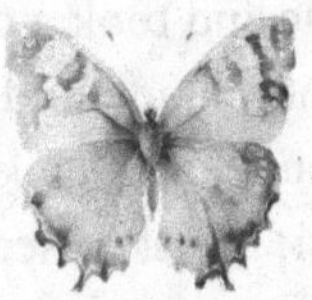

The fresh air in the hallway was a relief after the stuffiness of the dining hall. I inhaled deeply and imagined it clearing the fog settled around my thoughts.

I watched my father shuffle down the long corridor, cane tapping and Charles dogging his every step. As my father reached for the handle of his study door, it hit me. Of course!

I waited until they disappeared inside then hurried after them. The room next to the study was used to store my father's furniture acquisitions, most of which he sold to other wealthy landowners. The room was always cold, the hearth empty and the furniture shrouded beneath cloth to keep the dust at bay. I shivered as I slipped inside, grateful that there was still light enough outside to find my way through the towering maze of ghosts to where the panelling was loose.

As a child, I'd spend hours here whenever Nain was called away on coven business or to tend to the sick. Back then, I'd been able to sit on the floor of the narrow opening, my legs like a frog's as I listened to my father conduct his business. The tenant farmers who paid him in tithes each year and the merchants who arrived and haggled over the price of everything from horses to linens to wheat. There was much I didn't understand, but I just liked to listen to his voice. He barely ever said more than two words to me, and so I used to pretend that I was a man, here to sell him something, playing out the entire conversation in my mind, or sometimes with the corn dolls that Nain made for me.

I eased the panel aside and took a deep breath. I had been ten, listening to my father, alone and weeping in his study. Although I was forbidden from even knocking on his door, I wondered if I should risk it just to see if I might be of some comfort to him.

My thoughts had been stunned to stillness as his keening words sliced through me. 'Why, Lord? Why take my precious boy and beautiful wife and leave the useless girl? Why?' he'd wailed.

If his god had replied, it hadn't been an answer that satisfied him. That had been the last time I'd sneaked into the panelling.

I buried the memory as I crept sideways, positioning myself in the spot that I knew to be directly behind my father's desk, my nose just an inch from the wooden panel that divided the rooms. The darkness was choking here and the air stale. I bit my lip against the stirring panic and forced myself to focus on my task.

'Cousin, I will get to the point,' Charles said, clearly eager to say his piece. 'You know I have your interests at heart – and those of the Llewellyn line. Gwen is a fine young woman, but she is not an heir. If you are to rest easy in your dotage, then you will need to find her a suitable husband or ...' He trailed off. 'Make other arrangements for the good of the family name.'

My father scoffed loudly.

'Name you my heir? Not bloody likely, cousin.'

My father's voice might be frail these days, but he'd found enough steel to deliver that message with force. I felt a bubble of pride rise in my chest.

Charles's sigh was loud and affected. 'You misunderstand me.'

'I think not. I think I understand your intention here all too well,' Father replied, his voice growing stronger, although it was still no match for Charles's pompous boom.

'I will not insult you by pretending that the bequeathment of the estate would not be welcomed – we are neither of us fools. You love your daughter and want the best for her, that is clear,' Charles said.

I felt tears prick at my eyes, although I wasn't sure why. Did my father love me? If he did, he had a strange way of showing it. Then again, he had long repelled all suggestions that I should be married by now. He had, I suppose, gifted me a freedom denied to other girls my age, although I couldn't say whether that was an act of love or indifference. More likely, his reluctance to cross swords with Nain.

Charles pressed on. 'We, Prudence and I, want the best for her too, and the family name, which is why we suggest you find her a suitable match now, while ...' Charles faltered, biting off the words mid-sentence with an awkward half-laugh.

'Before I wither and die?' Father said tartly.

'Those are not the words I would have chosen, but the meaning is correct, cousin, yes.'

The sound of a chair scraping hesitantly told me that my father was struggling to his feet. If he paced, then it meant he was entertaining the idea. I screwed up my eyes and prayed to the Goddess that the next sound I'd hear would be Father putting Charles in his place for even daring to suggest such a thing. My heart thumped in my chest, marking out the seconds.

Tell him to leave! I willed the words through the wall and imagined them floating in through my father's ears and out through his mouth. *Tell him—*And then I heard the tap of a cane.

'No.' The word was more a breath than a whisper, escaping my lips before I could rein it in, but it was too late.

'Did you hear something?' Charles boomed.

My father's cane paused in its tapping.

'Hear what?' His voice was sharp.

'No matter. I thought I heard a noise.'

'It serves no man to be the type who jumps at shadows,' Father remarked pointedly, but without the sharp edge of just moments ago. My heart sank.

Why was he even entertaining this man? He detested him and his awful, money-grabbing wife. He knew they only cared about the money – he'd said as much to Nain for years. And sitting in this very space, I'd heard him complain to her that the cousins' eyes lingered on objects as if they were mentally calculating the value of every stick of furniture, right down to the spoons. And yet here he was, listening like a fool.

The tapping cane continued. Charles moved in his chair, which groaned under the weight of the monstrous man.

'I suppose you have someone in mind?' Father asked.

My eyes widened in alarm. *What is he saying?*

'We have several good men in our circle, yes, and we would be happy to make introductions, of course, but I think you would be happier to find your own match for the girl.'

My father made a noise that was part grunt, part snort. Tap. Tap. Tap.

A fresh chill crept across my skin. There was a plan here. I could all but smell it, mingled with the stench of Charles's rotten feet, which seemed capable of reaching me even here.

'The one thing I would suggest, if you would permit me,

is that whoever you choose is a godly man. These are dangerous times, and you are, of course, aware of the rumours surrounding your mother-in-law and your late w—'

A loud crack of wood on wood reverberated around the room and I jumped, heart thundering, my teeth biting into my lip to stop myself from making a noise.

'Hold your tongue in my house, cousin!' Father bellowed with a strength I had long doubted he still possessed.

'Forgive me. Forgive me, dearest Thomas,' Charles grovelled. 'I meant no offence. I hope only that the child is protected from the idle gossip of small minds. I will speak no more about it.'

Father snorted. The tapping continued, growing closer. *Take your rest, then send him on his way, Father.* I willed the words through the wall, clenching my hands into fists even though Nain had told me a thousand times that tension serves only to interrupt the flow of magic.

The tapping stopped and Father's chair creaked as he lowered himself into it with a groan. *Tell him. Tell him to go, Father. Tell him now.*

'The brandy is there,' Father said, and I could picture him pointing at it with his cane. 'Pour one for yourself,' he added with a sigh so heavy it all but crushed my heart.

CHAPTER 8

GWEN, 18TH SEPTEMBER 1612

I burst out of the front door and plunged headlong into driving rain, half blind with tears, nose streaming, my heavy skirts fisted in my hands. By the time I reached the end of the drive, the sodden dress felt like lead around my legs.

As I turned into the lane, a blast of wind slammed into my back, dislodging a thick strand of hair which wasted no time plastering itself across my face. I swiped it away, remembering the skirt only as it slipped from my fingers. I made a grab for it, but it was too late. The wet linen and silk twisted gleefully around my legs like serpents, conspiring to take me down.

I tried to break my fall, but the sleeves of the dress pinned my arms. I fell forward, my useless hands sliding through the mud and grit, doing little to save my face.

I struggled to my feet and marched the rest of the way to the cottage. I had just reached the front gate when a flash of lightning lit the night sky. I looked up just as a barn owl slid over the thatched roof and disappeared into the trees, silent as a ghost.

My teeth were chattering by the time I stepped into the cottage and closed the heavy oak door against the first rumbles of thunder.

I stood beside the hearth, dripping dark pools of water onto the flagstones as I tried to take in some steadying breaths, but the dress felt determined to smother me where I stood.

I scrabbled at the lace at my throat, trying to free myself. I reached for the fastenings on the back of my neck and heard the satisfying rip of wet silk as the seams of both sleeves split under the arms. My reach extended, I pulled, sending buttons flying to the four corners. My neck finally free, I took a breath, drinking in the familiar smell of home.

I tried to pull my arms free from the long, wet, filthy sleeves, but they refused to yield. My breaths grew shallow as the panic rose in my chest. I pitched forward, bracing my hands on the back of the chair for support, but cried out as the tight bodice bit into my abdomen.

I thought of Cousin Charles's straining waistcoat and how every man I had ever met had buttons on the front of their shirts and jackets. Who decided that men had control over their clothing but women were to be trussed up like joints of miserable meat ready for the oven?

Taking the top of the bodice in both hands, I let out a roar as I yanked it down over my breasts, sending yet more buttons flying. A thread at my wrist caught my eye and, desperate now, I ripped at it with my teeth, barely registering the mud and grit on my lips and the tang of earth in my mouth. The seam surrendered and loosened to the elbow. Emboldened, I crossed to the dresser and pulled open the drawer. I chose our sharpest knife.

My hands shook as I guided the blade, first through the limp fabric of the collar and then down, between my breasts to where the bodice pinched the flesh around my ribs. The fabric split like the skin of a ripe plum at the touch of steel, and I groaned with relief as my ribs returned to their natural position.

The sleeve on my right arm refused to yield, binding itself to my flesh as if it meant to follow me to my grave. I cursed under my breath and took the knife to it. It was awkward in my left hand, and by the time the sleeve fell away, a thin rivulet of my blood ran down my fingers, but I didn't care.

Finally free, I stepped out of the spent dress and stretched my arms wide. The ruined gown slumped to the floor; the heavy skirts held it upright, as if it still hoped I might step back into the hollow shell it had woven for me. I screamed as I kicked it into the corner.

When Nain arrived sometime later, she found me huddled in a blanket in front of the fire, Sage purring in my lap. My tears spent, I felt too numb to even clean the blood from my face and hands. From the stinging on my chin and cheek, they were at least grazed, my lip too, judging by the taste of copper on my tongue. I didn't want to look too closely at my hands.

It was the first time Nain had held me since I was a child. She had never been the hugging type. Once I had grown too big for her lap, I turned to Tân or Sage whenever I craved touch. As she rocked me in front of the fire, as my tears fell afresh, I eventually felt some strength creep back into my bones.

All too soon, she helped me to my feet and steered me to a chair at the kitchen table. Sage retook her seat in my lap, and I stared, blank-eyed, at the tabletop.

'Here,' Nain said, placing a bowl of hot water the colour

of moss in front of me. I angled my nose towards the rising steam and caught the slightly bitter smell of wood sage.

'Chwerwlys,' I mumbled, the herb's name out of my mouth before I could think of anything better to say.

'Is it only your face and hands?' Nain asked, placing a stack of linen clothes next to the bowl, her keen eyes scanning me.

'My arm too, I think.'

I let the blanket slip from my shoulders and examined the cuts on my right arm where I'd accidentally nicked my pale skin. The long, thin line of blood had crusted like rust, but the cuts were thankfully shallow.

'Get on then, before it cools too much,' Nain said, her tone gentler than usual.

I cleaned my hands and wiped the blood from my arm. Nain helped me wrap a bandage around a flap of skin on my right palm that, while not deep, would take a day or two to rejoin the rest of the surrounding flesh.

To keep the bandage dry, she cleaned the cuts on my chin and right cheek before smearing them with a yarrow ointment. The earthy, camomile-like smell reminded me of Tân. I kept a jar in the yard for him, to treat any scratches or angry fly bites. It had been the first thing Nain taught me how to make. I couldn't have been more than four.

Nain's instruction echoed in my mind, even after all these years. *Always with beeswax or pine tar, Gwen, never horse grease or lard. Nothing made from the misery of one innocent can ever heal another.*

'I think I know what you overheard. Prudence told me most of it, but I want to hear it from you, Gwen,' Nain said, taking the seat next to mine.

I recounted the conversation, surprised at how calm my voice sounded.

'And then I ran back here and ...' I glanced sheepishly at

the mud-caked bundle of rags in the corner. 'I know it was wrong, Nain, but I couldn't get it off me.'

Nain got to her feet, and I hung my head, bracing myself for the lecture. I heard the rustle of fabric and looked up just in time to see her throw the dress onto the fire.

My jaw dropped, but I couldn't think of anything to say.

'I will speak to your father,' she said quietly, stabbing at the fabric with the poker so that the flames could do their greedy work.

'About the dress?'

Nain frowned at me and replaced the poker.

'Hell no! About his wretched plan for you, of course!'

I felt my shoulders soften.

'Let's see to this hair,' Nain said, coming to stand behind me.

We fell into silence, the only sounds coming from the spitting fire, the purring cat and the clink of hair pins hitting wood as Nain threw them on the table.

My hair finally freed, Nain squeezed my shoulder before taking the seat opposite me. My scalp felt sore, but it was a relief to have my hair, wild and unruly as it was, feeling like my own again.

'If he refuses to see reason, cariad, we will have to make other arrangements.'

Nain wasn't looking at me when she spoke, and her tone was all wrong. She'd stood up to my father before – why did she sound so cautious now? My pulse quickened.

'Like what?' I asked. My tongue felt clumsy in my dry mouth.

'Gwen,' Nain said slowly. 'You are not a child anymore. You know that my protection will not be enough forever. If your father refuses to name you as his heir, then you will have to marry or commit yourself to a religious life.'

My blood began pounding in my ears at such a volume I

could barely think straight. I made to get up but froze as Sage sank her claws through my shift and into the flesh on my thighs. I sat down again quickly and stroked her head as I mumbled an apology.

'Listen, child!' Nain said, exasperated. 'Women have few choices in this world, but we are not totally without power. If you marry one of our kind, then you will at least be safe to live freely and never suffer the indignity of being sold off like a poor heifer. Marry on your own terms and you get to decide the cut of your own clothes,' she said with a nod to what was left of the dress in the hearth.

'But I don't want to marry anyone!' I screamed the words as my fury rose out of nowhere. The cat sprang from my lap and sprinted out of the room. 'Just tell my father that! Tell him I want to be free to live as I please! He won't dare cross you!'

Nain looked away from me.

'That might have been true once, child, but with Charles whispering in his ear, I believe he may try to find ways to outwit me.'

I snorted at the thought of him even trying, but when I glanced up at Nain, I saw real fear in her eyes, and in that second, my entire world seemed to tilt on its axis.

'Charles is sinking in debt. He gave up asking your father for loans years ago, but I have it on good authority that he now has creditors at his door, and they are not the type of people one argues with. He will stop at nothing to get his hands on this land, Gwen.'

'But it's not even my father's to bequest! It's your land! Llewellyn land! Why does it always go to men? It's not fair!'

'I don't care about the land, Gwen,' Nain said with a dismissive wave of her hand.

'Charles was fool enough to gamble away his own fortune, and he'll just do the same if Father gives in!'

Nain pursed her lips into a flat line and got to her feet. I watched her suck in a deep breath before she replied.

'You are not safe here, Gwen. Don't you see? This talk of suitors is a ruse. He may well produce some eligible bachelors for your father's consideration, but—'

Nain shook her head and changed tack.

'Gwen, we have evidence that the men in the woods the night of the spell were working under Charles's orders. He plans to accuse you of witchcraft.'

The laugh escaped me before I could check myself. Of all the ironies.

'Well, good luck to him,' I snorted, 'because as we know, I appear to not have a magical bone in my body.'

'Stop it!' Nain snapped, whirling around and bracing her hands against the back of the chair. 'Don't you see, child, he doesn't need actual evidence of magical ability to do you harm. Have you not heard a word I've said? Did the story of the poor souls from Pendle teach you nothing? People are being killed as witches, some for no greater crime than being old, female and having a cat!'

'But not here in Wales,' I said weakly.

Nain sank heavily into her chair and reached over the table to clasp my hands in hers.

'Gwen, listen to me, please. Whether he accuses you or sees to it that you meet with some sort of accident, he means you great harm.'

I huffed out a dry laugh. 'Nain, please. The man is monstrous, but he is no common murderer.' But even as the words left my lips, I knew I was wrong.

I lifted my gaze to hers and immediately wished that I hadn't. The fear that swirled in my grandmother's eyes made me feel sick to my core.

'What am I going to do?' I croaked out the words.

'You have my protection, and so long as there is breath in my body, I will let no harm come to you. You are safe here too – your great-grandmother and her coven warded this house and your father's so that the magic contained here will forever be hidden from those who seek it, though sadly it offers no protection from more earthly foes,' Nain said, squeezing my hands.

I squeezed back, grateful for the connection.

'If your father will not officially name you as his heir, then I have a letter from Rhys Morgan asking your father's permission to marry you.' Nain dropped her gaze to the table as she spoke the words.

'Rhys? The one with pimples and an obsession with caterpillars?' I asked, incredulous, remembering the annoying young boy we once visited in Builth.

'I think you'll find he has grown some since we last visited,' Nain replied. 'But the Morgans are our people, Gwen. Their magic goes back generations, and they are powerful and well respected. You will be safe there with them. Rhys is a kind boy with a good heart who would never dare dictate to you.'

'Is that where you've been this past week?'

Nain nodded slowly. 'Believe me, child, this is not what I want – of course it's not – but if there is no other way of keeping you safe, then we must consider it. At least if you married Rhys, after your father's days you could both return here.'

I opened my mouth to scream my reply. To tell her that I would never marry anyone, let alone a pimply kid I barely remembered, but, strangely, I couldn't find the words nor the fury.

This was all madness of the worst kind, but I knew too that what Nain said was the truth. There would be no reasoning with my father; he had made that clear tonight in his study. And if I was a risk to Charles's plan, then what might he do to Nain or Tân?

'What about you? I'm not going anywhere without you, Nain.'

She smiled at that and gave my hands a last squeeze before sitting back.

'There is a cottage in Builth for me if you decide that is what you want to do,' she said.

'You'd do that? You'd leave your home? Your land? For me?'

Nain smiled a little sadly as she shrugged. 'I'd prefer to stay, of course I would, but home is a feeling, Gwen, not a place. And I'd wander the Earth for an eternity if it meant keeping you safe.'

'Thank you,' I said. My voice was a dry rasp.

Nain frowned at me. She had clearly been expecting more of a fight.

I cleared my throat, suddenly desperate to free words that felt like caged birds that had just spotted the sky through an open door.

'Thank you for always taking care of me. For teaching me. For protecting me. For believing in me even when you have no evidence to warrant it.' I tried to smile, but the motion just misted my eyes again. I pressed on. I hadn't planned to say all this, but now I was speaking, I couldn't stop. It was my turn to hold up my hand when Nain made to reply.

'And now for all this. Trying to keep me safe and free.' I swallowed. 'I know you have always done your best for me, Nain, even though this wasn't the life you had planned for yourself. I want you to know how grateful I am. And how much I love you.' I bit my lip as my voice cracked on the last sentence. I would not ruin this with more tears.

Nain stared at me for a long beat. I saw her neck move as

she swallowed hard. She nodded briskly and cleared her throat.

'You will always have my love, cariad. Always. You remember that no matter where you are or what age you are, okay? Get yourself to bed now,' she said as she got to her feet and busied herself brushing non-existent crumbs from the tabletop.

'I will speak to your father in the morning, and we will make our plan from there,' she added, not looking at me.

I watched her for a long moment. The childish urge to run back and wrap my arms around her was almost over-whelming, but I held myself back. The last thing Nain would want now was me making a show of myself. So, I stood a heartbeat longer and then said, 'Goodnight, Nain.'

I had no idea then as I climbed the stairs, my heart sore and my head heavy with the weight of my troubles, that I had just said my final farewell to my beloved grandmother.

CHAPTER 9

GWEN, 31ST OCTOBER 1612

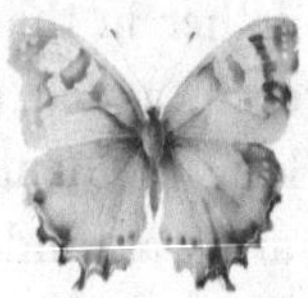

The thud of the book hitting the floorboards jolted me back to alertness. I stretched my back as I reached to retrieve it. The window seat was far from comfortable, but it was the only place in the room where the light was good enough to read.

I longed to be at home in the cottage with Nain, but so much had changed. I bit my trembling lip as the crush of remembering bloomed in my chest. Alone in my draughty room, away from my father's disapproval, I let the tears fall as I gazed out of the window.

Outside, the rain pounded the ground as if the land had somehow wronged the sky. I had never seen rain like it, despite living all my eighteen years in Wales. The lane beyond my father's driveway flowed like a river.

Mal would have Tân and the other horses safely tucked into their stables, despite it being barely midday. I hoped Sage had had the good sense to stay indoors too. A lump rose in my throat as I thought of her. Cook would give her a good life, I knew that, but I missed her almost as much as I—

'Hurry, child.' The voice was so close and so familiar that I caught my breath. Nain had been gone barely six weeks, and I could still hear her as if she were standing next to me. A movement in the glass caught my eye. I peered out and saw nothing but rain. Refocusing, I gasped when I saw my grandmother's outline reflected in the window.

I turned so quickly I toppled out of the seat, landing hard on the floor. There, just inches from my nose, were Nain's boots. The hem of her dress. This couldn't be. I jumped to my feet and staggered at the sight of my grandmother, whose body I'd cleaned and wrapped with her coven sisters before committing her to the earth.

I clamped my hand over my mouth to stop myself from crying out. If this was a dream, then I never wanted to wake again.

Nain smiled at me, but there was such sadness in her face it all but broke me anew. She reached a hand towards me, but her touch was as insubstantial as a butterfly's wing against my cheek. I saw the disappointment in her eyes and knew it reflected my own.

'I don't have time to explain, child, but you need to leave this house now, this minute.'

'What? Why?' I stammered.

'The man Charles recommended to your father as a future husband for you is on his way here. Only the storm delays him, and when he gets here, he will take you away with him. Your father has agreed to it,' Nain said, leaning close to my face to whisper the words.

'But Father said I could move back to the cottage,' I stammered, my heart hammering.

Nain shook her head. 'Men lie, cariad. Remember that. Few men can bear a powerful woman, even if that power lies only in the right to keep her own hearth.'

My mind reeled. Everything had happened so quickly after the night of the dinner. I had climbed those stairs as one person and descended as another.

I had heard Nain fall on the landing outside my room, but Sage had reached her first, yowling loud enough to wake the dead as she butted her head into Nain's waxy-looking cheek.

Unable to wake her, I ran to get a cloth and some vinegar for fainting. She was exhausted, that was all. I'd get her into bed, and once she was comfortable, I'd fetch a tincture of valerian root to help her sleep. But by the time I got back, she was gone. Sage confirmed it with a long hiss and then a yowl so pitiful it crushed my already ruined heart.

'I'll just refuse to go with him,' I said, my voice shaking.

'Then he will take you – by force if necessary! With me gone, there is nothing to stop Charles from enacting his plan. Leave now, Gwen, or mark my words, you will be joining me in that churchyard!'

Nain's voice cracked on those last, terrifying words.

'But where would I go?' I wailed, my hands trembling now.

'Ride to Talybont. The Owens will keep you safe tonight then help get you to Builth.'

'But Nain, I don't want to leave! This valley is my home!'

'I know, cariad, but sometimes life is not how we choose it to be.'

My grandmother dropped her gaze as she spoke her next words. 'They told you about the blood bind?'

I nodded miserably, remembering the conversation with Morvith and Anne. The grim business of washing and dressing my grandmother's body complete, they had lingered after the other coven women had filed mutely out of the cottage.

Still numb with shock, their words slid off my skin like

flat stones across a frozen pond. Morvith made me repeat what she'd told me twice.

'The spell contained a blood binding, so Nain's burden falls to me until the coven can meet again and undo it all.'

I'd spoken the words but hadn't given the spell a second thought since.

'This is important, Gwen. Has any magic arrived yet?' Nain asked, her brows pinched into an anxious frown.

I shrugged.

Nain's expression relaxed. 'You would know if it had.' She lifted her hands to my cheeks. 'Oh, that I was blessed to cross the veil and see this face one last time,' she whispered.

I pressed my hands over hers and tried to hold them to my cheeks, praying that by some miracle, if I just loved her hard enough, I could make her flesh and blood again.

'There's something else you need to know, Gwen.' Nain dropped her gaze and turned away from me, filling the air with the familiar scent of sun-warmed lavender.

A flash of lightning lit the room, and Nain jumped, cocking her head as if listening to something.

'Damn him! He's found a way around the swollen ford,' she said. 'Go now, child. Please, before it's too late,' she pleaded, her eyes wide and panicked.

I ran to the door and pulled my cloak from the peg.

'You said one last time. You mean you won't come to me again?'

Nain shook her head, her lips pressed to a thin line, her grey eyes brimming with tears. The sight was so unexpected that I made to rush towards her, determined to hug her one final time, but the sound of voices from downstairs stopped me in my tracks. Nain waved a hand, and the bedchamber door swung open.

Taylor's voice drifted up the stairs.

'Yes, sir, he's coming up the long road now, he is. Told me to come ahead to get things ready, so to speak.'

My heart leapt into my mouth. I turned back to Nain. She mouthed, 'Go!' And then she vanished before my eyes.

I took off, running for the back stairs.

CHAPTER 10

GWEN, 31ST OCTOBER 1612

The stairs lay shrouded in darkness, the storm having smothered the last frail light of autumn. Heart pounding, I rushed the last step and stumbled into the kitchen, almost careering into Cook.

She staggered back, a hand clamped to her mouth and her eyes wide as saucers.

'There's a man here,' she hissed, leaning in to whisper in my ear. 'Your father just sent me to fetch you. You can't be here, Gwen. He's bad blood! I can tell!'

'I know,' I said, my voice cracking and fresh tears stinging my eyes.

Cook sniffed and pulled me into a fierce hug. She took a shuddering breath, squeezed me hard and then, all too soon, stepped away.

'They're in the front parlour. Go out the back to the stables. Be quick – he said he has men coming behind him. I'll tell him you went to the cottage,' she said, wringing the handkerchief in her hands.

I hesitated, but the sound of Taylor's heavy feet slapping on the floorboards in the passageway sent a spasm of fear through me. I ran to the back door and flung myself through it, fighting to close it behind me as the wind tried to wrestle it from my grip. Cook threw her weight against it, and I exhaled as I heard her turn the key in the lock. Chest heaving, I pressed my back to the wood, trying to catch my breath.

'Didn't he ask you to bring Gwenllian?' Taylor bellowed from inside the kitchen.

'Well, if I'd found her, I would have brought her, wouldn't I?' Cook retorted, matching him in volume and her voice sharp as thorns.

After a beat, Taylor spoke again. 'She's not in her room, then?'

'Didn't I just say as much? She must be at the cottage,' Cook said irritably.

'Well go and fetch her!' Taylor snapped.

'Fetch her your bloody self! Or do you want to make the tea for his lordship?'

The possibility of Taylor leaving by the back door galvanised me into action. I hurled myself into the gale and ran through the kitchen garden, my dress and cloak already soaked and heavy as lead around my ankles. I headed for the long thicket of bramble bushes that connected the garden to the orchard. Once amongst the fruit trees, the stables would be in sight.

Although the rain was strangely warm, the strength of it landed like needles on my skin. The wind, fierce as a wolf's howl, snatched my breath when I risked a glance over my shoulder. It seemed to follow me, shifting as I changed direction so that it was always at my back again, propelling me forward.

At the stables, Mal was standing under the cover of the open hay barn with Tân already tacked up. For a moment, I thought I was dreaming. Take away the storm and my pounding heart and this could be any normal day.

Tân whickered softly when he caught sight of me. Mal followed his gaze, and his shoulders dropped.

'How did you know?' I asked him.

Mal gave me a sad smile. 'Your gran told me to get him ready. Saw her as clear as you are now,' he replied, shaking his head as if he still couldn't quite believe it.

'She always trusted you,' I said, touching my hand to his arm, then regretting it when I saw his cheeks flare with colour under his freckles.

Tân reared up. While his feet were just inches off the ground, his meaning was clear. I wasted no time in mounting.

As Mal tightened the girth, I said, 'Thank you, for everything. Please go fetch your mam from the house. I don't think it's safe—' I might have said more, tried to explain where the thought had appeared from, but Tân took off as if all the devils of hell were on our heels.

When we neared the lane, Tân veered off to the right, into the field that, back in the summer, had been full of swaying wheat. Given the storm, it should have been a quagmire, and yet the ground beneath Tân's feet was firm, without even a trace of a puddle. The rain had stopped too, and the howling wind was now a lilting breath stirring the air. The storm had passed, then, which meant they might already be looking for me.

Tân thundered the length of the field, only slowing when we reached the break in the hedge that led back to the road. He stood, chest heaving, ears swivelling. Once we were both satisfied with the silence, we crossed, heading straight for the woods on the other side.

We rarely took this path. It was far easier to cross directly opposite the house and take the steeper but more direct route up the mountain. This path was much wider, the incline more suited to the workhorses that brought felled trees down the slopes.

Once we were in the woods, Tân took off again, not slowing until we reached what had always been our secret lookout point. It was a large flat boulder that, as a child, I had imagined was the palm of the mountain goddess bursting out of the earth. As it was directly opposite my father's house but concealed by the trees, I spent many a happy hour here, watching the comings and goings and daydreaming about one day sharing my secret spot with my father. That never happened, of course.

'Shall we risk it?' I asked Tân. There were still enough leaves on the trees to conceal us should anyone think to look up, but I'd only get sight of the house from the ground.

Tân answered by inching forward then planting his feet.

I slipped from the saddle and crept towards the boulder, flattening myself onto my belly then wriggling to the edge.

I gasped, unable to believe my eyes. The house remained caught in the jaws of the raging storm.

'Nain.' I breathed her name, my heart tightening at the thought of her. Nain had sent the storm to keep me safe.

I was about to creep away when a movement at the house caught my eye. A tall man in grey emerged from the front door, my father hobbling in his wake, Taylor hovering behind him. My father was bracing himself against the door-frame and waving his cane down the lane towards Nain's cottage, but the grey man was paying him scant attention. His gaze was on the old coach house. As I watched, three dark figures on horseback peeled away from its shadows. The grey man, one hand pinning his hat to his head, used the other to stab a finger at the first man, then pointed towards the orchard. He directed the second man to the lane and the third – my heart dropped like a stone – to the mountain.

'No. No. No!' I mumbled. 'They're coming after me!' My hands slipped on the flat rock as I tried to push myself back from the edge.

Tân fidgeted, throwing up his head and snorting.

I tasted bright copper on my tongue a heartbeat before my skin prickled. I turned back to the house just in time to see lightning strike it. The horses on the driveway below all reared, depositing their riders in the mud before bolting. Just as the men scrambled to their feet, another fork pierced the sky, and I watched in horror as a majestic old oak, still smouldering from the direct hit, flung itself across the lane, blocking the shortcut to the mountain path.

I sprang from the rock into the saddle, and Tân took off the moment my boots found the stirrups.

CHAPTER 11
GWEN, 31ST OCTOBER 1612

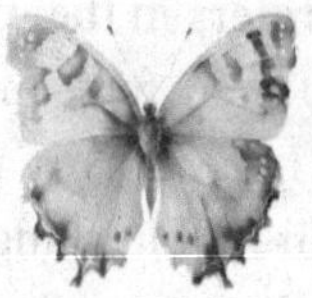

*H*ad there really been a time when, standing in this very meadow, gazing down at the valley below, my greatest fear had been my lack of magic?

Being here now, I feel like some ancient crone remembering her childhood. What I would trade for a chance to go back to my old troubles. I would gladly fail every magical test she set for me just to spend a day cooped up with Nain, failing at spell work. I wiped a tear from my cheek. We didn't have time to linger.

I took one last look at my beautiful valley and feathered my fingers against the left rein, giving Tân his cue that I was ready to go.

As we walked along the ridge, heading east, I looked up into a pale blue sky untroubled by clouds. While the sun wasn't strong, there was warmth enough to make tiny wisps of steam rise from my sodden skirts. I tied the reins and let them drop so I could wring the water from my skirts. It wouldn't be good for Tân to have wet cloth against his sides.

Still focused on the task, I tipped forward in the saddle when Tân stopped abruptly. The trees were thin here, providing a clear view of my father's house in the valley down below. My skirts slipped from my hands as I stared, wide-eyed, slack-jawed and too stunned to even breathe.

The grand house stood encased in a bubble of torment. What I had taken for a raging storm was, from this vantage point, a dragon woven from shadow and fury, twisting and howling around the house as lightning split the sky again and again and thunder rolled like a battle cry. It had to be a trick of the light, surely?

The stables were untouched, of course. I could even see my father's horses grazing contentedly in the neighbouring fields. I hoped that Mal and Cook were safely in their cottage, Sage on someone's lap, purring.

The storm was the most peculiar and fantastical thing I had ever seen. As if someone had dropped black writing ink onto a pretty watercolour scene. I didn't know how such magic worked, but I was certain that other members of the coven would have had a hand in raising this much energy. They did this for me. Risked themselves to give me a chance to escape. I swallowed the lump in my throat and asked Tân to walk on.

We had only taken two steps when I felt the air pressure change around us. I cast around me, panic suddenly rising, but we were alone on the mountain top. Suddenly, Tân leapt backwards, and I rocked in my seat, grabbing the saddle to steady myself.

He planted his front feet wide and leaned down, neck craned low to the ground. He snorted, but it was the kind of sound he reserved for children and small animals, soft and curious. I leaned forward in my stirrups, craning to see what had caught his attention.

I blinked at the sight of what looked to be a small white cloud, no bigger than an apple, hanging in the air just above the ground. As I stared, it drifted up towards me. Tân turned his head to follow it. My pulse quickened as I felt the magic growing nearer. Heart hammering, I held out my palm. The cloud felt more like the fur of a kit than the cool, damp air I had been expecting.

It moved like a cloud, though, shifting and undulating as if buffered by invisible internal winds. I leaned closer, my eye caught on something darker within its swirling layers.

The wind picked up, taking wisps of the cloud with it, and the shape within grew clearer. I held my breath, afraid to even blink in case I missed a moment of whatever this might be. And then, I saw it. A small meadow brown butterfly encased in the last tendrils of drifting cloud.

'Oh, no,' I groaned.

I hadn't meant to speak aloud, but I wasn't ready for this. Less than an hour ago, I'd assured Nain that the spell hadn't sent any magic to me, but now, here I was looking at what could only be the physical manifestation of orphaned magic. Magic that Nain had sworn to protect. I might have laughed at the irony, let alone the timing of its arrival, but as I looked at the small, helpless creature, all I wanted to do was take care of it.

'You're safe now, little one,' I said, extending my hand and using the same tone I'd use with any wounded creature I found in the woods. After a moment's indecision, the butterfly settled on my palm with a weight it shouldn't have possessed, and my entire hand tingled at the touch.

'I'm sorry for what happened to your witch,' I said, my voice thick with emotion as I tried not to think about what some poor soul might be suffering as we spoke. 'You have my word of honour that I will do everything in my power to protect you and then return you to your line as soon as it is safe.'

The butterfly fluttered up to my eye level, looped in the

air and then vanished. I gasped, and Tân stopped walking, turning his head to meet my eye.

'She's gone,' I breathed.

Had I said the wrong thing? Inadvertently turned the poor thing away. Was it because I didn't have magic? Was I not worthy?

Panic fluttered in my chest. It was an odd sensation but somehow familiar. I frowned until I realised that I'd felt this before, but in my cupped hands as I rescued a moth or butterfly from the cottage or stables. The breath of wings, ephemeral against my skin. But now that sensation was in my chest.

I barked out a laugh.

'It's okay,' I said. 'She's still here. I can feel her here.' I tapped the flat of my palm against the skin just beneath my collarbones.

I gasped as the fluttering turned to a tingling warmth that radiated through my body, then outwards into the energy that surrounded me, softening the world as if I had just plucked a fresh rainbow from the sky and thrown myself into it.

Tân snorted and stomped his foot. He was right. Magical miracles or not, we needed to keep going. I picked up the reins, and I didn't need to ask for the canter or the gallop that followed it. As we thundered across the spine of the mountain, all I could think about was keeping my promise to Nain – and to the orphaned magic I had just sworn to protect.

CHAPTER 12

GWEN, 31ST OCTOBER 1612

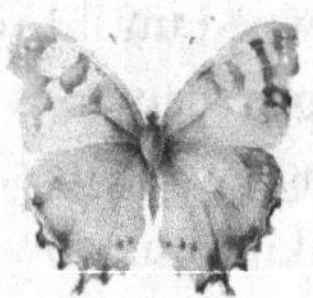

Tân didn't slow for anything on the ride to Talybont. I tried to persuade him, concerned about his legs on such a long ride, but he wouldn't listen. While I'd visited the Owens many times with Nain as a child, it had been years since I'd been here, and I couldn't picture the whole route to their house in my mind.

Thankfully, Tân remembered the way, but he seemed to be avoiding the roads, opting instead to race across country, through woodland and, on more than a few occasions, jumping the thick hedges that divided the fields. Despite his fiery reputation, he had never been one for jumping, and I didn't enjoy it much either.

When we reached the edge of an old stone wall, Tân slowed to a decisive walk, his ribcage heaving and his hot breath misting in the cooling air. While our daily rides took us for miles, this distance at such a speed must have exhausted him.

'I can walk now,' I said, patting his sweaty neck and slipping my feet from the stirrups.

Tân snorted his reply and lengthened his stride. Stubborn

bloody horse. Well, two could play at that game. I leaned forward and swung my leg from the saddle. With an exaggerated snort, he planted his feet as I slipped to the floor. My muscles felt as stiff as rusty hinges, my legs wobbly as a foal's.

I pulled the reins over his head and stepped in front of him. He was still breathing hard, but one look at his eyes told me he had lost none of his determination. I leaned my forehead to his, stroked his damp cheeks and breathed him in.

'Thank you, my friend,' I whispered.

He snorted gently, and I moved his forelock so that I could plant a kiss on the star that lay hidden behind it. When I stepped back, he took a half-step forward, nudging my shoulder with his nose. He was right. We needed to keep going. The sun was already sliding behind the hills and the shadows were lengthening. I walked at Tân's side, following his lead as he turned off the lane and onto a narrow track flanked with chestnut trees. Their leaves, turned golden in the autumn sunlight, carpeted the ground, a few nuts encased in their spiny burs amongst them.

John and Birdie Owen were not regulars at our coven – it was too long a journey to make regularly – but had they been there on the night of the spell? How much did they know? How much should I tell them? They were family friends, but I didn't really know them like Nain did. Could I trust them? And what danger was I bringing to their door? My head throbbed, joining the fiery ache in my back and seat as I hurried to keep pace with my beloved horse. Goddess knew how Tân must be feeling, having carried his own weight and mine for so many miles. I reached over and stroked his neck, glad to see that, while still damp, he wasn't sweating now.

Up ahead, the tree-line opened to reveal a modest house and farmyard sitting to the right of what was clearly the end of the track. There would be no passing visitors to this house. Getting here would always be a deliberate choice.

An old collie lay in a patch of sunlight across the front door, paws twitching in sleep. A black-and-white flash appeared from the side of the house, and before I could take another step, there was a younger dog weaving around my feet, tail wagging so enthusiastically it was nothing more than a blur.

I dropped to my knees as Tân planted his feet to avoid stepping on the dog.

'Well, hello to you,' I said, my fingers sliding through a sleek and shining coat. I relaxed a little. People who cared properly for their animal kin were good souls. Nain had drummed that into me from the cradle.

'Oh, thank the Goddess!' The voice was deep but edged with a shadow of approaching frailty.

I looked up to see John stepping carefully over the old collie. I recognised him at once. He was more stooped than I remembered, and he moved as if his joints pained him, but he was still the small man from my childhood memories who used to carve dolls for his daughter, Bethan, and horses for me when we played together here.

I raised my hand in a wave to hide the fact that I didn't know what to say now that I was standing here on their land.

'You got away in time then, girl,' he said, putting a gnarled hand over his heart.

He smiled, crinkling up his eyes and ploughing deep grooves into his skin, his expression a tangle of sadness and relief.

'This is a bad business. Bad business indeed, but Mary's delivered you safe, God rest her soul. I knew the minute she appeared to us that—'

'Gwenllian!'

There was no mistaking Birdie's sonorous voice. She was a head taller than her husband, with the robustness that spoke of good harvests and hard physical work. Her pale curls poked out from her headscarf like curious hens.

'We were beside ourselves with worry,' she said as she hurried across the yard, the old collie finally awake and tottering at her side.

John stepped around me and addressed Tân.

'Come on, lad. You've earned a long drink and a soft bed tonight,' he said, offering his hand, palm up, for inspection. Without hesitation, Tân pressed his nose into it and leaned in when John reached up to scratch his neck. I relaxed. If Tân trusted the Owens, then I could too.

CHAPTER 13

GWEN, 31ST OCTOBER 1612

*L*ater, with the dogs snoozing at my feet in front of the hearth and my stomach full of the stew Birdie had persuaded me to eat, I felt some of the tension slip from my shoulders. When I closed my eyes, I could almost believe I was back in Nain's cottage, the warmth from the fire heating my cheeks, the smell of drying herbs and beeswax mingling with the ghost of bread baked that morning.

Could buildings have a soul, or did they just reflect the energies of the people who inhabited them? I had never felt at home in my father's grand house despite its comforts, and yet this place, just like the cottage, seemed to hold me in invisible arms.

The young dog, May, began wagging her tail long before John pushed open the back door. A chill breeze took its chance and swept into the kitchen, nipping at the back of my neck.

'He's got a yawn the width of a barn door, that one,' John said with a smile as he closed the door, banishing the cold.

'His legs are still fine though. He told me it was time to leave by lying down.' John chuckled. 'He's a good soul, that one.'

I felt another knot loosen from my chest on hearing the news. I'd been out to the stables to see Tân three times since we'd arrived. The first to check that his legs hadn't swollen from the day's exertions and the second to take him an apple before supper. I'd stayed to brush him, even though John had already done a thorough job of it. John wouldn't have known the itch spot that made Tân pull funny faces, or that he enjoyed having his cheeks stroked as you whispered to him.

'Thank you, John,' I said. 'For taking care of him and—' I faltered, unsure of what to say next.

John pursed his lips and looked like he was about to reply, but Birdie hurried into the kitchen carrying an armful of blankets. 'The night's taken a chill to it, so best warm these before you turn in,' she said, stepping carefully around the dogs and piling the blankets next to me on the old settle.

There were so many questions buzzing around in my mind. The most pressing was what would happen if the men came here looking for me. I could hide, but what about Tân? What if they took him? Claimed he belonged to my father. The thought was like an iron hand around my throat, and I couldn't find the breath to ask. Why hadn't I thought of this before? I should stay in the stables with him, so that if we needed to flee, we could.

Birdie spoke, stemming the haemorrhage of thoughts that had just erupted into my mind.

'You're safe here tonight, Gwen. You and Tân,' she said, emphasising the 'and'. Had I spoken my fears aloud? I was too weary to remember.

'We have magic enough to conceal the farm for a short while. I'll do you a tea to make sure you get a good night's sleep, and in the morning, we'll talk about the plans to get you on to Builth,' Birdie said, leaning in so that she could squeeze my shoulder as she spoke.

The reminder, so gently delivered, still landed like a slap. I didn't mean to cry out, but the sound, part whimper, part sob, escaped before I could stop it.

Birdie pushed the blankets aside and sat beside me, pulling me into her arms and rocking me, just as Nain had that last night I'd spent with her. Just like Nain, Birdie soothed me with promises that everything would be fine. May nosed my hand and then sat, her back pressed into my leg. I cried. For Nain, my long-dead mother and my home. Was I to add my freedom to the list of losses too? Perhaps even my life? I cried next for the witch whose magic I now carried. A small part of me even cried with the joy of being held and rocked and comforted by a near stranger.

When the tears finally dried up, May jumped to her feet and put her paw on my leg. When I leaned in to stroke her head, she licked the inside of my wrist. I smiled at the gesture.

'Settle now, May,' John said kindly.

The dog glanced at him over her shoulder but kept her paw on my leg.

'That's telling you, then,' Birdie said with a laugh.

'She's a wise one alright,' John said, the pride clear in his tone and the way he looked at the dog.

'She knows when folk need her. Does the same with lambs that need watching. Never wrong,' Birdie said, reaching over to stroke the dog's head. 'Come on, cariad, I'll show you your bed,' she continued, getting to her feet and gathering the blankets.

May ran to the foot of the stairs and waited.

I smiled. 'I'd love the company. Is she allowed?' I asked, mentally crossing my fingers.

Birdie and John exchanged a smile.

'Go on then, girl. You mind her,' John said to the dog.

May vaulted up the stairs and was sitting by the bed, tail thumping, when Birdie showed me into the tiny room moments later. I could never explain to May how much I appreciated her at that moment. Or perhaps she already knew.

Despite the tea and my bone-deep exhaustion, sleep danced just out of reach. The small bed, tucked beneath weather-worn rafters, was warm and comfortable thanks to the freshly stuffed straw mattress and the small mound of hearth-warmed blankets Birdie had pressed into my arms.

May had claimed the end of the bed the moment Birdie's footsteps had faded. As the fragile slice of moonlight tracked across the tiny window, the silence broken only by the screaming of owls and foxes as they claimed the night for their hunting, May inched closer until she lay curled against my side.

As dawn broke, my head at last heavy with sleep that I couldn't give in to, I felt a strange fluttering at the edge of my consciousness. I levered myself up to sitting, leaning my back against the cool wall. I had all but forgotten the butterfly, my mind so tangled with the journey and hard reality that was crystallising around me.

The pressure shifted around me and May lifted her head, ears cocked, eyes trained on something I couldn't yet see. The meadow brown butterfly appeared in front of me just as the first rays of the watery morning light picked their way around the edges of the curtains. May thumped her tail rhythmically against the blankets.

'You can see her too, then,' I whispered, and somehow, in that moment, I didn't feel so alone.

CHAPTER 14

GWEN, 1ST NOVEMBER 1612

I must have drifted off, because I woke to the sound of raised voices. The sun was stronger, the morning fully upon us, and I had the sense that I'd slept far later than was usual for me. Beside me, May wagged her tail lazily and, upon seeing that I was awake, rolled onto her back. Stroking the dog's soft fur, I strained my ears to hear what was being said downstairs.

There were at least three people, maybe more. Their conversation was muffled and too quiet for me to make out, save for the occasional outbursts, which were followed by a chorus of hushings.

Unable to stand it any longer, I threw back the covers and pulled on my clothes as quietly as I could.

I had planned to listen from the landing, but May ran off ahead of me, tail waving like a flag in a summer breeze.

Birdie appeared at the foot of the stairs. She smiled up at me, but she looked wound as tight as a twisted knot.

'Morvith and Owain are here to see you, Gwen,' she said, beckoning to me.

I'd seen neither since Nain's funeral.

We buried Nain on Mabon. A sliver of moon still hovered in the palest of skies, the morning cold and full of drifting mist as if the dragons too were sighing their last farewells. In the trees, the birds were silent, but that night, a lone robin had sung outside my window even after darkness fell.

On seeing me, Morvith struggled to her feet, one twisted hand on the table and the other leaning heavily on her walking stick. She tsked and flapped away John's offer of help.

Nain had been apprentice to Morvith when she was a girl, and I had grown up in awe of her power and more than a little intimidated. Morvith was loved and revered in equal measure, and there wasn't a witch in Wales who would dare cross her, even now. Despite her good heart, just like Nain, she had a whip-sharp tongue and no time for fools. That time was slowly drawing her away from this world and into the next was why she had stepped aside two years ago, insisting that Nain lead the coven and ensure a smooth transition once her time came. But then Nain, at least twenty years her junior, had died and left us all adrift.

I stepped forward quickly to save the old woman from having to take too many steps on knees that made her wince with every one.

Morvith smiled at me and, with great care, touched my cheek with her arthritic hand. Her bright blue eyes, one clouded with a thick white mist, searched my face. After a moment, the old woman nodded and patted my cheek before turning, this time accepting John's proffered arm as he guided her back to her seat.

'Morvith and Owain have come with news, Gwen,' Birdie said, twisting the front of her shawl with restless fingers.

I sank onto a stool at the end of the table and May stationed herself next to me, leaning her body against my leg. I stroked her fur and tried to ignore my dry mouth and the sick feeling in my stomach. I looked from one face to the other. Nobody, save for Morvith, seemed to want to meet my eye.

The silence stretched out between us until Morvith huffed loudly.

'Owain,' she snapped. 'Tell her.'

Owain shuffled in his seat and ran his hand nervously over his thinning hair. He had always been pale, his hair and even his eyebrows so blond as to look practically white, but he usually had more colour to his cheeks than he had today. He rubbed at the back of his neck as if he needed to coax the words from his throat. Morvith tsked loudly, and after casting her an anxious glance, he cleared his throat and began.

'As you know, Gwen, I am the coven scribe, and it is my duty to write out all spells of import twice. One copy stays with the coven and the other is sent to Aberystwyth for safe-keeping in the archive,' he said earnestly.

I nodded.

'I did as much for the safe harbour spell we cast, the one where you ...' Owain paused and licked his lips.

'The one I interrupted by fainting,' I mumbled.

'The one where you prevented us being discovered by strangers,' Morvith corrected, pointing a crooked finger at me.

Owain pressed on. 'We didn't get to complete the spell that night, but we tried again on the Hunter's Moon.'

I snapped to attention and felt the flutter of tiny wings against my ribs.

'You did?'

In the weeks since Nain had passed, I had given little thought to anything besides trying to remember how to breathe in and out each day.

'Owain!' Morvith said, banging her stick on the ground to

add an exclamation mark. 'Tell her the important part and make quick about it. This is all taking too long.'

'There was a mistake in the spell, Gwen,' he said.

'Nain told me before she died,' I interrupted, so that he wouldn't get told off again for telling me something I already knew. 'I didn't know you'd tried again, though,' I said, feeling suddenly self-conscious as I realised it sounded like an accusation. Why would they have invited me? Everyone knew I had no magic.

'You needed time to grieve, Gwenllian. We wanted to respect that. But, as we discovered, we couldn't redo the spell without you,' Morvith sighed.

'There's something else, see, Gwen,' Owain said quickly, echoing Nain's words from the day before. 'We were in a hurry to help, what with the killings and all, and so we—'

'You,' corrected Morvith.

Owain sighed and hung his head. 'Aye. Me,' he said miserably.

Birdie stepped towards Owain and rested her hand on his shoulder. 'This isn't your fault, Owain. We all missed it, even Mary, Goddess rest her,' she said, aiming a steely look at Morvith, who appeared entirely unfazed.

I swallowed hard at the mention of Nain's name and the rising tension in the room.

Slumping forward in his chair, Owain said, 'I'm not talking about the mistake in the spell, Birdie,' he said, glancing up at her before dropping his gaze to the floor.

The skin on my neck prickled in warning. If this was something the Owens didn't know about it, it was unlikely to be good news.

'Here's the thing, Gwen. I thought I was saving time, you know, seeing as how important the work was and all, but—' He sucked in a breath and let it out slowly before continuing. 'I sent the claiming spell with the original.'

John's jaw dropped and Birdie's hands flew to cover her face as she let out a high, broken sound.

'Oh, Owain!' John said, sinking onto a stool and resting his head in his hand.

'Do you understand, Gwen?' Owain said, his eyes, full of pleading, finding mine.

'Of course she doesn't understand, man. You're talking in riddles.' Morvith spat the words and thumped the wooden table with her fist, making everyone jump. 'Gwen,' she said levelly, 'what Owain is trying to say is that because you are now the sole recipient of these displaced magics, should anyone be so minded, they can claim whatever magic you hold for themselves.'

'What?' My brain felt like it was running to catch up.

Morvith's face softened into something that looked like pity, and my stomach dropped. I pushed to my feet, needing to move and wanting an excuse not to look at her. May whined from where she sat by my now empty stool.

'I fear, Gwenllian, that you do not fully grasp the grave nature of your situation,' Morvith said sharply. 'Did Mary tell you that our messenger was attacked on the road to Aber?'

I hesitated. 'No,' I said tartly as I kneaded my palm with my thumb, trying to focus on my hands and not the cold, oily dread coiling in my stomach.

'The flaw in the first spell means that any orphaned magic will come to you and only you, now that Mary is gone. It is a beacon in the magical world we have so far been unable to extinguish, but that much you know already.'

I bit my lip as I paced, sensing with every step that what came next would be even worse.

'The claiming spell was a safeguard to be squirrelled away in the archive in case future generations needed to claim ancestral magic from their line. However, that too had a flaw, didn't it, Owain?'

He nodded, speaking to the floor without looking up. 'As I said, Gwen, I was rushing and …'

'What he's trying to say is that anyone can claim the magic that comes to you for safekeeping, not just the kin of those who sent it.' Morvith curled her lip as she spoke, her flinty gaze on Owain's still-bowed head.

I stopped my pacing and took a breath. My head was spinning. 'But what does this have to do with my cousin and that horrible man?'

Morvith cursed under her breath and rubbed a gnarled hand over her temple.

'Charles means to do away with you so he can inherit your father's land,' Morvith said, speaking slowly and with an obvious effort to rein in her frustration.

'It was your mother's land,' Birdie said bitterly. 'Thomas Maddox was nobody before he married her, Gwen. Why do you think he took your family name as his own? All that talk of him being a long-lost Llewellyn cousin was pure invention! You remember that, my girl! And it was your mother's quick mind and kindness that made the farms successful,' Birdie said bitterly.

'We are getting away from the point,' Morvith huffed.

I smiled at Birdie as I tucked that new piece of information away. My heart was hammering now, my mouth dry as old bones and my back clammy beneath my shift. I already had all the pieces of this nightmarish story, but somewhere in my panic, my mind was refusing to put them all together.

It was John who spoke next. 'I think what we're saying, Gwen, is that whoever attacked the messenger on the way to Aber now knows we cast a spell to shelter other witches' magic. If they've got half a mind, they'll spot the mistake and realise that the magic went only to one person. And as they've got the claiming spell too …'

I finished for him, my lips moving even before the thought had fully crystallised in my mind.

'If they know about Nain, then they'll know it's come to me.'

'It's worse than that, my girl,' Morvith said.

I stared at her, wondering how this nightmare could get any more terrifying.

'We think the attack on the messenger was planned by a magic hunter. We still don't know for sure who the men in the woods that night were – we assumed they were working for your cousin – but these are dangerous times, and it seems we have many foes.'

'You think this magic hunter will come looking for me?' I asked, rounding the table and forcing myself to look Morvith in the eye.

'He will. And if he finds you, he'll keep you locked up like a brood mare as you gather in orphaned magic, and then, when you're full to bursting, he'll rip it out of you and use the claiming spell to take it all for himself,' Morvith said with a disgusted growl.

'Morvith!' Birdie cried, banging her fists on the table. 'She's just a child!'

'She is not!' Morvith snapped. 'The girl needs the truth, Birdie. Not fairy stories. There is no comfort in lies. She needs the hope that only truth can deliver, no matter how hard that is to hear.'

Morvith turned to me. 'We have put you in grave danger, Gwenllian, and for that I am sorry, but there is more than your life at stake now. If this hunter, or the next, finds you before we can undo the spell, then every member of the magical community is as good as dead.

'Once it is known that there is a witch sheltering the magic of others, you will become the Holy Grail of magic hunters the world over! If one claimed the orphaned magic for himself then he would possess enough power to enslave the world!'

'Or heal it,' I stammered.

Morvith snorted. 'Don't be naïve, child.'

The world seemed to still in that moment. Even the spitting logs in the fire held their breath. I felt something wither inside me, like a cloud blotting out the sun and casting me into a permanent shadow.

'What do I do, Morvith?' I asked. My voice felt strange, like it belonged to someone else.

'Live, child. If you die, the magic you carry will be lost, remember that,' Morvith said with a heavy sigh.

I swallowed hard, balling my hands into fists to hide their trembling, the butterfly in my chest hurling itself now against my ribs as if they were the bars of a cage.

I took a deep breath. 'But if I am a risk then maybe it would be better for all if—'

'Never let me hear you finish that thought, Gwenllian!' Morvith slammed her cane onto the tabletop to emphasise her point.

I flinched, screwing up my eyes against the threat of tears and pressing my nails into my palms.

'Mary arranged for you to go to the Morgans in Builth. They are the only family with power enough to protect you until we can reconvene the coven. But tell them nothing of this, do you hear me? Not even Rhys. They are good people, but they didn't get where they are today without a more than healthy dose of ambition. You tell them nothing of us.'

My hand drifted to my chest as I listened. The butterfly settled at the mention of the Morgans, her wings soft against my still-racing heart as if she meant to soothe it. She liked that plan, then.

'And share the burden among us,' I said absently.

Birdie sighed, and when I looked up, everyone but Morvith dropped their gaze to the floor.

Morvith took a moment to reply. 'I think that option is now lost to us, Gwen. I will not ask my brothers and sisters to risk such a thing. When we meet, we will undo the spell and put an end to this matter once and for all.'

'But what will happen to any magic already sheltering with me?' I asked, pressing my hand to my chest.

'I'm sorry, Gwen,' was her only reply.

I had so many more questions, but Morvith was already struggling to her feet. I tried to focus. Tried to order the jumble of thoughts in my mind, but only one made it to my lips.

'Morvith,' I called out as she shuffled towards the door, Owain following behind her. 'How long before the coven can meet again?'

Morvith turned and smiled kindly. 'We will send word to Builth. If not the next moon, then certainly by Yule.'

I nodded, rubbing the top of my chest, desperate to feel the flutter of wings that had grown suddenly still. I could wait a month. Even two if I had to.

PART II

1975

CHAPTER 15

GWEN, OCTOBER 1974

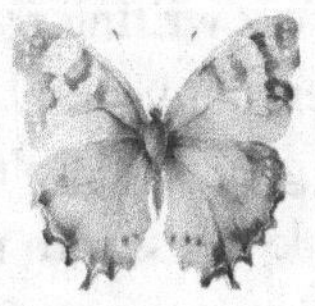

An arc of light swept across the bedroom wall, startling me from a fretful sleep. Someone had turned off the high road. While it couldn't have been the car's headlights – the drive was almost a mile long – I had long ago stopped doubting the portends the Goddess sent my way.

The raven's feather on the doorstep, blue-black and misted with raindrops, the flames in the hearth that all danced like demons, refusing to warm my stubbornly cold flesh, and then, this morning, a barn owl drifting through the waking sky just as I stepped out of the house. That was a sign I'd learned never to ignore.

Anxious wings rattled within my chest – they could feel it too. I pushed my feet into the boots next to my bed and was up and running even before my heart quickened. I sprinted into the empty bedroom on the east side of the old mansion, where I had a clear line of sight to the long, winding driveway. Nobody came here, and yet, under a pale sickle of a moon, there was now a car stalking towards the house.

The butterflies surged in my chest, and I braced my hands

against the windowsill, holding them back. It was all the confirmation I needed. Just before I turned from the window, I saw the car's headlights blink out.

I moved on instinct, racing down the stairs and bouncing off the walls at the half-landings to save precious seconds.

My boots crunched against broken tiles and fallen plaster as I landed in the once grand hallway and turned for the kitchen that doubled as my writing room. I snatched up the typewriter's ribbon cover, hooked my finger under the inky strip to free it from the guides and plucked the spools from their pins. I balled the inky mess into my pocket, writing off another pair of jeans.

I couldn't take the typewriter; it would only slow me down. I should have bought the lighter Olivetti, but the shop assistant insisted the Royal was the model preferred by Ian Fleming, and the reference to that other gentleman spy turned author had dropped a little pebble of grief in my throat.

I flicked the cover closed and swept up the tightly bound folder containing my almost finished manuscript. The journey from the main road to the house would take them less than three minutes, and I was already down to two.

I bolted through the old scullery to the boiler room and stopped at the back door, listening hard. Although my heart was pounding, I felt no frenzy of wings, so I inched the door open and stepped out into the darkness. I had time to register the faintest crunch of tyres on gravel from the front of the house before I took off again. I didn't stop running until I reached the old coach house, slipping in through the side door.

A casual glance at the building from the house suggested it was derelict. More than a third of its roof had long since lost its tiles, and its windows were boarded and black with mould. The first time I stayed here, I parked an old, rusting tractor in front of the main doors and planted a bramble bush beneath its wheels. After fifteen years, a wall of thorns now buried the old machine, exposing its skeletal outline only in the depths of winter as the plant conspired with me in my deceit.

The double doors at the back of the coach house were another matter. They opened onto a steep, tree-lined private lane that connected the house with the main road. I allowed the summer grasses and annuals to root around their base, but anything that might impede the doors, I swiftly removed.

The two small ramps in the coach house had perplexed me when I'd first seen them until I realised that backing the car up onto them meant I could release the handbrake and roll into the lane without starting the engine. I'd laughed when the realisation dawned, and sent up a silent thank you to the one and only person I'd ever had the privilege of calling a friend.

I pulled open the heavy double doors, then flung myself into the driver's seat. The Cortina slid obediently from the ramps the moment I released the handbrake. I turned the wheel, angling the car down the steep hill and into darkness so thick it might have been tar.

It would take them a while to search all forty-eight rooms in the crumbling old house, and I prayed they'd be thorough. The last thing I needed was for them to search the grounds.

I felt wings, heavy as rain-battered roses, in my chest. They were right. There would be no coming back to Tintagel now. Pendarrow House was compromised. I thought of the first time I'd come here, heartsore and lost in the world once again after all too brief a respite from my miserably long life. How many times had I come since? I'd lost count. A lump rose in my throat, and I swallowed hard. Sentiment got you killed. Or worse.

When I felt the car's momentum slowing, I turned the key

in the ignition and pressed hard on the accelerator, but didn't switch on the headlights. While they'd be almost impossible to see from the house, I wasn't about to take the risk. I could drive this route blindfolded if I needed to.

Up ahead, the solitary street light that marked the T-junction flickered as if its bulb might blink out at any moment. I flicked on the headlights, checked for traffic, then sped away into the night.

CHAPTER 16

GWEN, JUNE 1975

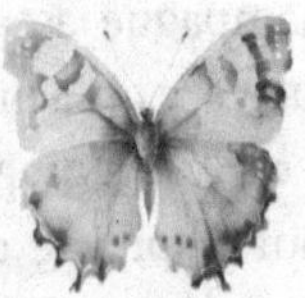

The double doors to the ballroom creaked on their hinges as I pushed them open. There were thirty-two interior doors in this house, and they were all reassuringly vocal under even the slightest pressure.

I'd arrived in Wells last night, just after dark. The old house was on the far side of town and backed onto open fields and woodland. It was half the size of the Tintagel house, but still large enough to provide multiple escape routes. A high stone wall around the half-acre garden did what it could to disguise the fact that unlike so many of the others, this house had neighbours.

Stonefields House sat in the crook of a curving street on the outskirts of the small, quaint cathedral city. Had it not been for the wall, the grand old house would have looked out of place amongst the neat, three-storey terraces with their wrought-iron front gates and freshly swept steps.

Contractors maintained the gardens to keep complaining neighbours at bay, and from the outside, the place looked presentable enough. Just like the others, however, the inside told a story of abandonment and quiet, dignified decay. The old house deserved better. They all did. It deserved a family with a gaggle of children to slide down the banisters, maraud through the wide hallways and romp around the gardens with a troop of happy dogs.

Especially this room, I thought, as I stood in the entrance of the vast, hollow ballroom. It needed to be filled with partygoers, all decked out in the finest clothes, laughing, dancing and sipping champagne as a live band played the night away. It was as if the very air ached for it.

The molten light of early evening tumbled through the long wall of French doors, spilling across the floorboards and flinging itself up the peeling walls.

Even the cobwebbed chandeliers remembered how to glow, their crystals tinkling as they moved in the draught. I felt a tug in my chest. They remembered this place too.

I sighed. I couldn't give the house children, people or dogs, but I could at least provide the music.

I carried my cello and bow to the lone chair in the middle of the room. I had barely taken my seat before they surged upwards, a crush of wings against my ribs that stole my breath.

'Okay. Okay. I know it's been a while,' I laughed.

In fairness, it had been more than a while. After fleeing from Tintagel, I'd spent close to nine months traversing the country, staying no longer than a week in any one place. I'd switched cars eleven times and had only come back here after three weeks of surveillance. It was highly unlikely that someone had unpicked the complex web of holding companies and trusts that protected me, but I needed to be sure.

There was a chance, of course, that the car I saw stalking towards the house that night contained nothing more than common burglars, but it wasn't worth the risk.

If they were hunters, then I likely only had myself to blame. I had stayed too long in Cornwall, and as the summer faded and the nights drew in, I'd given in to my loneliness. To my desires. Arnot had been a French PhD student on a research trip from St Andrews. He was tall and lithe, with the floppy hair of a poet, and while he wasn't classically handsome, he was interesting enough to catch my eye.

In hindsight, the three nights we spent together in his rented cottage, fun as they were, were definitely not worth losing my favourite house over. It was hard to see how he might have betrayed my presence, but if the wars I'd lived through had taught me anything, it was that you never could tell how people might betray you. *Or save you.* I smiled at the thought. It was true. Whenever I feared the Goddess had abandoned me, I reminded myself that she had put Walt in my path.

I adjusted the spike on my cello and wound my bow.

'No sadness today,' I said aloud. 'We've all waited a long time to do this again.'

I closed my eyes, slipped off my shoes and felt the warmth of the honeyed-oak floorboards beneath my bare feet. The pressure beneath my ribs ratcheted up, and my breath hitched. Was this what a shaken bottle of champagne felt like?

'Okay, out you come,' I said, slightly breathlessly.

The pressure changed for a heartbeat, and then with the force of a freed cork, they burst free, surging up and out into the ballroom as one joyous murmuration of iridescent wings.

I tipped my head back to watch them and wondered if I'd ever get bored with the sight. It hadn't happened in three hundred and sixty-three years, so I assumed it never would.

The spell had brought me the orphaned magic of 23,809 lost witches since that first day, and I tried not to think of the trauma and suffering that had sent each of them to me.

As I wound my bow, my newest arrival, a Giant African Swallowtail with a wingspan larger than my palm, fluttered into my eyeline. The newcomers never danced with the others, too traumatised and grief-stricken by their separation from the witch they'd known and loved.

I often wondered if, in creating the spell, my grandmother had chosen to represent magic as butterflies or whether magic had done that of its own accord.

I wondered too how the spell reached out to those in mortal danger. Morvith had called it a beacon, but could anyone with magic see it, or did it appear with the angel of death in a witch's last moments?

I had so many questions and nobody to ask.

In the early days, I wondered if magic ever refused to leave its witch, choosing oblivion and loyalty above all else. I was naïve, then, and more romantic than my circumstances should have allowed.

As I grew to understand my charges, I saw magic for what it truly is – an elemental force with one primary driver: survival. And yet, it isn't the brutal, clawing kind that rules over the forests and the jungles of the world, rather a quiet, gentle determination to live, no matter what.

The butterflies still grieved for their lost witches, and when they did, I felt it as a deep, bottomless ache that reverberated down the tether of the spell that bound each one of them to me. Some, even after centuries, still had days when their wings didn't shine as brightly and when they chose to perch and remember rather than dance.

The Swallowtail lingered, looking lost and unsure. Its black-streaked tangerine wings were beating too slowly to have kept it aloft had it been a corporeal butterfly.

'Come on,' I said, tapping the end of the cello's scroll with my finger. 'I've never met a butterfly yet who doesn't love the vibration of the strings through their feet.'

The Swallowtail hesitated. 'If you don't like it, you can sit here, with me,' I said, tapping my right shoulder.

I waited until the Swallowtail made its choice, and then, with it settled tentatively on the scroll, I closed my eyes and let out a slow, deep breath.

I levelled my bow, smiling as the butterflies above me stilled. I glanced up, glorying at the sight of their lacquered wings shimmering in the golden light. The air was electric. Their expectation and excitement palpable.

Without taking my eyes off them, I pulled my bow slowly across the C string, grinning as they quivered in the air. As I launched myself into the music, they swooped as one ecstatic murmuration that sent shivers of pure joy thrumming down the bond.

I played, and they danced, their wings reflecting the light like petals dipped in sunshine and rolled in rainbows. I thought of the top meadow, the forest and the Pont Nefoedd valley, and for a few glorious hours, I was home.

CHAPTER 17

DAN, NOVEMBER 1975

$\mathcal{I}$ was about to push open the pub door when two young men barrelled out. I heard them laughing before I saw them, stepping aside just in time to avoid a collision.

'Sorry, mate, sorry,' one said to me as he clapped his hand against his buddy's bent back.

I raised a hand. No harm done.

I watched them stumble down the street, whether through the lunchtime drink or the sheer joy of being young and laughing until your sides hurt, I couldn't tell. Best friends, I decided. Buddies to the end.

Man, the taller kid reminded me of Bobby. Maybe it was just the crew cut, a sharp contrast to the collar-length hair of his pal. And that laugh, like the whole world was there to entertain him forever. The image of him lying in the mud, the left side of his face and skull blown off and his glassy eyes frozen in terror, leapt into my mind before I had time to distract myself. I felt my heart rate kick up and balled my fists to hold off the tremor that I knew would come next if I didn't control it.

I sucked in a deep, deliberate breath, set my jaw and pulled open the pub door with a little more force than was necessary. Now was not the time to lose my shit, when I had so much riding on this meeting, not least the frickin' roof over my head.

The pub, a wide horseshoe shape with a curving central bar, was almost deserted. A large man in an off-white shirt straining over a beer belly stood behind it, smoking and talking animatedly to an elderly man with a Jack Russell at a nearby table.

I scanned the rest of the pub. Gents' toilets to the left of the bar, which meant the ladies' would likely be the other side. No stairs, meaning access to the yard out back and the flat above was through the bar. I already knew there was only one set of doors to the street – it was why I'd chosen the place.

'Afternoon, guvnor. What can I get you? Pint of …?' the barman asked cheerfully, his hand already resting on one of the pumps.

'Just an orange juice,' I said, adding, 'Thanks,' as an afterthought.

'On a Friday, mate?' he snorted. 'You sure?'

I should be used to it by now, but it still irritated me. The Brits loved their beer. Preferably tepid and in glasses with handles. I'd have killed for a cold one, even suffered the pond water they served over here, but that road only led to one place, and I wasn't going back there again.

I said nothing, just used my old parade ground stare.

The barman's smile slipped from his face as he came to his own conclusion.

'Ah, sorry, mate,' he said. 'On duty, eh?' he added, tapping the side of his nose and giving me a conspiratorial nod.

I didn't reply. The guy was free to draw his own conclusions, and it wouldn't be the first time that I'd been mistaken for a cop. Sometimes the assumption got me into trouble – my jaw hadn't been the same since that thug in Whitechapel had taken a swing at it – but right now, I planned to press the advantage, not least because the little charade was a useful distraction from the flashback I'd had outside.

I paid for my drink and found a table as far away from the bar and the cloth ears of the barman as possible. I checked my watch. Fourteen fifty-one. I sipped my tepid orange juice and watched the doors.

At just after fifteen hundred, a group of around ten men, ties loosened and overcoats unbuttoned, burst into the pub, the noise level ratcheting up with their arrival. Salesmen, I thought. Ending the week early and no doubt about to drink half their weekly bonus.

'Early today, lads. Who got target first then?' the barman asked cheerily.

The men turned as one and pointed to a short man with a thick moustache. As a cheer went up, I saw a tall, thin man wearing a camel-coloured coat the sales guys could only dream of slip into the pub. He scanned the bar, and when his eyes locked on me, I answered with a brief nod.

He was maybe early sixties, with a rich man's suntan and a shock of perfectly combed silver-grey hair. He walked like a man used to deference, his pale eyes scanning the pub as if everything offended him.

He'd likely be more at home at a private members' club, or had he lived in another time, cracking a whip on a planta-tion somewhere. There was a time when I'd have chided myself for my snap judgements, but my instincts had kept me alive – even if others hadn't been so lucky.

So, this was Reggie Briggs. It was the name he'd given on the phone, but it hadn't rung true then and it certainly didn't match the man I was looking at now.

As he came closer, I caught the hint of cologne, something subtle and expensive mixed with the rich scent of imported cigars, the kind smoked in a wing-backed chair with a glass of oak-aged cognac.

'Daniel Quinn,' he said. His voice was disarmingly soft.

I got slowly to my feet and extended my hand.

'Mr Briggs,' I said, looking him in the eye and finding in his hard, flinty gaze the confirmation that my gut instinct was right – he was bad news.

Had times been easier, I would have told him on the phone that my client list was already full, but he was the only prospect I'd had in months, and I wouldn't ask for another extension on the rent. I was in the wrong line of work if I wanted to work only for people I liked, I reminded myself.

'I don't, I'm afraid,' he said, glancing briefly at my outstretched hand.

'Drink?' I asked grudgingly, nodding to the bar.

'No,' he said, unbuttoning the bottom buttons on his suit jacket and lowering himself reluctantly onto the stool opposite, as if he feared the seat might leave a stain on the cashmere. He pulled a long, thin envelope from his inside pocket and held it out to me.

I added 'no manners' to my mental list of reasons to dislike the man perched awkwardly in front of me.

I opened the envelope and pulled out two sheets of paper and a cheque. I forced myself to look at the first printed sheet despite the almost magnetic lure of the cheque, which, at first glance, seemed to have too many zeros in the amount box. I slid it to the back and worked hard to keep my expression neutral.

The first sheet was a neatly typed profile of the woman he'd mentioned on the phone. Gwenllian Llewellyn. Approximately twenty-one years old. Five feet four. Dark hair. Known to have family in Pont Nefoedd, Wales. Last sighted in Tintagel, Cornwall, October 1974. I flipped the page over, looking for more information. It was blank.

'Why is her age an approximation?' I asked, frowning.

'Typing error,' he replied mildly. 'She's twenty-one.'

'Why is there no address for her family in Wales?'

'They have asked me to handle this as they do not want to be bothered by more detectives.' He spoke quietly, his voice low, smooth and almost breathy, yet there was no warmth in his tone and the contrast was unsettling.

I opened my mouth to ask another question, but my eye snagged on the corner of the second sheet, peeking out from behind the first. I pulled it out and saw a pencil drawing of a beautiful young woman. She had long dark hair, large, almond-shaped eyes, sharp cheekbones and full, well-defined lips.

I frowned. Photographs were the norm in a missing persons case. Granted, sometimes they were years out of date – I once tracked a guy in his thirties based only on a high school picture – but who didn't have at least one photograph of a loved one? There was something else about the image that bothered me too, but Reggie interrupted my train of thought.

'As I explained to you on the telephone, her family is desperately worried about her. She suffers with her nerves and needs treatment at once,' he said.

'I thought you were her family,' I said. 'On the phone, you said she was your niece.'

His pale eyes flashed with irritation, and for a second, I felt like I'd glimpsed the real man behind this quiet, refined facade. Like someone had snapped closed the pages of a book, but not before you caught sight of the monster in the fairy tale. He smiled before he replied.

'I meant her immediate family. She is, of course, my niece.'

I let the silence stretch until he continued.

'You come highly recommended, Mr Quinn, and while I have to confess I have reservations about Americans' – he articulated the word as if it left a bad taste in his mouth – 'you are the last in a long line of private investigators who have all failed to find her.'

'And why is that, do you think?' I asked, taking a sip of my orange juice without breaking eye contact.

'Well, that, of course, is obvious, isn't it? She doesn't want to be found,' he said, smiling.

I worked hard to maintain the eye contact even though my skin was crawling. If Vietnam had taught me anything, it was that the men to fear most are always the ones who light up when you give an order that makes the decent guys sick to their stomachs.

I'd seen enough. 'As I said to you on the phone, she's a grown woman. She has every right to disappear if that's what she chooses.'

I pressed my lips into a flat smile. I could pick up a few night shifts in the flower market to cover the rent this month. Maybe I'd say yes, this time, to making it more permanent. Until then, I should at least enjoy reminding pompous assholes that not everyone had a price sticker on their forehead.

Decided, I picked up the envelope, intending to stuff the pages and the cheque back inside, but when I looked at the drawing, the skin just below my collar bone prickled.

The memory of Linh's beautiful face, pinched in concentration, as she inked the small tattoo just below my left clavicle hit me with such force that I froze.

The prickle intensified until the tattoo burned as if Linh's needle were still scratching at the skin. I swallowed hard and resisted the urge to touch the spot. I glanced up at Reggie Briggs and sucked in a breath. Whoever this woman was, she didn't need monsters like this guy hunting her down.

The burning on my chest vanished and the words were out of my mouth before I could stop them.

'I'll take the case,' I said, already on my feet and tucking the envelope into the inside pocket of my jacket.

My new client bristled, thrown off guard, as I'd intended. He'd likely planned to leave first, but now he'd have to wait, or risk being seen leaving with me. I paused next to him, enjoying the shift in his body language as I stood a fraction too close, looking down at him.

'I'll need an address for the contract and my weekly progress reports,' I said, already knowing it would be a postal box.

'My secretary will be in touch,' he said, without looking up at me. 'And don't waste your time and my money looking in Wales; she's never been sighted there.'

I frowned, but didn't bother pointing out the obvious. Instead, I said, 'As I said on the phone, this may take some time. Like months, not weeks.'

'Just find her, Mr Quinn,' he replied smoothly.

I hurried out of the pub, pushing open the doors just as another gaggle of office workers filed in. The newsagents across the street offered a clear view of the pub doors, and I lingered, turning a rack of postcards, until I saw a silver Rolls Royce pull up to the kerb. Thirty seconds later, Reggie Briggs strode out and plunged into the waiting car.

I stepped out of the newsagents just in time to memorise the licence plate before the Rolls sped away. Time to find out who my new client really was.

CHAPTER 18

DAN, NOVEMBER 1975

The phone box stank of stale urine and spilled beer. Thankfully, the man I'd just called wasn't known for his chattiness. I asked my question. He said he'd call back within ten minutes, then hung up.

I shoved open the door and sucked in a breath. London air wasn't the cleanest, but anything was better than the smell of piss. I checked my watch. Sixteen-oh-three. My stomach growled, reminding me I'd forgotten to grab something for lunch.

I eyed the café opposite, but they were already mopping the floors, the chairs overturned on the tables. I scanned the street, looking for other options, but then the phone rang. It had been less than two minutes. I dived into the phone box and picked up.

'Identify yourself,' the voice ordered.

'Doodle,' I replied, suppressing a sigh. For such a serious man, DI Colin Heath had a strange sense of humour when it came to code names, or perhaps he was a secret fan of old musicals, who knew.

'Tread carefully on this one,' the detective said, his voice muffled as if the receiver were brushing against his moustache. 'The car is registered to the Mayfair Imperial hotel, which is owned by Sir Reginald Benedict Augustus Devlin.'

'Bad news?' I asked, pushing my luck.

There was a long pause on the line before he spoke again.

'Not a man to have as an enemy,' the detective said quietly.

'Got it. Thanks,' I said.

DI Heath made a 'huh' sound, and I pictured him nodding on the other end of the line, just before he hung up.

Tempting though it was to go straight over there, I needed time to put a plan together. The streets were crowded now, workers heading home after a long week mingling with shoppers weighed down with bulging bags. The first drops of rain sent everyone scurrying for the Tube, and I joined them, making it down the steps just as the heavens opened.

The rain had stopped by the time I got to Clapham, but the wind had a fresh bite now that the sun was officially absent from the sky. I shivered in the thrift store coat I saved for client meetings and picked up my pace, turning away from the common and jogging up the high street until the neon glow of Friar's came into view.

My stomach growled at the sight, so instead of heading for the door to my flat, I tapped my knuckles against the window of the chippy. Charlie would already be frying, and with any luck, I could buy the first portion of the evening.

It was Precious who opened the door for me, sporting her cleaning overall and cap.

'Hello, handsome. Don't tell me, you're starvin', right?' she said, grinning at me and showing off the impressive gap between her front teeth.

'Always,' I said, grinning back. 'How's trade been?'

'Bloody mental. Friday, innit. You sure you don't want a job, kid? The face on you, we'd have every woman for a square mile on a chip diet,' she teased, beckoning me to sit at one of the Formica tables while she bustled through the gap in the counter and disappeared behind the hot food cabinets that were already stacked as if awaiting the return of an army.

'The wanderer returns!'

I looked up to see Charlie making his way towards me, his white apron splattered with batter. He held up the mug of tea in his hand and raised his eyebrows. I shook my head.

'Give him this,' Precious said, thrusting a plate into her husband's other hand. 'I'm popping back to the house to have half an hour of peace before the chaos begins,' she added.

Charlie planted a kiss on her forehead, and she swatted at him.

'Get off me, you crazy man,' she giggled, before heading out to the kitchen and the back door beyond.

Charlie delivered my plate then sank into the seat opposite. He pulled off his cap and ran his fingers through his thinning dark hair.

'Busy again today, I hear,' I said between forkfuls of chips.

'Mental,' Charlie said with a sigh, but I could hear the pride in his voice. 'We had a queue down the road waiting for us to open from half past eleven. We sold out of our dinner time stock by quarter to one and had to use the stock put by for the teatime shift. The lady wife had to leg it over to the market to restock in time for tonight,' he added, taking another slurp of his tea.

'Best chippy in London,' I said, nodding to the framed newspaper article that sat in pride of place on the opposite wall.

Charlie beamed and tried to hide it behind his mug.

'How'd it go with the prospect? Was he as much of an arsehole as you suspected?' he asked.

My mouth full, I nodded emphatically.

Charlie rubbed his hand across his chin. 'I take it he left with your metaphorical boot up his arse, then,' he chuckled.

'Believe me, I wanted to, but—' I began, but stopped when Charlie's expression changed.

'Look, son, if it's the rent you're worried about, we can work something out. Pay us next month, it's fine. Don't go working for scumbags just to make ends meet. You've got to sleep at night,' he said, waving a finger at me.

I smiled. If only he knew the terrors that ambushed me when I gave in to sleep.

'Thanks. I appreciate it,' I said, meaning every word. Charlie and Precious were more than landlords; they were my friends, despite being nearly old enough to be my parents.

'He's looking for a young woman, and I don't like the idea of him finding her, if you get my drift,' I said. I didn't make a habit of discussing cases – my clients paid me to keep their confidences – but I wasn't breaking my own rules if I didn't share names and details.

Charlie snorted and pulled a face.

'Well, let's hope you find her first, eh,' he said, getting to his feet and untying his stained apron. By the time they opened the doors to the queue in less than twenty minutes, both the Walkers would be decked out in whites so bright the punters would need sunglasses.

I speared the last of my chips and shoved them into my mouth. At the counter hatch, Charlie turned and frowned.

'Just be careful, kid, alright,' he said, his tone unusually serious.

I nodded and gave him a thumbs up, but when I tried to swallow, my food seemed reluctant to slip down my throat. I succeeded on the second attempt, but as I rubbed slow circles over the tattoo on my chest, I wondered how often life hands you two warnings in less than an hour.

CHAPTER 19

GWEN, NOVEMBER 1975

My three hundred and eighty-first winter and I still hated the cold, I thought as I wound a thick scarf around my neck and tucked the ends into the top of my coat. And yet, as a child, I'd barely noticed, too enthralled with the world and too secure in my warm bed and full belly to worry. It took only one winter bundled in rags and sleeping in stables to teach me how to fear the season for the killer it often is.

The butterflies loved every season, of course, so their irritation was palpable on mornings like this when the darkness took an age to yield and I waited in the window for a reluctant dawn. They scattered the moment I released them, and I lost myself in my memories, my heavy boots crunching on the hard frost underfoot as I wandered around the edges of the frozen fields.

I turned for home when my stomach growled, reminding me that coffee alone was not enough to sustain me. I cut through the narrow strip of woodland, taking the shortcut to the long path that wound around the back of Stonefields House. A movement up ahead caught my attention – three roe deer bounded away from me through the trees, their white behinds bobbing in the brittle light. I raised my hand, overcome by the urge to call after them. *Wait for me!* I swallowed down the longing that lodged in my throat, cursing myself for my weakness.

The small meadow brown butterfly appeared at my side, fluttering at eye level as I left the trees and stepped onto the path. I smiled at it, knowing that where it led, the others would soon follow. I'd taken only a handful of steps before the air was thick with wings.

'Thank you, but I'm fine,' I lied, my breath misting the frigid air. 'Go play.'

When they didn't move, I searched for a happy memory, settling on the day Tân and I galloped for the first time, my spindly legs hugging the top of his ribs and my small hands fisted in his long black mane. It was the closest I'd ever come to flying, and I hadn't wanted the moment to end.

Reluctantly, the butterflies moved away, but the meadow brown stayed with me. Maybe it was because I was still so lost in the memory, but I didn't notice the old man leaning against the tree stump until it was too late.

He raised his walking stick in welcome and smiled. I should have turned and walked the other way, but something about the sadness in that smile propelled my feet towards him.

'Best time of the day, isn't it?' he said, leaning forward, his gnarled hands pink with cold and cupped over the top of the stick. He wore an old, waxed jacket that looked much too big for him, a flat tweed cap and brown corduroys that had ridden up around the ankles to reveal thin, papery shins above thick, mustard-coloured woollen socks. The meadow brown fluttered over to him, curious. I relaxed a fraction.

'It is indeed,' I replied, trying not to break my pace.

'Aren't you the young lady from the big house?'

I stopped in my tracks and fixed my smile in place. I nodded, careful to meet his eyes and not watch the butterfly only I could see fluttering around his head.

The old man held out his hand. 'Cyril Loveday.'

I swallowed, waiting a beat before shaking his hand awkwardly, my gloves and his twisted fingers making the movement more complicated than it might have been.

'Arthritis,' he said with a shrug.

'Do you want my gloves?' I offered, already tugging at the fingers. His hands looked so cold.

'Very kind, my dear. Thank you, but I can't get them over these.' He held up his misshapen hands and shrugged again.

I nodded, not knowing what else to say.

'I'm your neighbour from five doors down,' Cyril said, brightening again.

'Ah. Nice to meet you, Cyril,' I said. That was the problem with staying in one place for too long. People noticed things. Especially lonely old men. The meadow brown landed on his cheek. Honoured indeed, I thought, smiling. If only he knew.

'Just you, is it? At the house?'

'I'm back and forth. It's not my house.' I gave a little laugh. 'I'm house-sitting for my employer while he decides what renovations he wants.' I added an eye-roll.

It was a well-used lie, but one that helped people dismiss me. Better they thought of me as the hired help. It made me easier to forget.

Cyril nodded, as if I'd just answered an unspoken question.

'Well, if you are ever in need of a chat and a cup of tea, give me a knock at number seven. I have a granddaughter your age. Not that I see her much. Young people are always busy these days ...' He trailed off, his eyes lowered to the ground.

Young people. I felt my heart pinch. If only he knew I was old enough to be his, what, twelfth-great-grandmother?

'Thank you, I will,' I said, already hating myself for letting him down. For being yet another person too busy to ease his loneliness with an hour of their time.

When he looked up at me, I could tell that he knew it too, and my heart ached for him. In the distance, a cloud of bright wings headed my way. I dropped my gaze.

'It was lovely to meet you, Cyril,' I said, unable to meet his eyes as heat crept up my neck, shame prickling under my scarf.

I tried to smile, but it felt hollow and insubstantial. I turned for home, the butterflies trailing in my wake. The meadow brown was the last to catch up.

CHAPTER 20

DAN, NOVEMBER 1975

I sat in Charlie's beige Morris Marina opposite the Mayfair Imperial hotel and tried not to shiver. I rolled my neck and arched my back as I yawned, my breath visible in the frigid air.

Across the street, lights twinkled on the Christmas trees that flanked the hotel's wide marble entrance. The door man looked half frozen too, despite his thick grey overcoat, hat and gloves. The Brits sure liked their uniforms.

Thanks to a bored bartender studying to be an architect, I knew the building was made from Portland stone and was a fine example of the Edwardian Baroque style. I'd feigned an interest just to keep him talking, but to me, it looked like a lot of old London buildings – all pillars, marble floors and fancy ironwork balconies that screamed wealth and privilege.

At least I wouldn't have to play the part of the lonely American business traveller today. After a full week of late afternoons and evenings spent propping up the bar and spending an eye-watering amount on soda, I had enough information to be getting on with.

I'd spotted Devlin only once, stalking through the foyer, but he'd not given me a second glance. It's surprising what a moderately good suit and a pair of spectacles can do to make you invisible, especially to someone who's not expecting to see you on their home turf.

I felt bad about Cathy, the cute receptionist I'd taken for a drink after her shift one evening, but she had been all but bursting to share the hotel gossip once the first gin and tonic had passed her lips. Maybe in a different universe I might have taken her up on the offer of going back to her place, but I put her in a cab instead and promised to call. It was hard to see the hope in her eyes as I lied to her, but I'd done worse – much worse.

I wrestled my thoughts back to what I knew about my client. Devlin not only owned the hotel, he lived in its penthouse, supposedly with his wife, Annabel, but according to my chatty Cathy, she spent most of her time 'abroad', although nobody seemed to know exactly where. It seemed like the staff were happy for her to be anywhere but screaming orders at them at the hotel.

It took another three gins before Cathy dropped her voice and told me that, far from being bereft at his wife's absence, Devlin was rarely without female company in his penthouse suite. After waving Cathy off, I got talking to the escorts in the area, who, thanks to a recent bust-up with the concierge over his 'guest introduction fee', were more than happy to dish the dirt. They told me about the women who walked past them, heading up the back stairs to the penthouse. 'Snooty bitches in designer threads,' they'd said, but they'd been adamant they were still escorts.

I checked my watch. Twenty-two hundred. My stomach rumbled, reminding me the only thing I'd eaten today was the tinfoil-wrapped sandwich Precious had thrust into my hand with the car keys that morning.

How I lucked out on friends like these was a constant mystery to me, but maybe even the damned need something good in their lives.

My stomach growled again just as a fat raindrop hit the windshield. I froze, ever alert to the trigger. If the heavens opened, the rattling of rain on the roof might—I bit off the memory, but my hand was already circling the scar on my wrist. I let go immediately and gripped the steering wheel as I focused on slowing my breathing. I looked down at my wrists. It was too dark to see the pale, silvery bands of scarred, puckered skin, but it was what I didn't see that reassured me.

I let out a long breath and slumped back in my seat, suddenly aware of how tired I was. I reached for the key in the ignition, but just as I started the engine, the silver Rolls pulled up in front of the hotel.

Something in my gut told me it would be Devlin hurrying down the red-carpeted steps, and a second later, there he was.

He leapt into the car, and within moments the Rolls pulled off at surprising speed – and I followed.

CHAPTER 21

DAN, NOVEMBER 1975

I followed the car, heading east, for over twenty minutes, the bright lights and palatial homes of West London fading as we entered the East End. Tower blocks loomed like obituaries to hope. When people abandoned beauty for functionality, everyone lost out, or so said the architect barman, and I had to agree.

Up ahead, the Rolls turned onto a terraced street. I drove on, turning to watch as it pulled up to the kerb about halfway down the street. I parked the Marina behind a Bedford lorry in the next street, then jogged back, my head bent against the relentless rain.

I peered around the corner to see Devlin's chauffeur, rain bouncing off his shoulders and cap, on tiptoes as he held an umbrella over his stooped boss.

They stopped at a house in the middle of the row, and a second later, the sidewalk flooded with a harsh, bright white light. Devlin stepped inside and the door banged shut, leaving the chauffeur in the sodium glow of the street lamps.

It was only then that I realised what was wrong with the

scene. Every house was boarded up. Windows and doors were covered with plywood like pennies on the eyes of the dead. There was no good reason a man like Devlin would be in a place like this. Unless … The thought that they might have already found the woman in the picture twisted in my gut. I had to find out.

I turned and jogged to the alley at the back of the condemned row, wondering how I'd figure out which house he'd disappeared into. The ring of razor wire around the garden wall and the faint light seeping from around the boards on the first floor of the fifth house down told me exactly where I needed to be.

Dealing with the wire would take too long, so I headed for the house next door. Its gate was hanging by its hinges, and with any luck, the dividing fence would be in a similar state. I threaded myself through the gap and turned the beam of the flashlight onto a solid brick wall, complete with more razor wire. I cursed under my breath. Maybe I could pick up something useful just by listening to whatever Devlin said when he left the building.

A muffled scream stopped me cold. No. I had to get in there – right now. Hadn't there been a story in the paper about a burglar who used connected attics to rob houses? It was beyond a long shot, but it was the only one I had.

I turned the flashlight towards the house, dimly aware that the tattoo on my chest was prickling, like someone was dragging a nettle across my skin. I crept through the backyard, picking my way around fallen trash cans and a tangle of metal that might once have been a bed frame.

I lifted my flashlight to the kitchen window. The plyboard hung limply, but the window was still largely intact, save for a small hole in its centre, only big enough for my fist. Damn it. Knocking out the rest of the glass would be too noisy.

Just then, something darted from inside the house. I turned the flashlight just in time to catch the end of what looked like a fox's tail disappearing around the back gate. My pulse quickened as I edged towards the back door and realised that it wasn't even on its hinges, just propped against the top of the frame.

I crept into the kitchen, glass crunching under my boots as the sour smell of defeat mingled with the all-pervading stench of damp. It was hard to believe that this rotting, despondent shell had once been a home.

I went into the living room, the sodden carpet squelching like a sponge under my feet. At the stairs, I focused my weight at the edges, where the wood would likely be stronger and quieter. Water ran in rivulets down the wall, coaxing what was left of the wallpaper towards its inevitable end. I heard muffled voices. A man shouting and then a softer, female voice. Was that her?

The attic stairs, as steep as a ladder, were just visible behind a door on the landing. I inched it open and froze as the rusty hinges screeched in complaint. Just then, I heard a man gasp in pain and start to cough. Not her then, but whoever they had in there still needed help.

A flash of lightning lit up the stairwell, confirming my hunch that half the roof tiles were likely missing. I clicked off the flashlight and waited, counting the seconds. When the thunder boomed, I yanked open the complaining door and climbed the sodden stairs.

The drywall that had once separated the attics was now a pulpy pink mess and there was a hole in the ceiling of the house next door big enough for a man to jump through. The light in the bedroom was unnaturally bright, and I spotted the base of the kind of arc lights used on building sites. I smelled diesel on the air, and somewhere out of sight, a generator hummed.

I crouched on the A-frame, figuring it to be the strongest beam left in the rotting corpse of a house, and watched as Devlin strode into view below.

My heart pounded and my stomach churned as I leaned closer. Some of my men used to claim to love the rush of adrenaline before a fight, but it always made me feel sick to my stomach – not that I ever told them. All leadership is lies, as someone once said.

A pitiful moan from the room below pulled me from my thoughts. I shuffled further forward on the beam to get a better look.

'Tell us about the girl and you'll be able to go home to your family,' Devlin said levelly.

'I keep telling you, I don't know her,' croaked a man, his accent carrying the hint of the Caribbean beneath the refinement.

Devlin braced his hands on his hips and stepped back, giving me my first clear view of their captive.

'Again,' he said, waving his hand.

The man tied to the chair was older than his voice suggested, his close-cropped black hair greying at the temples. He was bleeding from the side of his head and one eye was swollen closed. Bastards.

A guy in a suit big enough for a gorilla stepped into view and pulled off his jacket to reveal a handgun strapped to his side. Then, he pulled back and punched the man full in the face. I winced at the sound of knuckles on flesh and the spluttering, agonised groan that followed.

I had to save him, but how? The only way in was through the ceiling, and it was at least an eight-foot drop to the bedroom floor. I might have had a chance one to one, but only the truly suicidal take a fist to a gunfight. There had to be a way.

'I know nothing of this girl,' the man said, spitting blood onto the floor. 'Please. I have my family and patients to think about,' he added.

Devlin snorted. 'Please save us the sob story, Clement. Show some dignity, at least.'

Clement didn't react to the barb, save for a tightening of his jaw.

'Let's go through this again, shall we. I've heard you coloured types are a tad slow,' Devlin said, tapping his knuckle against Clement's skull.

I clenched my teeth as I added 'racist prick' to the long list of reasons to despise my new client.

Clement shook his head, his teeth raking his bottom lip.

'Something funny?' Devlin asked, his tone still terrifyingly relaxed.

Clement shook his head, but his tormentor was not about to let it go.

'You really think being a surgeon makes you better than me, don't you? You might have the old school tie, but don't think you're—'

A small female hand appeared on Devlin's back, interrupting whatever he was about to spew out next.

'What?' he snapped, turning towards the woman, who was still out of my sight.

'He ain't going to tell us, Reg,' she said, laughing as if the man were simply withholding the punchline to a joke.

Devlin sighed as he straightened up, and he swept a hand over his silver hair.

'We'll do it your way then,' he huffed, stepping away from his captive.

It was then that I saw the first flicker of genuine fear on Clement's face.

'Look. I've told you. I don't have magic. I don't even know

what you're talking about,' he said, his words coming quicker now.

'You can drop the party line, Clement. We know all about you. We know all about your little Council of the Elders,' Devlin mocked. 'We also know you currently chair it. We know about the magical community and your hidden libraries and your ongoing spat with the government's secret department for all things magical.' He sounded almost bored.

Devlin stepped out of sight. There came the sound of a chair being dragged across floorboards, followed by the striking of a match.

'You could have made this easy for yourself.' Devlin's words were spoken between puffs as the smell of cigar tobacco drifted up to meet me.

He pressed on. 'You could have protected your family and your precious little community of misfits and miscreants, but instead you chose to lie to us. I don't like liars, Clement.'

Clement gave a wry laugh. 'Tell me, Reginald. Why do you seek this woman, anyway? I am telling the truth when I say I have no knowledge of her, but I'm curious why a man who clearly detests magic and – what did you call us? Misfits and miscreants, wasn't it? Why would a man like you be chasing such a myth if it wasn't to gain for yourself the magic you appear to hate so much, eh?'

'You make too many assumptions, Clement,' Devlin retorted. 'What I loathe is seeing power in the hands of those who don't deserve it.'

What the hell were they talking about? Had it not been for the violence, I'd have hoped they were playing some twisted party game, but no. This was all too real.

A flash of lightning lit up the sky just as Clement lifted his eyes to the hole in the ceiling. Our eyes locked for a fraction of a second, but it was long enough for him to give the slightest shake of his head.

'Angie, do your thing. I'm bored with this,' Devlin said flatly. 'Goodbye, Clement, you'll not be missed.'

What? I pitched forward towards the hole, holding on to the beam. But it all happened so fast. A small woman with a brittle blonde perm stepped behind Clement and hovered her hands on each side of his head as he thrashed desperately in his chair. On my chest, my tattoo burned like a fresh brand.

'You'll pay for this,' Clement snarled.

A blinding white light ringed his temple and then, inexplicably, shot out of his eye socket, then his nose, ears and finally, with the kind of scream you only hear on battlefields, his mouth. When I opened my eyes again, I stared not at a man but at something that looked more like a steaming bag of filleted meat.

I rocked back on my heels, felt my balance slip and grabbed on to the beam to steady myself. I hadn't even registered the darkness until I heard the woman bark out an order. 'Well, fetch a ruddy torch, one of you, for Christ's sake. And then see to the bloody generator.'

'Well, Angie? Did you retrieve anything?' Devlin asked with a sigh.

'I'm sorry, guv,' she said hesitantly. 'He was tight as a duck's arse, that one. I got a few flashes of his wife and kids. Him standing with some award or other at a fancy do and some surgery stuff I'd have rather not seen, if I'm honest, but nothing about magic and nothing we don't already have. Fair play. He was a tough old bastard, I'll give him that much.'

Devlin tutted. 'Get this mess cleaned up and report back in the morning. I've got dinner reservations now.'

I slumped down onto the beam and swallowed hard, trying to control my breathing. That look. That shake of the head. I'd seen men with their guts spooling out on the ground screaming for their mothers and had never doubted I'd be any different, but not him.

Whoever Clement was, his family deserved to know what had happened to him and, more importantly, who was responsible.

CHAPTER 22

DAN, NOVEMBER 1975

I sat in the darkness, my heart racing and the taste of bile in my throat. In the room below, the gorillas with the sidearms mumbled instructions to each other as, presumably, they set about the grisly task of moving Clement's body. Devlin's and Angie's voices, chatting as casually as if they'd just met at a party, faded, and I heard the clip-clop of heels descending the wooden stairs.

The muscle waited until they were gone before flicking on a radio. I couldn't place the song, but I had the strangest sensation that it would have been something Clement might have danced to with his wife. I took my chance and groped my way to the stairs.

When I reached the car, I collapsed into the driver's seat and leaned my head against the steering wheel, gripping it hard to stop my hands from shaking. The memory of Clement's face loomed in my mind, and I swallowed hard, knowing he'd join the other men I saw in my nightmares. Another life I'd failed to save. I had to get to a phone.

I pulled the car out of the parking space and headed for the main road. The rain had eased up into a persistent drizzle that was so typical of England. I flicked off the wipers just in time to realise that the silver Rolls had stopped up ahead, in the middle of the street. The driver's door cracked open a few inches, but moments later, it closed again, and the car backed up and swerved around something lying in the road.

It was the body of a dog.

I was out of the car and running before I could think about it, surprised to feel tears prick at my eyes.

I slowed as I drew nearer. Man, she looked so much like Lucy, the collie mix I'd grown up with. Thick toffee-coloured fur with a white chest and belly, or at least, fur that might have been white once. My heart leapt into my mouth as I saw her chest rise and fall.

'Hey, girl,' I said, dropping to my knees and using the kind of voice men only use for animals when there's nobody around to hear them. 'You're gonna be okay, alright. I'm gonna get you some help.'

The dog wagged the tip of her tail, and when I inched my hand towards her, she stretched her head forward and licked it enthusiastically. I stroked her head, feeling the grit and grime from her coat.

'Need any help, mate?' The voice from behind me made me start. An old man in a long overcoat and flat cap hovered, staring down at the dog. The scent of his chip supper, vinegar soaking through the newspaper, was strong, and the dog tried to struggle to her feet but slumped back to the floor.

'Steady, girl,' I whispered, stroking her head and earning myself another wag of that bushy orange tail.

'Do you know this dog? Does she live around here?' I asked.

'Used to. Her owners moved out to the sticks when the houses was condemned last year, but they left her. She still sits on her old doorstep, waiting for them to come back, so she's not the brightest of dogs. Few of the neighbours feed her from time to time though,' the man replied with a shrug, as if that somehow made up for it.

I clenched my jaw, feeling slighted on the dog's behalf. Bastards abandon a loyal dog to fend for herself on the streets and then she gets sneered at for her hope and loyalty by this asshole.

The dog tried again to get to her feet. Maybe it was the smell of food or the fact that some of the initial shock had worn off, but this time, with only the aid of my steadying hand, she made it to standing. Three of her four paws touched the ground, but she held one of her back legs aloft. She turned her head to look at it, then looked up at me. The thought of her trying to run off, maybe getting hit by another car, was too much.

'Good girl, you wanna come with me?' I asked, holding my arms out.

She took a faltering step towards me, her head down, eyes soft, and with that fox's brush of a tail wiggling at the tip. As soon as she was within reach, I lifted her as gently as I could, scooping my arms around her chest and butt before pushing myself to standing. For a medium-sized dog, she weighed next to nothing. Apparently, the neighbours hadn't done a great job of keeping her fed. I stroked a hand across her side and felt protruding ribs.

'Is there a veterinarian around here?' I asked the man.

He snorted out a dry laugh. 'Not at this time of night, no, mate. And it'll cost a packet to get her fixed. The pound is your best bet. They'll see to it for you.'

I bit back what I really wanted to say to the heartless old git and said instead, 'Can you just open the back door for me? My car's back there.'

'Aye,' he said, but sounded none too pleased about it. He

followed me, moaning about the state of the neighbourhood, the developers and the government, but I tuned him out. The dog lay quietly in my arms, too quietly, and my mind raced with how she might be injured. Had I done the right thing in even picking her up? What if there was spinal damage? Or internal bleeding? But there was no way I'd have left her there.

The old man opened the car door, and I laid the dog carefully on the back seat. When I turned to thank my helper, he was already hurrying home, no doubt worrying about his cooling chip supper.

I turned back to the dog, reaching in to stroke her. She pressed her head into my palm then licked my wrist as she thumped her tail, more energetically this time. I felt tears burn the backs of my eyes again. I'd not cried since I was a kid. The dog whined, waving her paw as if to motion me back, so I shook the emotion away and forced a smile.

'It's okay, girl. It's all gonna be okay, you'll see. Come on, let's get you fixed up,' I said before carefully closing the back door.

I had only driven a mile across town before she joined me in the front of the car. I gave her ten out of ten for stealth, because busted leg or not, she was on the passenger seat before I clocked her.

She lay down carefully, her head resting on my thigh, tail thumping against the passenger door. I reached down and stroked her ruff, my fingers finding sodden, matted fur.

I drove the rest of the way home with her head on my lap. She thumped her tail every time I glanced down at her. What my landlords would say, I had no idea, but I'd find out soon enough.

CHAPTER 23

DAN, NOVEMBER 1975

*I*t was after midnight by the time I reached Charlie and Precious's house. I felt bad for doubting their reaction, because a minute after explaining the situation, they were both in the back seat of their own car, Precious wearing her coat over her nightgown and Charlie still in his whites from the late shift. Running the chippy meant they knew just about everyone in the neighbourhood, and, as I'd hoped, we headed to a veterinarian who had a reputation for never turning away an animal in need.

He worked out of his house, which looked like a much bigger, grander version of the Victorian terrace the Walkers called home. While Precious rang the bell and Charlie sat in the car with the dog, I sprinted to a payphone on the corner to call DI Heath.

He picked up on the second ring and waved away my apology about calling so late.

'Give me an hour or so,' he said before the line went dead.

I jogged back to the car to see Charlie standing on the pavement, the dog in his arms. She lit up when she saw me, paddling her front legs as if Charlie were a boat she could steer towards me. A wave of warmth spread through my chest like sunlight breaking through a leaden sky.

'Hey, sweet girl,' I said as I ruffled her head and followed Charlie up the stone steps to where Precious and the doc were waiting.

'What's the verdict, Doc?' I asked, after the man, who'd introduced himself as Arnold, had given her a thorough examination.

He smiled at the dog as he handed her a biscuit, which she practically inhaled.

'She's one very lucky girl. Looks like the car clipped her back end, but I can't find any obvious breaks. She's only young, judging by her teeth, so she's got youth on her side. My guess is that the back leg's badly bruised – she's certainly sore there – and I've given her something to help. I'll give you tablets to take home for her too, but I'd like her back in a day or two for X-rays to make sure. For now, though, I prescribe lots of rest and a few square meals. I'd say she's half the weight she should be,' he said, shaking his head.

'Thank God for that, eh?' Precious beamed, reaching over to stroke the dog.

Arnold's expression turned serious. 'Now technically, if she's a stray, I have a duty to inform the dog pound,' he said with a sigh, his eyes on the glasses he was polishing on his sweater.

'She's my dog,' I said without missing a beat. 'Some friends were taking care of her and she ran away and got into a state, but she's home now.'

Charlie gaped at me with what might have been admiration or just sheer surprise at how quickly the lie had fallen from my lips. As if to cement the story, the dog chose that moment to hook her paws over my shoulder. I lifted her from the table, and she licked my face enthusiastically.

'Excellent news,' Arnold said, grinning at me in a way that

told me it was exactly what he'd wanted me to say. 'In that case, keep a close eye on her and don't hesitate to come back if anything changes, but otherwise, I'll see you in a few days.'

We were nearly at the door when he called after us, 'By the way, what's her name?'

I thought of Clement. His ruined eye. The blood. The flash of terror that crossed his face. That light that had—'Her name's Clementine,' I said.

'Ah, very good. After her colouring,' the veterinarian said with a smile. 'Very apt indeed.'

Charlie and Precious had just left my flat when DI Heath arrived. It had taken three of us to bathe Clementine with the flea shampoo Doc Arnold had given us and then snip away the worst of the mats on her belly, legs and tail. The rest could wait for another day and a more expert hand than mine, but as she raced around the flat on three legs, it was obvious that she was already feeling a lot more comfortable.

Clementine drank a whole casserole dish of water, then wolfed down the leftover dinner Precious had given me the day before – I tried not to notice the arched eyebrow that had earned me from my landlady. I carried her down to the small yard behind the shop to relieve herself, the three of us standing around her with a flashlight, which I'm pretty sure just delayed the inevitable.

After thanking my friends again for their kindness, and the unspoken understanding that my lease now allowed pets, I carried Clementine back upstairs and settled her on the makeshift bed of old blankets Precious had made for her.

When the flat's buzzer sounded, I pulled the door closed and hurried down the stairs. DI Colin Heath was a man who polished his shoes, never lost his keys and remembered the names of every kid he'd ever been to school with. He must have just scraped the minimum height requirement back in the day, and despite being, at a guess, still a few years off forty, he was bald but for a smattering of dark, curly hair still clinging to the edges of his skull. His horn-rimmed glasses and thick moustache made him look more like an actuary than a cop. He'd once told me that nobody ever guessed his profession, partly, I think, because he just looked too nice. That people often mistook me for a cop told its own story.

'This must be a biggie, given the hour,' Colin said, his voice low.

I stepped aside and motioned for him to come in. 'Doesn't get much bigger,' I said as I followed him up the stairs.

'Since when do you have a dog?' Colin asked as he pushed open the door into the flat.

'Since tonight,' I said, noting the empty pile of blankets on the floor. 'Her name's Clementine.'

Colin was already lowering himself onto the sofa, where a softly thumping tail was beating out a welcome.

I snorted. Somebody had wasted no time making herself comfortable then. I made a mental note to buy her a bed and immediately dismissed the idea. She'd already found one.

'Tea?' I asked, one hand on the frame of the doorway that led into the kitchen.

'Please,' Colin replied, without looking up from fussing the dog.

Ten minutes later, with Clementine snoring beside me and Colin in the armchair, I began my story. I considered holding back the bollocks about magic, not wanting to besmirch the victim's good name or give the police an excuse to write him off as a fantasist, but in the end, I laid out the whole thing.

It was only when I'd finished that I realised that Clementine's head was in my lap again. I looked down at my hand resting on her still-damp fur.

'Golly,' Colin said, placing his empty mug on the coffee table. 'This is going to be a bit of a shitshow, as the boys say down at the station.'

Colin looked to be weighing his next words. He let out a breath as he leaned forward and braced his forearms on his knees.

'I don't need to tell you that what I'm about to say is to go no further, but I can confirm that we have been investigating the disappearance of Doctor Clement Johnson. His wife made the report three days ago, after he failed to return home from a lecture he was giving. He worked at the Royal Holloway Hospital as a cardiac surgeon and was, according to his boss when I interviewed him, 'a shining light in medicine'. Your description matches the image of the man I have in his file. Poor beggar. Such wickedness.'

I let out a long breath and sat back in my seat. As an active case, things would likely move swiftly. Colin had said nothing about the magic stuff, though. I'd expected him to at least raise an eyebrow at that bit of the story, but he'd not so much as flinched. I opened my mouth to ask, but, without warning, Colin jumped to his feet, startling Clementine. She emitted a low, throaty growl as she fixed her eyes on the policeman.

'Shhh, it's okay,' I said, stroking her head. The growl vanished and she licked my chin, her body soft again, tail wagging.

'My fault,' Colin said, holding up his hands and heading for the door.

'What will you do?' I asked, getting up to join him.

'I'll get the wheels in motion. Get a team over there, although from what you said about the clean-up crew, I doubt we'll find his body,' Colin said with an irritated shake of his head.

'What about Devlin and that Angie woman? I'm a witness and I'll happily testify.'

Colin's face turned serious. 'On that front, my friend, I caution you to keep your counsel for now. This may take some time.'

'What?' I said, trying not to raise my voice but failing. All I wanted to hear was him telling me he'd be knocking down their doors to haul their asses to jail before the sun rose. The injustice of them seeing another day of freedom after what they'd just done to a man was simply too much.

'Daniel,' Colin said firmly, stepping towards me and putting his hand on my arm. 'If you want to stay alive long enough to protect this Gwen woman from a similar fate to Doctor Johnson's, and if you want to see justice done, then you need to trust me on this. Find the woman, stay safe and keep me posted.'

Colin blinked at me from behind his large glasses, and I saw it. The tell. The merest of twitches at the corner of his left eye. He knew much more than he was letting on.

'What else, Colin?' I asked. 'There's something you're keeping from me. Is it about this magic bullshit?'

He regarded me for a long moment, and I caught the tiniest quiver of his moustache. 'You're still young enough to join the force, you know. You're not even thirty yet,' he said.

I held his gaze. It was a distraction, and I wasn't falling for it. He knew well enough that I had no interest in ever being part of a government machine again.

Colin sighed. 'There is, of course, something that I am withholding, but you need to trust me when I say it is nothing that will prevent justice being done.'

I barked out a laugh. 'Come on. Magic? Are you shitting me?'

'There are more things in heaven and Earth, Horatio, than are dreamt of in your philosophy,' Colin said, his hand already on the door-handle.

I sighed. Pressing the point was hopeless once he started quoting Shakespeare.

After saying our goodbyes, I stumbled, heavy-footed, back to the couch, meaning to collect up the mugs and head to bed. Clementine cracked open an eye and wagged her tail sleepily. I thought about my bed in the room next door, but instead pulled a blanket from the floor and slid myself in next to her on the couch. She wriggled until her head tucked under my chin and sighed. I smiled and planted a kiss on her damp head. She smelled of medicated soap and the wet dogs of my childhood, soaked from playing in the sprinklers or splashing in the creek.

I thought of Clement. Maybe the news Colin would deliver might ease some small part of his family's torment. It wasn't nearly enough, though. If only I'd gotten there sooner, or—I screwed up my eyes, stopping the train of thought just like the army shrink had taught me. I'd been down this path so many times I'd worn the stones to a polish beneath my feet.

War taught me the depths of human depravity, but nothing in my twenty-nine years had prepared me for what I'd seen tonight. That woman had killed him with nothing but light that poured from her hands. It made no sense.

I didn't expect to sleep. But when I finally drifted off, for the first time in years, the faces of the dead didn't haunt my dreams. Instead, bizarrely, I dreamt of butterflies and the woman from the picture riding a black horse.

CHAPTER 24

GWEN, APRIL 1976

I woke to a gentle breeze on my cheek and groaned. For incorporeal beings, the butterflies knew how to stir the air when it suited them. I cracked open one weary eye, already knowing what I'd see. Sure enough, the outline of the meadow brown, my first ever charge, swam into focus as I squinted against the bright morning sunlight. Maybe it had drawn the short straw, or perhaps being first to arrive gave it first dibs in the pecking order, but whatever the reason, it was always the messenger.

'Morning,' I croaked, still groggy from the late night at my typewriter.

It responded by landing on my nose with a weight more fitting for a seagull.

I sighed. *Bang goes my plan to catch up on the lost sleep.*

'Okay. Out you come,' I said hoarsely, bracing for the moment that, even after all these centuries, always left me breathless and sometimes a little light-headed.

They burst into the room, delighting in their freedom and turning the air into a living kaleidoscope of colour so vibrant I screwed up my eyes against the glare. It would pacify them for a while, but I knew what they really wanted – a walk. 'Nature and magic are one and the same, child. One cannot exist without the other.' Nain's voice echoed in my memory.

I flung back the covers and my skin goose-fleshed in the chill air. The energy in the room ratcheted up a notch as the butterflies fluttered excitedly and dived around me, stirring the air and making me shiver again.

I pulled on my clothes and pushed my feet into the boots by my bed. Then, with a train of butterflies in my wake, I headed out onto the landing. I shielded my eyes from the sunlight pouring in from the central glass dome that sat above the sweeping grand staircase. Force of habit made me stop and listen intently to the house before I took another step.

There was an intermittent tapping. The sound of a wisteria branch against the bathroom window a few rooms down, moving in the breeze. The old boiler was already awake, judging by the hiss and clank of the pipes. In the distance, I heard the tinkling of bottles as the milk float drove by. The butterflies circled around me, hurrying me along.

I descended the stairs, avoiding each squeaky tread and reminding myself that caution had kept us all alive until now. I didn't need to be herded like a wandering lamb, although I'd long since tired of telling them as much. The thought reminded me of May, the Owens' collie who had comforted me that first night. I still remembered her silky soft fur and those gentle, intelligent amber eyes. The weight of her next to me, anchoring me in the here and now and reminding me that, no matter what, there was still love in the world.

Walt had suggested I get a dog in his letter, but I knew my heart couldn't bear another loss. After finding Tân forever asleep in his stable one morning, I swore never to torture myself with such a bond again. He had lived an unusually long life for a horse, and I often wondered if he'd held on for me. It was clear, even back then, that the spell was protecting me from the normal passage of time. But in the end, the Goddess had called him home, and he'd left me, just like everyone before and after him.

I headed for the kitchen, following a bright stream of dancing butterflies. The old kettle never boiled quickly enough as far as they were concerned. Some fluttered at the windows, others perched on any available surface, and the truly restless just flew laps around my head, the draught blowing my hair into my eyes, a sure sign I was due a haircut. Wearing it long always invited too much attention, so I was relieved when pixie cuts had become fashionable. I'd take the scissors to it later.

The butterflies dogged my every step, and I sighed, wafting a hand in front of my face. 'Come on, play fair. You know the deal, coffee first,' I said irritably.

The troop circling my head backed off a few inches, but didn't go far. Muttering, I shook a ring of Holly Blues from my mug and repeated the process with the coffee canister. I gave in and laughed when I opened the drawer for a spoon and released a cloud of wings, a giggle rippling down the bond as they revelled in their joke.

'You're all hilarious,' I said, crossing to the sink and adding a generous splash of cold water to my mug. I drank the coffee in three quick gulps.

Picking up my latest manuscript from the table, I walked towards the back door and crouched beside the last cabinet in the row. I slid back the side panel and pulled out the old, battered satchel from its hiding place. I placed the manuscript inside and stood up.

The air quivered as, teasing them now, I slid back the bolts with the haste of a snail. I felt a bubbling in my chest as their excitement and anticipation built. I smiled. My mood improved with the caffeine, the promise of fresh air and the chance to see my charges back in their element, where they belonged.

I turned the key in the lock, swung the door wide and took a step back. They darted, arrow-like, over my head, flying out and up until they all but disappeared into the morning sky, stretching the spell that connected us to its very limit. Despite bracing for it, the snap of the tether in my chest still made me rock forward in my boots.

How many times had I prayed for that tether to break? Dreamt that one day, that snap wouldn't come, and I'd be able to just stand and watch them reclaim their freedom. Free to find the descendants of their lost witches or to do whatever else orphaned magic did in a world that seemed to have forgotten it even existed. What that would likely mean for me, I didn't like to dwell on.

Stonefields House backed onto open fields and woodland. There were two gates connecting the high stone wall with the rarely used footpath beyond. The one visible from the path looked old enough to have survived both wars, its green paint faded and peeling. Only its padlock and sturdy chain suggested it was still up to the job of keeping the uninvited out.

I chose the other one, as I always did when I stayed here. Accessed through the old summerhouse, the door opened onto a thick wall of hedging. There was usually plenty of room for me to slide into the gap between hedge and wall and walk, concealed from anyone who might be on the footpath, to the narrow gap a hundred yards away. Today, though, I had to fight my way through the foliage, which meant I'd need to return with the shears this evening. In an emergency, every second counted.

The butterflies were, of course, oblivious to my predicament, already enjoying their freedom, such as it was. I scanned the sky as I stepped out onto the main footpath, then turned in a circle, deciding which way to go but also checking to see where they might be. While I knew they were in no real danger, I still liked to know where they were, especially the new arrivals.

Heading away from town, I set off, enjoying the crispness of the morning air and revelling in the sight of nature bursting into life all around me. Back in Pont Nefoedd, the coven would have been preparing for Beltane, and I, being little use on the magical front, would have spent my time weaving wildflowers into circlets and baking oat cakes. How I'd resented it. Hated myself for my lack of magic. And yet now, I'd do anything to go back to those times. To be back in the cottage, safe with Nain, grumbling through my lessons. To be part of a coven in any capacity at all.

As I rounded the first bend, I spotted a few common blues playing together near an ivy-covered oak, then, to my delight, two Giant African Swallowtails swooped past. I smiled to myself. The newcomer had found a friend then. That would make things easier – it always did.

A tingle in my chest slowed my march. The butterflies were excited about something. I turned back to the old oak, but the common blues had vanished. The tingling intensified, and I stopped in my tracks, focusing on the bond to make sure I had interpreted the sensation correctly – excitement and fear were different sides of the same coin. No, definitely excited, I decided after a few more beats. I let my shoulders relax as I walked on. Maybe there was a horse in a field nearby. They got excited by creatures in general, but horses were their favourite. I liked to think maybe it was Tân's influence all those years ago, but it was a romantic notion at best.

I left the path and plunged into the woods, drinking in the smell of old leaves, rising sap and slowly warming soil. I noticed the wind rise but didn't pay it much attention, too wrapped up in my forest bathing to register it or the dimming light, so the first rumble of thunder made me start. The tingle in my chest turned into a fizzing a hive full of bees would be proud of.

That explained it then. I turned slowly, focusing on the sensations in my chest. Usually, when we were out walking, the connection felt like a maypole with butterflies off exploring in all directions. But now, when I concentrated on the bond, it felt like they were all woven together into a single, quivering thread.

I followed the thread, almost running now, until I stumbled into a clearing. At its heart sat a tumble of stones – all that remained of what was likely a forester's cottage, long abandoned and sinking into a sea of nodding bluebells. The butterflies were all here – I felt it – but I couldn't see them yet.

The trees swayed, their new green leaves whispering in the wind. The sky, iron grey and spoiling for a fight, pressed down on the clearing. I licked my lips, the taste of metal and electricity sharp as a knife on my tongue. Another boom of thunder rolled in, a low growl that vibrated through my bones like the roar of something ancient and hungry.

And then I saw them.

A storm of butterflies lifted into the air, their wings impossibly bright against the leaden grey sky as the heavens opened and the rain fell in a torrent.

I stepped back into the relative safety of the trees and crouched low, my breath mingling with the scent of rain-soaked earth as I clutched my satchel to my chest to protect it from the downpour.

The butterflies' excitement pulsed through me – a shared thrill that quickened my heartbeat and made my breath hitch. In all our years together, this had only happened a handful of times. The last time was the day Walt died. A familiar ache, heavy as a boulder, settled in my chest as I thought of my friend. It felt like yesterday.

Lightning forked, splitting the heavens in jagged silver lines, and I gasped as the butterflies' unbridled delight surged down the bond. I watched in awe as they danced with the lightning, their jewelled wings a blur in the storm light, tracing wild, electric arcs through the tempestuous sky. The storm had arrived, and despite the spectacle unfolding before my eyes, I couldn't shake the sinking feeling that Time had, at last, found me again.

CHAPTER 25

GWEN, JANUARY 1938

The woman from the secretarial agency hadn't wanted to give me the job. While I'd not exactly begged, I was ready to. I was almost out of money, having spent the last of what I had on a train fare and a cheap hotel room in Kings Cross.

Maybe there was something in my demeanour that made her take pity on me, or perhaps she was just past caring, but she handed me a folded sheet of paper with the address.

'Keep your wits about you. Our last girl left because of his roaming hands, and I want no more drama. Understood?' the woman said frostily.

I squared my shoulders, lifted my chin and nodded. 'Understood,' I replied, my insides twisting at the thought of having to fend off the advances of another entitled man, but I was out of options, and I only had until the end of the week before I needed to pay my hotel bill.

The day was bitterly cold, the sun a pale excuse in an anaemic sky and the pavements frosted and slippery underfoot. My feet were numb thanks to holes in the soles of both boots, but repairing them was an expense I couldn't afford to worry about. I needed to look respectable for secretarial work and had spent some of the money the baker's widow had forced into my hands on the day I left on second-hand clothes that did the job passably well.

I'd not had enough left for gloves, but the assistant found me a mismatched pair and gave them to me. I had long ago sacrificed my pride on the altar of survival, so I took them gratefully. The black woollen coat was by far the most expensive item, but it was well cut and respectable, which meant I could make a good first impression – if only during the winter months.

I'd lived in London before, of course, but never for very long. I told myself it was easier to hide in big cities where you could disappear into a crowd at a moment's notice. I'd stay until the paranoia set in, but once I started suspecting everyone I saw of being a hunter or an informant, I'd bolt for the nearest station and head for somewhere small, preferably a village where everyone knew everyone else and strangers stood out like sore thumbs.

Being a low-born woman meant I'd soon pale into invisibility, blending into the community so long as I knew my place, held my tongue and worked hard enough. The hunters were always men, and men were always seen.

Now, as I walked through Belgravia on my way to my new temporary role as secretary to Lord Walter Middleton, I couldn't help but notice the contrasts. Every age had its kings and paupers, and I'd seen it all.

I'd left the misery of Kings Cross behind me for a few hours. The beggars on the street and the women forced to sell themselves to survive might have broken my heart had there been anything left of it to break. I was nobody to judge them.

Here in the smart part of London, I saw nannies ushering rosy-cheeked children to school, their boaters and blazers pristine, shoes polished to a shine. Men in suits, umbrellas cracked over their arms as if they might be shotguns, hurried past, tutting as if the very pavements belonged only to them.

The shiny black door to the smart regency townhouse was opened by an elderly butler with a pronounced stoop and eyes so milky I wondered if he could see at all. He was hard of hearing too, and I had to raise my voice to an improper volume to make myself understood.

After my second attempt, a man I presumed to be my new employer hurried from an adjoining room. He was unusually tall, well over six feet, with thick salt-and-pepper hair neatly combed and swept to one side. Broad of frame, he had an oval-shaped face, and a wide forehead above dark, deep-set eyes that crinkled when he smiled. I liked him at once, which was so unusual a feeling it unsettled me.

The butler scowled, turning with the speed of a rusted clock to his employer.

'Miss Lloyd, I presume. Please. Come in,' Lord Walter said.

I nodded and stepped inside, feeling my cheeks pink at the lie. Lloyd. Lewis. Lovell. How many names had I had over the years? For some strange reason, when filling out the paperwork at the secretarial office, I'd caught myself about to write my real name. I stopped after Gwen, annoyed at myself, and plucked Lloyd from the air. I was never usually so careless. Careless got you caught.

'Before you tell me off,' Lord Walter said loudly to the butler, 'I was on my way to the lavatory.'

The butler mimed an 'Oh' and nodded stiffly, apparently mollified.

'Villiers, this is Miss Lloyd, our new secretary,' he said, his voice still loud but, I noticed, without a hint of the patronising tone most adopt with the elderly or hard of hearing.

'Pleased to make your acquaintance,' Villiers said with a smile and a little bow.

'How do you do, Mr Villiers,' I said, loudly but, I fear, not loudly enough, as he didn't seem to hear me. I smiled and mirrored the little bow.

'Your coat and hat, miss?' Villiers asked, extending an unsteady hand.

'Let me do that, Villiers, but if you can ask Cook to sort out the tea, that would be marvellous,' Lord Walter said.

Villiers pursed his lips before nodding his goodbyes and retreating slowly down the wide tiled hallway.

A while later, sitting in the elegant drawing room, Lord Walter said, 'Villiers has been with the family almost seventy-two years. Came to us as a boy, and before you imagine me a monster, he point-blank refuses to retire. There's a cottage on the coast waiting for him, a generous pension, and a younger sister who would love nothing more than to fuss over him, but he swears he'll not last the week if he stops working.'

I smiled politely but said nothing. It wasn't my place. I was here to do a job, collect my salary and save enough to leave the moment the paranoia set.

If the Goddess was feeling generous, I'd have six months, maybe nine. A little later, watching Lord Walter pour spilled tea from saucer to cup and mop milk from the tray only once Villiers had shuffled from the room, I had the overwhelming feeling that I might like to stay a little longer. I had no idea then that this would become my home for the next twenty-two years.

CHAPTER 26

GWEN, SEPTEMBER 1938

'Bottom pinching, my arse! I dismissed her when I caught her pocketing three silver teaspoons,' Walt huffed into his brandy glass. 'I thought she was a very nice young woman too. Always typed well, and she even laughed at my terrible jokes. I'd have given her the ruddy spoons it she'd asked, or just upped her pay, but to steal from me. Just hurtful, Gwennie. And why pinch three? It's not even a bloody set!'

Archie, Walt's nephew, snorted so hard from where he lounged on the floor cushion his wire-rimmed spectacles slipped down his nose, and had it been full, his wine glass might have deposited what remained of his claret on the rug.

'You need to let it go, Uncle Walt,' he said, laughing. He drained his glass then said, '"Acqua passata", as they say in Italy.'

'Passata? Isn't that a tomato sauce?' Walt asked, frowning.

I giggled from where I sat curled on the sitting room couch. 'Walt, darling, in this context, it translates as "water under the bridge", although you're not entirely wrong about the tomato thing,' I said.

Walt frowned. 'Explain yourselves at once,' he commanded, affecting his best upper-class-gent tone. 'And don't do that ganging up on me thing either,' he chided with a pout.

Archie got to his feet. He wasn't as tall or as broad as his uncle, but they shared the same scholarly look.

'I will leave the explanation to the signorina,' he said, patting Walt on the shoulder. 'I'm heading up to Oxford in the morning, so I need my own bed tonight. And on the subject of the stolen silver, just be thankful that the actions of Miss Light Fingers delivered you this angel in her place,' he added, giving me a theatrical wink.

I smiled at Archie and allowed the compliment to settle over me like warm velvet on a chilly night. *You're getting too comfortable*, whispered a quiet voice in my head. It was right. Walt had offered me a live-in position the moment he learned that I was boarding in Kings Cross. I hadn't hesitated. The Belgravia townhouse was more secure than the wretched hotel, and it had more escape routes. Nine if you included the route via the attic and the service ladder over the roof to the neighbouring terrace. But it was more than that, too. I felt safe here with Walt. It was a feeling so unfamiliar to me I spent many a sleepless night dissecting it. There was no logic to it, just this bone-deep knowing that he was perhaps the one person on Earth I could trust – if not with my secret, at least with my life.

Comfort breeds complacency, trilled the quiet voice. I felt my smile falter, but when I reached for the butterflies, they too were perfectly content. Had they been cats, they would have purred. The epitome of 'flighty', the slightest hint of danger set them off, yet they'd not had a moment of even mild distress in nine months. I ignored the voice. I would enjoy this respite for however long it lasted.

'What's happening in Oxford?' I asked to distract myself

from my brooding. I hoped he might say a party or, better still, a date.

While we were technically of a similar age, it had been clear from the beginning that Archie had no romantic leanings in my direction. Walt either, for that matter. Maybe that was why it was so easy to be friends.

Archie twisted his mouth the way he did when he was trying not to smile, then, with a toothy grin, said, 'I've been offered the position of research fellow at Magdalen College.'

Walt and I erupted into cheers, but Archie raised his hands, holding us off. 'It's not official yet, but I'll know more after I meet with the college president tomorrow,' he said, pulling a face and making his outstretched hands shake in a parody of fear.

'They would be fools not to hire you,' Walt said, on his feet now and standing in front of his nephew. Putting a hand on the younger man's shoulder, he said in a voice that wobbled around the edges, 'Your mother would have been so very proud of you, Archie, my dear boy. So very proud indeed – as am I.'

Archie nodded, then dropped his gaze to the carpet.

After he'd gone, Walt sank heavily into his chair.

'Penny for them?' I said.

Walt smiled sadly before he met my gaze. He shrugged, and I knew his thoughts were with the siblings he'd lost. His brothers, save for the one who hadn't lived a week, to the Great War and his beloved youngest sister, Cissy, who had died from consumption when Archie was just a child.

'I was hoping he might say he had a date with an eligible young woman,' I said, trying to lift his mood.

Walt huffed out a laugh and shook his head. 'I fear he takes after me in that regard,' he said, reaching for his glass of port. 'He's just not that bloody interested. No, it'll be books and bachelorhood for young Archie, I'm afraid.'

'Does it bother you? The end of the Middleton line? Archie not passing on the peerage to a son?' I asked.

Walter scoffed. 'Not a jot. He's already told me he doesn't want it, anyway. Wish I'd had the gumption to tell my father that. He'll be better off without it. Let him make his own way in the world.'

'Would you like me to ask Mrs Small to order in some more champagne?' I asked.

Walt brightened. 'Damn good idea. Or maybe dinner out, somewhere extravagant. He likes that French place over on Berkley Square, as I recall. Can't think of the bloody name though.'

'I've got a note of it. Leave it with me,' I said, glad to see his malaise seemed to be shifting. I got to my feet, suddenly sleepy.

'Shall we play in the morning, before we start?' Walt asked, looking hopeful.

'Let's,' I said, smiling as the butterflies stirred in my chest at the mere suggestion of music. It was a novelty for me to have someone accompany me on the piano, and, thanks to Walt's generosity, I once again had a cello of my own.

'But then we need to finish plotting the next book or else your delightful publisher will …' I paused, tapping my finger against my temple, pretending to rack my memory. 'Oh yes. That was it. He said he'd nail your hide to the nearest barn door.'

'I'd like to see him try!' Walt guffawed.

'Good night, Walt,' I said, laughing.

'Good night, Gwennie dearest,' he replied.

I smiled before walking to the door.

'Archie's right, you know,' Walt said.

I stopped and turned.

'About being an angel, I mean. You saved me, Gwennie. I was bored to tears of this writing lark until you arrived. I even considered coming out of retirement and going back to the ruddy Home Office,' he said, snorting at the idea. 'But then you walked in, so chock full of ideas and enthusiasm, and it's like the light went back on and I fell in love with writing all over again.'

I'd heard this before, but I'd never tire of it. He had given me so much, and so it felt wonderful to know that, for once in my life, I'd been able to give too.

'I couldn't have wished for a better writing partner,' he said, raising his tumbler of whiskey in a silent toast.

I made to reply, but he shook his head.

As I started up the main stairs to the first floor – neither I nor Villiers had to suffer the attic rooms usually reserved for the servants – I sent up a silent prayer to thank the Goddess for the gift of my friend Walter Middleton.

CHAPTER 27

GWEN, FEBRUARY 1939

'You'd be doing me the most generous favour, Gwennie dear, you really would,' Walt said, pressing his palms together and smiling hopefully.

We were sitting in his study in the pair of winged-back armchairs that flanked the fireplace, him with his slippered feet on the fender, nursing a whiskey in one hand and his pipe in the other. I sat curled into the belly of the other chair with a mug of cocoa and a blanket over my knees.

I stared at him blankly, still trying to process the bombshell he'd just delivered at the end of a perfectly ordinary day of writing, dining and playing cards until it was time for our respective nightcaps.

Walt pressed on. 'I'd shuffle off this mortal coil content in the knowledge that my little books would still be rolling onto the shelves while my earthly remains were keeping the High-gate worms well fed.'

I recoiled at the grisly image and made a face. *This is what happens when you get attached,* I thought. I couldn't think of Walt dying. Or of my leaving, for that matter, although I knew I had to – and soon. I had already broken the promise I'd made to myself after fleeing Norfolk, but here I was living in luxury with a kind man who wanted nothing more than my friendship.

'I'd hardly call eleven best-selling espionage novels "little books",' I said with a pointed look.

Walt conceded the point with a shrug.

'But think about the benefits, Gwennie, darling. You love writing and you're damn good at it. This way, after my days, you can just carry on scribbling while pocketing the royalties. It's a genius idea,' Walt said, looking smug.

'I can't possibly write a whole novel on my own,' I protested. 'Besides, your readers would know it wasn't you.'

Walt snorted. 'Oh, piffle. They don't care a hoot. They just want the next Gideon Lockwood book. They don't give a fig if it's written by yours truly or the Queen of bloody Sheba, although sadly, having said that, we might have to keep your real identity from Larry.'

My flesh crawled at the mention of Walt's creepy publisher with the wandering hands.

'It's an incredibly generous offer, Walt, dear, but we don't need to talk about this now. You're only just sixty, for heaven's sake. You've got years left,' I said tightly, before taking a sip of my cocoa.

'I'm rather afraid that we don't,' Walt said seriously.

I sat forward with such a start that I slopped hot cocoa onto the blanket. My mind raced. His last check-up with Dr Carmichael was just a few months ago, and he'd been fine. But had he been again without telling me? He had been going to a lot of meetings lately, returning grim-faced with what looked to be the weight of the world on his shoulders.

Walt's expression morphed from confusion into horror. 'Oh, goodness no. I'm quite well. Fit as a flea, I promise,' he said, placing his hand over his heart.

Relief washed over me, and I sank back into the armchair, feeling as if I'd just finished a hundred-metre dash. I placed the mug on the side table and pulled a handkerchief from my sleeve to mop at the drops of spilled cocoa.

'War is coming, Gwennie,' Walt said with a heavy sigh.

'Again?' I asked, my heart like lead in my chest.

I'd spent the last one in Scotland, working as a governess to three children in Perthshire and tutoring their eldest, Claudia, in cello. A tall, quiet child who longed to study music but who had instead found herself packed off to a finishing school in Switzerland after the war. I hoped she still played.

'There is talk of a conscription bill for young men, and ...' Walt paused, his eyes on his whiskey. 'I'm under quite a bit of pressure to return to the service. I've said I'll consider it if things worsen, but I fear that my comfortable retirement may be coming to an abrupt end.' Walt met my eyes briefly before turning his attention to the hearth.

I followed his gaze and watched the flames consume the logs. How many wars had I lived through? Most had happened in faraway lands, but they always brought a rush of new arrivals. Lost magic beating a path to me on fragile, tattered wings.

I'd had no choice but to return to Wales during the first English Civil War, carted off with the other servants to my master's country estate. I passed myself off as a boy and slept every night in the gardener's loft with my fingers curled around the handle of a knife. I could have worked in the stables, but there would never be another Tân, so I told them horses made me sneeze.

I fled after the head gardener caught me binding my breasts to flatten my chest. I ran away into a snowstorm before they dismissed me – or worse. The nuns found me collapsed on the road, half frozen to death. And so began my period of not so divine cloister. I shuddered, dragging myself from the jaws of the memory and uncurling my legs to rest my feet on the fender beside Walt's.

'If we begin now, then it will give you time to get into your stride before I'm called back to Whitehall,' Walt said, framing the statement as if it were a question.

I bit my lip, conscious that the butterflies were swooping excitedly in my chest. I had to admit that though the thought of trying to write an entire novel terrified me, it thrilled me too. I had thought that nothing compared to my music, but writing opened a whole new world for me. On the page, I could be anyone. I could live a thousand lives or simply be the woman I might have been. That I might one day have the means of earning money without skivvying for others felt like a dream.

Before I could put my thoughts into words, Walt placed his whiskey tumbler on the table and leaned forward, his expression serious.

'I know you're hiding, Gwen.'

My body moved on instinct. My feet were on the floor, hands braced on the arm of the chair, even before I felt my adrenaline surge. I expected to feel an answering rush of frightened wings, but now that the talk of ghost-writing had passed, they were utterly still.

Walt held up his hands.

'Just wait, please,' he implored. 'I will never ask you what, or whom, you're hiding from. I don't care if you're on the run for murder, you have my solemn word that I will always keep you safe.'

I lowered myself slowly back into my chair, unable to speak around what felt like a shard of glass in my throat. If only he knew.

'If things go as we expect them to, then London won't be safe.'

I said nothing, still preoccupied with my memories.

'I have friends in Canada you could stay with—' he began.

'I want to stay here,' I said, cutting him off.

Walt regarded me and nodded. He opened his mouth to say something else, but I leapt in.

'I would prefer to stay with you, if that's alright,' I said, annoyed at how my plan to leave by the summer had been so easily cast aside. But in my chest, the butterflies gave an approving flutter. While my judgement was humanly flawed, I had the feeling that magic never made mistakes.

'I'd like that very much,' he replied, smiling. He sat a moment before pushing to his feet and ambling towards the door. He turned before opening it.

'I know a man who can sort out papers, birth certificates and the like, as I'm assuming yours were lost ...' Walt let the statement trail in the air.

'The first of August, 1916,' I said hoarsely. It was the date I'd put on the form at the secretarial agency.

'Place of birth?' he asked lightly, his hand on the door-knob but his gaze on me. The question caught me off guard. It must have shown on my face because he waved his hand in the air as if the question were drifting smoke he needed to waft away.

'Leave that one to me then,' he said with an affable smile. 'Anywhere to avoid?'

I cleared my throat. 'Anywhere but Wales,' I breathed, feeling like a traitor to my country and every ancestor who had lived and toiled before me.

I turned towards the fire just as the tears spilled down my cheeks and something tugged in my gut as surely as if the land of my fathers had pulled on the knotted cord that connected us.

'Understood,' Walt said. He opened the door wide, and I

felt the cold rush in from the hallway. Even with my head turned to the fire, I knew he was watching me.

'The Welsh have a word for it, don't they,' he said gently. '"Hiraeth", isn't it?'

I nodded, emotion smothering my voice. Images of Nain and Tân slid into my mind, quick as butter in a hot pan. The view from the top meadow overlooking the valley, the wind in my hair as we stood and gazed at land that was ours, not because my father owned it but because it was in our blood and bones. Because the very air we breathed felt like a mother's embrace. Wales made me but then betrayed me. What a cruel irony then, that the memory of my homeland could still bring me to tears even now.

CHAPTER 28

GWEN, MARCH 1942

The sound of Walt shouting was so unusual that I rushed to his study without even taking off my coat or muddy boots. I'd crept out of the rambling old country house at dawn to check on the greenhouse after a night of howling winds. I had half the village waiting for the cabbage and tomato seedlings hardening off in there, and they were the last of the seeds.

After making sure all was secure, I'd stayed to sow some perennial flowers. While my own butterflies had no need of nectar, the native ones relied on it, and if the local bees went hungry, so did we all.

Flower seeds sown and labelled, I'd cleaned some pots, thinned some parsnip seedlings and hunted around the kitchen garden, looking for the tin watering cans the wind had claimed.

It wasn't until my stomach growled that I realised the time. Poor Walt must be ravenous too. I stopped by the henhouse to collect the eggs and let the ladies out to forage. Since the start of the war, both the London house and this one, Walt's old family home in Wiltshire, had run with a skeleton staff. Villiers had passed away during my second summer in London, slipping quietly from sleep into that other place just before midsummer. Walt had sobbed like a child when he found him.

Villiers had been gone nearly three years now, and neither house felt quite the same without him. As Mrs Small had stayed in London with her family, I had taken charge of the cooking, such as it was. A young woman called Daisy came in daily to help with the cleaning, and when Walt needed to go to London, the Ministry sent a car.

Walt shouted again. I was just about to push open the study door when I realised he was on the phone. Relief washed over me, but before I could take a step back, his next words pinned me to the spot.

'You killed twenty-three innocent civilians. British subjects who volunteered – *volunteered* – to serve queen and country in the war effort.' Walt ground out the words as if he hoped the dust of them might fly down the telephone and choke whoever he was talking to. 'You *knew* the chances of the experiment working were slim to non-existent and yet you persisted!'

I could hear him heaving in shallow breaths, like a boxer back in his corner, biding his time.

'Of course I shut it down, man! If you'd followed procedure and sought my approval in the first place, I'd have refused you, and twenty-three members of the magical community would still be alive and well and living the lives they were damn well entitled to live!' He was almost screaming now.

My heart hammered beneath my ribs.

Magical community. Had I heard him correctly?

'You can expect charges over this, Simpson,' Walt growled. Then I heard the receiver slam back on the telephone with such force it would be a miracle if it remained in one piece.

The next noise to reach my ears broke my heart. It was the sound of Walt weeping. I flung my hand over my mouth as I hurried to the front door, opened it quietly and then slammed it loudly. I strode, my steps as heavy as I could make them, to Walt's office, knocked once and pushed open the door.

The curtains were drawn and the lamps still lit despite the brightness of the morning outside. Walt's desk was a sea of paper and files, and the man himself sat slumped, his head in his hands.

He stood up swiftly when I entered and turned away, making towards the curtained window. 'Good morning, dear heart,' he said cheerfully. That was the art of the spy, I suppose, the ability to project whatever was needed in the moment despite what one felt in private. He'd never admitted as much; we were both allowed our secrets, after all. My heart ached for him.

'You made an early start, I see,' I said.

Walt opened the curtains, flooding the room with early-morning cheer that neither of us felt. He pulled a handkerchief from his pocket and blew his nose without turning.

'More a late night that turned into an early morning.'

'You've been here all night?'

He shrugged. 'There were times in my early days at the Ministry where sleep was a luxury saved for high days and holidays.'

I gathered my courage. 'Did I hear you shouting?'

He studied me for a moment before answering.

'Probably,' he said, trying for a nonchalant shrug, but the smile that went with it was eggshell thin.

I should have pressed it, asked him to explain what he meant when he mentioned the magical community, but the pain in his eyes was just too much. I headed for the door and spoke without turning.

'Boiled eggs okay?' I asked, chiding myself for my cowardice. I should just come out with it. If anyone could help me, it was Walt, and yet I couldn't seem to form the words. The butterflies, always so eager to protect me from danger, were utterly still. Did that mean I should ask him or hold my tongue?

'Gwen, you know I'll do anything and everything in my power to always protect you, don't you?'

I froze, my hand reaching for the doorknob. I took a deep breath before turning. I forced a smile, but I wanted to weep at the sadness in his expression.

My words abandoned me, so I simply nodded and left the room.

CHAPTER 29

DAN, MAY 1976

'Ever get the feeling we're wasting our time?' I asked Clementine as we sat in the car, watching the home of the late Dr Clement Johnson. As I'd feared, DI Heath's officers didn't find the victim's body when they searched the derelict house. Forensics found traces of blood and, crucially, a piece of fabric caught on barbed wire in the backyard that was a perfect match to the overcoat Clement wore on the day he disappeared, but that was it.

His family knew the police were treating the case as a homicide, but how could anyone begin to grieve without a body to bury? My hands tightened on the steering wheel as I thought of his killers still walking the streets.

Clementine whined and pawed my arm. Only then did I realise that my knuckles had turned white. I let go of the steering wheel and slumped back in my seat with a sigh. Seven months since I'd taken this case, and I still had nothing on the missing woman. Gwenllian Llewellyn, if she existed at all, was a ghost.

I'd ignored Devlin's warning not to waste my time going

"

to Wales. In a missing persons case, you always start from the place they called home, but nobody I spoke to remembered a young woman matching her description or recognised her name. The long drive to Tintagel in Cornwall yielded nothing either. I'd pulled in favours from every contact I had, as had DI Heath, but we always came up blank. Had it not been for the dreams, I might have convinced myself she didn't exist.

Through the fabric of my T-shirt, my fingers traced the outline of the tattoo on my chest. It hadn't burned since the day of the murder, but I noticed it a lot more now. I'd wake from another dream where Gwen felt so real I could smell her perfume, my chest aching and the tattoo feeling like a bruise that refused to heal. I knew in my gut she was real – despite what the evidence suggested.

The only positive was that I was still on the case and still getting paid. There was something poetic about using Devlin's own money against him. I mailed my reports each week to the PO Box his secretary had given me, but it was one-way traffic. That suited me fine. I wasn't sure how I'd hold myself back if I ever met my client face-to-face again.

So, here I was, parked in an affluent, tree-lined street in West London, watching the home of another man I hadn't been able to save. What had seemed like a good idea this morning now, with my body stiff from four hours of sitting down, felt more like a penance.

I glanced over to where Clem sat on the passenger seat, peering out the windshield as if she too were on surveillance. Then again, I guessed she was. Maybe I needed to put her name on my business cards.

She turned her head and wagged at me, and there it was, another piece of my heart handed back to me courtesy of a stray mutt I'd pulled from the road.

'We saved each other, didn't we, Clem,' I said, reaching

over to run my hand down her silky fur. She was a far cry from the filthy bag of bones I'd found that night.

I checked my watch. She was probably hungry by now. I retrieved the bag I'd stowed behind the passenger seat this morning. While my sandwiches weren't to Precious's standard, they'd keep us going until dinner. I broke the first one in half and held it out for Clementine, who took it like a lady choosing fancy cakes at the Ritz but then ruined the effect by choking it down without chewing.

I ate my half with a little less enthusiasm, then handed her half an apple which, to my surprise, she made a half-assed attempt at actually chewing.

Lunch complete, I picked up the field goggles to take one last look at Clement's front door. There had been no movement in over four hours. Maybe this was a fool's errand after all. Just as I lowered the goggles, I glimpsed a figure striding towards the house.

'What the—' I said, not trusting my eyes.

I lowered the goggles and rubbed my eyes before lifting them again. There was no doubt about it. It was him. Leaf, or Lieutenant Jackson Brady back when we'd served together, jogging up to Clement's front door and pressing the bell. He was out of uniform, wearing a crisp short-sleeved white shirt and camel-coloured slacks, his dark, curly hair still regulation short, but he was still the soldier I remembered.

A moment later, he disappeared into the house and the door closed behind him.

Clementine gave a low whine.

I exhaled a long, slow breath before I spoke. 'I just saw an old friend, Clem, and if I'm not mistaken, he could be the break we've been waiting for.'

I spent the next ten minutes wondering about the odds. I didn't like coincidences, but I'd learned never to spit in the face of good fortune. I jolted back to the moment as the front door opened and Jackson stepped out. I clipped Clementine's leash to her collar, and we jumped out of the car.

Jackson stood talking to whoever had seen him to the door. From his body language, it was clear he was reluctant to leave and still politely pressing his case, whatever the hell that could be.

'Time to sniff,' I whispered to Clementine.

Like a pro, she dropped her head and began inspecting the nearest tree while I waited, my head bent as if looking at her but keeping one eye trained on Jackson. When I saw his shoulders fall, I knew he was about to give up.

'Time to go, kiddo,' I whispered, and Clementine abandoned her sniffing.

Jackson was jogging down the steps as we approached, his lips flattened, his jaw tight and one hand already reaching into his top pocket for his sunglasses. Not a successful meeting then.

'Leaf?' I said, using the lame nickname we'd given the only Canadian in our platoon.

His head snapped up, a scowl narrowing his eyes and knitting his brow. I saw the moment recognition hit him. His face broke into his famous thousand-watt smile, and he jumped the last few steps and hurried towards me.

'Captain Dan Quinn!'

'At your service,' I replied, grinning. 'It's been a long time, Jackson.'

When I stuck out my hand, he raised his eyebrows, and we stepped in for the swift back-patting hug men reserve for brothers in arms.

'Man, I was only talking about you last week! I told a bunch of new recruits that if you'd not saved my ass in Nam, some other, way scarier mother would be yelling at them instead,' Jackson said with a laugh.

My throat tightened at the memory, and I looked away.

Jackson and six others had survived, but nine good men didn't make it home because of me.

Jackson put his hand on my shoulder. 'Hey. Don't go there, man. None of us could have done anything different – and if it'd been down to me, we'd all be pushing up daisies right now.'

I nodded but couldn't think what to say next. Thankfully, Clementine chose that moment to press her nose into Jackson's leg.

'Well, hello,' he said to her, dropping to a crouch and offering his hand for her to sniff. It gave me a moment to collect my thoughts and refocus on why I was here. I glanced up and noticed the gates to a small park in the distance.

'Got time for a stroll in the park?' I asked, inclining my head.

Jackson checked his watch, but I already knew he was going to say yes.

'For you, man, I've got all the time in the world,' he replied.

I unclipped Clementine's leash once we were through the gates, and she immediately dropped her nose to the ground. Maybe when I had more time, I'd teach her how to track.

'So, you're clearly still serving,' I said with a smile as I made a thing of looking him up and down. 'What brings you to London?'

Jackson didn't stop, but he missed a beat in his pace.

'I live here now,' he said carefully.

'Really?' I said, stopping and turning towards him. I needed to see his face.

He nodded slowly, his teeth already raking his bottom lip the way they did when he was thinking.

'I didn't think we had units stationed here, save for maybe some intelligence guys in the north,' I said, trying to sound as casual as I could manage.

Jackson's forehead tightened, and he closed his mouth, his lips pressed shut. He eyed me for a long moment before he spoke.

'Tell me, was meeting you today a genuine coincidence?' he asked, and I saw something close to hurt flash in his eyes.

'Straight-up coincidence,' I replied, putting my hand over my heart. 'Had anyone asked me, I'd have said you were back in Ontario.'

Jackson nodded slowly, his eyes raking over my face, looking for the tells I'd taught him how to spot. His expression softened again.

'So, you're working a case,' he said.

I nodded. 'And I'm out of leads,' I said with a heavy sigh. 'Coming here today felt like a last crazy toss of the dice. I was about to call it a day and go home, and then you show up.' I shrugged.

'The famous Dan Quinn intuition,' he said, the wide smile back in place.

We walked in silence for a while, and I weighed up my options. Deciding that I had little to lose, I gestured to a nearby bench.

'What if I tell you a story and you tell me whether you think I'm losing my mind,' I said.

Colin's warning rang in my ears, but I silenced it. Clementine raced back to join us and sat at my feet as I told Jackson an edited version of the story, starting with my new client and his hunt for a missing woman. I didn't name either, but I did describe the murder of the poor doctor by means I couldn't explain.

Jackson remained silent throughout, his forearms resting on his knees, his eyes trained on the tree-lined horizon. 'Tell me again what this guy said to the victim. Exactly what he said.'

'He said something like, "We know you lead the Council

of Elders. And we know all about your secret libraries." He seemed to think the victim knew the whereabouts of the missing woman, but Clement denied it until the end.' I shook my head to dislodge the image of that ruined husk of a man.

'They talked about magic as if it was a real thing,' I said, throwing up my hands and shaking my head.

'And what information do you have on the woman they're after?' Jackson asked, his eyes still fixed on the trees.

Deciding to leave out the part about the sketch, I said, 'An approximate age of twenty-one, dark hair, attractive. Has family in a little town in mid-Wales. But that's a dead end too. There's no trace of her.'

'Where in Wales exactly?' Jackson asked slowly.

'A little place near the Brecon Beacons called Pont Nefoedd,' I said, no doubt still mangling the pronunciation.

Jackson spun around to look at me, his jaw slack. With a sigh, he leaned back against the bench and lifted his head, gazing skyward for a long moment.

'Magic doesn't make mistakes, my friend,' Jackson said, turning to look at me. 'Man, just when you think you've seen it all,' he added wryly.

'What the fuck?' Had I misheard him?

Jackson sat forward, resting his elbows on his knees, and lowered his voice.

'You're not losing your mind, man. What you saw in that house, it's real. That's all I can say without breaking my vows, but trust the evidence of your senses, not the bullshit beliefs you've been force-fed since the cradle,' he said, his expression deadly serious.

I hissed out a long breath. So, this was likely some top-secret weapon or something equally as shady. I didn't really care.

'Look, I don't need to know. I just need to find her, Jackson. Before she becomes their next victim.' I didn't like the note of desperation in my voice.

Jackson dragged his teeth over his bottom lip. 'You asked me which unit I'm with, and I can't tell you because it doesn't have an official name. In fact, it doesn't exist. And our mission is investigating other things that don't, technically, exist. Do you get me?'

I didn't, but I nodded. 'Kind of.'

'You already know I'm here visiting the widow of our high-profile victim in my official capacity. And now you've shared your story, I also know that you're the source DI Heath refused to name in his official report,' Jackson said.

I made a mental note to get Colin a good bottle of Scotch for Christmas.

Jackson checked his watch.

'Meet me at the George on Borough Road tonight at twenty-two hundred hours. Tell the bartender you've booked the upstairs room. I have something you'll want to see,' he said, already on his feet.

He lingered a moment, stroking Clementine on the head as she gazed into his eyes and wagged her tail like he was her new best friend.

'I guess I'd be wasting my breath telling you to walk away from this,' Jackson said.

I shrugged. He knew me better than that.

'I figured. Just watch your back. You have no idea how deep this shit goes or how far some powerful people will go to keep their secrets,' he said.

As I stood, he caught himself mid-salute, his hand freezing before he let it drop. He rolled his eyes. I smiled and placed my hand on his shoulder.

'It's good to see you, Leaf.'

'You too, my friend,' he said. 'I'll see you tonight.'

I had time to register the hint of a smile on his lips before he strode away, pulling his sunglasses from his pocket.

CHAPTER 30

DAN, MAY 1976

I could still feel the weight of Clementine's loaded stare as I backed out of the flat. She hated being left behind, but I didn't know if the pub allowed dogs, and I wasn't about to take the risk.

I took the Tube to Borough and arrived at the galleried old pub half an hour early. It was a warren of small, interconnected rooms, and I strolled through them all, getting the lay of the place. Nothing made me uneasy, so I returned to the main bar and found a seat in a corner by the window from which I could watch the punters and staff. At twenty-one fifty-five, I took my glass to the bar and told the barman what Jackson had instructed.

'First floor, room on the right. Stairs are that way,' he said with a quick jerk of his head before turning to serve the next customer. 'Just move the rope,' he called after me.

After unhooking and replacing the rope that closed off the polished-wood staircase to the public, I ascended slowly, listening intently. When I reached the top, I found the door to my right cracked open.

'We're clear,' Jackson said from inside, and I stepped into

a large, dark-panelled room that looked like it was being used for storage. There were enough chairs piled against the opposite wall to seat everyone in the pub. To my right sat a row of tables, stacked top to top, their legs reaching skyward like skeletal arms. To my left, a run of old leaded windows looked out onto the courtyard below, the sodium glow from the street lights defiant against the night sky.

Jackson rose from his seat at a small table in the middle of the room and greeted me in the same way he had that morning, but there was no thousand-watt smile tonight. He looked coiled as tight as a box of springs.

He gestured to the other chair as he stepped past me to lock and then bolt the door. Next, he pulled the curtains over the windows, making sure to cover the joins. I frowned. Either Jackson had been here more than half an hour or he'd slipped in another way.

'I came in the back,' he said as he took his seat. He had always been good at reading people.

I sat down slowly, my eyes on Jackson. He blew out a slow breath, then reached down to pluck an old knapsack from the floor. He paused again before he opened it, as if some part of him were trying to hold back his every step. I clenched my jaw, resisting the urge to hurry him. Whatever this was, he was in two minds about it. He finally pulled out a thin manila folder and, after another careful exhalation, slid it across the table to me.

'Read first and then ask your questions,' he said with a heavy sigh.

I nodded, flipping open the folder and noting the military-style indexing on the cover that told me the yellowed pages inside dated back to 1960. My frown deepened as I read. This had to be an elaborate joke. While it looked official enough, right down to the paper, what it detailed read like something out of a fantasy novel. They even had crime scene images of the shootings. I closed the folder abruptly and slid it back to Jackson.

I huffed out a laugh. 'Really, man? Is this some kind of joke? Because I can assure you, I wasn't laughing as I watched that guy die.' My voice was tight with the effort of trying to contain my anger and disappointment that my old buddy would pull a stunt like this.

Jackson was shaking his head.

I flung up my hands. 'You're seriously telling me your unnamed unit investigates real-life magical activity.'

Jackson kept his eyes on the table as he nodded slowly.

'Oh, come on,' I snapped, hitting my palm against the tabletop. 'I saw a tortured man murdered in cold blood and you want me to believe in fucking fairies?'

Jackson turned his head away and pulled in a long breath.

He turned back, looked me in the eye and said flatly, 'Witches, actually.'

'Oh, great. Because that's so much more fucking plausible!' I snorted, and pushed to my feet, knocking over my chair.

Jackson tipped back his head and groaned. 'Man, will you just sit down, please.'

I stared at him. 'What, for a lecture on the occult and why Siegfried and Roy really did make that goddamn tiger vanish into thin air?'

'Fuck's sake, just sit your ass!' Jackson barked, a flash of anger shadowing his face.

Had it been anyone else, I'd already have been out the door, but it was Jackson. I'd saved his life, yes, but when they'd pulled me half dead from that hut in the jungle, it was Jackson who cut the wires from my wrists, then carried me, literally carried me, to the chopper.

I studied him. He wasn't lying to me – he really believed

this shit. I picked up the fallen chair, sat back down and folded my arms, waiting.

The silence stretched between us, and I rubbed absent-mindedly at a tingling on my chest. I let out a long, exasperated breath and scrubbed my palms across my face. I'd had enough of this.

When I pulled my hands away, I couldn't make sense of what I saw. I was looking at the top of Jackson's head. He lifted his eyes and gave an apologetic shrug.

'What the—' I yelled, gripping the sides of my chair and scanning the room, my brain desperately trying to find a rational explanation for why I was hovering five feet in the air.

Jackson waved his hand like he was doing tai chi, and the chair lilted from side to side. I launched myself onto the floor, landing in a crouch. When I looked up, the chair was still hanging in mid-air.

'What the—' I repeated, stumbling backwards and crashing into a stack of chairs.

'You said that already, man,' Jackson said wearily.

'What the fuck?' I rasped.

The chair floated to the ground, and I snatched it up, flipping it over, looking for wires or anything that could rationally explain what had just happened. I found nothing.

Jackson gestured for me to sit, but I kicked the chair across the room and pulled another at random from the stack. While I wouldn't admit it, my legs felt like Jell-O. I slumped into the chair and braced my elbows on the table. Had he drugged me? But how? I'd watched the bartender open the bottle of Coke. No. It had to be something else. I opened my eyes as an icy breeze prickled the skin on my forearms, and I felt my jaw drop at what I saw.

Spinning between Jackson's outstretched hands on the table was a perfectly formed tornado, no bigger than a box of matches. The pages in the file ruffled with the force of the wind. I watched, transfixed, as the file edged across the table, blown by the tiny tempest. Jackson turned his palms up, and the tornado morphed into a cloud the size of a watermelon and the colour of a battleship.

'Is that actual fucking snow?' I gaped, unable to drag my eyes away from the flakes dusting the tabletop.

With a flick of his fingers, Jackson sent the cloud upwards, fat snowflakes falling onto my outstretched hands as it grew. They caught in my eyelashes and melted on my cheeks. When I looked down, it was already quietly blanketing the table and floor around us.

'I know it's a lot, man, but believe your senses, remember,' Jackson said, reaching over to briefly clasp his hand over my forearm. He squeezed it once before letting go.

I glared at him, fury building in my gut even as my mind struggled to process it all.

'If you can do this shit, then why didn't you save them?' I growled.

While I was looking at my friend in a London pub, in my mind I could still see my men lying dead and dying as the Viet Cong soldiers dragged me, barely conscious, through the jungle.

Jackson swallowed and looked away. He bit his lip, and I caught the tremble of his chin. When he turned back to me, his eyes were glassy.

'I was knocked out, remember? You dragged me to the Jeep and went back for Cooper. By the time I came around, it was too late. But this magic shit, as you call it? It's how I got you out of there in the end,' he said, tapping the snow-covered tabletop with his finger.

I stared at him as if I were seeing him for the first time. So much about my rescue had never made sense – how they found me, for one, but also how Jackson and just two others had overpowered the dozen or more enemy soldiers at the camp.

The army sent me home to recover from my physical injuries, but the mental scars had taken the longest. Six years on – three of them sober – and I had an answer to a question I'd never thought to ask.

'They don't give out medals of honour for nothing, Quinn. You went above and beyond, and it's high time you focused on the men you saved and not the ones who were never destined to make it home. You hear me, my friend?' Jackson stabbed his forefinger into the tabletop, adding exclamation points.

My chest heaved as shame and grief knotted up like a fist behind my ribs. I closed my eyes, expecting to see the faces of the dead swim before my eyes, but instead, I saw the woman in the picture.

It might have been my imagination, but as I sucked in the next breath, it felt like I had more room in my lungs. I opened my eyes and nodded at Jackson. Maybe it was time.

When I stepped out of the pub an hour later, it felt like stepping into a whole new and even more terrifying world. But I had a full notebook and, most importantly, I had my first real lead.

CHAPTER 31

GWEN, MAY 1960

I eased open Walt's bedroom door and peered inside. He was sleeping, his head turned on his pillows towards the French doors and the balcony beyond. I swallowed against the lump in my throat. He looked so frail now. So unfathomably old.

The faint sweetness of human decay lay beneath the sharp tang of disinfectant. I lifted my nose, searching for the fragile scent of the freesias I'd placed by his bedside this morning. They weren't enough to mask the other smells, but I loved the way his eyes lit up whenever he saw me approaching with another new offering wrapped in florist's paper.

I should have been used to death by now, and yet I tried so hard to avoid it, staying nowhere long enough to get attached, or so I told myself.

The children were always the hardest to leave behind. I'd worked for many years as a governess, trying and often failing to never stay more than a few months. When my positions ended well, I'd be called away by an urgent family emergency with a letter of recommendation tucked into my bag, but when the butterflies woke me in the middle of the night, hurling themselves against the cage of my ribs, I'd flee with only the clothes on my back, my heart breaking at the thought of the children's faces come the morning.

Even the planned goodbyes left their scars. Memories of distraught, red-cheeked little ones clinging to my skirts still haunted me, even though those children lived to make old bones and were long since in their graves.

The only other option available was skivvying, but even rising at dawn to scrub floors and empty chamber pots was sometimes a relief from the heartache and the bittersweet reminder of what would never be.

I saw plenty of death during the last war, slipping out of the house to volunteer during the Blitz while Walt was occupied at the Home Office.

It was soul-destroying work, but in some ways, I'd never felt more alive. I helped in soup kitchens and mobile canteens, administered first aid and took down the names of the lost and dispossessed, whatever was needed in the moment. Several times, that meant searching for survivors in the rubble. I always longed to find someone still alive, but I never did.

Walt was furious when he found out. I'm still not sure how he did, but it was the first time I'd ever heard him come close to raising his voice. When his fury dissolved into tears, my defiance melted away. Our darling Archie had been killed in North Africa just months before, and when Walt, choking out the words, said, 'I can't lose you too,' we had sobbed together.

We'd moved to Walt's country house in Wiltshire the next day. For the first time in my life, I was sorry to leave London, but when I felt the butterflies settle for the first time in months, I knew it was the right decision. My first duty was to them. I couldn't risk them to a Nazi bomb, or even an unfortunate accident with a lump of falling masonry. So, I spent the rest of the war digging for victory by day in the extensive gardens and knitting and sewing clothes for those in need by night.

Standing here now, back in the London house, on the threshold of Walt's bedroom, it occurred to me that this was my first deathbed vigil. Nain, Tân, even Rhys had all passed on without me. I rubbed a hand over my throat, tasting bile even at the thought of his name.

'You would make a terrible spy if that's your idea of covert surveillance,' Walt rasped, then burst into a fit of coughing.

I rushed into the room, but he was already replacing his beaker of water on the bedside table.

'Serves me right for thinking myself witty,' he said, settling back onto his pillows.

'You are wit personified, my love. Can I get you anything?'

Walt shook his head. 'The nurses left just a few moments before you came home.'

I didn't tell him I'd watched them leave. I perched on the side of the bed, leaned over and swept a stray lock of wispy white hair from his forehead. His skin felt cool and waxy under my fingers.

'I see you're bone dry today, at least,' Walt said, cracking open an eye and grinning. He had insisted I take at least an hour's walk each day when the nurses gave him his bed bath, and I had reluctantly agreed, but only because I knew it pleased him to think I was getting some air.

I forced a smile, but a lump rose in my throat at the thought of yesterday's sudden thunderstorm. The butter-flies had danced with the lightning, and while I had wanted to scream my grief and fury into the storm, like all prey animals, I had swallowed my pain and bolted for home, arriving soaked to the skin and dripping onto the parquet in the hallway. Today, I'd spent the hour sitting in a café across the road, counting down the minutes until I could return.

'Will you play for me, dear heart? And open the doors. I fear the nurses mean to suffocate me.'

I stroked his head again and leaned down to plant a kiss on his forehead before getting to my feet. As I pulled open the double doors to the balcony, a gust of fresh spring air barrelled into me, bringing with it a flurry of cherry blossoms from the trees in the garden beyond. I bent to scoop up a handful.

'The trees send their love,' I said, gently turning Walt's hand and dropping the petals onto his palm. He raised it slowly to his nose, sucked in a breath and held it, his face softening into a contented smile.

'Archie always wanted to go to Japan to see the blossoms. Had a book about it when he was a little boy. He was quite obsessed for a time.' He swallowed, his eyes still closed but squeezed more tightly shut now, against memories or tears, I didn't know.

I bit the inside of my cheek, trying to distract myself, but it was no good. I just didn't know how to say goodbye like this. It felt like each breath he took was another step away from me.

'Tell me again what you are to do when the time comes,' he said.

My heart sank. There would be no hope of holding back the dam if I had to recite this again, and every time I cried, I felt as though I was letting him down. I needed to be strong for him, and yet I was already grieving.

When I opened my mouth to protest, he just mouthed, 'Please.'

'You are a tyrant,' I joked feebly, squeezing his hand and

settling back onto the edge of the bed. I swallowed hard and licked my lips, mouth like ash, as I began.

'I am to go immediately to your private safe and take the satchel with my name on it. I must then go directly to the railway station and buy a ticket to the place specified in your instructions, which will be in the bag.

'If the nurses are here' – I cleared my throat – 'I am to tell them I must leave to enact your orders in the event of your —' I stopped abruptly and turned my head from his face, but not quickly enough to miss the tear leaking from the corner of his eye. My chest heaved, and I took a shaky breath as I felt my hands tremble.

'If they are not,' I pressed on, speeding up to get the ordeal behind me, 'then I am to telephone Doctor Carmichael and, as soon as he has confirmed' – I paused again, took a deep breath – 'what's required, I am to tell him the same thing. That you have entrusted me with urgent business.'

I braced my hand on the edge of the bed, feeling as if I'd just run a marathon.

'Good girl,' he said, his lips curved gently.

'You wanted me to play,' I said, standing, desperate to find firmer ground.

Walt patted my hand in reply and his smiled broadened.

After retrieving my cello and bow from my room next door, I hurried back to Walt's side. He looked so peaceful I almost crept out again, fearing he may have fallen asleep, but as I peered at him, he cracked open an eye.

'Not sleeping, old girl. Just waiting patiently for my serenade,' he wheezed.

So long as he was still trying to be funny, I thought, there was hope still. I pulled out a chair, adjusted the spike on the cello and wound my bow. The butterflies were already fidgeting in my chest, as they always did whenever they sensed the instrument. I still didn't know exactly why they loved it so much, although I suspected music and magic are closely entwined.

Out you come then, I thought, slipping back the mental bolt in my mind that released them. I felt the familiar pull as they surged upwards, and then, with a cool shudder from the breath of invisible wings, they were free. I closed my eyes and levelled my bow.

I had no idea what I was about to play; having long abandoned sheet music, I now just trusted my hands to make manifest whatever I needed to say. Sometimes familiar melodies surfaced, fragments from those early days when coaxing a single tuneful tone from the infernal instrument had felt like chasing an impossible dream. And yet, the butterflies had never minded. They had danced from the very first wailing note.

As I played, I lifted my head to watch them soar. They usually flew as high as the confines of the room allowed, but today they circled back to me. Some fluttered only inches away from my body while others settled on my hair, shoulders, hands and arms. I felt gossamer wings against my cheeks, and when I glanced down, the body of my cello had disappeared under a sea of bright wings.

When my gaze drifted to Walt, his eyes were open wide and there were tears streaming down his cheeks. A mile-wide smile lit his face, and I glimpsed the gentle, enchanted boy he had once been. I stilled my bow, ready to go to him, but he shook his head urgently.

'Play,' he mouthed. My own eyes clouded with tears, and pushing every ounce of love in my heart into the music, I played.

When the piece ended, he whispered, 'There you are. Ma sorcière papillon,' as he wiped the tears from his cheeks. I laid down my cello, sending the butterflies soaring once more, and climbed onto the bed next to him, wrapping my arm around his frail frame and holding on as if my presence alone might be enough to keep him here.

'I saw them,' he whispered into my hair. 'I saw your butterflies. Thank you for trusting me with your magic.'

I had no reply because it hadn't been my doing. So instead, I just said, 'I love you, Walt.'

'I love you too, dear heart,' he said, his voice cracking on the last word. We both cried, and when he at last fell asleep, I lay there, wondering what might have been had I just told him everything years ago.

CHAPTER 32

GWEN, MAY 1960

I woke, still curled into Walt's side, my arm flung over his chest like he was a life raft. The warmth of the spring day had vanished, the breeze from the open doors sharp-edged and indifferent now that the sun was so low in the sky. I shivered, and felt for Walt's hand, suddenly fearful that he'd slipped away while we slept, but thankfully his skin was still much warmer than mine. I loosed a quiet breath and eased myself from the bed, wincing as my muscles complained at the movement. Walt stirred but didn't wake.

The grand room lay in shadows now, with only a fading splash of sun fire lingering on the wall and ceiling above the bed.

I closed the balcony doors and secured them, then gathered up my cello and bow and crept quietly back to my room. After stowing my instrument in the case, I headed for the bathroom. The nurses were due soon, so I'd sit with him until they arrived, then make us all a pot of tea.

As I was washing my hands, I looked at myself in the mirror. I'd heard people say that grief ages a person, and even though I looked no different to the eighteen-year-old who fled her home during an unholy storm, when I focused only on my eyes, I barely recognised the girl I used to be. So long as I carried this magic, death passed me by, but time still raked me with its claws as if it meant to rend the flesh from my bones. We none of us escape this life unscathed.

A movement in the mirror caught my eye. The meadow brown appeared above my left shoulder. I stared at her for two whole heartbeats before realisation dawned. Not stopping to dry my hands, I ran from the room, slipping and falling to my knees when I caught my foot on the long rug on the landing as I raced back to Walt's bedroom.

I knew the moment I saw him; he was gone.

I didn't bother to put on the lamps.

I sat holding his hand, my forehead resting on the side of the bed, my gaze on the floor. I expected to cry now that this long-dreaded moment had arrived, but the tears didn't come. I don't know how long we stayed like that, but I jumped when a hand touched my shoulder.

Bernadette, his favourite nurse, stood behind me. She gave me a sympathetic smile and squeezed my shoulder.

'I only stepped out to put my cello away and use the lavatory.'

'Sometimes they wait for a little moment like that to make their move,' she said, her soft Irish accent lending her words the feel of a soft woollen blanket. 'You stay with him as long as you want. I'll just go telephone for Doctor Carmichael.'

'No,' I said suddenly. 'He gave me very explicit instructions in the event of his—' I couldn't say the word, not even now. 'I promised him. I'm to do something for him – it's important. Connected to his work,' I stammered, going off script a little but barely caring.

Bernadette nodded. 'You can leave him safe with me, Miss Gwen.'

I nodded, then realised that I was still sitting down, his hand still cupped in my own. I looked at Walt. He already looked so much less like the man I had known and loved. As I pulled my hand from his, the cherry blossom petals fell to the floor. A sob caught in my chest, but I heaved against it, refusing to give in to it. I would not let him down now. I gathered up the petals and stared at them in my hand. *The trees send their love.*

'Leave them with me and I'll make sure they go with him, if that's what you'd like?' Bernadette said from behind me, her hand hovering over the telephone in the corner.

I nodded mutely. I pulled three petals from the pile, one each for us and another for Archie, and tucked them into my pocket.

I leaned forward and kissed Walt's forehead. His skin was already cool to the touch. I pulled the blanket up to his neck and tucked it in around his shoulders. 'Goodbye, my friend,' I said, arranging the remaining petals on his chest. I glanced up, but the sun fire on the wall had gone.

Bernadette was replacing the receiver when I turned around.

'Can I get you anything? A cup of tea, at least, before you do your errand?'

I shook my head. 'No. Thank you,' I said, wanting to say more to this woman who had cared so diligently for Walt but not having the words.

Beneath my ribs, my heart hammered in my chest. I frowned, shock numbing my senses. No. Not my heart. The butterflies rising in alarm.

I mumbled my excuses and ran from the room. When I reached my door, I flung it open, skidding on my knees as I knelt to pull my already packed case from under the bed. I threw in the novel I was reading, the perfume Walt bought me every year for Christmas and the small framed photograph of the three of us.

I shoved my arms into my overcoat and pulled my cello case onto my back. I hurried towards the stairs, but paused when I heard Bernadette's sweet, lilting voice drift down the landing.

'Doctor Carmichael will be with us soon, Mr Middleton,' she whispered. 'He's just around the corner, as you know. He'll do the paperwork, and then little Bridget – you remember her, don't you, the sweet one with the ginger curls – well, she'll be over to help me get you ready.'

I clamped a hand over my mouth to stop myself from crying and hurried down the stairs, wondering why I'd never noticed how infernally long they were. Walt's study was at the foot of the stairs to the right. He'd not used it for months, but once I stepped inside, I could feel his presence everywhere I looked.

I put my head down and marched towards the picture that concealed his private safe. It took me three attempts to make my shaking fingers spin the dial to enter the combination.

Inside was a battered old satchel, my name inked on a luggage tag in Walt's looping script. I pulled it out with trembling hands and closed the safe, spinning the dial to lock it again.

Sliding the satchel's long handle over my head and shoulder, I headed back to the door, peering into the satchel as I went. I stopped in my tracks when I saw thick wads of cash still bound in cashier's wrappers, several manila folders and three long envelopes – two fat with folded sheets. I pulled them out. On the thin one were the words 'read me first'.

I ripped it open with shaking hands.

· · ·

Dear heart,

If you're reading this, I'm gone, and I'm sorry to leave you. There is much to explain, but first you need to get out of London as quickly as possible. <u>You are not safe in London!!</u>

Take the train and then head to the place we were going to send Gideon Lockwood in book fourteen before we changed our minds. <u>Go straight away.</u> You can read the next letter on the train.

Stay safe, my wonderful girl.

Much love, always,

W

PS. Sorry again for the being dead bit. Chin up though, old girl. Be strong for me.

He'd intended to make me smile with the PS, but it just made me want to curl up in a ball and howl. The peel of the doorbell stopped me in my tracks, and I rushed to close the study door before Bernadette could come down the stairs. The bell sounded again before I heard the creak of the steps and then her soft-soled shoes shuffle over the tiles outside.

Dr Carmichael wasn't a man used to hushed tones.

'He's in his room?' he asked crisply.

'Yes, Doctor. Do you want a cup of tea while you do the paperwork?' she asked.

'Good of you, yes, please,' he replied. 'Tell me, is his assistant still here?'

'No, Doctor. She left a little while ago. She said Mr Middleton left her with instructions to do something urgent in the event of his death.'

'Good,' Carmichael said.

I waited, expecting to hear the creak of the stairs, but he crossed the hall, his shoes sounding against the tiles. For one terrible moment, I thought he was about to burst into the study, but the footsteps halted outside the door. The telephone on the hall table pinged as he lifted the receiver.

'It's Doctor Carmichael. You instructed me to call when Lord Walter—' He stopped abruptly and snorted. 'Well, if you already know, I'll bid you good day,' he said tersely. The next words out of his mouth made my blood run cold, the butterflies rising in a panic.

'I'll do no such bloody thing. The young woman is free to come and go as she pleases, and anyway, I've just been told that she left the property hours ago on an errand,' Carmichael snapped, but I could hear a note of fear in his voice.

'Suit yourselves, but don't rush. She told the nurse she wouldn't be back until after ten p.m.'

I clamped my shaking hand over my mouth and tried to telegraph a silent thank you to the good doctor through the door. I waited until he and Bernadette had climbed the stairs, the boards squeaking under their feet and the teacup rattling in its saucer, before slipping out of the house.

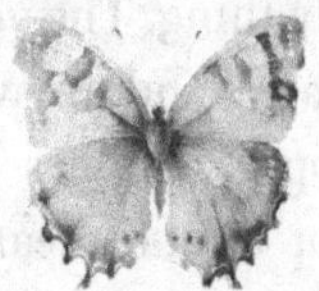

Just an hour later I was sitting on the last train heading to Plymouth, my cello beside me and the satchel in my lap. I tapped the second letter against my hand and caught the ghost of old pipe tobacco in the air. Walt had complained loudly when Dr Carmichael had suggested he give up his evening pipe habit, but he had complied. That was almost three years ago. My throat tightened at the thought of him sitting down to write this, pipe clamped between his teeth, the sweet scent of tobacco drifting into the air of his study.

I searched in the satchel for something, anything else, to delay the moment. I pulled out one of the thin manila folders and froze at the words 'Top Secret' stamped in red ink on the front.

Even though I was alone in the compartment, I folded back the cover to hide the stamp. At first, I couldn't quite take in what I was reading. My name stared back at me from the paper, along with my date and place of birth. Not what appeared on the passport Walt had procured for me but my actual date of birth, the fifteenth of March 1594.

My mouth went dry as my pulse pounded like a raging river in my ears. I had not breathed a word to a living soul in over three centuries, and yet, here it was in black and white.

Below those scant details, a neatly inked family tree. There was my name, next to Thomas, my older brother who hadn't lived to see his first birthday. Two terminated stumps on a family tree that, if my grandmother was to be believed, once held the most powerful magical lineage in Wales. At least it had until I came along and ruined it.

I touched my fingers to the page, tracing first my mother's name, Catrin, and then my grandmother's, Mary. My mother's father, Tyron, was long dead even before my brother drew his first breath. These were the people I owed my existence to, and yet even Nain felt like a stranger. The woman who had loved me in life, cursed me with her death and long since abandoned me to my fate.

I flicked through the rest of the file and stopped dead when I saw my likeness staring back at me. My hand flew reflexively to my throat, massaging away the bruises that, even three centuries ago, had faded unnaturally quickly.

The memory sank its talons into me and ripped, stealing the very air from my lungs. I saw Rhys's face, half shadowed in the soft autumn light, as he sat next to the table, pencil in hand. I remembered lowering my book and smiling at him from the window seat, for in that moment, I saw the echo of the awkward, pimply boy I'd played with as a child, the one who collected interesting rocks and who loved horses almost as much as I did. I also saw the handsome young man I'd fallen in love with and married. But when he'd lifted his head from the paper, his flint-eyed gaze had struck me like a hammer. I'd run for the door but hadn't been fast enough.

Later, as I lay on the floor, my dress torn, my face bleeding and my throat burning with each raw, rasping breath, I'd seen the sketch lying beside me. I'd wanted to shred it, but that would only make him angrier, and so I stayed there, staring at it as the butterflies thrashed furious, futile wings against the cage of my bruised ribs.

But now, inexorably, here it was.

Suddenly, the carriage felt unbearably hot, and I jumped up to yank open the window. The night air had turned cold, but I was glad of it. Holding on to the window, I heaved in deep breaths until the memory of his hands closing around my throat and the weight of him pinning me down faded back into the shadows.

Collapsing back into my seat, I slid the picture to the back of the file and forced myself to read on. Along with the family tree and the page with my details, there were two pages of reports detailing suspected sightings of 'the subject'. At least three of them were from places I'd never been, but the others, at least a dozen, could have been me.

All these years I'd imagined myself running from the magic hunters, but it seemed the British government had been tracking me down too. The last date was 1938. The year I began working for Walt.

I shoved the file back in the case, pulled out Walt's second letter and tore it open.

Dear heart,

If you've not already, please pause here and read the file marked 'Top Secret'.

I know today will have been a shock to the system, and I'm sorry to say that you need to brace yourself for more revelations. As you'll have read, the Unit, the government's hush-hush department for the investigation of all things magical, and I must confess, the department I headed up on my return to service at the start of the war, has been trying to find you for some time.

I think the gods were smiling on us both when I stumbled on your file in the archive. I removed it, of course, and replaced it with one of my own invention, but I can't be sure there aren't copies.

While I likely went to my grave never knowing your secret (Good girl! You would have made a wonderful spy, did I ever tell you that?), the Unit will use any power they have to discover it.

As far as I know, their interest in you is related to your abnormally long life, but I can't be sure. Whatever you do, DO NOT TRUST THEM! Too many in your community have already died at their hands.

I lifted my gaze to the ink-dark window, seeing only my own reflection and the occasional passing street light stretched to a sodium streak.

I had never thought myself part of a community. I had barely been part of a family, not until Walt and dear Archie. I dropped my head back to the letter. It was only then that I noticed that, unlike the first letter, this one was dated. The sixteenth of April 1960.

My vision blurred, and I lowered the file to my lap as I leaned my head against the stiff fabric of the seat and rubbed my eyes. I sighed and read the last paragraph.

I've gone to elaborate lengths to keep you safe, as you'll see from letter three, but be on your guard – ALWAYS, dear heart! The bonds of loyalty I enjoyed in life will not, I fear, stretch into the great hereafter, so what little protection I was able to afford you will vanish once I'm gone.

· · · ·

I smiled as I thought back to Dr Carmichael's blatant lie on the telephone. Walt would have been pleased to be wrong about the bonds of loyalty on that score.

I leaned against the side of the carriage. Twenty-two years of peace. Days when, had it not been for the butterflies, I might have convinced myself that I was an ordinary woman, living an ordinary life, but here I was, facing the unfathomable depths of life alone, once again.

There was nothing else in the letter of note, save for Walt's entreaties to keep myself safe, play my cello daily and consider getting a dog. He signed off with, *Now read letter three.*

Fearing that I might run out of energy if I delayed any longer, I tucked the second letter into the satchel and opened the third envelope, marked 'The Future'.

Walt's third and final letter detailed everything regarding my new position as his ghostwriter.

There is money enough for you to be comfortable for several more lifetimes, but comfort without occupation is a dull affair, my dear, so I encourage you to pursue your talent so long as it is safe to do so.

I'd teared up at that. Walt taught me all I knew about writing craft – enough to write the last nine Gideon Lockhart mysteries with minimal input from him, save for some spy craft, of course. When the first of 'my' books, as he called them, went to number one on the bestsellers list, Walt beamed with pride and waltzed me about the drawing room before insisting on champagne.

The royalties alone meant I'd never have to work again, but the real coup de grâce was the fat folder held together with two large elastic bands marked 'Operation Magic Carpet'. I giggled through my tears when I read the name, but after seeing what was inside, I felt like the genie of the lamp had just granted me a wish.

Inside were the deeds to sixteen properties dotted the length and breadth of the British Isles, five passports, all containing my image but bearing different names, plus a half dozen bank books containing eye-watering balances.

A handwritten sheet even provided the details of Walt's contacts skilled in the creation of new identification documents.

I'd need to read the lengthy explanation in his letter to fully understand the complex web of holding companies and trusts set up to protect my identity, but the headline was that they all belonged to me. Some were, in Walt's words, 'in deliberate states of disrepair', but all were at least partially habitable, and they'd all been chosen with concealment and ease of escape in mind.

Walt had written the name of the first property at the end of the letter: Pendarrow House. I rocked back in my seat, unable to take it all in. There was even a car for me in the car park of a pub near to Plymouth station, although he suggested I buy new ones for cash as soon as I could.

I scrabbled in the satchel and found the heavy bag of keys Walt referred to in the letter. Each bore a numbered label which I assumed corresponded to the properties. I pulled the keys marked 'House #1' and 'Car #1' from the bag and slipped them in my pocket.

A few hours later, I found the beige Ford Cortina in the far corner of the pub's car park, exactly where Walt said it would be. Bone-weary, I briefly considered taking a room in the pub for the night so that I could find Pendarrow House in the morning but dismissed the idea almost at once. Walt had moved mountains to keep me safe – I'd not fail at the first hurdle. Besides, I reasoned, I'd be more comfortable in a nice little cottage, hopefully, on the edge of a village than in a busy pub with – I did a quick scan – only three exits.

Two hours and countless wrong turns later, I pulled into a lay-by to interrogate the map for the hundredth time. The house should be here, but I looked to be in the middle of nowhere.

A movement outside caught my eye, and I glanced up just in time to see a fox. It looked up at me without breaking its stride, then turned and trotted down a tree-lined lane I'd not noticed when I parked.

I pulled my torch from the glove compartment and got out of the car. The fox was already nowhere to be seen, but as I turned back to the car, my eye snagged on what might have been an old name plate built into a half-demolished pillar. I pushed a tumble of ivy out of the way and sent out a silent thank you to the Goddess and the fox. This was it. Pendarrow House was at the end of this lane.

Five minutes later, I sat in the car, jaw slack and eyes like saucers, staring at the colossal Pendarrow House.

CHAPTER 34

DAN, MAY 1976

Thanks to Jackson and his top-secret file, I now had the name of a family with known connections to the magical community. Trouble was, the incident neatly typed up in December 1960 bore no resemblance to reality. Days of searching archives and death records turned up no evidence to corroborate what was in that report. And yet, the Unit had held on to it as if it were genuine. Why?

I'd spent a couple of days in Cardiff searching archives there, but coming back to Pont Nefoedd felt like the only other option. Maybe the Lewis family could shed some light on things – if I could find them. Trouble was, everyone around here was pretty tight-lipped. I'd seen it before: small towns closing ranks when a stranger started asking questions. It was noble – if frustrating. Directing me to the family's bakery was all the help anyone seemed willing to give. So here I was, sitting in the bakery's small café, for the third day running, feeling guilty for leaving Clem back in the guest house.

I pulled the picture of Gwen from my notebook and stared at it. I knew every pencil stroke by heart now, but sometimes it just helped keep me going. I still dreamt of her. Crazy, fragmented dreams where I'd often see nothing more than a glimpse of her face or hear her laughing. Sometimes I just woke with a feeling that she had just left the room. I sighed. I had been so sure back in London that I had my first real lead, but now I wasn't so convinced. The tattoo on my chest prickled, derailing my train of thought.

Just then, the bell above the door tinkled. I looked up to see a young woman back into the café pulling a wheelchair in which sat a frail, crumpled-looking man in his eighties, a tartan rug tucked across his lap despite the warm day. He had a beaky nose and wild, curly white hair that stuck up in all directions when he pulled off his cap.

The woman was something else. Long dark curls framed a fine-boned, porcelain face that looked like it belonged on the cover of *Vogue*, but the way she scanned the café, appraising the staff and the smattering of customers, suggested she was more bodyguard than nurse. I'm difficult to intimidate, but when her icy gaze fell on me, I quickly dropped my eyes back to the novel that sat open but barely read in my hands.

The woman chose a seat across the café, near the window. The staff swarmed around them like they were royalty, and the waitress announced loudly that anything they ordered would be Mr Lewis's treat.

The woman inclined her head graciously, but her companion didn't appear to have even heard, his attention already fixed on the bustling little high street beyond the window.

Could that be the same Hywel Lewis named in the file?

I could feel the woman's needle-sharp gaze fall on me every time she scanned the small café, and each time, my tattoo prickled in reply. I resisted the urge to rub at it and instead focused on my book, remembering to turn the pages regularly. When the waitress asked if I wanted anything else, my stomach rumbled loudly, making us both laugh. I ordered a sandwich and more coffee and went back to my reading pretence.

I had just taken my first bite when a lumbering young man in baker's whites yanked open the door with the neat 'staff only' sign. Red-faced and flour-dusted, he stood in the doorway and called across the café in a voice that had never learned to whisper, 'Miss Seren, Mrs Short's on the phone for you. Says it's urgent.'

I looked from the young man to the table where the young woman, Seren, and her companion sat. Only amateurs fail to react to an interruption, and it's always a tell. Seren threw a concerned glance towards the old man.

I feigned disinterest and went back to my book.

The waitress who had served me stepped from behind the counter.

'You go, Seren. I'll sit and keep him company,' she said as she wiped her hands on a tea towel.

Seren hesitated for a moment and then rose from her chair, graceful as a dancer.

'What's his name again?' the waitress asked as she settled into the vacated chair. Either Seren didn't hear her or she chose not to respond. Somehow, I guessed it was the latter. I focused on the book as Seren swept past my table and disappeared through the door.

'What's your name, love? I forgot,' the waitress said, her voice too loud and too slow.

'My name is Morgan.' His voice was shaky but clear. 'And I am not deaf.'

'I'm Maureen,' said the waitress, still at an unnecessary volume.

'I know who you are, Maureen. We were here last week,'

Morgan said, sounding irritated. He turned his attention back to the window, and Maureen laughed awkwardly.

I studied Morgan, wondering who he was and why he had such a stunning-looking pit bull for a companion. She might be his granddaughter, but if she was, I couldn't see a similarity in their features.

As I watched, his expression softened. 'Do you know about magic, Maureen?' Morgan asked, his tone boyishly excited and his eyes twinkling with mischief. 'It's real, see. I've dedicated my life to keeping it secret. I probably shouldn't be telling you now, but you have an honest face, so I know you won't tell anybody else.' Morgan tapped the side of his nose and then pointed a crooked finger at the waitress.

Maureen laughed and threw a wide-eyed look at her colleagues over her shoulder as Morgan watched her.

'Is that right,' she chuckled.

Morgan frowned, the lines on his face knitting together into deep furrows, but the excited schoolboy had vanished under a cloud of indignation.

'I don't tell lies, Maggie. You should know that. You've known me all your life. And you the apprentice Keeper of the Pont Nefoedd Library too. I'll be telling your mother.'

Maureen rolled her eyes again. 'I'm not Maggie Lewis, Morgan, I'm Maureen from the baker's,' she said patronisingly.

I gritted my teeth as I saw the old man's expression crumple and cycle from reproachful to confused in the space of a breath. He slumped forward, chewing on his thumbnail.

'Her married name is Short, anyway,' said a smug voice from behind the counter.

I didn't hear Seren return. The first I knew of her presence was the movement of the air as she swept past me on feet that didn't seem to make a noise on the wooden floor.

'There you go, love, your friend is back now,' Maureen

said, patting Morgan on the shoulder as if he were a well-behaved Labrador as she got up.

Seren knelt next to Morgan's chair and touched a handkerchief to his cheek. She murmured something inaudible, then rose to her feet.

'Did he say anything?' Seren asked.

'Oh, we had a lovely chat,' Maureen cooed, addressing the top of Morgan's now bowed head. 'Just some old nonsense about magic and libraries. Mistook me for Maggie, the boss's daughter. It happened to my old dad. The mind goes and then it's all downhill from—'

I felt the air pressure shift around me the way it does on an aeroplane, and then everything seemed to stop, including the babbling of the waitress. My tattoo burned like a fresh brand on my chest, bringing the flash of memory. My last day in Hanoi. Linh, naked beneath her blue silk robe, her long dark hair falling across her narrow shoulders.

'Something to protect you from witches,' she had said as she dragged the needle over my skin. I barely felt it thanks to the half a bottle of rum I'd downed on my way over. I'd reached up to cup her cheek and said, 'Thanks, but can I get some protection from bombs and snipers instead?' I could still hear her laugh.

My throat grew tight at the memory, as it always did when I thought of her and what happened next. But why had that memory surfaced now? Maybe it was because there was something about Seren that reminded me of Linh. On my chest, the tattoo pulsed in time with my heartbeat, and I focused on keeping my breath steady. I couldn't afford to lose my shit to a flashback, not here.

The bell above the door snapped me back to the moment and I huffed out a long breath. I looked up to see Seren and Morgan already on the street. Maureen stood at the closed door, waving to their backs. I shook my head, annoyed with myself that I'd been so lost in a memory I might have missed something important.

The waitress turned from the door, and spotting my empty plate, came over to clear it.

'He had some tall tales,' I said, giving her my best smile.

She frowned and eyed me suspiciously. 'What? He didn't say a dickie bird. Been drinking, have you?'

I held up my hands. 'Sober three years,' I said honestly. 'I just thought I heard him say something about a library in town,' I ventured.

Maureen shook her head, looking more confused. 'Closest library is in Brecon,' she said, but her speech was stilted.

'Hey, are you okay,' I asked, noticing that she'd lost the colour from her cheeks. I jumped up and pointed to my chair. 'Here, sit a while, maybe.'

Maureen sat down heavily and held her head in her hands.

I went to the counter to ask for a glass of water, and two of the other staff hurried over to her. I settled my bill with the lumbering kid who had announced the phone call.

'They seemed nice,' I ventured.

'Who?' he asked, staring at the cash register like a man looking at the flight deck of a plane.

'The old guy in the wheelchair and his granddaughter.'

I turned and pointed to the table they'd just vacated. Their cups and the plate that had contained Morgan's cream cake were still there.

He frowned, looking even more confused.

Maureen, still pale but looking better, bustled behind the counter and shooed him out of the way. Her hands flew over the register, and she announced my bill. I handed her the money, adding a generous tip.

'Are they regulars here?' I asked, again pointing to the

table in the window. 'The man in the wheelchair and his granddaughter,' I clarified.

She frowned, her hand hovering over the tips jar. I saw the moment the confusion settled around her. She shook her head and smiled as she opened her hand and let the coins fall into the jar. 'You must be mistaken, love. We've not had anyone in here in a wheelchair today.'

The skin on the back of my neck prickled as my tattoo pulsed in time with my racing heart. What the hell was happening here?

I hurried out into the street, but there was no sign of Seren or Morgan, which, after what had just happened, was almost a relief.

I marvelled at my luck. I was here to find people in the magical community, and they'd just found me. Plus, thanks to Morgan, I was now pretty sure there really was a hidden library in Pont Nefoedd. I was halfway down the street when a barking dog made me glance up. Across the way, gold lettering on a black storefront caught my eye: *Short's the Chemist.*

CHAPTER 35

DAN, MAY 1976

$\mathcal{I}$ stared at the shop, my pulse quickening. It was a long shot, but something told me I had to try – and now. I crossed the street and headed for the Post Office next door. After buying an envelope, I tore a page from my notebook and wrote a hurried message. I printed her name on the envelope, added 'Private and confidential' to the top and then licked the gum to seal it.

The file said she was a librarian, but as I pushed open the door to the drugstore, I was kind of hoping I might find her standing behind the counter, but there was nobody in the store at all. I waited a few moments before ringing the bell on the counter. A head of brunette curls popped up, meerkat style, from behind the dispensing area. I could barely see her eyes as she craned her neck to peer over the dividing wall.

'Be with you in a sec.'

Could it be her? No, Maggie would be in her late thirties by now, and the voice had sounded younger than that.

The assistant, a young woman in her early twenties, clopped down the steps and stopped dead when she saw me. She was pretty. Petite with a wide mouth, nice teeth and long lashes framing bright blue eyes. In another world, I might have been interested.

'Sorry about that,' she said, grinning as if she'd just won a raffle and I was her prize. 'Mr Short is out delivering, so it's just me here.'

I smiled back, dropping my gaze for a second and biting my lip in a parody of bashfulness that used to work like a charm when me and my buddies hit the bars back home.

'It's kinda delicate,' I said slowly, ramping up my accent.

'Oh, you can tell me. We see all sorts in here,' she said, dropping her voice to a whisper as she took a step closer.

I held up my hands. 'Nothing medical,' I laughed, feeling heat climb up my neck. 'My folks wanted me to look someone up while I was visiting. She'd be all grown up now. A Maggie Short.'

'The boss's wife?'

I shrugged, tapping the envelope against my free hand.

'All I know is that they were friends back in the sixties, when my dad was stationed nearby. She was Maggie Lewis back then, they said.'

'That'll be her!' the assistant said, her grin widening.

'Gee, that's great. They wanted me to deliver this,' I said, holding up the letter.

When her smile faltered, I pressed on. 'It was with their last effects,' I said, dropping my gaze to the floor.

I heard her suck in a little breath, and when I looked back up, she was the picture of compassion.

'Are they both gone?' she asked gently.

I nodded. 'They both passed while I was serving in Vietnam.' At least that was the truth.

'I'll see she gets it.'

I was thanking her when the door behind me opened.

'Oh, no need,' the assistant said, looking past me and

waving. 'You can deliver it yourself,' she said, handing the envelope back. 'Hiya, Mags.'

When I got back to the guest house, Clementine was waiting by the front door. Mrs Dean, the landlady, had taken a shine to her the day we arrived, and so she got to potter around the old Victorian town house, apparently 'helping' with chores. I suspected it was more about Mrs D having a dog to fuss over again, but I was grateful.

'She's been sat there waiting for the last five minutes,' Mrs D cooed as Clem launched herself at me.

'Thanks for watching her,' I said, pulling Clem's leash from the hook by the door.

'It's her been watching me,' she chuckled.

We headed out of town, towards the woods. After the day's events, I needed some quiet to get things straight in my head. I replayed the scene in the drugstore. As I'd figured, Maggie was in her late thirties. She had shoulder-length straight hair pulled into a low ponytail the colour of damp sand and bright, intelligent eyes. What I hadn't been expecting was the kid.

A toddler with a riot of blond curls wearing a pink chequered dress had waved at me from her stroller like I was an old friend. I grinned and waved back.

With the assistant listening in, I had no choice but to repeat my story about my dead parents' wishes. I held out the envelope and glanced at my watch. 'I'm sorry. I need to be somewhere else right now, but it's all in there,' I said, smiling as I gave the envelope a wiggle. Maggie had just stared at me, her eyebrow slightly cocked, and in an instant, I was back in third grade, being scolded by my elementary school teacher.

'Nice man,' the toddler giggled, wrinkling her button nose and bunching her hands to cheeks.

I laughed as a little bubble of tension popped around us. As I smiled down at the kid, I felt the envelope pulled from my fingers.

'I'll read it, Mr …'

'Quinn,' I replied, meeting Maggie's appraising gaze.

I'd said my goodbyes and fled. I was only a hundred yards away when someone called, 'Wait!'

I turned, hoping to see Maggie, but it was the assistant.

'Mags is covering my lunch break,' she said, standing uncomfortably close and looking up at me through thick, black lashes. 'You can buy me a ploughman's at the pub, if you like.' She smiled, and I noticed the fresh coat of lipstick.

I had to repeat my excuse of having somewhere to be, but she just shrugged and tucked a folded piece of paper into my shirt pocket. I forced a smile and nodded when she asked if I'd call. I hope she's not the kind of girl to get disappointed.

I sighed, trying to force the memory from my mind. Clem glanced up at me.

'Good girl,' I said, quickening my pace to put some distance between us and the town. Even if Maggie read my note straight away, she was stuck watching the drugstore for the next hour, at least.

The top road, as the locals called it, beckoned me like an oasis in the desert. The winding, flat road was a welcome respite from the hilly little town perched between a river at its toes and a mountain for a crown. It felt like a quiet standoff between mankind and nature: old stone houses on one side, nothing but trees on the other.

I crossed without hesitation, plunging into the wood and letting the trees swallow my tension. I unclipped Clem's leash, and she shot forward, tail like a sail in the breeze, tongue lolling and her nose to the ground.

CHAPTER 36

DAN, MAY 1976

$\mathcal{M}$aggie's reply to my note arrived three days after our encounter in the drugstore. I'd almost convinced myself she wouldn't get in touch at all until, returning from an early-morning hike with Clem, I found a letter addressed to me sitting on the hall table.

My relief that she had agreed to meet me quickly turned to frustration when I saw that she wanted to meet on Monday. While the prospect of yet another weekend in Pont Nefoedd wasn't the worst thing in the world, I couldn't shake the feeling that Gwen was running out of time.

I spent the weekend hiking with Clem, exploring the mountains on the other side of the river. There were incredible views over the valley if you took the trail up through the woods; we'd even found a wildflower meadow and sat amongst flowers I couldn't name, sharing sandwiches and listening to the birds sing, the bees buzz and the wind sigh through the leaves.

Weird as it sounds, sitting there, it felt like Gwen could just walk out of the trees and come join us at any minute.

When Monday finally rolled around, I arrived at the park a full twenty minutes early, Clem at my side.

The park sat at the top of the main street, a flat parcel of land in the mountain's lee, with a small copse of trees off to the right and acres of gently rolling parkland stretching out into the distance.

The sun was still low in the sky but already busy burning off a thin mist carpeting the ground. The entrance to the copse looked like a doorway to another world, its sentinel trees glowing golden against the shaded stillness beyond.

In her letter, Maggie had told me to meet her at the bench nearest the main gate at six a.m. I was glad she was the cautious type. I knew I was no threat to her, but she didn't. I stood as I waited, not wanting to risk my jeans to the damp-looking bench.

I unclipped Clem's leash, and she dropped her nose to the ground as she headed off to sniff. It was a beautiful park. Rolling grassland, if a little parched-looking, but perfect for picnics and summer fairs. I was just letting myself imagine what it might be like to live here when I spotted her.

Her step faltered when she saw me, but only for a second. Her walk was purposeful, her back straight, her hands shoved into the pockets of her lightweight jacket. As she drew nearer, I took in the set of her jaw and the tightness around her eyes.

I smiled and tried to make myself less intimidating, relaxing my shoulders and turning side-on as I waved. It was a tactic that sometimes worked, but clearly not today.

'Mr Quinn,' she said, my name an accusation.

I nodded, widening my smile. 'Mrs Short.'

'Call me Maggie.'

She strode to the bench and pulled a rag from her hand-bag, wiping away the dew from the length of it, then sat at the end nearest the entrance. I took the seat at the opposite end.

'You came prepared, I see,' I ventured with a laugh. 'Impressive.'

'I don't flatter easily, Mr Quinn. Please get to the point,' she said flatly.

Clem chose that moment to bound over, wagging her whole body as if she were nothing but tail. She sat and held up a paw, which Maggie shook in a greeting that was a lot warmer than the one I'd received.

'That's Clementine,' I said. 'And please, call me Dan.'

Maggie gave me a curt nod. I cleared my throat, ready to deliver the speech I'd been practising in my head for the best part of a week as Clem sat leaning against Maggie's knee, getting her neck stroked.

'First off, thanks for coming, Maggie. As I said in the note, I'm a private investigator,' I began.

'Yes, Colin Heath tells me you're a very good one too,' Maggie said, turning towards me, her expression unreadable.

That stopped me in my tracks.

'I wasn't about to meet a stranger in a park based on a cryptic note,' Maggie said with the lift of an eyebrow.

I waited a beat. Took a breath. The how wasn't the point. I needed to stay on track.

'I was hired to find a young woman by a man who means her great harm.'

'He *told* you this?' Maggie's lip curled.

'Hell no. He told me some cock and bull story about her being mentally unstable and needing to get her back to her family, but—' I took a breath. 'Look, the guy who hired me is bad news. Stinking-rich bad news, which in my experience is the worst sort imaginable. I followed him one night, and I saw an innocent man executed on his orders.'

I hadn't intended to share that, regretted it the moment it

was out of my mouth, but the softening of Maggie's expression told me I'd done the right thing.

'What I saw that night and what I've discovered in the course of my investigations since has convinced me that ...' I huffed out a laugh and rubbed a hand over the back of my neck, some part of my brain still unwilling to say the words out loud. I sighed and started again. 'Look. As crazy as this sounds, what I've seen suggests that magic is real.'

'What makes you think I can help you?' Maggie asked sharply, all traces of softness gone. But she'd not made a move to leave, nor had she laughed at me.

'Because I have a friend who works for some secret military unit who showed me a file that shouldn't exist. A file with your name and your father's in it. It even mentions a Siamese cat.'

Maggie froze – her eyes fixed on the path. When she eventually looked at me, her face seemed drained of colour.

'What sort of file?' she demanded.

I clearly had her full attention now. I lowered my voice and turned towards her. 'A file about a raid on the secret library in the basement of your home in December 1960 that ...' I sighed, unsure how to say what I had to say next without looking like a total nutcase.

'Tell me,' Maggie demanded, a note of desperation in her voice.

'It lists you, your father, Hywel, a young woman named Seren, three security personnel and a Siamese cat as fatalities. It also notes that the house was then set on fire and demolished three months later.'

Maggie went so still, Clem turned around and whined.

'Shot.'

'Yes.'

'Did it say I was shot three times? Two in the chest, one in the temple?'

I rocked back in my seat. 'How did you—'

'What about my mother?' she whispered, cutting off my question.

'Your mother was listed in the file as missing since July 1960, but the police have no record of it. Our friend DI Heath checked.'

Maggie let out a breath with such force I feared she might be about to scream. She braced her elbows on her knees and held her head in her hands. Clem shot me an anxious look, unsure what to do. Before I could call her to me, she decided for herself, covering Maggie's hands in frantic kisses.

'Thank you, Clementine,' Maggie said, her voice shaky.

'I'm sorry. I didn't know how else to say it.'

Maggie smiled at me then, all traces of her earlier hostility gone.

'I always knew there was something. Never this, whatever the hell this is,' she said, throwing up her hands, 'but something. I had nightmares for years. Saw the gunman. Stared down the barrel. I even felt the bullets. Two in the chest, one through my skull. I'd wake up screaming.' She touched her hand to her chest and forehead as she spoke, her gaze on the ground.

I let the silence settle between us, fixing my eyes on the horizon. The mist was all but gone now, the sun gaining strength as it rose. In the distance, a handful of crows stalked across the grass, poking their beaks into the ground.

Maggie let out a long sigh. When I turned, she was studying me. I got the feeling she had come to some sort of decision.

'I'm sick of lying, Dan. Tell me, do you know what I do for a living?'

'According to my friend's file, you're the apprentice Keeper of Pont Nefoedd Library of Magical Texts, but I'm guessing it's a little out of date.'

Maggie laughed wryly, but she sat back against the bench, then patted the seat next to her. Clem wasted no time, hopping up and laying her head in Maggie's lap.

'The file was correct. I was an apprentice back then. And until last year, when my mum passed away, I was the assistant keeper,' she said, and it was hard to miss the grief in her voice.

'I'm sorry,' I said, meaning it.

'I was twenty-one in 1960. My first boyfriend had just asked me to get engaged, and I was at sixes and sevens because I didn't think he'd take well to my family's secret.'

'The library?'

She pursed her lips and closed her eyes for a moment but then nodded slowly.

'There are things from that summer that just don't add up. They never have done. I thought at the time I might have a brain tumour – I was a bit of a drama queen back then, mind you. But my memories were all so jumbled up. Look, nothing I'm going to say now will make sense to you, but I'm going to say it anyway.'

I held up my hands.

'There were little things, like books in the collection that weren't catalogued and that neither I nor my mother had seen before, which isn't odd unless you know what a stickler she was usually. But the weirdest thing was the camera.

'A close friend of the family gave me a Polaroid camera for my twenty-first birthday. It was a big deal because that model wasn't available over here. He'd got it from America for me along with about a year's worth of film. The memory is clear as a bell because while I was over the moon, my mam and dad were going on at him because it was an expensive gift. We both ignored them, obviously, and I clearly remember getting my mam to take the first photo of me and him together.

'My dad was taking photos on the day too, with his big camera like he always did on birthdays, setting the timer and then running into the shot.' She smiled at the memory. 'We've got albums full of birthday photos, but in the one from my twenty-first, Uncle Morgan is missing.'

Morgan! I didn't think it was a coincidence, but I wanted to keep the conversation on track.

'But you remember the Polaroid of you together?'

'Remember it? I've still got it! It's faded, but you can still see the birthday cake in the background.'

I rubbed at the stubble on my chin as my brain tried to process everything.

'When I asked my parents, they were both adamant that Morgan didn't come to my twenty-first because he was called away on business.'

'What did they say about the Polaroid?' I asked.

Maggie sighed and dropped her gaze. 'It caused no end of arguments. They said it must have been from another birth-day, but I know that it wasn't. Your twenty-first is a big deal,' Maggie said emphatically. 'I overheard them after one partic-ularly heated bust-up, wondering if I needed to get psychi-atric help. That scared the life out of me, so—' She shrugged. 'I let the subject drop.'

'But you're still adamant that Morgan was there?'

Maggie smiled down at Clem before she answered.

'I know Morgan went to Boston, Massachusetts, in January 1960 on business. I checked. Years later, mind, and without mentioning it to anyone. It was his first and only trip to the US, and that's where he would have bought the camera.'

'So, what do you think happened in 1960?' I asked.

'In truth, Dan, I have no bloody idea. I'm just grateful to you for finally confirming that, whatever happened, I wasn't losing my mind. I don't suppose I can get a copy of that file, can I?'

I shrugged. 'I'm sorry, but I don't have it. I had ten minutes with it in a London pub while my friend kept an eye on the door. They'd likely throw the Official Secrets Act at him for even telling me about it.'

Maggie went quiet for such a long time I was afraid she was about to leave.

'Is Morgan in a wheelchair now?' I blurted out the question.

'Yes. He has dementia, poor love, and terrible arthritis.'

'I think I saw him last week in the bakery. He was with someone called Seren. Is she related to the young woman mentioned in the file?'

Maggie pursed her lips and turned her head away. Her hand stilled on Clem's side, and I saw her jaw tighten.

'Look, I shouldn't even be talking to you about this. I'm breaking my oath,' Maggie said, her face crumpling into an anxious frown as she shuffled forward on the bench, readying herself to stand.

'What does your oath swear you to?' I asked quickly.

'I'm sworn to protect magic.'

'And what if finding and protecting this woman is protecting magic too?' I asked, no longer caring that I sounded slightly desperate.

She stilled. Clem whined and thumped her tail until Maggie smiled down at her and resumed her stroking.

Turning to me, she said, 'Look, I don't know why, but every sense I have is telling me to help you, Daniel. Give me your mystery woman's name and I'll see what I can find out.'

I tried to contain my relief, but judging from the smile that pulled on her lips, it was written all over my face.

'Thank you, Maggie,' I said. 'Her name is Gwenllian Llewellyn.'

CHAPTER 37

DAN, MAY 1976

*M*aggie had said she'd be in touch once she had something to tell me, but three days later, I was still waiting. With temperatures rising, me and Clem had started hiking earlier in the day, tackling the long, steep climb through the woods while the morning air still had a coolness.

We explored the mountains, walking for miles but always finding a route back to the high meadow to take in the view as we drank barely warm tea from the flask. I would have preferred coffee, but as I shared it with Clem these days, I figured tea was better for her.

The Pont Nefoedd valley really was something else. The drought was biting into the landscape, making spring look more like autumn in places, but it was still breathtaking. We had beautiful country back home, but there was something else here. A sort of … I hesitated to even use the word given everything I'd seen recently, but yeah, it was sort of magical. I wasn't just seeing the land; I was feeling it too.

When this was all over, I decided, we'd come back for a

visit. I stopped myself before the daydream turned into a fantasy that included Gwen.

Back in the hallway of the guest house, I scooped up the handful of letters from the doormat, sifting through them in the hope there'd be one from Maggie. There wasn't.

I trudged up the stairs, wondering how much longer this would all take. It felt like time was running out, and yet Maggie was the only hope I had left of finding Gwen. I didn't doubt Maggie when she said she'd help me, but patience had never been my strong point.

I unlocked the door to my room and reeled back at the sight of Seren, the woman from the café, sitting in the armchair, staring right at me.

Clementine growled, but it was more of a gesture than a sign of any actual intent.

'What the—' I bit off the expletive.

Seren rose to her feet in a movement so fluid I wasn't sure I'd seen the transition. One moment she was sitting, straight-backed and regal, in the grubby old chair, and the next she was on her feet, her hands raised in placation.

She beat me to the first word too. 'Please forgive the intrusion, but it was necessary given the circumstances.'

'What kind of circumstances?' It was my turn to growl now.

'Circumstances in which you, Captain Daniel Quinn, begin asking questions about—'

I snorted, interrupting her flow as I tossed my key on the vanity. Clementine pulled towards her water bowl, but I held her back.

'I'm not here to threaten you, Daniel, and witches are not in the habit of hurting animals. Clementine is quite safe, as are you.'

I looked at Clem. The dog gazed up at me, her eyes soft, tongue lolling as her tail swished low against my legs. One of us trusted the witch, at least. I unclipped the leash and watched Clem ignore the water bowl and gallop over to greet the intruder. When Clem hopped into her lap and licked her chin like they were long-lost friends, I tried not to take it as a betrayal.

I topped up the water bowl from the sink and set it on the floor, then pulled out the desk chair and sat opposite Seren, crossing my legs at the ankle.

'I'm listening,' I said, opening my arms wide.

Seren gave a nod but continued fussing Clem, who was acting like she'd never been patted in her life. Just as my patience thinned, she began.

'Our relationship with the authorities is … complicated,' she said carefully. 'But they have their uses, especially when we're investigating the murder of one of our leaders.'

'Doctor Clement Johnson,' I said, the memory of his ruined face swimming into my mind before I could even try to block it out. That almost imperceptible shake of his head as he locked eyes with me.

Clem slid from Seren's lap and padded over to me, settling at my feet.

'My source tells me you witnessed his murder,' Seren said matter-of-factly.

I took a deep breath before answering.

'I was in the attic space next door, observing through a hole in the ceiling. It all happened pretty fast, and I didn't have time to …' I trailed off, hating how pathetic it sounded.

'You were not there to save him, Daniel. That you wanted to speaks volumes about your character, but had you tried, you'd be dead now too. Life means nothing to magic hunters.'

'Magic hunters?' I said, my head snapping up.

'If we seem a little defensive as a community, it is because we are constantly under threat. Our sacred libraries are raided in the belief that there is a book that can grant magical ability to anyone – it's a myth, of course, but so was the Holy Grail, and look what devastation that caused.

'Sir Reginald Devlin is searching for another myth – a young woman who carries immense power – power that he, of course, plans to claim for himself.

'Do you ever wonder, Daniel, why these myths never involve fat old men with one foot in the grave?' Seren's eyebrow lifted, the curl of her full lips, more a smirk than a smile, like the kid who always raised their hand in class.

She sighed a little theatrically, her expression serious once more. 'That these quests are usually tied up with youth and beauty tells you all you need to know about the veracity of the stories. But,' she added, suddenly on her feet again, 'delusion or not, he is obsessed enough to kill. Poor Clement wasn't his first victim, nor will he be his last if we don't stop him.'

I stood too. 'Who's we?'

She ignored the question and stepped towards me. 'So, you were impervious to the memory spell. What is it? An amulet?' Her eyes raked the front of my T-shirt.

I considered denying it, but it was obvious now that my tattoo was doing something, if only warning me about danger.

'A tattoo.'

'Even better. Amulets are too easy to lose. Has it faded?' she asked, her head tilted, looking genuinely interested.

I thought of the image of a twisted knot that looked just the same as it had the day Linh inked it onto my skin over six years ago. 'Not one bit,' I said truthfully.

Seren's expression softened into what looked to be a genuine smile.

'Had the magic not found you worthy, it would have faded. Whoever gave you this gift must have loved and trusted you very much to bestow such a thing.'

'Does this mean you'll help me find the missing woman?'

Seren looked amused. 'No,' she laughed. 'You're chasing a myth, Daniel. Our real work is putting Devlin behind bars, and that's why I'm here. I'd like to hire you.'

'You're looking to hire me?' I asked, incredulous.

'We are. In my capacity as acting head of the Council of Elders, I would like to formally offer you a twelve-month retainer at double the rate Devlin is paying. We'll review it at the end of the year and extend as needed.'

I scrabbled for something to say, but she pressed on.

'Details are in here along with an emergency number,' she said, holding up a large cream envelope I swore hadn't been in her hand a moment ago. 'I took the liberty of making the first payment into your bank account.'

I gaped at her.

'Will you take the job?'

I nodded. I'd do anything I could to help put that bastard behind bars.

'Good. Importantly, don't stop working for him – he doesn't take resignations well, and we don't want you befalling a mysterious accident like the last two investigators who tried to leave his employ.'

She was at the door before I registered her even moving.

'Wait,' I said. 'What about Gwen?'

Seren pursed her lips.

'The only Gwenllian Llewellyn in Pont Nefoedd was born in 1594, and while I know a thing or two about extended life spans, not even the strongest witches live that long. Please, just focus on putting Devlin behind bars.'

The door was closing before I could reply.

I couldn't have been more than five seconds behind her, but by the time I reached the hallway, Mrs D was already closing the front door.

'Such a lovely girl, Seren,' she said when she saw me.

I was about to ask my landlady why she'd let her into my room without my permission, but before I could speak, she thrust a hand into her overall pocket and pulled out a long cream envelope. She held it out to me, my full name written on the front in the sort of calligraphic font reserved for wedding invitations. I took it, feeling the bulk of something much heavier than just paper inside.

'She said to tell you that it's parked around the side behind your old one,' Mrs D said, leaning down to fuss over Clem.

I shook my head. 'What is?' I asked, confused.

'The car,' she replied with a roll of her eyes.

Confused, I mumbled my thanks and ripped open the envelope, pulling out the note and just catching the set of silver keys contained within its folds.

. . .

Dear Mr Quinn,

Please forgive the presumption, but your vehicle's age and state of repair are a risk to you successfully completing your commission. We hope you will accept this more reliable alternative as part of your remuneration package. Insurance and registration papers are in the glove compartment.

Regards,

S

'What the f—'

'Oh, and Maggie called. Said to tell you your tablets are ready to collect from the chemist if you get there before eleven,' Mrs D said over her shoulder.

I turned my wrist, only to realise that my watch was still by my bed. Reasoning that the morning's activities couldn't have taken anything more than a half hour, I headed for the door, Clementine at my side.

Hurrying to the side lane, I spotted a brand-new Jaguar XJ6 in British racing green parked right behind my battered old Ford.

'You have got to be kidding me,' I mumbled as I eyed the car.

Clementine wasn't as cautious. She rushed over to it, tail wagging expectantly.

Stunned, but not wanting to waste time going back to my room, I slipped the new key into the lock of the Jaguar and felt the satisfying click as I turned it.

Clementine didn't stand on ceremony, hopping into the car as soon as I opened the door and claiming her shotgun position.

I got in, still not quite believing any of this was true, but sure enough, I found the registration and insurance papers, listing the keeper as some JDL Holdings Ltd, in the glove box. I glanced at the clock on the dash, shoved the documents back in and slammed it shut. I had ten minutes.

'Come on, you know the score, kiddo. It's safer in the well,' I said, trying to ignore the pleading look in her eyes.

I shook my head. 'No time, Clem. Footwell or the back seat.'

After a pause, just to make her point, she slunk into the footwell and lay down, resting her chin on the gear stick console. Five minutes later, I was pulling up outside the drugstore just in time to see Maggie come out the front door.

I jumped out of the driver's seat, but before I could say anything, she said, 'Are you two heading to the park too?' Her smile was casual, but I read the meaning.

'We sure are,' I replied. 'Enjoy your walk.'

I counted to fifty before I got back in the car, turned it around and headed to the place we'd first met.

CHAPTER 39

DAN, MAY 1976

I saw Maggie as soon as we turned into the park, talking to an elderly man in a flat cap, a small black cocker spaniel sniffing around the base of the bench where we'd first met. I unclipped Clem's leash and headed over.

A flash of caramel and black blurred past me before I could say hello. I turned, rocking back on my heels as Clem tore across the grass. She was playing. Actually playing. She'd always been polite with other dogs, sometimes firm if they pushed their luck, but had never shown this kind of unbridled joy. My heart squeezed at the sight of her wrestling and rolling with the little spaniel, their bodies a tangle of fur and paws. I caught my breath when she grabbed the underside of the spaniel's neck, but the old man lifted his hand before I could yell.

'Don't tell her off,' he warned. 'That's the best sort of play, that. My Benny's letting her know he trusts her. You watch and he'll do the same to her in a minute too.'

Sure enough, after the next round of chasing and rolling, the spaniel grabbed Clementine's neck, and then off they went again. I watched, transfixed by this whole new side of my best friend, and made a mental note to spend more time at the park when it was busy with other dog walkers.

The old man chuckled as the spaniel flopped down in the shade from a tree. 'And that's his sign that he's tuckered out for the day. Thanking you and your lovely girl for making the old boy happy,' he said, touching his cap to me. 'Ta-ra, Maggie, love.'

We watched him walk slowly away, his dog waiting until the last moment before getting up and lumbering after him. Clementine stood, tongue lolling, staring after them.

'There's a little stream over there,' Maggie said, pointing past the expansive lawns and tulip-stuffed flower beds to the foot of the tree-covered hill that bounded one side of the park. 'It's a bit low these days, but she can have a drink and a paddle.'

We walked in silence, and I wondered if I should mention Seren's visit.

'I hear you had a visitor,' she said, glancing sideways at me, a smile pulling at her lips.

I laughed. 'Wow. News travels fast.'

Clem lifted her nose from the grass long enough to throw me a questioning look when we neared the stream.

'Go paddle,' I said, pointing. She shot off before the last syllable was even out of my mouth.

'Seren's heart is in the right place. Power would corrupt lesser mortals, but I think in her case, it's just blinded her to certain truths.'

'How come?'

Maggie shrugged, as if she felt awkward about what she was about to say. 'The thing I told you last time, about the Polaroid. Seren was the one pushing hardest for me to drop it.'

When I shot her a confused look, she said, 'Oh, she's

much, much older than she looks. The Seren I knew growing up looked exactly the same as the woman you met today.' She shrugged again, as if that was just the way of the world, but I was still having a hard time adjusting.

'Seren wants Devlin put away for his crimes, just like we all do, but she also believes he's just another power-obsessed magic hunter wreaking havoc on his wild goose chase.'

'And you don't believe that?' I ventured.

'Oh, he's a lunatic alright, but I don't believe this Gwen is a figment of his imagination. And I might have found something that proves it.'

I stopped in my tracks and faced her. She was clearly trying to stay professional, but there was a definite twinkle in her eye.

'I told you there were things from that summer that didn't add up. New books in the collection, the Polaroid, but there was something else too. Look, this is going to sound strange,' she said with a snort. 'I found a cardigan in the spare bedroom. It was nothing like anything I'd have worn back then as I was a bit of a diva about my clothes. It wasn't one of my mother's, and nobody had stayed with us for months.'

I kept walking, unsure about where this was all heading.

'Anyway, before I put it in for the jumble sale, I went through the pockets and found, of all things, a piece of parchment that looked like it belonged in our archive. It was dated 1612.'

My pulse quickened even before my brain did the calculation.

'It was a spell. And not just your run of the mill "bless the harvest"-type spell either. This one was designed to allow a witch in mortal peril to send her magic to another for safe-keeping. It's called a safe harbour spell and is incredibly rare – not to mention ambitious.'

'Hang on, 1612 would've been prime witch hunt time in

Europe, right?' I asked, trying to remember the class project we'd done on the witch hunts in high school.

'Yes. It was the year of the Pendle witch trials over here. Twelve people, two men and ten women, were accused and tried in Lancashire, England. It was one of the most notorious cases on record. Ten were convicted and hanged, and all on the testimony of a child of nine to boot!' Maggie said with a shudder. 'Horrific.'

'So how come an ancient spell ended up in the pocket of a cardigan?' I asked.

'No idea, but the spell itself looks to have originated here, in Pont Nefoedd. I can't be one hundred per cent certain, but it appears to be the same handwriting as examples we have from around the same time. They are just fragments, though, so it's hard to be conclusive.

'That's not the interesting bit,' Maggie said, and if I wasn't mistaken, she was trying not to look too pleased with herself. 'I took a trip down to St David's to see an old friend of mine. He's a witch and a gifted seer – someone who has visions,' she added when she saw the blank look on my face. 'My friend told me two important things. One he read straight from the parchment, which had me kicking myself that I'd not spotted it too – the spell has a monumental error in it, but I'll come back to that.'

'And the second?' I prompted.

'The second came to him as a vision. The spell was started but never completed,' Maggie said, raising her eyebrows and nodding.

I waited, trying not to look as underwhelmed as I felt.

When she didn't elaborate, I shook my head. 'I don't get it.'

Maggie huffed. 'Sorry, I'm not explaining this very well. The spell kept another witch's magic safe. They needed a full coven of thirteen or more because carrying someone else's magic is a huge thing energetically – a bit like adopting a few dozen kids, I suppose. The safe way to do it was for the magic to be shared. The high priestess goes first, then her second, third, fourth, et cetera, until all members of the coven receive a share. If more arrive, they go around again, layering the burden only once each member has learned to adjust their own energy to cope with it,' Maggie said, drawing out a circle in the air.

'But that's not what happened?'

'The error in the wording meant that all orphaned magic would come first to the high priestess, who then had to call upon each member of the coven to accept a share of the responsibility, and only once every coven member had agreed would the burden shift from her to them. It's poetic the way it's written, but fatally flawed, because until every witch accepts their share, it pools within the high priestess.'

Realisation slammed into me like a ton weight.

'Meaning that the high priestess unwittingly turned herself into, what, some kind of super witch?'

Maggie nodded slowly. 'Sort of, which explains why Devlin is hunting for someone he believes to be the most powerful witch to ever walk the Earth.'

'So, this Gwen was the high priestess?'

Maggie shook her head emphatically. 'No. We have records of local covens. It was her grandmother, Mary Llewellyn. Gwen was only eighteen, and not even the exceptional are given positions of leadership so young, not even now. Mary died suddenly a few weeks after the spell, which is probably why it wasn't repeated. After Mary's death, Gwen disappears from the records. No marriages, at least no church-registered ones. No children born to her. No property in her name. No death certificate. No grave. Nothing. We know she lived, but we've no evidence that she died.'

My heart thumped in my chest, but I wasn't ready to ask the obvious question.

'But if none of the coven had accepted a share of the burden and the high priestess, this Mary, died, then …' I left the sentence hanging as I struggled to keep up.

'That was the other flaw in the spell. It was blood-bound in the casting, which meant when Mary died, her obligation went to her closest surviving relative – Gwen.'

I cleared my throat, my eyes on Maggie as I asked my next question. 'And you really believe she's still alive? After, what' – I did the math quickly – 'three hundred and sixty-four years?'

'It seems to be the most logical explanation,' Maggie said with the straight face of someone who'd lived her life amongst the impossible.

I blew out a long breath and raked my hands through my hair. 'Man, that's …'

'I know it's a lot, Dan. You need to give yourself some time to adjust. It can be scary. Knowing that there are people out there with such power. My husband walked around like a zombie for a week after his oath.'

Nam had taught me all I needed to know about being powerless, I thought, but said nothing.

'Well, if that is true, it explains a lot,' I said, picking up a stick and tossing it into the stream for Clementine to chase. 'Devlin isn't about to square up to the most powerful witch in history, is he? She'd fry him on sight, or turn him into a toad or something,' I said, trying to be funny but not managing to. And here I was thinking she needed rescuing.

'Oh, you misunderstand, Dan,' Maggie said. 'The safe harbour spell had one very useful safeguard – the receiving witch or witches can't use the magic in their care. So, Gwen, if she is still out there, will only be able to use her own magic to defend herself.'

'So why is Devlin so hell bent on finding her?' My head was starting to pound.

Maggie sighed. 'The spell is so full of holes it looks like Swiss cheese. While the receiving witch can't use the orphaned magic, there's nothing in its wording to prevent someone else taking it from them and claiming it as their own.'

I spun around. 'What? Like magical small print?'

Maggie nodded, her expression grim. 'It's easy to be critical now, but we need to remember that people were likely terrified. Imagine being in the magical community and seeing ordinary folk tortured and murdered for the very thing you possessed.'

I admired her attempt to protect her ancestors, but something she'd said a moment ago scratched at me.

'You said there was nothing to stop someone else taking the orphaned magic. Take it how?' I asked, already sensing that I wouldn't like the answer.

Maggie pulled a face. 'Well, that's the bit my seer friend was decidedly unhappy about witnessing. He said the vision was too horrific to even describe, but as he needed to make a bolt for the bathroom to be sick, I think it was pretty bad.'

'Your seer friend can see the future?'

'Sometimes, but not in this case. He saw flashes of the past, which is how he knew the spell wasn't completed. The worst news is that Devlin's been having a few practice goes at ripping magic from people.' Maggie spoke the words through gritted teeth. 'Inhuman bastards,' she added in a growl.

'Wait. Devlin has magic now?'

'Apparently so, although it's practically unheard of for an ordinary like you and me to acquire magic. And if that gets out then God help us all. The libraries will never be safe again.'

Gwen's face flashed into my mind. Not the drawing but the flesh-and-blood woman I kept seeing in my dreams. Immortal witch or not, I needed to find her. Help her, although I had no idea how.

'What now?' I asked, my impatience building. 'Knowing the history is great, but how do we find her?'

Maggie brightened a little. 'There were a couple of things that might be helpful. My seer friend said that she was somewhere in England. He saw her surrounded by waves and by music. He also saw a tall man with a pipe in spirit form watching over her.'

I waited a beat until the smile faded from Maggie's face.

'That's it?'

She nodded miserably. 'I'm sorry. He said if anything else comes to him, he'll call me straight away.'

I watched Clem as she hopped in and out of the stream, dropping her stick up current and then running along the bank and diving back in to retrieve it downstream.

'She's survived this long,' Maggie said, putting a tentative hand on my back. 'She must have some pretty powerful magic of her own.'

I scuffed the toe of my sneaker into the ground, unable to dredge up anything positive to say.

'Oh, nearly forgot,' Maggie said, pulling a wad of folded pages from her bag. 'My seer friend made notes as he tried to scry for her. There's not much there, but you might as well have them.'

I tucked them into my pocket and tried not to look as defeated as I felt.

'Maybe I'm just not meant to find her,' I said, the words out of my mouth before I could stop them.

Maggie shook her head. 'If I've learned anything from all my years studying magic, it's that it never makes mistakes. People, yes, even witches, but magic itself? That essence that keeps the flowers blooming and the rivers running, it always has a plan. That you're here, Dan, that you witnessed what you did – everything, in fact, that brought you to this point – none of that would have happened unless magic enabled it.'

'What does that say about Devlin, then?'

Maggie threw up her hands. 'That I don't have an answer for, but he has a part to play in all this, and magic knows it.'

'You make it sound conscious,' I said with a tired laugh.

'Maybe. Or maybe like the river, it just has a direction of flow that it corrects each time we humans do something stupid to interrupt it. Don't give up on her, Dan. Every bone in my body is telling me that Gwen is still out there, and she needs your help,' she said, her expression sad.

Maggie's words still echoed in my ears as me and a soaking wet Clementine headed back to the guest house. I'd arrived in Pont Nefoedd chasing a phantom. Now I was searching for a needle in a haystack, but maybe that was still progress.

CHAPTER 40

DAN, MAY 1976

I'd dreamt of Gwen again last night. She was standing on a clifftop, looking out over a furious grey sea, her long dark hair flying around her face. Lightning split the sky, the wind stealing my breath as I ran, screaming her name.

She turned to me, a ghost of a smile on her lips. I felt her presence like a weight in my chest, anchoring me to the spot. I laughed as a joy I'd never known burst up out of my lungs. But then she was falling into darkness, my useless hands scrabbling in thin air.

The dream was still with me hours later when I spotted the sign for Tintagel, the windswept Cornish village perched on the North Atlantic coast, its ruined castle a magnet for tourists thanks to the legend of King Arthur.

My previous trip here had been a bust, but over the years, I'd learned the value of the second pass. Last time, I was looking for a vulnerable young woman. Now I was looking for a – I could still barely bring myself to use the word – a witch who'd survived over three hundred years. That changed things.

I broke off from the line of holiday traffic and turned towards St Nectan's Glen, a secluded woodland valley, that, according to the guy in the tourist information centre, was one of the most spiritual sites in Cornwall.

A temperate Atlantic rainforest with ancient, ivy-covered trees and waterfalls felt like a more fitting place for a witch to hide out than a busy tourist town selling cheap figurines and wooden swords amongst the postcards and ice creams.

I parked in a lay-by, grabbed my backpack and Clem's leash, and we headed out.

As I trudged back to the car a few hours later, I wondered what the hell I'd been thinking. The valley was certainly a reprieve from the open, wind-lashed landscape that surrounded it, but I was no closer to finding Gwen.

Clem had loved it, sniffing every inch and paddling in the streams and pools like she was living her best life, but I couldn't shake the disappointment. While I'd not been expecting to see Gwen strolling through the forest, I had expected … something. An idea. A gut feeling. Anything.

Not wanting to admit defeat, when we reached the lay-by, I crossed the road, heading north towards the coast. The dream played in a loop in my mind. Gwen's face as she turned. That sad smile pulling at her lips. My scream as I watched her fall. It had left me feeling sick to my stomach all day.

Maybe the dream was a clue. Maybe if I stood on a clifftop, I could figure out what the hell it meant. Clem's leash pulled taut, cutting off my train of thought. I backed up, giving her the slack to sniff whatever had caught her attention, and glanced around.

Up ahead was a long, unpaved lane flanked by old trees. It

was easy to miss from the road, whichever direction you came from. Clem was still sniffing around the same patch of greenery. What she found so captivating was beyond me.

As I looked closer, though, I saw that what I'd assumed to be an old tree stump was, in fact, the remnants of a stone pillar.

I reached up to touch it, finding first brick and then the cold press of metal, hidden beneath the thick blanket of ivy. I pulled it aside and gaped at the nameplate: Pendarrow House.

I recognised the name, but where from? Devlin hadn't mentioned it. Neither had Maggie. Had the guy in the tourist office?

Clem pulled on her leash, urging me towards the lane.

'Hang on, girl,' I said, not wanting to move an inch until I remembered.

I pulled the wad of folded pages from my back pocket and sifted through them. I stopped when I got to the third page.

Music all around her.
Clifftop.
Big house.
Pen-something?
Tall, older man in spirit. Pipe smoker.

I caught my breath. It wasn't much, but this couldn't be a coincidence, could it? Of all the lay-bys in Cornwall, I pull in here and just stumble across a 'Pendarrow House'? The cynic in my head had already answered for me, but I ignored it.

'Come on, Clem,' I said, setting off up the lane at a jog. My feet crunched on gravel just as I made the last turn and a grand old house loomed into sight.

I counted sixteen bone-white shuttered windows to the front of the property, which stood alone in the middle of an ocean of gravel with neatly trimmed lawns beyond. With the sinking sun at my back, I jogged the rest of the way, but still not fast enough for Clem.

My gut told me the place was empty, but I rang the front doorbell anyhow, just in case. After the second try went unanswered, I headed around the side, cursing myself for leaving my lock kit in the glove box. It would only take twenty minutes to get back to the car, half that if I ran, but every second felt like a delay I couldn't afford.

Shutters covered the windows at the side and the back of the house, too. I ducked my head around the corner, just in case someone was out back, tending the garden, but all I saw was a wide terrace, steps green with mould, and the corner of an old coach house fifty yards away, its roof half collapsed.

I tried the first door I reached, using the bottom of my T-shirt to make sure I didn't leave any prints, and to my amazement, the knob turned without complaint. Just like that, I was standing in the boiler room of Pendarrow House, my heart pumping and blood pounding in my ears. Gwen's face flashed into my mind again, visions from a dozen dreams and that bittersweet ache in my chest. She had been here. I could feel it.

In the old scullery, a black typewriter sat at the end of a long kitchen table. I hurried over, flipping up the cover, but the reel was gone. I opened the cupboards one by one, finding enough tinned food to get someone through a war. A bowl of shrivelled brown apples sat next to a bread bin that emitted a cloud of green mould when I lifted the lid, and at the sink, a single plate and mug stood on a bone-dry draining board.

As I searched, I rubbed at my tattoo. It wasn't burning or

even prickling like it had done before; this time, it felt more like warm feathers against my skin.

Clem whined and pulled at her leash.

'Okay,' I whispered, unclipping her. 'But stay close to me, alright?'

She dropped her nose to the dusty floor, then trotted out of the room as if I'd not spoken.

Cursing under my breath, I followed her out into the grand central hallway. The place would be perfect for one of those arty photographer types, all crumbling plaster, peeling paint and cracked floor tiles.

I caught sight of the end of Clem's tail as she slunk past the foot of the sweeping staircase and disappeared. I didn't bother calling her. There was no point once she got a scent, so I just followed.

A set of wooden double doors faced me, one cracked open. I don't know what I was expecting to see, but it sure wasn't a ballroom, complete with fancy chandeliers. Clem was standing in the middle of the room, sniffing the only piece of furniture – a plain wooden chair.

The light was low now, the sun sliding steadily westward, and I could see why the architect had put the ballroom here. The golden light from the long line of windows gave the place an almost otherworldly feel. I swallowed around the lump in my throat, feeling like Gwen's presence was suddenly enveloping me. I turned in a circle, heart thumping, mind reeling, until Clem let out a sharp bark.

I jumped. What the hell was I doing? I forced myself to focus and think like a detective. I didn't want to put a name to the other behaviour – it was too ridiculous. I studied the chair, wondering why anyone would place it in the middle of such a vast room. Sure, the light was incredible, but if she'd wanted a view of the grounds and the ocean beyond, wouldn't she point it towards the windows?

When I ran out of ideas, I sat down, hoping the change of height might reveal something. It didn't.

'I don't get it, Clem,' I said wearily, dropping forward to rest my hands on my knees. 'Why sit in the middle of the room facing side-on to the only view?'

It was then that I saw the small cluster of indentations on the wooden floor a few feet in front of me. A memory hit me like a slap. Patty May Bridges getting yelled at by our teacher in tenth-grade band class for not putting a mat under her cello spike. Miss Pearson going on and on about the dent she'd left in the newly varnished floor of the music room.

I dropped to my knees to get a better look. Some were deeper than others, and up close, I saw faint scratches too. Maggie's seer friend had said Gwen was surrounded by music. I'd dismissed the idea, but what if it was music she played herself?

'Come on, Clem,' I said, jogging to the door. 'I think I know how to find her.'

PART III

1976

CHAPTER 41

GWEN, JULY 1976

I woke at dawn, reluctant to leave the dream in which I shared my bed with my Italian lover. I'd left Pietro asleep in a beautiful clifftop hotel in Poole in 1936. He was, without doubt, the most beautiful man I had ever seen. Michelangelo's *David* made mortal and blessed with glossy dark curls and eyelashes that rested on high, sun-kissed cheekbones dusted with the faintest of freckles. I had spent hours gazing into those gold-specked green eyes, wondering how I might this time find a way to stay. To make a life with this man who, in the throes of passion, granted, had told me repeatedly that he loved me. I had heard it before – men will say anything to get what they want – but there was something in the deep pools of his eyes that told me he truly meant it. When I found that small red velvet box in his jacket pocket, I knew I had to leave.

Lying in my bed, a tear escaped. He would be an old man by now – if he'd survived the war and the internment. I prayed he'd had a good life. When I met him, I would have sworn myself immune to love. My heart no longer a fertile soil but the crumbled dust that precedes a desert. And yet, I'd felt it from that first look – that stirring that whispered a promise of the impossible. The butterflies didn't help, their love of pleasure spurring me on, sending me deeper into the oblivion of my own making.

I shouldn't have let myself fall. I told myself it was only lust, a brief interlude to slake my desire before I moved on, but I'd known that I'd love him – and I did. It consumed me in a way I'd not felt since Rhys, my husband, which terrified me and thrilled me in equal measure. Maybe if I could love Pietro enough, I could atone for what I did to Rhys, but of course, life doesn't work like that.

I'd left a note, hastily scribbled on the hotel stationery, telling Pietro not to look for me, then boarded the first train out without even checking its destination. I spent the journey crying for all I had lost: Tân and Nain, the mother and brother I never knew, the father who never loved me. I wept for the murdered witches and innocents, for the butterflies, even Rhys. For the children I'd never have. The woman I'd never become. And for all the years I'd existed but never truly lived.

That's the thing about grief. It doesn't fade into silvered scars like they say. It's a scab, fragile and paper thin, waiting to be ripped off when you least expect it, leaving nothing but raw, tender flesh.

I clenched my teeth, angry at myself for giving in to the emotion. I flung back the sheet, determined to put my mind to less distressing tasks. With my latest manuscript already with Walt's agent, I couldn't busy myself with editing today. Maybe that was why I'd had the dream, memory sneaking into the space where fantasy and imagination usually held dominion. I thought back to my practice yesterday, noticing how my cello's neck had shifted – subtle but unmistakable. I'd take it to the luthier this morning. Then I'd spend the day walking in the woods, trying to forget.

I spent the short walk into town trying to ignore the grumbling from the butterflies. While our communication had always been limited to feelings, I knew full well what they thought about the prospect of being without my cello, even for a few days. Like me, they had grown used to having it at hand all these years – being able to escape reality and soar whenever the mood took us.

There was a beautiful grand piano in this house, and while I was a reasonably talented pianist, not a single wing stirred when I sat down to play. Only the cello had a call on my soul, and maybe theirs too, because they refused to dance to anything else.

It was market day in Wells, and so I weaved through the cobbled streets, busy with traders and shoppers. In some ways, it had changed little since my last visit – or indeed my first, travelling as a maid to the mistress of a minor nobleman who sent her to pray for his soul every Friday in the cathedral which towered over the pretty little town. There was still the scent of bread in the air, fruit and vegetables piled high on carts and the calls of traders plying their wares. The heat wasn't familiar, though. My T-shirt stuck to my back, my cello case pinning it in place.

I turned into the side street, glad to be away from the crowd and the glare from the sun. The street was shaded, but there wasn't a breath of wind to move the luthier's sign above the small, bow-fronted black-and-white shop. The bell above the door announced my arrival, the sound too loud for what felt like a hallowed place. A few instruments lined the lime-washed walls, but this wasn't the place people came to browse. The real magic happened in the workshop.

A small, fine-boned man with close-cropped grey hair and half-moon glasses poked his head around the archway that connected the back of the counter to the workshop. He smiled politely and shuffled towards the counter, a hint of tightness around his eyes the only sign that at least one of his old joints was complaining. I'd not been here since 1960 – the year Walt died.

As that long summer drew to a close and the shadows lengthened at Pendarrow House, I'd left Cornwall and the biting Atlantic winds that rattled the shutters and howled like banshees down the chimneys and wintered here in Wells, where the Mendip Hills met the Somerset Levels. It wasn't Wales, but the sight of the hills brought me some comfort.

Time hadn't been kind to the luthier. He looked up at me, his pale eyes narrowing and his brow furrowing as if trying to place me. I smiled, readying my story, just in case he asked, but after a moment, the frown vanished, and he shook his head as if dismissing whatever bell of recognition had chimed in his head. Thankfully, it was my bow that had needed attention back then.

The luthier was just closing the lid on my cello case when I felt the first fluttering in my chest.

'It might well be this awful heat, but I'll take a proper look at it once I get it on the bench,' he said, addressing the counter. His head dipped as he wrote out a receipt.

I was barely listening, my attention fixed on the butterflies and trying desperately to interpret their sudden animation. The skin on the back of my neck goose-fleshed, and I spun around. I strode to the front of the small shop and peered through the leaded windows. A few sun-weary people ambled by. A woman bending to keep pace with a ponderous toddler. Two elderly ladies with tight grey curls in summer dresses, one waving a lace-edged fan while the other patted a handkerchief to her brow.

When I turned back, the luthier had vanished. I caught

my breath, but before I could speak, he reappeared, still talking as if there'd been no break in our conversation.

'You were wise to bring it in now. I find the particularly old ones can be too stoical sometimes, hiding their aches and pains until something serious occurs.'

He misread my blank expression for a question.

'I can't look at it until the morning, I'm afraid, but it's safely locked away in our strong room. I don't like to take any risks, especially with such valuable instruments.'

I let out a breath, but the butterflies were still on the wing, beating a slow, steady rhythm against my ribs. It made no sense. 'What?' I wanted to scream the question, but I knew they couldn't answer me. I tried to calm myself. If I was in danger, they'd be in full panic mode, but they weren't. This was a good sign, so why was the urge to run so damn strong?

'Do you have a back door?' I blurted. My heart was hammering now, my voice shaky.

The luthier stared at me, motionless.

'My ex-boyfriend isn't allowed to come near me, but I think he might be following me,' I said, glancing towards the door.

Without a word, the luthier dropped his pen, handed me my receipt and then lifted the top of the counter, beckoning me through. I followed him into the workshop, past the long benches with their clamps and angle-poise lamps where disassembled instruments waited for their miracles. Neat rows of chisels and gouges lined the wall, and I drank in the familiar scent of wood shavings, varnish and glue, transported back to York when desperation had driven an old luthier to teach a young woman a man's trade.

The luthier stopped at the blue steel door at the back of the shop.

'Go through the yard into the lane. Turn left and left again and you're back on the high street.'

We both jumped when the bell above the front door jangled to announce a new customer.

'What does he look like?' the luthier asked. 'Your ex-boyfriend?'

I couldn't answer him. If it was another hunter, it would be the latest in a long line of mercenaries hired to track me down.

'Don't worry,' I said, already edging into the yard. 'Even if it is him, he won't hurt you.' I prayed it was true.

My pulse slowed the further I got from the luthier's shop, but the experience had unsettled me. Why had I sensed danger but the butterflies hadn't? They were never wrong.

Abandoning my plan to walk in the woods, I headed back to the house, calling in to a café on the way to buy a sandwich and a bottle of water, my eyes appraising every passerby and my ears alert to every sound.

I sighed. When even little old ladies started looking like possible threats, I knew it was time to move on. I'd already stayed too long, using the edit of my latest manuscript as an excuse, but now that it was safely with Larry, it was time to face facts.

Decision made, I slowed my pace and took the long route back to the house, trying to enjoy the walk despite the heat and the fact that my pumps stuck to the tarmac each time I crossed the road. Sandals would have been cooler, but I'd learned a long time ago that sometimes, staying alive depended on shoes you could sprint in.

The butterflies shuffled beneath my ribs like disgruntled

residents at a parish council meeting. I didn't really want to leave either, but I'd long since given up on the idea that life was fair. But that didn't mean we couldn't enjoy one more afternoon here before packing up.

I walked past the house without even glancing at it, heading instead to the car at the end of the street, already pulling the keys from my pocket.

Less than an hour later, I sat at the top of Glastonbury Tor, my chest heaving, my shorts and T-shirt damp with sweat. The heat was relentless, but at least up here, there was a breath of wind – though nothing like the elemental force that usually howled through the three large, pointed Gothic arches of St. Michael's Tower.

I'd released the butterflies the moment I stepped out of the car. They loved it here, just as much as I did, although our reasons differed. It reminded me of the view of the valley from the top meadow back home, but I think they just loved the energy of the place. They'd not stretch the limits of the spell's tether as they usually did when we walked. Instead, they stayed close, some swirling and shimmering overhead, while others rippled across the ground like a shifting, delicate tide. Standing stones were a favourite of theirs too. I wished there was a camera capable of capturing the sight of Stonehenge enveloped in a quivering mass of adoring magical butterflies.

I sat on the ground, my back pressed to the tower as I sipped my water and took in the view. The heat made everything look like the world had been rendered in chalk, the edges blurred and indistinct. The vast, rolling patchwork of fields, yellowed by the drought, made for a melancholy sight. The land begged for water, its pleas ignored by a stubborn sky. I prayed to the Goddess to send rain.

I sat for hours, moving with the shifting sun to remain in the shade. I ate my sandwich, trying to imagine the wind delivering a sky full of rain clouds, but I knew it to be a fool's errand. Nain had summoned a raging tempest to help me escape, and yet I couldn't even conjure a single raindrop.

As I stood up, dusting crumbs from my shorts, I noticed a tiny, wilted daisy at the base of the tower. Crouching, I unscrewed the lid of the bottle and let three fat drops of water fall. I waited until they soaked into the dust before repeating the process. I smiled. I couldn't do magic, but I could do this.

Later, on the drive back to Wells, I decided that my reaction in the luthier's was likely just the heat and the agony of having to part with my cello for a few days. It had long felt like a friend, but even more so now that I was alone again.

While my life today was a dream compared to my pre-Walt era, I missed those years when it felt like I actually belonged somewhere. Back when I had someone to care about me. I tsked at the thought. If I was throwing myself a pity party, it was a sign that I needed to clear out – immediately.

Back in Wells, I parked the car at the end of the road, turning first so that I was pointing in the direction of the main road, and walked back to the house.

Once inside, I pulled the satchel from its hiding place and slung it over my shoulder. In the bedroom, I threw a few essentials into my overnight bag and left the rest. I'd pick up some new clothes in the next place.

In the kitchen, I emptied the cupboards and fridge of anything perishable, adding what was salvageable to my bag. I dried the plate and mug that sat on the draining board and stowed them back in the cupboard, folded the cloth and draped it over the neck of the tap. Leaving was a ritual now. A series of practised moves designed to tie up the loose ends of another brief chapter in my ridiculously long existence.

Turning, my eye snagged on the shiny red Olivetti typewriter on the kitchen table. It was a delight to use, its keys light and as keen to get words on the page as I was. I took a half-step towards it, my hand outstretched. I snapped it back. I had rules for moving on – take only what you can carry in one trip. I brushed my fingers over the keys as if in doing so I could sweep up some of its energy and carry it with me. I threw the dust cover over it, picked up my bag and strode to the front door.

After dropping the house key into the satchel, I stepped out into the early evening. After the relative cool of the house, the heat closed in around me like a fist. The sun was sinking now, the pale blue sky streaked with ribbons of candy pink and orange and reminding me of the jars of sherbet in the newsagents.

It felt strange to be leaving without my cello. I felt the absence of it on my back, a snail without her shell, but maybe it was safer in the cool of the luthier's strong room than inside a hot, sticky car for who knew how long.

As I headed for the car, I wondered if instead of going to another of the safe houses, I'd stay nearby in a hotel until my cello was ready to collect. Shaftesbury was nice, or Castle Cary.

The butterflies surged in my chest, stopping me in my tracks. I spun around, but the street was deserted. A noise to my right made me turn, just in time to see Cyril, the elderly neighbour I'd met in the woods months ago, teetering on a chair outside his front door, watering can half raised to a hanging basket.

Frantic wings strained in my chest as if calling out a warning, but it happened before I could even take a step. The chair wobbled on the uneven paving, he lost his footing and then he was falling.

I dropped my bag, flung open the gate and bolted up the half dozen steps, but I wasn't quick enough. I heard an ominous crack beneath his cry of shock as he landed on the unforgiving stone path.

'You're okay,' I said, realising at once what a ridiculous thing that is to say to someone who's just had a nasty fall. 'I've got you – Cyril, isn't it?'

The old man groaned and tried to get up but cried out with the movement.

'Steady. Steady,' I said softly. 'Stay still for me. Have you got a telephone, Cyril?'

Chest heaving, he gave a small nod and pointed a gnarled index finger in the direction of the house.

'I'm going to be a few minutes, okay? It's all going to be fine though,' I said, looking around at the deserted street as I rose, desperately hoping to see someone else who could help.

The telephone was on a small, polished table in the hallway next to a notebook with 'Telephone messages' printed at the top of the blank, dusty page. I bit my lip as the weight of the loneliness I'd felt when I first met him huddled around me like an accusing crowd.

After giving the address and the basics of what had happened, I hurried back to sit with Cyril. He looked pale as chalk and his breathing was laboured. I gingerly took his hand.

'Help is on the way, Cyril,' I said, unable to disguise the quiver in my voice. The butterflies had stilled as if they were waiting. I swallowed hard. 'Your baskets are a credit to you though,' I said feebly. 'I can find someone to water them for you while you're getting better.' I had no idea where that had come from, but he looked to be fading before my eyes. Was it the shock, perhaps? His heart? Such a gentle old soul. Such a stupid accident. I thought of Walt before I could stop myself, and the emotion reared up.

The wail of an approaching siren was like a balm to burnt

skin. I craned my neck, desperate to see help sweeping around the corner.

'Cyril, the ambulance is nearly here now,' I said, glancing back to him. But there was something wrong. Cyril lay completely still.

'No, no, no!' I cried as I fumbled at his neck, trying to find a pulse.

The butterflies chose that exact moment to explode out of my aura, snatching every ounce of breath from my lungs as they flew into full panic mode.

I bent forward, putting my ear to Cyril's nose. Nothing. I locked my arms and started chest compressions, talking to him the whole time, although what I said, I have no idea.

Time slowed as I focused on counting, then, blessedly, I felt firm hands pull me away. Dazed, breathless, and with the butterflies straining at the end of the spell's tether, I stepped back willingly to allow the ambulance people to take over. It was only when a hand clamped over my mouth that I realised my mistake.

Screaming against the man's flesh, I kicked and fought, my eyes on Cyril as the hunter dragged me, my heels bouncing off each step. A flash of blue light and another blare of the ambulance siren gave me just enough time. The hunter's grip loosened for a fraction of a second, but it was all I needed. He wasn't much taller than me, and so I snapped my head back into his face. My stomach churned as I felt cartilage collapse under the weight of the blow.

'Oi! Leave her alone!' called a man's voice from the street.

I took off running, risking a glance over my shoulder. One of the ambulance men was already crouching over Cyril, while the other stood on the steps, looking towards me. The man who had grabbed me was nowhere in sight. I just needed to get to the car.

I heard something crack a fraction before a sharp pain

lanced though my left ankle. I crumpled to the floor, my hands skidding along the hot stone pavement as I tried to break my fall. The second hunter was much taller than the first. He snorted out a dry laugh as he stepped from in front of a black van, a long police night stick in his hand.

I tried to crawl, but the beefy hands of my first assailant lifted me under my arms and dragged me backwards as I screamed. My chest felt about to burst as the butterflies strained at the limits of the spell, desperate to escape. A sweaty hand slipped around my mouth, and I bit down as hard as I could, the coppery tang of blood mixing with the bile rising in my throat.

The slap to my face snapped my head to the side, shocking me into silence.

I heard the van door slide open and my panic reared again.

'What the f—'

Whatever my attacker was about to say was lost. He leapt backwards, releasing me, but I had no time to prepare. I crashed onto the pavement, the pain in my ankle so blinding the world began to dim at the edges.

I was vaguely aware of a dog. A flash of snarling orange-and-white fur. I heard a man scream and then something heavy hit the ground. As consciousness left me, I prayed it hadn't been the dog.

CHAPTER 43

GWEN, JULY 1976

J opened my eyes to semi-darkness. The pain in my
ankle felt like a hot, throbbing, twisted blade. I
swallowed hard against the nausea and panic rising in my
throat and took a slow, quiet breath.

I tried to focus and assess the situation. I was in the back
of a strange car, moving at speed. A motorway then.
Passenger seat empty. One man driving. I could only see his
arm and profile, but he wore a denim jacket, not the black
fatigues of the men who had attacked me. So a different
hunter.

I reached down the bond to the butterflies, but they were
oddly calm, given the situation.

The radio was on low, playing some rock ballad I couldn't
name. I uncurled my fingers and felt the weight of my satchel
on my chest. That was something, at least. While I'd scattered
its original contents in safety deposit boxes around the country, the case itself was my last connection to Walt. My
reminder that I had once had a friend in this wretched
world.

Beneath the case, I felt the rough wool of a travel rug. I

rubbed my fingers over the fringe, trying to breathe through the searing pain in my ankle as I looked around the car.

Three hundred and eighty-two years and I'd never broken a bone, which, given how I used to ride Tân, was probably a minor miracle. Had I thought myself indestructible? Perhaps. But what else was I to think when everyone around me lived and died while I existed like a fly in amber, never sickening with so much as a cold?

I didn't know if it was the spell or the butterflies themselves that protected me from sickness and the ravages of time. Did this mean my luck had finally run out? Or would the magic heal me? Deciding it had to be the latter, I turned my leg gingerly, but only just stifled a scream as the pain, white-hot and furious, all but blinded me.

When I opened my eyes, I saw a dog's face peeking around the passenger seat, tongue lolling, eyes bright in the reflected streetlights.

'Clementine. Back in the footwell. Let her sleep.' The driver sounded exasperated. He was an American, his accent soft, the vowels rounded at the edges. I felt my flesh go cold at the memory of that other hunter from across the pond.

His pursuit had been relentless. Months and months spent running from one town to the next until, inexplicably, the handsome couple I'd careered into as I fled my employer's house in Cardiff appeared like avenging angels in York, just in time to save me. Whatever happened next, it was the last I saw of the man who called himself Silas Thorne.

The dog shot the driver a pointed look and compromised by lowering herself so that just her elbows were on the front seat. She watched me, mouth open, and from the draught, tail wagging. I squinted at her. There were smears of something dark around her muzzle. I leaned forward, and it was all the invitation she needed to clamber into the back seat.

'Clementine!' the driver hissed. 'You'll hurt her—' He glanced over his shoulder to look at me.

I felt a twist of something in my gut as I saw him clearly for the first time, and for a moment, I was back in a clifftop hotel room in Poole.

His hair wasn't quite the raven's black of Pietro's, but just like my Italian lover, he was that one step beyond handsome that made sculptors sighs and reach for their chisels.

He had high cheekbones, a strong jawline and light-coloured, deep-set eyes. His chin was stubbled with a few days' growth and his wavy dark hair brushed the back of his collar.

The butterflies surged in my chest, swooping and diving as if they'd just arrived at a carnival. I never forgot a face, especially one like his, but I couldn't shake the sense that I knew him.

I set my jaw as I glared at him.

The dog clambered into the well behind the passenger seat and leaned her head into my hand. I stroked her. She had the same silky soft fur as May, the Owens' dog, although May hadn't had what looked like dried blood around her muzzle.

'Is your dog injured? She's covered in blood,' I snapped.

'I'm sorry she woke you,' he said. 'I checked her all over and there's not a scratch on her. The blood is from the guy who busted your leg. Her name's Clementine, by the way.'

I dropped my eyes to the dog, who thumped her tail in the confined space.

'Thank you,' I mouthed to her as I tickled her ear. 'And who the hell are you?' I said, pushing every ounce of confidence I could muster into my words. Until I could run, I'd have to negotiate.

'My name's Daniel Quinn. Dan. I'm here to help you, Gwen,' he said.

I snorted at that.

'I don't need saving, thanks,' I snapped.

I saw his jaw tighten as he pressed his lips together. At least he didn't point out the obvious.

The memory of Cyril lying on his garden path landed heavy as a lead weight.

I cleared my throat.

'The old man who fell. Did you see what happened to him?' I was careful not to call him a neighbour.

Dan shook his head. 'I'm sorry. We pulled up just as the big guy was dragging you to the van, and, well, it all got crazy from there.' He frowned. 'You know, I think he had an oxygen mask over his face when they stretchered him to the ambulance. I only saw it for a second, though, as I grabbed your bag off the street, but that's a good sign, right?'

I saw it then. My overnight bag was tucked into the well behind the driver's seat.

'You helped him back there?' he asked, glancing over his shoulder.

I didn't reply.

He tried a different tack.

'So, do you know the men who came after you tonight?'

I pursed my lips, letting out a careful breath. If I stayed silent, he might stop talking, and I needed to know who he was and what he intended to do to me.

'No.'

'Does it happen a lot?' His tone was lighter now, almost playful.

Did he think this was a joke?

He shook his head. 'I'm sorry. Bad taste. I'm kinda nervous, and I can't quite believe you're actually here.'

'Who hired you, Daniel Quinn?'

He sighed and didn't answer right away. I saw him twist his mouth as if he were chewing over what to say next.

'I should say that I'll tell you everything I know once we get your leg looked at,' he replied.

'I heal fast. I'll be fine,' I said, the last word ground out through gritted teeth as the car hit a pothole in the road, which was enough to send a red-hot poker of pain through my ankle. It was, though, an improvement on my last attempt at moving. Maybe it was healing fast.

'I can't go to a hospital,' I added, suddenly worried that was where we were headed.

'No. That's the first place they'll look. I'm taking you to someone else who can help,' Dan said evenly. 'Look, we have a couple of hours on the road before we get there, so I'm just going to lay it all out for you. If I've got it wrong, then you can call me a whack job and call the police once your leg's fixed,' he said with a nod in my direction, but without taking his eyes from the road. 'But if I'm right, then we can figure out a plan together.'

I bit back the retort. Whatever he thought he knew, he was wrong. The silence stretched out between us. I saw his shoulders fall and his jaw set, then he shifted in his seat, pulled a folded sheet of paper from his back pocket and handed it to me.

I took it, my heart thumping as if some part of me already knew what I was about to see. He flicked on the overhead lamp, and just as I'd feared, my own eyes, rendered in Rhys's precise hand, stared back at me from the sketch. I thought of the three times I'd laid eyes on it. The first on the day Rhys had created it, the second in the top-secret file Walt stole for me – and now.

My mouth went dry, but before I was ready for it, Daniel launched into a story about a baby girl born to a renowned witch who died on the birthing bed in the pretty little town of Pont Nefoedd. A spell that went wrong and a wealthy man called Devlin obsessed with claiming orphaned magic for himself.

He spoke of seeing things he couldn't explain, a kindly librarian, how fate had delivered him right to the gate of Pendarrow House and his revelation in its abandoned ballroom. He finished by telling me how he'd visited almost every luthier's listed in the phone book before finally catching a break this afternoon.

My head swam with the impossibility of it all.

'It was you in the luthier's,' I mumbled, remembering how the flesh had prickled on my neck.

Daniel snorted a laugh. 'For about ten seconds, yeah. The guy threw me out the shop and threatened to call the police.' He sounded ... I struggled to find the word. 'Pleased' felt incongruous given the situation, but it was the closest.

'His reaction convinced me I was on to something, but it was more than that. It felt like you had just walked out the door ahead of me.'

The butterflies fluttered their wings, and I rolled my eyes, glad that he had his eyes on the road.

He laughed awkwardly, shaking his head.

'So how did you find me?'

'I figured you might have been there to pick up a cello or something, so I asked the folks on the market if they'd seen a young woman carrying a cello case. One guy said he'd seen you on his way to work walking towards town earlier that morning. I got to wondering if you lived locally ...' He shrugged, a smile tugging at the corner of his lips.

I swallowed hard. Only a hunter would go to this much effort. Bringing a dog along was a nice touch, I thought sourly. I dropped my hand from Clementine's head, and she nuzzled my arm. I looked down into her soft, gentle eyes and went back to stroking her ears. It wasn't her fault if she was being used as a pawn in his sick game.

'So, you spent the day kerb-crawling,' I sneered, intending it to sound as seedy as I could make it.

The smile dropped from his face. 'I was about to call it a day when I saw the big guy take you down. Look, I know it's a lot,' Daniel said. 'Until all this happened, I'd have laughed at anyone talking about magic. But what I've seen with my own eyes …' He trailed off. Long seconds passed.

'And what do you intend to do now?' I asked.

He glanced back at me just as the street light sent an amber glow drifting across his face. His brow knitted into a frown, and he looked genuinely confused.

The butterflies danced under my ribs, sweeping and soaring on unhurried wings. What the hell was wrong with them? This man was likely driving me to my death and their annihilation, and they were swooping and swooning like a bunch of lovesick teenagers.

It was pointless telling them to settle down, and when they surged in my chest, stretching at my aura until my vision blurred and my head spun, I gave in.

Fine, I thought as I slid back the mental bolt to release them.

The butterflies exploded, filling the car with iridescent wings before melting through the roof and taking to the night sky. They often did this as I drove, using the tether of the spell to trail behind the car like so many impossible balloons. Clementine lifted her head slowly, eyes wide and tongue lolling.

'Sweet Jesus! What the hell was that?' Daniel gasped, head turning this way and that.

I stilled. 'What was what?' I asked, careful to make sure my voice was as flat and as disinterested as I could make it, despite my hammering heart.

He faltered. 'I don't know. There was like a rush of something, like … Forget it. I'm jumping at shadows now,' he said, sounding unconvinced.

'I asked what you intended to do with me,' I pressed, desperate to divert his attention.

'We need to get your leg fixed, then we go hide out somewhere until we can figure out how to free you.' He said it as if it were the simplest thing in the world.

I gritted my teeth. So that was his plan. Offer me the comfort of lies until he handed me over to whoever was paying him.

I shifted a fraction in my seat, freezing when another lance of pain coursed through my ankle. I bit down hard on my lip, squeezing my eyes shut as I tried to breathe through the pain. When I opened them again, I noticed the meadow brown still perched on my captor's shoulder.

CHAPTER 44

DAN, JULY 1976

'You brought me to a vet!'

Gwen huffed out the words as I pulled up outside the veterinarian's office and killed the engine.

'He has an X-ray machine. He helped Clem,' I said lamely, twisting in my seat to look at her properly.

She was glaring daggers at me, but it was the fear in her eyes that felt like a gut punch. What the hell had I been expecting? Open arms and a thank you card? She'd spent centuries running from men who meant her harm. In her eyes, I guess I was no different. That thought came as a blow too. She didn't know me. And despite my weird dreams and the strange feeling of familiarity they left me with, I didn't know her either. Not really. It hadn't occurred to me before now that she might be a threat to me. Was she about to do to me what Devlin's witch had done to poor Clement? Or maybe she was more the make it snow indoors kind of a witch, like Jackson? I looked away.

'Let's get this over with,' Gwen snarled.

An hour later, a bewildered Dr Arnold stood scratching his head as he stared at the X-ray on the light box.

'You say this injury occurred earlier today?' It was the third time he'd asked.

'Yes.' Gwen sounded irritable now. 'I was hit in the ankle with a night stick. I heard the bone crack,' she repeated from where she sat, her left leg propped on a cushion and her swollen ankle the colour of a damson plum.

'Curious indeed. What I'm seeing here looks like a fracture that's had a couple of weeks to heal. It's what I'd expect to see on a follow-up after setting. How's the pain level?'

'Better than it was,' Gwen said carefully. 'I could probably walk on it.'

The veterinarian spun around, looking horrified. 'Oh, don't do that! Even a clean fracture such as this takes six weeks to heal. You need to stay off your feet or you'll risk more serious consequences.'

'Like what exactly?' Gwen snapped.

'Aside from refracturing the bone, there's the risk of malunion, which could lead to long-term deformity and a permanent limp. And, of course, we don't know yet if there's tendon damage. That's a wait and see job, I'm afraid.'

I watched as her eyes widened and her colour paled. She waited a beat before lifting her chin and nodding at the vet.

'Thank you,' she said, her tone formal but sincere. 'I appreciate you helping me, Doctor Arnold.' Gwen's eyes flicked to me. 'You too,' she said coolly.

It was after midnight by the time we emerged from the veterinarian's office, Gwen's lower leg encased in a fibreglass cast and a pair of cobwebbed old crutches under her arms that the doc had spent half an hour searching for in his basement.

'You know I'll run the moment I can,' Gwen said, her eyes

on the steps down to the sidewalk. She spoke so quietly, I wondered if she realised that she'd said it out loud.

'I know. But will you let me help you until you can?' I held out my hand. She stared at it for a long moment before lifting her eyes to mine, and I swear something broke in my chest.

She worked hard at trying to hide the fact that she was beautiful – the dark, roughly cut hair, the oversized clothes that swallowed her shape – and yet she still looked like a goddess to me. Long-limbed and coltish, she had an artistic, otherworldly air. But it was her eyes that mesmerised me. I couldn't tell if they were hazel or amber in this light, but each time I caught her eye, it left me feeling stripped bare.

I dropped my gaze and waited, hand still outstretched. When I glanced back, her eyes flicked to my left shoulder, the movement so fleeting I almost missed it. I turned but saw nothing.

'Look, you don't know me, Gwen, so you're right not to trust me yet. But I plan on earning your trust.' It wasn't much of a speech, certainly nothing like the elaborate ones I'd constructed in my head these last few months, but it was the truth.

Standing between us on the step, Clem leaned over and nuzzled at Gwen's hand. I watched as the edges of her lips softened, her eyes on the dog. Unfurling her fingers from the crutch, she stretched them forward and tickled Clem on the head.

'Look, our priority now is getting you somewhere safe,' I said. 'Can we just do that?'

'Fine,' she hissed.

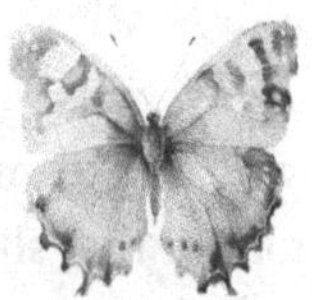

'I've already told you! I am not going to Wales!' I was shouting now, my words reverberating around the car, but I didn't care.

Why hadn't I asked before I got back in the car? He'd said it was on the coast and that it belonged to an old friend of his he knew from some flower market, but it was only when I saw the sign for the M4 that I thought to ask the most obvious question.

'I know. You've mentioned it,' Dan said tightly. 'What you've not said is why.'

He flicked his eyes to the rear-view mirror, and I glared at him until I felt the prick of tears. I turned away, fixing my gaze on the dark London streets as we sped through them.

How could I even begin to explain? I was far from ready to confess my sins, let alone to a complete stranger. It was more than that though. I wasn't ready to forgive my homeland for its false promises of family, belonging and, when I thought back to my time in Cardiff, salvation.

My heart ached to go home, to see my mountains and the valley from the top meadow. To ride through the woods, feel

Welsh soil beneath my bare feet, gallop back to the cottage to see Nain grinding herbs, Sage the cat asleep in a shaft of sunlight. I wanted so much to go back to those happier, simpler times.

But memory is a cruel thing. Even the very idea of 'home' was a thorn-wrapped lie masquerading as a truth, whispering of a time that had never really existed in the rose-tinted way I imagined it now.

People, too, weren't always what we wanted them to be. Even Nain, the woman who raised me to be wild and free, had cursed me. It didn't matter that she hadn't meant to. The punishment was the same: an eternity longing for a life I could never have. If you wait long enough, everyone abandons you in the end.

'I just don't,' I said, swallowing hard as I stroked Clem's head.

Dan made a sound somewhere between a sigh and a groan. He glanced in the mirror, then pulled into a side road. I breathed out. Maybe he was listening after all.

'Hey,' he said, turning in his seat once the engine was silenced and flicking on the overhead light. 'I don't need to know unless you think that's one of the places they'll look first. I only suggested it because Devlin warned me not to waste his money looking for you there, but if it's too much of a risk, we'll find somewhere else. Okay?'

I bit the inside of my cheek. If they were using past sightings to predict my movements, it was likely the last place they'd look, but I wasn't about to say that out loud.

He pressed on. 'I have no idea how you've survived this long, Gwen. I'm guessing your magic helps you defend yourself or something.'

I couldn't stop the snort of a dry laugh that flew out of my mouth. Did he really think I was a witch? That I had magic that could protect me? I watched as a vertical line grew between his eyebrows. Oh no. He actually did. I sighed. If he really was trying to help me and this wasn't an elaborate plan to deliver me to this Devlin man, then I should probably tell him the truth. But if he was just another hunter, maybe it didn't hurt to have him believe I had power.

I groaned, tipping back my head to rest on the window, my eyes on the roof of the car. I took a deep breath. Then another. The meadow brown appeared a few inches from my nose, but I couldn't even muster a smile for her.

When she fluttered off, I turned my head, careful to keep my eyes on Dan. I already knew where she was heading.

She settled on his hair this time, and I watched as he ran his hand over the spot, passing right through her. A quiver of excitement rippled down the bond, quick and light – like the first note of a jig across the strings. It fizzed in the hollow of my throat, then my ribs, stirring the other butterflies as it reverberated, bright and clear as a bell.

As I watched, she fluttered to his nose, spreading her wings wide. Dan wrinkled his nose as if he were about to sneeze, then rubbed at it with the edge of his finger.

I licked my lips, my mouth dry. Could he sense her? It had to be a coincidence, surely. But whether he sensed her or not, the message was clear: she trusted him.

I sighed. 'I don't have magic, Dan,' I breathed.

His frown deepened. And just like that, I was eighteen again, the weight of my inadequacy resting like a boulder in my gut. I looked away before I could see the disappointment register on his face.

'Wow,' he said. 'You survived, what, three hundred plus years just on your wits? That's incredible.'

It wasn't the reaction I'd been expecting, and it left me flustered.

'A friend helped me. During the war – and afterwards. I owe him a lot,' I said, suddenly defensive.

Then Dan did something that almost broke me. He smiled. A lump caught in my throat as I took in his expression. His lifted brows, the crinkled skin around his eyes and the subtle tilt of his head. He was genuinely happy for me.

'I'm glad you had a friend,' he said. 'Could he help again now?'

I shook my head. 'He's dead.'

'I'm sorry about your friend. But, look, what I said still stands. I don't know of a soldier alive or dead who could have survived like you have all this time.'

I dropped my gaze, not wanting my grief for Walt to show in my face.

'Do you have someplace better we could go?' he asked. It wasn't a challenge, just a concession.

I'd hoped the intruders at Tintagel were common thieves, but after tonight, it was more likely that someone was unravelling the complex web Walt had woven to protect me. None of the houses would be safe, I realised. I shook my head.

The meadow brown fluttered back to me and settled on my cheek, tenting her wings as if she intended to stay awhile. I sighed. This was why I endured, wasn't it? To keep my promise? To honour the spell and shelter orphaned magic that would otherwise be lost to the world forever? When I thought of it like that, my reluctance to go back to Wales felt almost childish.

I turned to Dan. 'We can go to this place you know in the Gower,' I said.

'You sure?'

I was anything but sure, but until my ankle healed, I was short of options.

'I'm sure.'

CHAPTER 46

GWEN, JULY 1976

I woke with a start, pain lancing through my ankle and bright spots dancing across my vision. I gripped the edge of the seat as the car bounced again over a rutted road – we had to be close now.

'You okay?' Dan's words cut through the semi-darkness.

'Uh-hmm,' I groaned as I fought back a wave of nausea rising up my throat.

'The track is a little bumpy from here, but we're nearly there.'

Annoyed with myself for falling asleep in the first place, I levered myself carefully up to sitting. Outside, a pale, uncertain light hovered on the horizon. I saw nothing but rolling moorland, tufted with gorse and heather and a few windswept trees standing like weary sentinels in the half-light, but I could hear the sea and smell it.

Clem, stretched out in the back footwell, yawned and wagged her tail as she lifted her nose and sniffed at the briny air.

So this was my first sight of Wales in more than – I did the sum quickly – one hundred and thirty-five years. I waited, expecting to feel something, but just then, the car rumbled over another patch of uneven ground. I bit back a curse as a fresh stab of pain shot through my ankle.

'Sorry,' Dan said, slowing the car to a funereal crawl.

As we turned to the left, I caught my first glimpse of the cottage. It was a squat, weather-beaten stone building with a sagging slate roof, set near the cliff's edge but buffered by a long windblown garden. Its once white walls were now a weary grey, streaked and stained where the rain had worn its defences thin. The small, boarded front windows flanking the central door gave it the look of a weary mole.

If Daniel Quinn – if indeed that was his real name – was a hunter, he'd picked the perfect place to make sure nobody heard me scream. I winced at the scratch of wings. Great. The last thing I needed was judgement from my would-be captor's new fan club.

We rolled to a halt, and I felt my muscles relax the moment Dan pulled the handbrake. He hopped out of the driver's seat and jogged around to the passenger side, hauling my crutches from the front seat and then gingerly opening the back door.

Clem wasted no time in leaping out of the car.

'Stay close, Clementine!' Dan warned as she sauntered off, her nose already on the ground.

When he turned back to me, my crutches in one hand and his other one hovering like a question mark, he looked at a loss for what to do next.

I sighed. Much as I'd have loved to refuse the help, I had no idea how I'd get out of the car without him.

'Lean the crutches against the car, then hook your fore-arms under my armpits and pull me out slowly. Stop when my foot reaches the end of the seat,' I said, trying to channel the matron I'd worked under during the First World War.

I straightened my back and lifted my bent arms out to my

sides, my heart hammering for reasons I didn't want to think about. The butterflies flew into a fit of excitement, and I rolled my eyes.

'Okay,' he said slowly from behind me.

He cleared his throat before he took a step forward and tentatively slid his arms under mine. His skin was warm against my sides, his forearms lean and tanned. The butterflies flew into a frenzy in my chest, giddy as schoolgirls and as carnal as only magic can be. I closed my eyes, trying to ignore the sensations rippling down the bond and the heat building in my core as he eased me gently from the car.

My foot snagged on the edge of the seat, and I winced as the pain stole my breath.

'Shit! Sorry,' Dan said.

'No. It was my fault,' I said between breaths.

The rest of the manoeuvre went to plan, and a few minutes later, I was balancing on my crutches in the cottage, my sides feeling unnaturally cool after the warmth of his skin through my T-shirt and my heart rate only just about slowing to a regular pace.

'Cottage' was perhaps a generous word for what appeared to be only three rooms. I stood just inside the front door, which opened straight into the main living space. To my right, a small kitchenette occupied the corner; to my left, I spotted the foot of a double bed through a half-open door.

A stone fireplace stood to the left of the bedroom doorway, about halfway along the wall, a clumsy oil painting of the cottage hanging above. Opposite it, a small round table and two mismatched chairs were tucked close to the wall next to a battered-looking armchair. The only other furniture was a long brown sofa at the far end of the room, just below a wide, boarded picture window.

I took a tentative step on my crutches and saw an interior door on the far left, which I presumed would be a bathroom, and, with a rush of relief, a solid-looking back door complete with internal bolts on the far wall to the right.

The sound of yielding plywood preceded a rush of watery daylight as, behind me, Dan removed the first window boards outside. Clem ran into the cottage, nose working overtime and tail waving as she explored. She barged open the bedroom door, did a circuit then hopped on the sofa.

I hobbled into the kitchenette and braced myself against the counter as I peeked inside the wall cabinets. The three I opened were all stacked full of tins.

I pulled open the drawers, finding not just the usual assortment of cutlery and utensils but boxes of batteries, first aid supplies, candles and waterproof matches. I raised an appreciative eyebrow. Whoever owned this place liked to be as prepared as I did.

I was about to open the next drawer down, keen to see what else might be squirrelled away, when the rattle of chains caught my attention. I looked up just in time to see Dan outside, lowering the board that covered the long picture window above the sofa.

I gasped. There she was – the omnipotent, endless sea, her waves catching the first spill of dawn sunlight like molten silver. Clem woofed at Dan from where she stood with her front paws braced on the back of the sofa, and he turned and waved at us. It was such a simple thing, but seeing him standing there, with the light hitting the sea – I had to swallow around the lump in my throat.

Clem was already at the front door when Dan stepped through it.

'There are chairs out back. Do you want to come sit?'

I nodded.

A few minutes later, we sat in silence on the long patch of scrubland that passed for a back garden, holding mugs of scalding black coffee. The hushed slap of the waves below was a quiet reminder that the moon was always at work.

Fifty feet ahead, the garden fell away to nothing, like a snapped tooth, long since lost. To the right, the rotting remains of a white fence lay tangled among the curling bracken; dried to a brittle yellow-brown, it gave the illusion of autumn even though it should still be months away. My eye snagged on what looked to be the start of a wide slipway to the left of the property which had to lead down to the beach.

The sun was still low on the horizon, its ascent lazy and unhurried as if it had all the time in the world. The cool morning air, edged with salt, made the skin on my arms gooseflesh. The butterflies strained in my chest, desperate for release, but I tried to ignore them. When had I stopped watching the sunrise?

'I suppose some things don't change, right?' Dan said, his gaze on the horizon and a slow, easy smile in his voice.

When I didn't reply, he looked at me.

'I just mean that the sea at least must have looked the same back when you were a kid.'

I shook my head, unable to meet his eye.

'Actually, this is the first time I've seen the sea from Wales, unless you count Cardiff docks, which I don't,' I said, trying to laugh, but it fell flat, my words landing like half-drowned birds unable to lift their wings.

Dan shot me a confused look.

'Pont Nefoedd is a long way from the coast. Too far for a child, even a daring one, to travel by horseback, certainly. And the only other place I lived in Wa—' I stopped, annoyed at how easily my lips were about to betray me. I still didn't know who the hell this man was. The butterflies might trust him, but that didn't mean I had to.

I clenched my jaw against their answering protest and,

too tired to argue, slipped back the bolt in my mind and let them fly. I didn't need their judgement on top of everything.

They surged upwards, their excitement as wild and untamed as the sea herself as they exploded into the air, thousands of wings dancing at the delight, not only of a brand-new day but the thrill of being next to the sea. I could feel their unbridled joy coursing down the bond, and my irritation at them melted away like mist in sunlight.

Beside me, Dan leapt to his feet, his hand rubbing circles over his chest. 'Shit! Did you feel that?' he asked.

My breath caught, and I didn't hurry to answer.

'Feel what?' I asked casually.

'Same thing I felt in the car. Like warm air and a, I dunno, like a tingling.' He spoke slowly, still rubbing at a spot high on his chest. He sounded as if he were already doubting himself.

I pulled a face and shook my head.

Clem let out two short barks. I followed her gaze, and it was clear that she was tracking the butterflies as they swooped and swirled over the shimmering sea.

Dan was watching the same spot now, and for a terrifying moment, I thought that he could see them too. I held my breath.

'Hey, girl, did you see a bird?' he asked Clem, his fingers ruffling her fur.

I let out the breath slowly.

'What's the plan from here, Daniel?' I asked, desperate to change the subject.

It took a few moments for him to drag his eyes from the sky and compose himself.

'Um, in a few hours, I'll head into the village for some supplies. I need to check in with my librarian friend too, so I'll call her from the phone box.'

I opened my mouth, but he held up his hands.

'And no, I won't be mentioning you.'

Strangely, I believed him. Now I saw him in daylight, his eyes were a golden hazel, not too dissimilar to my own. I doubted he was even thirty, but time hadn't abandoned him. His eyes were creased at the edges, and deeply etched lines ran the length of his brow as if he'd spent years thinking hard about the things that really mattered.

When I realised I was staring at his mouth, my eyes lingering on full lips hidden beneath a few days' worth of dark stubble, I hurriedly changed the subject.

'The cottage looks well stocked,' I said quickly.

Dan looked away. 'Yeah. The guy who owns it bought it as a bolt-hole for when the apocalypse hits. He paid me to fix it up for him a few years back, and I think I got the gig because at the time, I was planning on heading back to the States and he didn't want anyone knowing about it.'

'Why did you stay?'

'Nothing to go back for,' he said, his gaze on the horizon now. 'Both my folks are passed and I'm not close with my half-sister, so …' He shrugged, as if it were no big deal.

'I'm sorry about your parents,' I said, meaning it.

The silence stretched, and I filled it.

'It's a wonder he didn't have you killed to protect his secret,' I said with a laugh, trying to lighten the mood.

Dan looked up and smiled at me, his eyes joining in this time. With the butterflies already on the wing, I knew the fluttering in my chest was mine and mine alone. I swallowed hard and looked away.

Dan let out a breath and took a gulp of his coffee before he replied.

'We became friends, so I think I'm off his hit list,' he said, grinning. 'Plus, he has a bunch of kids now, so he's not so keen on the whole apocalypse thing.'

'You trust him?' I asked.

Dan turned serious. 'I do. He's as rich as hell but still dresses like he fell into a thrift store. He's good people, you know? A "my word is my vow" kinda guy. You know the type?'

I did, because Walt had been cut from the same cloth. Honourable to the end. I wondered if Daniel Quinn might be too.

Irritated with myself, I threw the dregs of my coffee onto the ground, then reached for my crutches. After Walt died, I'd vowed to never get that close to someone again. It was a promise I was determined to keep.

CHAPTER 47

DAN, JULY 1976

'Just get it X-rayed first,' I pleaded.

Gwen glared at me like I'd just suggested she run naked through the village on market day.

'I keep telling you – it's healed,' she growled.

'And that's the best news ever, so let's get the X-ray to confirm it! You heard the doc say six to eight weeks. It's barely been three.'

'It'll be four on Friday,' she snapped.

I threw up my hands and flopped down on the sofa beside Clem. Barely seven a.m. and the cottage was already stifling, even with the big window boarded and the side door propped open.

Gwen remained on her crutches, her cheeks hollowing – the way she did when she was fighting not to concede. She looked away, and I saw it then. The doubt. The memory of the doc's warnings of permanent impairment if she pushed it.

I got it. Being cooped up here and dependent on a complete stranger wouldn't be easy for anyone, let alone her.

As for me, I'd sleep on this sofa for the rest of my life if it meant I could breathe the same air as her. She worked tirelessly to keep me firmly at arm's length, but I didn't care. I was in so deep now I had no desire to ever be free again.

I'd take the arguments, the slammed doors and the cold shoulders, just for those moments when she forgot herself and sat next to me on the sofa, too engrossed in her book to notice the proximity. Or the days we'd stand together in the tiny kitchen, cutting vegetables, our arms almost touching.

I hoarded the lists she made, inked in a flowing, copperplate hand that was more art than shopping list, tucking them in the glove box like they were love letters next to something I hoped might put a smile on her face – if I could figure out a way to pull it off.

'Please,' I said, not knowing what else to say.

She shrugged, disappointment and frustration etched across her face. For a heartbeat, I thought she'd relent, but then the metaphorical shutter crashed back into place and she turned away.

I dropped my head, the sigh leaving me like it had just been knocked out of my lungs. Fine. Today was the day, then. I pushed to my feet.

'Look, I need to check in with Maggie, see if she's found anything yet. Wanna come?'

I already knew the answer. Since the attack at Wells, Gwen wasn't keen on going anywhere, not even to the local village.

She shook her head fervently.

'I'll be back this evening then. Can you watch Clem, please? It's too hot in the car for her,' I said, backing towards the kitchen.

'Of course I will!' Gwen scoffed, managing to make my question sound like an insult.

I topped up Clem's water and bent to put the bowl back

on the floor. I heard the clatter of crutches and a muffled huff as Gwen lowered herself onto the sofa. When I picked up my keys from the counter, Clem rushed over, tail wagging.

I knelt and stroked her chest, her silky fur thick under my fingers. 'You stay here, sweet girl. You guard her, okay? Keep her safe till I get back. I won't be long,' I whispered.

Gwen huffed. 'I don't need a babysitter, Daniel.'

That did it. 'Well, she saved your ass once!' I shot back.

I knelt back down and ruffled Clem's ears. 'You're a good girl,' I said, not bothering to whisper this time. Clem gave me her disappointed wag before slumping onto the floor, her head between her paws and her amber eyes on mine.

I knew she'd be safe with Gwen, but I strode out the door before I could change my mind.

The cottage was a silhouette against an inky, moonlit sky when I returned, tyres crawling over the rutted track baked hard as concrete by an unrelenting sun. Maybe I should ask Seren to swap the low-slung Jag for something built for rough terrain. But that would invite questions I wasn't about to answer, such as why I'd ignored her orders about looking for Gwen.

The golden glow from the small front windows felt like beacons, pulling me in. I parked around the side and stood for a moment, just watching the moonlight spilling out over a tranquil sea. My eyes were gritty, and hunger gnawed at my ribs, reminding me that the chips I'd picked up in the village on the way home were likely getting cold.

Clem was overjoyed to see me, of course. That's the beautiful thing about dogs. They just love.

Gwen was sitting on the sofa, her leg, still encased in the

cast she'd been threatening to cut off this morning, propped on the coffee table and a book open in her lap. I thought I saw relief flash across her face, but it was likely my imagination. She said nothing as I fussed Clem, and went back to her book.

'Hi,' I said, holding up the large parcel of hot, newspaper-wrapped chips. 'I brought us supper.'

'I've already eaten,' she said coolly.

'Suit yourself. I'm sure Clem will be happy to have yours,' I replied, unable to keep the irritation out of my voice.

'She's eaten too. Did you honestly think I'd not feed her?'

I ignored the attempt to start yet another fight and took a breath, although I was too tired to force a smile.

'Thanks for feeding her and taking care of her today,' I said, then walked back to the kitchenette.

I heard the book close with a thump.

'I could manage a small plate,' she said as if she were doing me a favour.

I pulled three plates from the cupboard, dished out the take-out and took mine and Clem's to the small table. I set the dog's on the floor, smiling as her butt hit the ground like it was magnetised. She pinned me with a wide-eyed stare, a fine line of drool already hanging from her mouth.

'Okay,' I said.

Clem had finished before I'd even chewed my first mouthful.

I could hear Gwen struggling to her feet, but I made a point of not offering to help this time. She walked to the counter and stopped. I knew she couldn't use her crutches and carry her plate to the table, and I suppose I was being a dick, but I was sick of being treated like a monster when all I'd ever done was try to help. She would just have to eat standing on one leg at the counter.

She sighed and cleared her throat. 'Daniel, would you mind helping me, please?'

'Sure,' I said, getting slowly to my feet. I picked up her plate and cutlery and carried it to the table, then retook my place and continued eating.

Gwen eventually broke the uneasy silence.

'What did Maggie have to say when you saw her?' she asked.

My pulse quickened as I recalled that morning's call. It was our first big break, but I wasn't sure how Gwen would react. I'd have to tell her the news Jackson had shared about Devlin too, and how that might land, I had no idea. But they would both need to wait until I confessed.

'I lied, Gwen. I didn't go to see Maggie today, but I did speak to her on the phone.'

Gwen froze, her fork hovering midway between her plate and mouth. I saw her swallow, the skin on her long, delicate neck bobbing with the movement. She dropped her gaze and lowered her fork slowly to the table.

'It's nothing sinister, I swear. I just—' I let out a breath. This wasn't going to plan. 'It's probably easier if I show you,' I said, pushing back my chair and heading out the front door. I didn't need to turn around to feel her eyes like daggers on my back.

The look on her face when I returned a minute later, cello case in hand, was worth every hour I'd spent sweating over how to retrieve it.

'But how?' she spluttered, her eyes wide as she held out her arms as if I were about to hand her a newborn.

'I found the receipt in your shorts pocket when I did the laundry that first time. Figured I'd try and get it back for you,' I said, feeling awkward.

'How did you ...?' Balancing on her good leg, Gwen didn't

finish the question, distracted by trying to push the dinner plates aside so that I could lay the case on the table. I dumped the plates on the kitchen counter and set down the case.

She opened it with deft fingers, flicking open the fastenings as if she'd done it a thousand times. She let out a soft, breathy sigh as she lifted the lid, and I felt like someone had just turned on a light.

'I went disguised as a delivery guy, but the old fella who kicked me out the first time wasn't there,' I said, running my hand through my hair.

She snorted, glancing up just long enough to raise an eyebrow.

'No, really. The uniform's in the trunk, along with the thick-rimmed glasses and cap,' I said, feeling even more ridiculous. 'I probably didn't even need it. There was a bored-looking kid behind the desk this time, and he just took the receipt and handed it over, no questions asked.'

She laughed then. It was such a tiny sound, small and fragile and fleeting, and yet it felt like a page turned. A wall demolished.

Gwen played for hours, insisting the vibrations would help her leg heal, but to me it looked like it was really her heart she was trying to fix.

I suppose it should have been the music that echoed around my head later. I'm no expert, but even I could tell that she played like she should be on the stage at Madison Square Gardens. It was like the bow was just an extension of her arm, the cello some externalised part of her soul.

If you'd asked me before tonight, I'd have said classical music was one hundred per cent not my thing, but hearing her play made my skin gooseflesh, and while I would never admit it, a few pieces brought me closer to tears than I believed possible.

Later, once Gwen had finally retired to bed and I'd collapsed on the sofa, it wasn't the music I replayed in my mind but the sound of something even more magical – her laugh. As I drifted into sleep, I remembered that I'd not told her about Maggie's breakthrough.

CHAPTER 48

GWEN, JULY 1976

I knew I was alone in the cottage the moment I opened my eyes. Silence was nothing new – I'd learned to revel in it – but today, it felt different. Not peace but absence. The kind that lingers in the air after the last note of a symphony fades into nothingness.

The room was brighter than usual, too. I glanced at the clock to see that it was almost seven a.m. I was so used to the butterflies rousing me before dawn, yet today, they lay still, as if the music last night had lulled them into a drowsy stupor – like newborns warm and heavy with milk.

I pulled on a pair of shorts before getting out of bed – it was easier to do lying down – flung on a T-shirt and then grabbed my crutches. I could probably walk without them. I hadn't been lying yesterday when I told Dan that my ankle felt stronger. It still ached, but the searing pain had only lasted a few days. I knew I was healing faster than was normal, but fear still gnawed at me like a hungry rat. The thought that I'd not be able to run when I needed to made me feel sick to my core. Maybe I'd risk an X-ray just to make sure.

I brushed my hand over my cello case as I hobbled past and smiled, remembering how wonderful it had felt to play again – like being handed a missing piece of my soul.

It was hard not to be touched by Dan's gesture – he'd gone to so much effort for me – and yet … I shook my head as if the movement could dislodge the unhelpful notion brewing there. I couldn't afford to read anything more into it than a nice man doing a kind thing.

I scanned the kitchen counter, but there was no scribbled note telling me he'd gone to the village, which meant he was likely on the beach with Clem. Coffee made, I added a generous splash of cold water and took a satisfying gulp.

The cottage felt stuffy, the heat of the day already building to what I knew would be an almost unbearable crescendo later, turning my cast into an instrument of torture in the process. I knocked back the last of the coffee and picked up my crutches.

A delicious rush of cool, salt-tinged air barrelled into me as I opened the back door, and I sucked in a long, slow breath. I stepped out into a pastel picture of a day, the sun melting into a cloudless powder-blue sky, the seam between it and the sea indistinguishable. Even the sand and cliffs blurred at their edges, as if smudged by an artist's practised thumb.

I stood for a long moment, enjoying the sun on my face and the play of the breeze on my hair, which, I realised, was already past my shoulders. If my bones healed as quickly as my hair grew, then maybe there was still hope left.

I walked the fifty yards to the start of the cliff path and leaned on the rail. Dan and Clem had the beach to them- selves. The smile was on my lips before I could hold it back.

I watched as Dan threw the ball, a powerful overarm that would make any cricketer happy. Clem chased after it, a blur of copper fur against the sand, but she skidded to a stop just before a wave crashed in and claimed the ball. Clem made to go after it, but a flick of her head told me that Dan had called her away. After throwing a last forlorn look towards the surf, she loped back to Dan, her tail held low.

Poor Clem. A memory sparked, and I hurried as fast as my crutches would allow to the side of the cottage, scanning the ground.

I grinned when I spotted the blue rubber ball lying beneath a patch of wilted bracken. After balancing on one leg to retrieve it, I shoved it in my pocket and headed back to the path.

The path down to the beach was wide and gradual enough to double as a slipway, but I'd not attempted it before now. I'd snapped at Dan the first time he'd suggested a walk, and for the last three weeks, I suppose I'd been trying to prove a point, although I had no idea what it might have been.

The soft sand was more work than the path, my crutches sinking a few inches with every step and slowing my progress. Dan was sitting on a rock, Clem leaning into his side, as they both gazed out to sea. The warm breeze brought me snatches of what he was saying to her.

'... get you another ball ...'

'... probably gonna make some dog fishes' day ...'

'... my fault for throwing it so far ...'

'Hello,' I said, suddenly feeling like an intruder.

Clem spun around and galloped over to me, tail wagging, tongue lolling, as if she'd not seen me in days.

I pulled the blue rubber ball from my pocket and wiggled it in the air.

'Would this cheer you up, Clem?' I grinned.

I didn't need a reply; she was already bouncing on the spot, her eyes wide and fixed on the new treasure.

'Gwen. Should you have ...' Dan began.

I tuned him out as I threw the ball up the beach, laughing at the sight of Clem, already running, her head tilted skyward as she went. She leapt into the air and caught the ball even before it hit the ground, then raced back to us, tail like a happy flag.

'Probably not,' I said, answering what I assumed had been the other part of Dan's question. 'But she looked so sad when she lost hers, and—' I shrugged. 'I enjoy seeing her happy'.

'Me too,' Dan said, his eyes on the dog, who was now on her back, the ball caught between her front paws. She released it, caught it in her mouth and then used both paws to pull it out again, holding it aloft as if admiring her new toy.

'How is she even doing that?' I asked, fascinated.

Dan laughed and shook his head.

We watched her play, and I sighed. It was like falling into a dream, the sunlight dancing across the waves, the gentle breeze pulling at my hair as it delivered the promise of faraway lands I'd never see. It felt like time had slowed to a crawl here, and it would be so easy to let myself imagine that it had somehow forgotten me altogether.

'Your ankle up for a walk?' Dan asked.

'Sure,' I said, and Dan fell into step beside me. In my chest, the butterflies stirred, their wings caressing my ribs. I fixed my eyes on the sand and tried hard not to notice that Dan's sun-kissed forearm was just inches from my own.

Clem trotted over and deposited the ball at my feet.

Dan bent down, but the dog was quicker, sweeping in to grab it and then sidestepping him to drop it near my foot.

'Ha! She doesn't trust me not to lose it again,' Dan snorted. 'Hey, I said I was sorry, Clem.'

I laughed as, with an effort, I bent to retrieve the ball. The throw was nothing like Dan's, but Clem seemed happy enough with the game. When she eventually wandered towards the rocks, sniffing, I tried to focus on just enjoying a moment in the sun, but my thoughts betrayed me, drifting into daydreams of what it might be like to have someone in my life. Not just a lover but someone to make a life with.

A piercing yelp propelled me back to the present moment. Dan was already running, arms pumping, legs kicking up sand. Clem stood a hundred yards away, her front paw raised and her head bent as she licked at it. As I hobbled closer, I saw blood on the sand.

Dan slid to a halt on his knees, and my heart pinched as Clem gave a feeble little wag and limped towards him.

'There must be broken glass somewhere,' Dan growled as he examined her paw. I scanned the sand but could see nothing.

'It's okay, girl, I've got you,' he whispered, yanking off his T-shirt in one quick movement and then wrapping it around her bleeding paw.

My eye snagged on the tangle of long, silvered scars on Dan's bronzed back, but then he scooped up the dog and turned.

I stepped in and stroked her face.

'Poor baby,' I whispered. 'Don't worry, I'll bring your ball.'

With the new toy safely in my shorts pocket, I followed Dan as he carried Clem back up the path to the cottage, her head resting on his shoulder.

I tried to focus on negotiating the path on my crutches, which would have been a challenge even without the distraction of Dan's bare back and all the questions it raised in my mind.

Back at the cottage, he lowered Clem to the sofa and grabbed the first aid kit. I sat next to her, and she wriggled towards me and laid her head on my knee. Dan cleaned and dressed the wound before bandaging her paw and leg with swift, practised fingers. It was only then that I saw the scars encircling his wrists. I'd spent so long trying not to look at the man for fear of what it did to my blood pressure, but I had missed so much.

'You look like a pro,' I said as I stroked Clem's head. 'Where did you learn to do that?'

A shadow fell over his face, and he kept his eyes on Clem as he replied.

'Nam.'

I opened my mouth, but closed it again, the pieces of the puzzle slowly drifting into place.

'It doesn't look deep enough to need stitching, but if it bleeds again, I'll take her to the vet in the city,' he said, planting a kiss on her nose before getting to his feet.

My breath hitched at the sight of his hard, flat stomach, the fine line of dark hair arrowing down below the waistband of his shorts. I lifted my chin, allowing my gaze to slide up his chest, past the dark stubble shadowing his jaw. But when I finally met his eyes, it was all too much to bear.

The butterflies flew into a frenzy of pure, unfiltered lust, their wings raking across my ribs like caged animals begging for release. I knew they were only responding to my own desire, but it was still unsettling.

Dan mumbled something and hurried out of the side door. I collapsed back on the sofa, flinging back the mental bolt to release the butterflies as I went. Maybe I'd get some peace from my own racing pulse if they were free.

They exploded like a bomb, and I had to grab Clem's collar to stop her jumping up.

'Try and ignore them,' I whispered as I stroked her back.

When Dan reappeared, he was wearing one of the T-shirts I'd spotted on the washing line. He stopped in the doorway and frowned, his hand rubbing at that spot on his chest again as he scanned the room. I was pretty sure he couldn't see what I could or else he'd surely be screaming, but there was no doubting that he sensed them.

'Coffee?' I asked, struggling to my feet.

'Sure.' He was still frowning and looking anywhere but at me.

I shuffled over to the kitchenette and grabbed the kettle with fingers that no longer felt connected to my brain. I caught it just before it slipped out of my hands, but when I fumbled for the tap, I shrieked as the old pipes coughed out a blast of icy water that soaked my vest top and face.

When I looked up, Dan was surrounded by butterflies, his hand clamped over his mouth. I laughed, and he let his hand fall as he joined me, rocking back on his heels, his laughter rolling around the room like music.

I felt something catch in my chest as if he too were now inexplicably tethered to me.

CHAPTER 49

DAN, JULY 1976

'She shouldn't be much longer,' I said to Clem as I checked my watch for what had to be the tenth time. I saw the end of her tail flick at the sound of my voice, but she went back to her snooze, lying underneath the bench outside Singleton Hospital.

Gwen had suggested the X-ray. Right after the wet T-shirt incident, she'd just come out with it. I replayed the events of the morning over and over. Gwen sitting on the coach. Her eyes sweeping up to look at my face as if it were the first time she was really seeing me, and the way all the air seemed to get sucked out of the room.

The sight of her standing at the sink, water dripping from her nose and chin, her T-shirt soaked. The sound of our laughter rolling around together like it was something we did every single day. Our eyes locked for the briefest of moments, and it felt like my entire world cracked open.

'I think I should get that X-ray, today.' She'd blurted out the words, her arms folded across her chest and her eyes on the sink.

I don't even remember what I said in reply. I think I probably just nodded. And now, here we were. Thankfully, the village GP was used to holidaymakers, and I guessed Gwen was used to telling people what they needed to hear. I checked my watch again.

'Hello.'

I jumped to my feet at the sound of her voice. She still had her crutches propped under each arm, but her cast was gone, her bare foot dangling above the ground.

'I didn't think to bring the other shoe,' she said with an awkward laugh.

When I looked at her face, she looked so much younger than before. Softer, somehow.

'I still need these until my muscles remember what they're meant to be doing,' she said, indicating the crutches, 'but the X-ray showed no sign of a break. The radiographer suggested I make a complaint about wrongful diagnosis ...' She trailed off as she rolled her eyes, but she was still smiling, her eyes dancing in the sunshine.

'Wow,' was all I could think of to say, my mind too captivated by that soft, easy smile I'd never seen before.

We drove back to the cottage with the radio playing and the windows open. Gwen had her elbow propped on the sill, her dark hair whipping around her face. She'd worn it cropped short when I first met her, but just a month later, it was already tumbling past her shoulders.

I wondered if fast-growing hair and healing fractures were normal for witches, but I didn't want to ruin the moment by asking. I ran my hand through my own, trying to remember the last time I'd been to the barber's, come to think of it.

I still needed to tell Gwen about Maggie's discovery and Jackson's news. I told myself that what with the cello reunion, Clem's paw and now the trip to the hospital, there hadn't been an opportunity, but that wasn't the whole truth.

Once I told her, everything would change, and I wasn't ready to lose this – whatever the hell this even was. Not yet.

I stole a glance at her and felt my heart twist at the contented smile pulling at her lips. I tried to capture the image in my memory as if one day, this might be all I had of her. The thought landed like a punch, and I cleared my throat.

'You okay?' she asked.

I kept my eyes on the road.

'Yep,' I said, forcing a smile. I couldn't keep this from her any longer. She had a right to know.

'I need to tell you what Maggie found,' I said carefully.

When Gwen didn't reply, I turned. She had her elbow propped on the sill again, but this time, I couldn't see her face.

'I said—' I began again, raising my voice a little.

'I heard you,' she said softly. 'Let's just wait until we get—' She halted. 'Until we get back to the cottage.'

'Sure,' I said.

She turned up the radio, and we coasted back through narrow country lanes as Lindsey Buckingham sang about a love that had finally found him.

After the relative cool of the car, the cottage felt like an oven, but I didn't care. It just felt good to be back here with Gwen. I'd carried Clem from the car, even though she was more than capable of walking on three legs. Once inside, she'd taken a long drink and slumped down on the cool flagstone floor.

'Lunch first?' Gwen offered, leaning her crutches against the kitchen counter.

'Great,' I said, hurrying over to pull things at random from the refrigerator.

I sliced up tomatoes and chopped a cucumber while she buttered bread, the silence between us as taut as one of her cello strings. Sandwiches made, I picked up both plates, but she put a hand lightly on my arm before taking one from me.

I hovered, just in case, but casting a dismissive look at her crutches, she took a tentative step, her lip caught beneath her teeth. I studied her expression as apprehension, determination and, finally, relief flashed in quick succession across her face. She broke into a wide grin, her eyes finding mine.

I grinned back and gave a cringeworthy double thumbs up as she took two more steps before flopping down into the chair.

A few minutes later, my plate empty and Gwen's sandwich half eaten, I decided that I couldn't delay the moment any longer.

'Maggie's found evidence suggesting that Devlin has recently acquired two incredibly valuable arcane spells. One for claiming magic and one for—' I sighed and took a deep breath before continuing. 'And one for taking it,' I said, unable to use its given name.

Gwen stopped chewing, then swallowed with an effort.

'What about releasing magic?'

I shrugged. 'We can only assume he has that too, but there's no concrete evidence.'

Gwen muttered a curse under her breath, her shoulders falling as she slumped back in her chair.

'But that doesn't mean he doesn't have it,' I said quickly. 'It stands to reason that if he has the original, he'll likely have the release spell too.'

She nodded, her eyes on the table, her gaze unfocused. From her expression, she was far from convinced.

'There's more,' I said grimly. 'The Unit has evidence of Devlin using magic himself, which means—'

Gwen snapped her head up, her eyes wide as she tipped forward in her chair, bracing her hands on the table as if she'd just been winded. I felt a rush of warm air sweep past me and rubbed at my tattoo as it pulsed.

Catching her breath, Gwen sat back in her chair, her eyes on the ceiling for a long moment. When she looked at me, her words drifted, light as feathers, from her lips as if she feared giving them weight might make the truth of them more real.

'He's already used the spell to take magic from others, hasn't he?'

I nodded but couldn't meet Gwen's gaze. I wasn't about to tell her that Jackson's team was busy trying to ID multiple victims through dental records after Devlin used his new ripping spell on them. My friend's voice echoed in my memory. 'Man, he leaves people looking like shredded trash bags after the coyotes have come calling.'

'If he finds me …' Gwen's voice still sounded like it was coming from somewhere far away, but the fear in it twisted in my heart.

I pushed myself out of my chair and knelt beside her. I knew I was close to crossing a line, but I'd soon know it if I had.

'We can't let him take them.' Her voice was still a whisper, but there was an edge of steel to it now that felt reassuring. She'd never talked about 'them' before, but I figured now was not the time to ask.

I touched her hand and kept my eyes trained on hers.

'He's not getting your magic, Gwen,' I said, curling my fingers around hers and squeezing gently.

'It's not mine!' she snapped, snatching her hand free. 'I don't have magic!'

'I know. I know,' I said, holding up my hands and backing off. 'We're going to get the release spell. Then nobody, not Devlin, not anyone, can ever hunt you again. Okay?'

She nodded tightly, her cheeks sucked in and her jaw set. A flicker of something – fear, fury – flashed across her beautiful eyes before vanishing behind the cold, unreadable mask I'd come to know so well. She straightened, putting a few more inches between us, and I suddenly felt like a creep, intruding on her space. I scrambled to my feet and retook my seat.

'Do you have a plan?' she asked coolly.

'Yeah, but we need help. So, plan A is asking Seren and the Council of Elders for help. Plan B is asking Jackson,' I said, bracing for her reaction. I didn't mention that I didn't like our chances with either.

CHAPTER 50

DAN, JULY 1976

I hadn't figured Seren to be the dramatic type, so it was a surprise when she chose Highgate Cemetery for our meeting. It had already been a long day. I left Wales before dawn, driving first to Clapham to drop Clem at Precious and Charlie's place.

Seeing Clem's nose pressed against the front window of the little terrace felt like a knife in my heart. They'd take good care of her – hell, they'd spoil her rotten – but how did she know I wasn't just abandoning her like her first family?

I'd talked to her practically the entire drive – telling her of our plan and how, when it all worked out, I'd be back to pick her up. How we'd celebrate with a trip to Pont Nefoedd, long hikes in the mountains and sandwiches from the bakery. I'd made it sound like a fairy tale with a guaranteed happy ever after, but even with magical help, I didn't like the odds, and even Clem had looked sceptical.

London felt like an assault to the senses after the peace of the Gower. Tempers frayed in the heat, horns blared, and more than one driver shot murderous glances my way when they noted the closed windows of the air-conditioned Jag.

I was a half hour early, but as I approached the imposing stone archway that marked the entrance to Egyptian Avenue in Highgate's west cemetery, Seren was already waiting by the heavy iron gates. She wore a long black sundress, her shoulders and forearms alabaster white against the dark fabric, her face partially obscured behind enormous sunglasses. Despite the heat, her long dark curls tumbled down her back, and I wondered how many artists might have begged to paint her.

She greeted me with a curt nod and strode away before I reached her. I jogged to catch up, taking in the high stone vaults on either side of the narrow, winding path. My feet against the gravel felt unnaturally loud. In the distance, a crow cawed. I felt the hairs on my arms lift a second before the tattoo on my chest prickled and the air thickened around me, muffling the sound of the bird and my footsteps.

'What progress have you made?' Seren asked without preamble.

I took a breath.

'I know that Devlin now has the power to take and then use magic.'

Seren kept walking, but I let the silence stretch.

'Would you like to tell me something I don't already know, Daniel?'

'I'm confident that the evidence we need to bring him down is kept at his country house in Berkshire. And I need you, or someone with magic, to help me retrieve it.'

I didn't see her move. I didn't even see her turn, but Seren was suddenly standing in front of me, her sunglasses pushed up into her curls. She looked older, somehow. Weary, even. I leaned back as something close to anger flashed across her eyes.

'Your job, Daniel, is to find legitimate evidence against

him. Anything you steal from him would be inadmissible in court.' She spoke slowly, as if I were a slow child.

'I thought you had your own justice system in the' – I lowered my voice – 'magical community.'

'There *is* only one British justice system,' she said icily.

I frowned, genuinely confused.

'Did you expect some kangaroo court with executioners?' Seren snorted.

I shrugged. Maybe I had.

'But how do you keep magic a secret then?'

Seren turned and continued walking. 'Magical cases are just dealt with by members of the judiciary from within the community,' she said flatly.

'Oh, come on. There must be exceptions. If this guy gets his hands on' – I stopped myself just in time, clearing my throat of an imaginary frog – 'too much magic, then he's an unprecedented danger, isn't he?'

Seren spun around to face me. 'Of course he is. But what you don't understand, Daniel, is that the magical and non-magical worlds exist on a knife edge, and right now, we're teetering close to all-out conflict.'

I reeled back. 'What? But why?'

She sighed. 'Maybe some context will help you understand,' she said, walking again. 'Until 1939, we had a strange but functional relationship with the British government. We refused to confirm or deny the existence of magic, and they pretended not to care so long as we kept out of their way.

'Then, with Hitler threatening all that was good and decent in the world, we put our differences aside and signed an historic agreement of cooperation. Our role was to use magic to help bring a swift end to the war with minimal casualties. That's what we believed, anyway, but it wasn't long before the government betrayed us, and good people died.'

'How?' I asked.

'That's a story I don't have time to explain, but there are members of the magical community who will never forget what they did to us. Some influential figures see the likes of Devlin, disgusting as he is, as the means by which we can take our revenge on an establishment that's persecuted our kind for centuries.'

'You're kidding, right?' I asked, stunned.

'I wish. But they're not our only problem. Outside of the community, there are still those who believe people like me shouldn't exist. Thanks to the 1939 agreement and the much-hated "Unit for Magical Affairs", our community isn't quite the Whitehall secret it once was. They quote from Exodus and hide behind their weak-chinned clergy as they petition the government for interventions to' – she mimed quotes in the air – 'deal with us. In the last few years alone, we've seen recommendations ranging from re-education programmes to containment operations, forced sterilisations and the resettlement of all magical people to secure camps for testing.'

I stopped in my tracks.

'What the f—' I shook my head, the word dying on my lips. 'Maggie didn't mention any of this.'

Seren shrugged. 'Maggie wouldn't know. The Council of Elders works hard to keep this from the wider community, but we're struggling to contain the rumours. I'm telling you this, Daniel, because I need you to help put Devlin behind bars before his cronies turn him into some sort of cult leader they can use to ignite an all-out war between magical and non-magical people.'

'But that's why I need to—'

Seren held up her hand, cutting me off.

'You'll need to find another way,' she said, shaking her

head. 'If we mess this up, it'll just embolden him and his supporters, and then he'll be untouchable.'

I dropped my chin to my chest as the fight left me. I scuffed at a loose rock on the ground and watched the dust eddy into the air. I'd seen enough of war to last me several lifetimes. I didn't want to think what a magical one might look like, especially one led by a maniac capable of ripping magic from people and wielding it himself.

'Any ideas what that other way might look like?' I said, my eyes still on the ground.

When I looked up, I was alone amongst the vaults.

CHAPTER 51

GWEN, AUGUST 1976

July melted seamlessly into August, the heat cruel and unrelenting. The news, when I bothered to switch on the radio, was dominated by the drought and, bizarrely, predictions of a harsh winter to come. It felt like an omen. A proclamation that our plan, such as it was, would never work.

'We've got a couple hours before we get there,' Dan said from the driver's seat. 'Get some sleep if you want.'

'I'm fine,' I said, my eyes on the lights of the hospital as we sped past on the almost deserted pre-dawn coastal road.

My thoughts drifted back to the day of the X-ray. I'd planned to run the moment the cast came off. I'd taken my satchel and had even persuaded Dan to bring Clementine along for the ride, so he'd have to wait outside the hospital with her.

The exquisite relief of cool air on my itchy, suffocating skin as the cast came off and the simple joy of feeling both feet flat on the floor had been short-lived.

As I asked the radiographer how to avoid the main exit where Dan and Clem sat waiting for me, the butterflies had rebelled, pounding furious, sandpaper wings against my ribs.

I'd ignored them, propelling myself down the corridor on my crutches as the meadow brown thrashed about in front of my face, passing straight through my palm each time I paused and tried to swat her away.

It was only when a nurse stopped to ask if I was okay that I realised I was sobbing. Every instinct I had told me to go back to Dan, and yet I knew with a certainty that I couldn't explain that if I did, my abnormally long life would finally end. I knew he would do anything to protect me, but he couldn't protect me from time.

I'd sat in the corridor and allowed myself to slide into self-pity. I didn't want to die, and yet I'd already taken so much more than I was due. I let the tears fall, and when the butterflies, gentle now that their message had been received and understood, pulled at the tether, I released them.

I expected them to flee as far as the spell would allow them, but they stayed close, cocooning me in soft, bright wings that felt like sun-warmed silk against my skin and made me wonder if this was what it was like to tumble into a kaleidoscope.

The stale food and disinfectant stench of the hospital vanished, and between my sobs, I caught the scent of summer flowers carried on a mountain breeze and the unmistakable smell of a coal-black horse as I pressed my nose to his warm, velvety muzzle.

I heard the distant echo of my cello, Nain calling me to supper and Walt laughing uproariously between puffs on his pipe. But it was the memory of Dan's voice that lingered. I'd laughed out loud when, after rummaging in my satchel for my other shoe, I realised I'd left it back in the cottage.

I stole a glance at him now as he drove, and the butterflies stirred as they always did when I allowed myself to look at him. Did he think I'd run that day? Or maybe he knew me better than I knew myself. I'd likely never know.

It hadn't been a surprise that the witch, Seren, had refused to help him. Maybe if she'd known about me, the answer would have been yes, but we'd agreed that it was too much of a risk, especially now, with the leaders of the magical community at loggerheads with the government. We were on our own.

There had never been a 'we' before. Not even with dear Walt. A bubble of sadness caught in my throat, and I reached for the water bottle in the footwell.

Was I betraying all he'd done for me? His letter had been unequivocal – don't trust the Unit – but it was only a matter of time before Devlin found me, and when he did, the magic I'd protected all these years would be his. I dreaded to think what he'd do with such immense power.

Dan trusted his friend Jackson and, while it still amazed me to admit it, even to myself, I trusted Dan. We had precious few options to begin with, and so here we were, travelling to a meeting with the man himself so that I – or more precisely, the butterflies – could decide for ourselves.

I leaned my head against the glass and closed my eyes. The next thing I knew, Dan was speaking to me.

'Hey, nearly there,' he said, touching his hand briefly to my shoulder.

I jerked awake, squinting at the bright sunlight.

'You sure about this?' he asked as the sign for the Little Chef diner came into view up ahead.

I wasn't, but I said yes anyway.

Moments later, we pulled into the car park, circling around the single-storey restaurant before choosing a space as close to the exit as possible.

'You're sure he's not expecting me?' I asked, scanning the car park.

'I'm sure,' Dan replied. 'I've not told him yet about finding you, so he's in the dark. But look, if anything feels off, if you don't trust him, then give me the signal and we'll get the hell out of Dodge, okay?'

A tap on the driver's window made us both jump, and the moment was lost. A tall, slim man with close-cropped Afro hair peered in at us. I had just a second to notice his surprise before he straightened up and stepped back.

Dan put his hand on the door-handle and raised his eyebrows at me.

'Let's just do this,' I said, already pushing open the passenger door.

Jackson dressed like he was worried someone might still bring him up on a charge for leaving a crease in his T-shirt, but his smile was genuine, and his handshake firm and warm.

I'd already decided not to release the butterflies just in case Jackson was able to see them; they could make their judgement well enough from where they were.

They fizzed about in my chest, excited by the stranger standing before us. But there was something else too. I frowned, trying to put a better name to the other feeling rippling down the bond.

As Jackson and Dan stepped into a back-patting welcome, the word I was searching for drifted into my mind. Recognition. Jackson was a stranger, but the butterflies recognised his magic. When the meadow brown appeared and settled on his forehead, I knew I had my answer.

We chose a booth at the back of the restaurant with a clear view of the entrance and the doors to both the toilets and the kitchen. I excused myself to use the bathroom while Dan and Jackson took their seats and ordered drinks from a uniformed waitress.

The toilets were off a long corridor with a fire door at the end, propped open with empty crates, presumably to help the smell of burnt oil escape from the kitchen across the corridor.

When I got back, Dan and Jackson were speaking in hushed tones, but they were clearly arguing, their heads bent together over the table so that they were just inches apart. They stopped talking when they saw me and sat back.

'So much for looking inconspicuous, gentlemen,' I said coolly. 'Do you mind filling me in?'

Jackson sat back against the bench and threw up his hands, his expression anxious.

'You shouldn't have come, Gwen,' he said gravely. 'What they'd do to you if they found you …' His face collapsed into a grimace.

I slid into the seat and shrugged.

'I don't mean to be rude, Gwen – in other circumstances it would be great to meet you – but I'm worried for you. Why did you even come?'

'I needed to see if I could trust you,' I said, looking him in the eye.

'I'm not sure I can say or do anything to prove that to you in the time we have,' he said.

I held his gaze. How long had it been since I'd allowed myself to sense magic? It had been a comfort once, a consolation prize for a wannabe witch with no magic of her own, but, I realised, I'd abandoned that along with my hope. Studying Jackson, I felt his magic like the buzzing of bees in the air around him. Focused and industrious, like every part of him was working towards the same goal.

When Dan turned to me, eyebrows raised in question, I nodded.

'We need your help to get into Devlin's country estate.'

Jackson groaned as he cupped his head in his hands.

'Please don't ask me to do this,' he said, looking up at Dan. 'You know I'd give you my life in a heartbeat, but Devlin's already too powerful. We need to wait for the Elders and the Unit to figure something out.'

'But I thought they were at each other's throats?' I put in.

'Oh, they are. I've never seen it this bad, but officially at least, they agree on the need to bring down Devlin,' Jackson said.

'What do you mean, "officially"?' I asked.

Jackson sighed. 'There are factions in both camps, but look, Gwen, he's not the only one looking for you,' he said, sliding a manila folder towards me.

It wasn't a surprise to see Rhys's pencil drawing of me when I flipped open the cover, but the next page stopped me in my tracks. It was the intelligence report Walt had stolen from the archive during the war.

My pulse pounded in my ears as I turned the pages. Pictures of Pendarrow House in Tintagel, complete with grainy images of me in the grounds. So, it hadn't been Devlin that time but the Unit. I was already struggling to take a full breath, but it stopped altogether when I turned the next page and saw Walt's photograph staring back at me. I didn't need to read the rest to know that it was all over. As I'd feared, I had nowhere left to hide.

Jackson's tone was apologetic. 'They didn't make the connection until a few weeks ago. Middleton did a brilliant job of covering his – your – tracks, but it's all there. The houses, the ghost-writing arrangement. I'm sorry, Gwen.'

I sat for a long moment, just staring at Walt's picture. Without warning, the butterflies surged upwards, straining at the tether, their blind panic arrowing down the bond like a shot of lightning.

Dan put his hand on my shoulder, but I shrugged free and bolted for the toilets. He called after me, and I heard Jackson curse, but I kept going. I felt the air shift behind me, like an insistent wave at my back, pushing me onwards and through the double doors into the corridor.

The dappled sunshine of the rear car park beckoned at the end of the corridor, but just as I broke into a run, I heard heavy boots, their steps too many and too regimented to be civilians', crunching over gravel. I flung myself into the kitchen and crouched behind the propped door, holding my breath as the footsteps, echoing off the walls like ricocheting bullets, jogged past. The kitchen staff raced after the operatives, hurling half-formed questions at their backs.

I stood up, curling my fingers around the door, ready to duck back out of sight. I heard someone scream from the restaurant and the unmistakable sound of crockery shattering on the floor.

'Police. I need everyone to stay calm, please.' The man's voice was deep and commanding as he addressed the room.

I took my cue and bolted for the exit but stopped short when I saw the back of a young man in black fatigues standing between me and the car park beyond. I turned left and hid behind one of the huge industrial bins, filled to the brim with black bags. I clamped my hand over my nose and mouth as the smell of rotting food, sweating in plastic, almost made me gag.

The restaurant was an island in the middle of a car park, sandwiched between the motorway and a busy A-road. There was no point trying to get to the car – they'd see me in an instant – and both left and right just led to more open car park. I eyed the steep, grassy bank directly behind the building; it was fifty yards away and there was no way of covering the ground without the guard spotting me.

The butterflies begged for release, but I shut them out. I needed every ounce of my focus if I was going to get out of here. Just then, a squeal of air brakes pierced the fetid air, and a bin lorry rolled past, coming to an abrupt halt when the guard stepped in front of it with his hand up.

I crept from behind the bin, my eyes fixed on the officer, who was shielding his eyes against the sun as he craned his neck to speak to the driver. From the snatches of conversation, neither was happy.

'… don't give a monkey's, son …'

'… ask you again to leave the vicinity while …'

I darted behind the lorry and crouched down, scanning the scene as I tried not to breathe in the choking exhaust fumes.

When I heard the driver's door screech open on complaining hinges, I sprinted for the bank, clambering up into the trees, only to smack my face into a hard wire fence at the top. I winced, but my hands and feet were already in motion, propelling me up and over the top. As I landed on the other side, my ankle gave way beneath me and I toppled down the steep bank towards the motorway, desperately grabbing at the scrub to slow myself down before momentum put me under the wheels of a car.

I stopped just before the white line, my heart jack-hammering in my chest. Up ahead, an old Morris Minor swerved onto the hard shoulder, and a thick-set elderly woman in a sundress and headscarf leapt out of the driver's seat and hurried over.

'Good god, girl. Are you okay?' she asked, peering at me.

I wasn't sure I was, but I mumbled something about being fine.

'Come on,' she said, putting a hand on my arm. 'Let's get you in the car.'

I hesitated, scanning the vast expanse of open fields around us, before climbing into the passenger seat. Behind me, a wagging West Highland terrier woofed a greeting.

My rescuer, Bernie, chain-smoking and tapping her ash

out of the car window, chatted amiably about the dog and her job as the headmistress of a girls' school in Kent. I tried to listen, but her words slid around me as I attempted to process what the hell had just happened.

I couldn't make myself believe that Jackson had set us up. He hadn't even known I'd be with Dan today; besides, the butterflies were never wrong about people.

Bernie was still talking, seemingly oblivious to my lack of responses, but then I heard a word that made my heart lift.

'Sorry, did you say Mumbles? As in the Gower?'

'Yes, dear. My sister has a caravan there. Murray and I are staying the week.'

I almost cried with relief. What were the chances? Had the butterflies not settled like lambs as soon as we were in the car, I might have doubted my luck, but maybe the Goddess hadn't abandoned me after all. She'd put Walt on my path and now Dan. Was this kindly teacher another gift? Or a bone thrown to a starving, already condemned dog by an indifferent owner?

When Bernie asked me how I'd come to be on a busy motorway, I told her I was running from a boyfriend who beat me. The story felt like a battered old book, the pages dog-eared and greasy from too many tellings, but it said something about the world that nobody ever questioned it. This time, though, the lie felt like a betrayal of the man risking his own life to help me. The man I'd just abandoned to his fate.

CHAPTER 52

DAN, AUGUST 1976

$\mathcal{I}$ called after her, but Gwen didn't turn. When I made to stand, Jackson grabbed my arm, his grip urgent. 'Trust her,' he said.

I froze, half standing in the booth, my eyes locked on the still-swinging doors she'd just disappeared through. A second later, we both turned as a line of blacked-out vans rolled into the car park.

'Shit!' Jackson cursed. 'This isn't me, okay?' he said through gritted teeth.

Before I had time to reply, I felt my tattoo nettle just as the pressure shifted around us.

'Quinn!'

When I glanced at Jackson, he looked meaningfully at the table. I followed his gaze, expecting the file to have vanished, but the only thing missing was Gwen's coffee.

I nodded my understanding as behind me, someone shrieked. I turned to see a slack-jawed waiter drop a stack of plates at the sight of a half dozen operatives bursting in through the front door. A woman in the next booth pointed to the toilet doors, and my mouth went dry as I saw another half dozen run in from the back.

'Police. I need everyone to stay calm, please.' A short man in a navy suit marched into the diner, waving his warrant card like a shield.

Jackson strode towards him, hands on hips and an expression of cold, hard fury etched into his face. I jumped up and stood behind my friend.

The man with the badge stopped short. His slicked-back hair and dated navy suit made him look like he'd escaped from a fifties cop show. The old guard, solving one last case before he retired to his cabin in the woods.

'You've got five seconds to explain yourself, Perkins,' Jackson said, slowly turning his wrist to look at his watch.

Perkins looked me up and down before flicking his attention to Jackson.

'Just thought we'd pop in and see if you needed any back-up, mate,' he said, his accent pure East London.

'And why the fuck would I need back-up?' Jackson growled, closing the gap between them with one long stride so he could glare down at the shorter man.

Perkins snorted but took a step back. 'Alright. No need to loom. You seem a bit on edge, Goose. You worried about something?'

It was my turn to snort. Was that the best nickname they could think of for the Canadian in their midst?

Jackson didn't rise to the bait.

'Here she is, sir,' said the operative, pointing to the waitress who had served us. The young woman looked furious rather than intimidated, and the sight cheered me.

Perkins marched back to the booth we'd just vacated.

'How many people did you serve at this booth?' he asked, jabbing a thick finger at the table.

The waitress rolled her eyes and huffed loudly. When she

spoke, it was in the sort of tone reserved for people who were hard of hearing.

'I'll say it again, shall I? These two,' she said, pointing first at me and then Jackson but not taking her eyes off Perkins. 'You check me bloody book,' she added, pulling it out of her apron, flipping furiously through the pages and then thrusting it at Perkins with such force he had to take a step back.

'See? Right there, sweetheart. Two orders. Table twelve. He had a cuppa tea' – she pointed to Jackson – 'and that fella,' she said, pointing a painted nail at me, 'had a coffee. They needed longer to decide on food.'

Perkins pursed his lips.

'And you lot don't look like any coppers I've ever seen,' she said, bracing her hands on her hips.

Perkins ignored her. 'Question the others,' he snapped at the operative.

'We already have, sir,' the man replied.

'Well do it again,' Perkins snapped, lowering himself into the booth. He motioned for me and Jackson to join him. We stayed standing.

'Suit yourself.' After a long beat, he looked up at Jackson. 'Look. I'm sorry, mate,' he said. 'I knew you two went back a bit so—' He shrugged.

'So what?' Jackson snarled, leaning over Perkins. 'Were you hoping to find me and Dan sitting here with the target getting wads of cash in brown envelopes while this fictional fucking tooth fairy character danced around sprinkling pixie dust over us?'

'Nah, nothing like that. I just thought you might need ...' Perkins trailed off, his hands making nondescript circles in the air.

Jackson shook his head but slid into the booth. All I wanted to do was go after Gwen and get her as far away from here as possible, but if I was going to keep her safe, I had no choice but to play along.

'I don't need to explain myself to you, Perkins, but just so we're clear, I asked Quinn to meet me so I could share the new intel on the target's favourite obsession and see what progress, if any, he'd made.' Jackson tapped the top of the file.

'Have you found her?' Perkins turned to me, his eyes hard and appraising.

I leaned back in the booth and shook my head slowly as I lied through my teeth. 'Until I saw that' – I pointed to the file – 'I wasn't sure if she even existed. Even now, all we have is surveillance images and a theory; there's no actual proof.'

Perkins's gaze drifted to the window, his head nodding almost imperceptibly as I spoke.

I pushed harder. 'If you ask me, the girl's a distraction. Word on the street is that things are about to get ugly between the communities. If that's true, then taking down Devlin needs to be the priority.'

'How'd you get the chief to sign off on this?' Jackson asked.

Perkins tried to hide his expression with a smirk, but he was too slow.

Jackson gave him one of his famous thousand-watt smiles as he leaned across the table.

'Man! I wouldn't want to be in your shoes when he finds out about this. Blowing the budget to go checking up on a fellow officer? You must really want to beat me to that promotion, huh?'

The smirk fell from the other man's face, and he slid out of the booth without responding.

Jackson and I followed. The diner was almost empty now, save for the operatives and the gaggle of staff huddled near the register.

Jackson paused as he drew level with Perkins and dropped his voice to a whisper.

'He won't hear it from me, but you go behind my back again and I'll end your career. Are we clear?'

The other man nodded but didn't meet Jackson's eye.

We strode out of the diner, Jackson pausing only to place a fistful of notes on the counter and apologise to the staff for the interruption. It was all I could do not to sprint to the car.

CHAPTER 53

GWEN, AUGUST 1976

I took the bus to Llangennith, my bare legs sticking to the hot plastic seat as it trundled through narrow country lanes, the driver muttering under his breath about the number of tourists on the road.

Bernie had offered to drive me to my fictional family, but I'd lied and said I'd call them from Mumbles. I should be used to lying by now, but it still went against the grain.

I walked the last few miles, footsore, thirsty and praying with every step that Dan would be at the cottage waiting for me. He wasn't.

There was a risk that the Unit might be lying in wait there instead, but when I reached down the bond to the butterflies, I felt nothing but a weary calm tinged with a weighted sadness.

The cottage was just as we had left it that morning. Two coffee mugs and the plate Dan had used for his toast sat on the countertop. I ran my fingers over the edge of the plate as I waited for the water to run cold from the tap. Tears welled in my eyes at the thought of what the Unit might have done to him. Were they above torture?

I thought of Walt, weeping in his study all those years ago, so no, anything was possible. I shoved the thought away as I downed the first glass of water and refilled it.

I pulled open the windows, leaving the shutters in place to hold back the sun, but the small space was still unbearably hot. I headed for the tiny bathroom, suddenly desperate to wash away the worst of the day. I stripped off my clothes and stood waiting for the warm water.

The sight of my reflection in the mirror took me by surprise. I knew my hair had grown – I was forever tying it up now – but I'd not realised how my skin had tanned in the sun. I even had a dusting of freckles across my nose and cheeks. I held out my arms. They too were a light golden brown when I compared them to my creamy-white ankle and shin. It was hard to believe that my skin had changed that much in just a month, but I couldn't argue with the evidence.

I washed my hair twice, not because it needed it but because when Dan had climbed into the car this morning, his hair was still damp from the shower and the appley scent of the shampoo we shared.

I sat in the garden with a book until the sun went down. I must have read the same chapter a dozen times, and I still didn't know what it was about. I jumped up twice imagining the sound of car tyres but slunk back to my seat disappointed both times.

Later, sitting at the table, the crusts of a half-eaten sandwich curling on the plate in front of me, I tried to think about my next steps. I couldn't use the houses, but I had money and identity documents in safe deposit boxes around the country, plus cars bought for cash that couldn't be traced back to Walt.

I pushed the plate away. I wouldn't be going anywhere without Dan. A wave of exhaustion broke over me, and I slumped down onto the old sofa. Dan's pillow sat on top of his neatly folded bedsheet on the armchair. I grabbed the pillow, hugging it to my chest and burying my face in the soft cotton as I lay down.

In my dream, I'm standing on the clifftop overlooking the beach. The sky is flushed with the pink kiss of dawn, but I am crying because I know I will not live long enough to see the sunrise. I know I'm dreaming, but I can't wake myself up.

The wind is strong, whipping tendrils of my hair skyward and sending the fabric of my long white nightdress billowing. I should be freezing, I realise, but I'm not. I'm nothing. Nothing but sadness, grief and regret.

I see the cottage in the distance, and Dan running towards me, calling my name frantically. I already know he won't reach me before it happens. Time has found me. The Goddess is calling in my debt.

The wind coils around me, stealing my breath. I glance down at my hands and see not my own flesh but the beating wings of thousands of iridescent butterflies.

I woke with a gasp, dimly aware that Dan's pillow was damp with tears. The thoughts landed in my mind like depth charges. There would never be a home or a family of my own. No new horses to love or faraway places to visit when this was all over.

Not every story has a happy ending, child. Nain's voice echoed so clearly around the room I sat up, expecting to see her. But there was only the sigh of the waves – and the crunch of tyres.

I rocketed from the sofa, flinging open the front door and not bothering to grab my shoes. If the hunters had come for me, they'd have to kill me right there and then, but it was Dan's car emerging from the trees. I kept running, arms pumping, tears streaming down my cheeks. The car jerked to a stop, and he leapt out of the driver's seat. He had barely taken a step before I jumped, wrapping my arms and legs around him and sending us both careering back into the side of the car. I raked my hands through his hair, kissing his face as he stroked my back and whispered, 'Hey, hey. It's okay, we're safe. It's all okay.'

But it wasn't okay. It would never be okay, but right now, all I wanted to think about was how to live, truly live, in this moment with him.

I pulled away and looked into his eyes as I ran my hands through his hair, my breathing coming in hard, short gasps. I traced my thumb over his bottom lip, my eyes locked on his. Then his lips found mine, and I kissed him, as if savouring my last moment on this Earth.

When the heat between us became too much, he made to walk us to the house, but I pulled him towards the garden, where we could make love under the stars and greet the dawn of what might be our first day, and one of my last.

CHAPTER 54

GWEN, AUGUST 1976

We collapsed onto our backs on the grass, spent and exhausted, our chests heaving. Despite the hour, the air was still warm, the breeze hot and sticky like slowly melting molasses. Every inch of me was bathed in our sweat and every cell in my body rang with a joy I couldn't even begin to describe.

The butterflies, always my carnal cheerleaders, had behaved strangely tonight. I'd felt their joy and relief as I kissed Dan for the first time and their anticipation as we hurriedly shed our clothes on the back lawn, but then they'd fallen unusually quiet.

The thought was fleeting, because all I could think about was Dan. His eyes in the moonlight, his arms around me. His hands on my skin. The feel of him as we rocked together. I'd begged the heavens for my release, and when it came, I threw back my head to the night sky just in time to see a flock of bright wings explode out of my chest and head for the stars. Had I consciously released them? If I had, I had no memory of doing so.

Dan traced his fingers up and down my arm. We'd be

cooler lying apart, but I couldn't bear it. As if he'd read my thoughts, he inched closer and planted a kiss on the top of my head. After how we'd just consumed each other, the tenderness of that kiss brought a lump to my throat. I turned onto my side, curling my leg around his and resting my head in the hollow beneath his chin.

'Do you think it's the heat?'

I laughed. 'What? Us?'

'Hell no. I've been dreaming of that since the day I set eyes on your picture. I meant the butterflies.'

I pulled back to look at his face. He was staring at the sky, his eyes wide as they tracked back and forth. I looked up, and there they were, a moonlit murmuration. Something close to a giggle reverberated down the bond, and I swear my heart skipped a beat.

'You can see them!' The words burst out in a tumble.

Dan frowned. 'Well, yeah. I've never seen so many types before, though. Is that normal? I mean, back home we get—'

I silenced him with a kiss as a purr rippled down the bond. I glanced up just in time to see the butterflies move as one, arrowing down to engulf us in a sea of bright, impossible wings before shooting upwards again and mingling with the stars.

Dan pushed himself up to sitting, his mouth hanging open and his eyebrows hitched high, deepening the creases on his forehead.

They *wanted* him to see them. My pulse quickened, pounding in my ears as snatches of my dream flashed into my mind. *This is the start of the end.* The thought was no more than a whisper on the wind, but in that moment, I decided. I heaved in a shaky breath, climbed into his lap and wrapped my legs around his waist.

'The butterflies are mine. Sort of. Dan, I need to tell you

everything,' I breathed, cupping his beautiful face in my hands.

He nodded, his eyes locked on mine and his hands tracing the length of my spine.

Dawn was breaking by the time I finished my story. We sat on the grass, a tangle of limbs, under the blanket Dan had pulled from the sofa. He'd pulled me closer, kissed my hair and caught his breath multiple times as I recounted my tale, but not once interrupted me.

I let out a long breath and laid my head on his shoulder, exhaustion claiming the last of my strength. The meadow brown appeared a few inches from my nose, and I smiled at her.

'Your first?' Dan asked.

I nodded against his shoulder. 'She took a shine to you even before I did.' I smiled. 'Sitting on your shoulder, settling on your face in the car after the others left. She's always been a great judge of character.'

He raised his hand tentatively, his index finger outstretched. The meadow brown landed at once, and he grinned, his eyes crinkling at the corners as he gazed at her.

'She's incredible,' he whispered. 'Just like you,' he added, his eyes back on mine.

The butterfly lifted into the air and we tracked her until she'd rejoined the others.

Dan's expression darkened. 'Why do you think they want me to see them? I mean, Walt saw them just before he passed, right?'

I turned quickly and put my hand to his cheek, traced my fingers over the stubble. 'You're not about to die, Dan.' I paused. I couldn't tell him what I really believed, so I said, 'I think they know we're coming to the end of this. It sounds bonkers, but I think the Goddess brought you to me because you have a part to play in releasing the magic back to where it belongs. Maybe the butterflies just need you to see them so that you know what we're trying to protect.'

Dan kissed my lips. 'It doesn't sound bonkers at all.' After a beat, he said, 'Can I ask you something?'

'Anything.'

'You came back to Wales briefly in, what, the mid–eighteen hundreds – why did you stay away so long? And you've never been back home? To Pont Nefoedd, I mean?'

My throat thickened with the all too familiar emotion. I took a breath and levelled my gaze on the brightening horizon, trying to draw strength from the dawn. In telling my story, I'd glossed over my time with Rhys, but how could I be true to myself if I didn't share this – my greatest shame – with the man who was risking everything to help me?

When I looked at Dan, he frowned and pulled me closer. 'Hey, you can tell me anything, you hear me. There is nothing you can say that will stop me loving you.'

I smiled despite myself. How long had it been since I'd heard those words? How long since I'd felt loved?

'I love you too, Daniel Quinn,' I breathed.

I let the moment stretch a few more beats, just two people declaring their love like lovers the world over. I tried to imprint the scene in my memory. The way the first rays of the new day made his hair shine and turned his golden-hazel eyes into pools of liquid amber. The scratch of stubble on his chin and the softness of his lips as I brushed my thumb across them.

He deserved the truth, but maybe I also needed someone to bear witness to the truth of my existence. I might have been a butterfly myself for all the mark I'd made on the world, but if I told Dan my story, at least a part of me would exist – after.

'I came back to Wales one other time too, during the English Civil War, but didn't stay long. Home is a difficult thing for me. The people who were supposed to love and protect me betrayed me. Even Nain.' I cleared my throat as guilt, hard and round as a river pebble, lodged there, choking back my words. I had to do this.

'She loved me fiercely and helped me escape, but she was also the one who, unknowingly, cursed me to this life,' I said with a sad shrug. 'To me, Wales was Pont Nefoedd, but it was also Builth and what happened there …'

Dan waited while I took a breath and forced myself to go on.

'As I said, the Morgan family protected me when I fled from Pont Nefoedd, but there was more to it than that. I married their son, Rhys.'

I felt my heart pinch as something close to pain flashed in Dan's eyes. He dropped his head and sighed.

'Jeez. Ignore me. Go on, please, while I put my ego back in the box,' he said, lifting his eyes to mine.

I smiled and kissed his nose.

'My father was furious, of course, but he wasn't fool enough to stand up to the most powerful magical family in Wales. My grandmother knew that, which was why she'd arranged it all. I can only imagine what my cousin thought about it. His plan to marry me off or kill me so that he could inherit my father's land was in tatters, which was probably why he started the rumours. I was a thief, fleeing my father's home with stolen jewels; I was a witch consorting with the devil. We heard it all.

'In the beginning, I waited for Morvith to send word about reconvening the coven to remove the spell. But one moon turned into two, and then three. The messengers I sent returned with scribbled notes telling me to wait. So, I did.' I shrugged, barely recognising the naïve child I'd been.

'But then my cousin targeted the coven.' My voice cracked, and I waited a beat before forcing myself to continue. 'I heard of Owain's death first. He was our scribe. Then Morvith just a few weeks later. Rhys told me I was being paranoid. Morvith was elderly and in poor health, but I just knew in my bones it hadn't been a natural passing. Increasingly desperate, I wrote to the Owens, but when the messenger arrived, he found their farmhouse burned to the ground.' I choked down the sob.

'He murdered them?'

I nodded, desperate to get to the end of my confession.

'I stopped writing after that. Four people were already dead because of me, so I just resigned myself to my fate.'

'Wait. If Rhys's family had magic, couldn't they undo the spell?'

I felt my stomach drop at the memory of my in-laws. Their politicking and their seemingly endless appetite for wealth and power.

'If I'd confided my secret, they would have taken the magic for themselves. As it turned out, the plague claimed them both within a year of my arrival anyway. Rhys was their only surviving child, so he took over the estate, and I suppose I was happy for a while. My heart broke when I lost Tân a few years later, but I had Rhys, at least.' I smiled at the memory of the kind, affectionate man he'd been at the start.

'And the butterflies still came?' Dan asked.

'Yes. There were quiet times, but then the witch fever would take hold again and they'd arrive, sometimes in flocks, from all over the world.'

'And Rhys didn't know?'

'He knew I didn't have magic of my own. His parents hadn't been happy about that. They didn't want to ruin their magical bloodline, but the promise of my father's lands sweetened the deal. Rhys knew I had a secret, but in the beginning, he said he didn't need to know what it was.'

Dan raised an eyebrow. 'I'm guessing he changed his mind?'

I pulled in another long breath, trying to gather my courage. This was the hardest part, but I had to say it.

'Rhys always said he didn't care about heirs. He said he planned to enjoy his wealth and then leave it to the poor after his days. It sounded very noble.'

Dan stroked my back as I pressed on.

'We'd been married for around six years by then. It was clear that we'd never have a child, but he said it was a blessing because he'd never lose me to the birthing bed. But as he got older and his hair thinned and the fine lines appeared around his eyes, he changed. He'd always been very proud of his good looks, and it hurt him – especially when I looked just as I did the day I arrived.'

'Sounds like a top guy,' Dan growled.

I pressed on, speeding up now so that I could get this over with.

'He caught a bad flu in the winter of 1619. I was afraid he'd die, but he recovered, and maybe it was the brush with death, but he became obsessed with having a son.' I looked away, not sure how to phrase the next line. I closed my eyes against the memory of his brutality. 'He was … relentless,' I said at last.

Dan's fingers closed gently around my wrist and pulled my hand away from my throat. I stared at it. 'Watch closely, and everyone has a tell,' Walt used to say. I stared at the scars on his wrist and dropped to kiss the silvered lines.

'You don't need to tell me this,' Dan whispered, his fingers caressing my cheek as he looked into my eyes.

'I need to.'

He nodded and pulled me closer, his hands stroking my bare back.

'The day I suggested he find a mistress to have a child with, he used his magic to fling me across the room.'

Dan opened his mouth to speak, but I put a finger to his lips and shook my head fervently. I saw hurt and fury burning in his eyes, and if I hadn't already loved him, I might have fallen right there.

'I lived to tell the tale; tens of thousands of women didn't. And tens of thousands still suffer at the hands of men every day,' I said.

Dan lowered his head. 'How did you get away?'

I closed my eyes, shame burning like a furnace in my cheeks.

I took a deep breath and closed my eyes as I whispered my reply. 'I killed him.'

CHAPTER 55

DAN, AUGUST 1976

Of all the things I had been expecting Gwen to say, that had not been on the list. I thought back to Vietnam and the faces of the men, some of them little more than boys, whose lives I'd ended during that bullshit war. Hell, I was the last person on Earth to judge.

'Hey, it's okay. He hurt you. He might have killed you, Gwen. Nobody would blame you for defending yourself, least of all me.'

Gwen was shaking her head, her eyes screwed up tight.

'It wasn't like that. I ran away. I got it into my head that if I could just find a coven to help lift the spell, I could be a proper wife to Rhys and give him the heir he craved. I went to London, but I didn't know how to even begin looking for magical people, so when my money ran out, I went back to Rhys. By then, he had men scouring the country for me. He'd given them every drawing he'd ever made of me.'

'So the picture Devlin gave me was a copy of Rhys's sketch?'

Gwen nodded. 'Rhys was overjoyed when I returned, but his mood quickly soured. He forbade me to leave the house

again, and for a few terrible days I feared I never would, but
—' She paused, her hand massaging her throat again, and I
clenched my teeth against the thought of what I'd like to do
to Rhys fucking Morgan had he not been dead for a few
centuries.

'There was plague in London that year, and while I've not
had so much as a cold in over three hundred years, I must
have carried the disease back to Wales. Rhys sickened within
a week. I sent the staff away the moment I realised what was
ailing him. I used every remedy I could think of, nursed him
around the clock, but he was still cursing me with his last
breath.'

'Wait. He died of plague?'

Gwen covered her face with her hands as she nodded, her
whole body shaking as she tried to contain her sobs.

'You know you didn't kill him, right?' I said, easing her
hands away so that I could take her face in mine and stroke
away her tears with my thumbs. 'Even if you'd wished him
dead, it was an accident.'

She was shaking her head, her face pinched with misery.
'I didn't wish him dead. Not once. I tried to save him.'

'Then you need to forgive yourself. It's time to let that
shit go, Gwen. It wasn't your fault. Do you hear me? It wasn't
your fault.'

I held her as she sobbed and wondered what it must be
like to carry a few centuries' worth of guilt and grief around.

Tomorrow, we'd figure out how to retrieve the spell from
Devlin. If it was the last thing I did, I was going to give Gwen
her shot at the beautiful life she had always deserved.

CHAPTER 56

GWEN, AUGUST 1976

'*Y*ou're sure they don't know about the cars?' Dan asked from the passenger seat.

I shrugged. It was hard to be sure about anything. 'As sure as I can be. I paid cash for the cars and the garage rentals and chose the locations by sticking a pin in a map.'

I stole a glance at him, taking my eyes off the road only long enough to register the look on his face. He was still brooding.

'I shouldn't have come home without changing the car,' he sighed. 'It was a rookie mistake.'

The fear that someone from the Unit might have followed him to the cottage had hit Dan hard as we sat in the garden this morning, planning how to retrieve the spell. He'd been self-flagellating ever since, despite my best efforts.

'You didn't come straight back here precisely to make sure nobody was following you,' I said for what felt like the hundredth time.

'Yeah, but the car is sort of distinctive,' he mumbled.

I flicked on the indicator and pulled out to overtake a slow-moving tractor in the country lane.

'Are we having our first argument?' I asked, grinning at him.

'Hell no,' he said, reaching over to trace a finger from my hairline to my collarbone. I tightened my grip on the wheel. 'I'm just mad at myself for not thinking straight. I shouldn't have put you in danger like that.'

'Enough! No more self-recrimination, okay?'

From the corner of my eye, I saw him give a reluctant nod.

'You called the cottage home,' I said, grinning as I glanced at him.

Dan laughed and rubbed at the back of his neck. 'Did I?'

'You absolutely did.'

'The cottage isn't home,' he said. 'You are.'

A flush of warmth spread through me, a gentle wave against a long-abandoned shore, but when it receded, I felt a stab of grief, knowing that I was going to break both our hearts. I swallowed, my throat closing around the emotion like it was trying to smother it.

'Hey, what's up?'

I shook my head and forced a smile. I should tell him. He deserved to know. But if I did, he'd try to talk me out of it. Or find another way, but there was no other option. It was only a matter of time before Devlin found me, and I couldn't risk him taking the butterflies' magic. I would never betray them.

'I love you,' I whispered, not taking my eyes from the road. We'd said it last night and again this morning as we'd made love, but I didn't want him to doubt me – not for a second. When this was all over, he'd need these moments. These memories would remind him that what we felt for each other was real.

'I love you too,' he said, serious now as he reached over to tuck a strand of hair behind my ear.

'I need a haircut.' I blurted it out, desperate for a distraction.

'Does it, like, grow way quicker than normal?' Dan asked.

'Yes. I think it's the spell,' I said with a shrug. 'A little magical side effect or something which is probably the least useful thing imaginable.'

'I'd love you even if you were bald as a coot,' Dan chuckled, and I let his words sink into me. I'd need these moments too when the time came.

We drove with the windows cracked open and the radio playing in the background, and I imagined what it might have been like to live a normal life. To be just another normal woman.

Later, as the Severn Bridge loomed into sight, Dan popped open the glove compartment, pulled out a notebook and pen and began writing. He ripped out the sheet, folded it and, with a grin that made my breath hitch, slowly tucked it into the back pocket of my shorts.

'Whoa, you had better take your hand back, or I'll be flinging this car into the nearest lay-by.'

Dan laughed but took his time drawing back his hand. I tried to focus on the road as memories of last night threw more kindling on the fire.

'What's on the note?'

'Phone numbers for Jackson, Maggie and DI Heath, my friend in the Met. Just in case.'

My throat tightened at the thought, but I'd have done the same for him, had there been anyone to call. I checked my speed as my eye snagged on the outline of a police car on the hard shoulder. The last thing we needed was a ticket. In my chest, the butterflies stirred, their wings rattling like dried leaves. I flicked my eyes to the rear-view mirror, but the police car hadn't moved. I watched it grow smaller as I pressed my foot on the accelerator, the scratch of wings under my ribs softening with every mile.

'Nearly there,' I said, indicating to leave the motorway and join the A46 to Tetbury.

'Pretty place,' Dan said as gently rolling hills and farmland gave way to a smart market town built in buttery, soft Cotswold stone. 'Where's the car?'

'In a garage on the north-east side of town,' I said. 'It's about two minutes away.'

Just as I spoke, the traffic slowed, then ground to a halt, as a lorry tried to do a three-point turn in the road.

Dan checked his watch and made a face.

'Problem?'

He shook his head. 'I wanted to call Jackson, but it can wait.'

'There's a phone box right there,' I said, pointing towards a side street. 'I'll meet you there in ten minutes.'

'Uh-uh!' Dan said with a slow shake of his head. 'I'm not leaving you unprotected.'

A flush of irritation nettled at the back of my neck, and I pursed my lips, but the words flew out anyway.

'I've survived three hundred and sixty-four years on my own, Dan. I'm with you because I choose to be, not because I need a man to protect me.'

He flinched and held up his hands.

Up ahead, a driver leaned on their horn as the lorry continued to manoeuvre in the narrow street.

'I'm sorry. Meet you back here in ten minutes,' he said, leaning over to plant a kiss on my lips. As he drew away, I grabbed a handful of his T-shirt and pulled him back, deepening the kiss.

'Ten minutes,' I said, releasing him only when I heard the blare of another car horn.

I watched him jog across the road, his hand already reaching into his pocket for change. When I looked back at the road, the traffic was finally moving.

The garage was big enough for a bus, let alone an Austin Allegro, but it was the only one available when I took the lease. After pulling up the rolling door, I parked the Jag and swept the contents of the glove box into my satchel, smiling when I found a fistful of my old shopping lists carefully folded. After checking the door pockets, I slipped the spare key from the keyring and tucked it under the driver's mat.

I popped the boot, and Walt's voice drifted in my memory at the sight of the small khaki knapsack he'd nicknamed his midnight kit.

'Well, sometimes, dear heart, one can't wait for an invitation to tea.' He'd chuckled as he'd pulled the items from the knapsack, placing them on his desk to illustrate what his character, the British spy Gideon Lockhart, might carry for emergencies.

My own kit, stowed in every car I owned, included binoculars, a mini bolt-cutter, lock pick set, Swiss Army knife, a slim Jim tool for popping car locks and, my least favourite of all, the Fairbairn-Sykes fighting knife.

I checked my watch as I headed back into town. At this pace, I might make it back to the phone box before Dan had even finished his call. My optimism cooled as the traffic slowed again a hundred yards before the turning to the side street. I thought of poor Cyril as my eye snagged on the hanging baskets wilting in the relentless midday sun. The whole country seemed to be locked in a bubble of inescapable heat.

Just ahead, a young woman skipped out of a bakery and dropped a string bag onto the passenger seat of her convertible MG. My stomach rumbled, so when she indicated, I flashed my lights to let her join the queue in front of me. If I was going to be late, then at least I could bring us lunch. I parked, grabbed the satchel and hurried into the shop.

'What can I get you, love?' the bakery assistant asked wearily, her face the same shade of red as the jam tarts on display.

I opened my mouth to reply just as the butterflies exploded out of my aura, pitching me forward into the sturdy glass counter. I pushed against it and raced out of the shop, my legs already pumping in time to my panicking heart.

A horn blared as I bolted into the road. Rounding the corner to the side street, I saw the last punch in a fight that Dan would never win. Before I could even scream, two men bundled his limp form into the back of a black saloon car and sped away.

I think I might have screamed then, but I can't be sure. My legs buckled, and I sank to my knees where I stood.

'I called the police, love,' said a thin, shaky voice from somewhere above me. I looked up into a face that was all wiry grey beard and wrinkles.

'I tried to stop them,' he said, 'but one of them punched me. I'm so sorry. Is it your husband they've taken?'

The man in shopkeepers' overalls held out his hand, and I took it but pushed myself to standing when I realised there was no strength at all in his grip.

'They hit you?' I stammered.

'What's going on, George?' said a small white-haired woman in matching overalls who came scurrying out of the shop.

'Thank you. I'm so sorry,' I said, backing towards the main road.

I ran to the car and jumped behind the wheel. Panic clawed at my throat, and I tried to swallow it down. *Think, Gwen, think!* I pulled out into the traffic, ignoring the blare of car horns. I turned onto the side street, retracing my steps, but the black car would be long gone by now.

Had the Unit taken Dan? Or was it Devlin's thugs? Dan trusted Jackson, and so did the butterflies, but did I?

Goddess, help me! I ground out the plea through gritted teeth, but as ever, silence was my only reply. The meadow brown hovered in my peripheral vision, and so, decided, I flung the car onto the kerb and ran back to the phone box.

CHAPTER 57

DAN, AUGUST 1976

I figured I could only have been out for a minute because when I came to, my head throbbing against the hot glass of the back window, we were just passing the 'You are now leaving Tetbury' sign.

My right eye felt sticky and swollen, I tasted blood in my mouth and my stomach reeled from the gut punches I'd taken, but it was the weight of steel on my wrists that threatened to break me.

The moment I registered the cuffs, I was back in that tin shack in the jungle. My heart jack-hammered and I felt the sweat erupt from my pores. If I didn't get a grip, I'd be hyperventilating in seconds. I wrestled down the panic, tensing my stomach so that I could distract myself with the physical pain long enough to think like the soldier I'd never wanted to be.

These had to be Devlin's men. The grab had been too blatant and too brutal for the Unit, but maybe this was what Jackson had warned me about on the phone.

'Watch your back, man. Target is escalating,' he'd said before promising to call back from a secure line.

I'd heard the phone ringing as I went down, my vision

blurring as consciousness left me, thanking the stars that Gwen hadn't been with me. The memory of her sprinting out of the cottage and leaping into my arms last night bloomed in my mind like dropped ink on wet paper, leaving no room for that other memory that was so desperate to claim me.

My heart rate slowed, and I focused on keeping my breathing light; the longer they believed me to still be unconscious, the better.

There were four of them. I'd gotten a good look at the three that attacked me on the street: one guy that looked a lot like Bluto from the comics; a walking slab of muscle, built like a brick wall; a middle-aged, stocky guy with a teddy boy quiff who jabbed like a boxer; and a short, weasel-thin kid with a wispy moustache and small, mean eyes. He'd grinned as he'd taken a swing at the old man who came out of his shop to help me. The driver was just a voice to me for now. He had an accent which might have been Russian, but I wouldn't have sworn to it.

They talked about football, of all things. Like regular guys driving to a match, not a bunch of psycho thugs. The thought that there might be a second team going after Gwen landed like another kick to my gut.

'Looks like pretty boy's awake,' said the big guy from the seat next to me.

I stayed still, but he didn't buy it. I heard a cork slip from a bottle, smelled the tang of chemicals, but then he was on me, crushing me against the door as he wrestled a wad of cloth over my nose and mouth and held it in place until everything slipped into darkness.

I came to with a start, gasping for breath like a landed fish. The sudden movement sent a cannonball ricocheting around the inside of my skull, and I screwed up my eyes against sunlight so blinding it felt like a blow torch on my retinas.

Panic reared again as I felt ropes biting into the skin across my wrists and ankles. *It helps to use your senses, Mr Quinn. Name things you can see, hear, touch and smell.* It had been the only piece of useful advice the shrink had.

I sucked in a few long, slow breaths as I tried to take stock. I was bound to a heavy chair. I smelled fresh paint and thinners, and beneath it, the stench of stale tobacco and ale-soaked wood you only find in old English pubs.

I heard voices. Men laughing. The scuff and crunch of gravel beneath their feet. They were moving but not walking. A thread of fresh, acrid cigarette smoke drifted in on a warm breeze. A car park then, or a driveway.

When the pain in my head subsided, I tried opening my eyes again, slowly this time. My right eye felt heavy and swollen, but at least it still worked. As my vision cleared, old, dusty floorboards swam into view, then a row of flagstones nearest the long, curving bar.

I lifted my head gingerly, taking in the paint-splattered sheets thrown over its surface, the beer cloths draped over the pumps and the back shelves devoid of glasses. In other circumstances, it might have been a nice-looking country pub in the middle of a make-over.

Outside, amongst the chatter, one word caught my attention. '… inside …'

I heard someone crunch across the car park, their footsteps drawing closer. Behind me, a door-handle creaked. The door stuck in its frame, wood screeching against wood until, with a grunt, someone shouldered it open, and a rush of hot, dusty air swept into the pub.

'Nice kip?'

I turned my head to see the short man with the quiff striding towards me. He did not look happy. Back in Tetbury, he'd been the first to swing a punch. I'd dodged it, but his second jab was the reason I could barely open my right eye.

I'd fought back, my knuckles slamming into flesh and bone, but it all happened so fast I wasn't sure who I'd managed to hit in the seconds before they took me down. Given his thunderous scowl and the swelling around his top lip, I had at least one answer.

He tried another tactic.

'You got some skills on you, fair play,' he said, leaning against the bar and folding his tattooed arms across his chest. As he waited for me to reply, he ran his tongue over the swelling on his lip.

'So do you. You box professionally?' I asked, deciding that any information was worth taking.

He caught the smile before it could fully form, but even beneath the hard-man scowl, I could see he was flattered.

'Devlin not here?' I asked, testing the water.

'He's been held up in London, hence the delay in proceedings,' he said, clearly pleased with his choice of word.

'Any idea what they'll be?' I asked, trying to keep the fear from my voice.

He made a face, then pushed himself away from the bar and ambled over to the window without looking at me. He was just tall enough to see out, the bottom panes obscured with the frosted glass that seemed to be a feature in British pubs. From where I sat, all I could see was trees and sky.

'I can tell you you're not gonna enjoy them, mate. If you want my advice, get it over quick like and tell him where the girl is. If you do that, he might show a bit of mercy and get Bobby to pop two in your skull. That said, he's been itching to try out his new voodoo shit, so nah, I take it back. Even if you spill your guts at the off, you're in for a mother-fucking load of pain,' he said flatly, still looking out the window.

'You don't fancy helping a guy out, do you?' I asked. Anything was worth a try.

He turned and stared at me for a long moment, then he laughed.

'You're funny,' he said, pointing at me and shaking his head. 'Tell you the truth, I'm sort of looking forward to the show. Pushes all my buttons, if you get my meaning,' he added with a grin.

He turned back to the window.

On my chest, my tattoo flared into life like a struck match.

'Ah. Speak of the devil. Here's his lordship now.'

The rush of hot, dusty air heralded Devlin's arrival, no squeaking door for him. He walked slowly, and I steeled myself not to turn around. On my chest, my tattoo turned to ice. I was used to it prickling, even burning, when it sensed magic, but this was new. A cold, hard, creeping frost that inched out across my skin with every clipped, unhurried footstep. I swallowed and stared ahead, channelling every ounce of energy into keeping my expression neutral. When I let out a breath, it misted in the air, and yet I could still feel sweat beading on my brow and trickling down my neck.

'Leave us, please,' Devlin said, his voice soft and edged with a practised smile.

Quiff man scuttled away, looking like he couldn't get out of the room quickly enough.

Devlin stepped into my line of sight. Today's offering from Saville Row was a three-piece light beige suit, a crisp white shirt and a thin sky-blue silk tie. He held his Panama hat, ivory with a black band, in one hand and a slim brown leather briefcase in the other.

He placed the case on the shrouded table opposite me

with a clergyman's reverence and gazed at it for long seconds while he smoothed down his silver-streaked hair. He was tanned, clean-shaven and apparently untroubled by the searing heat. A fresh bead of sweat rolled off my forehead, and I saw his lips twitch in amusement.

My temperature plummeted, fear frosting my chest and chilling my bones, but the sensation vanished as quickly as it had arrived, and the heat of the day returned. I forced myself to meet his gaze, and he smiled when I recoiled, his pale eyes dancing at the sight of my horror. I couldn't have described what I saw, but every cell in my body froze in that moment, and I knew with a gut-wrenching certainty that I wouldn't be walking out of this pub alive.

'Welcome, Mr Quinn,' he said, his voice so quiet I had to strain to hear him. 'It's good of you to visit at last.'

Not trusting my voice yet, I said nothing, just watched as he selected a bar-stool, wiped it with a clean handkerchief he pulled from his pocket and then perched on its edge, as if he still didn't trust it not to ruin his pristine trousers.

'I expected more of you. Given your service record, I assumed you capable of following orders. But that was my mistake. History teaches us that Americans love the limelight but often demur in the face of hard work. You have reminded me of that, so thank you.'

I bridled, thinking of my father's service in the war he was referring to – the war Devlin spent in a comfortable office in Whitehall – but said nothing.

Devlin sighed. 'Incompetence I may have tolerated. But I never forgive liars, Mr Quinn. Especially liars who take my money and then work for my enemies.'

I cleared my throat. It was time to try my first play.

'They approached me,' I said, aiming for a non-committal shrug. 'I thought the best way to find the girl was to get close to the community.'

Devlin mouthed an 'Oh' as he nodded.

'You mean to say this is a clever tactic then? Pretending to work for them just to get intelligence.' His tone was mocking, and despite the ghost of a smile, his eyes were hard as marble.

I couldn't go back now.

'I told you when I took the case I thought it was a wild goose hunt. If the connection with the community had yielded anything, I'd have reported it, but so far it hasn't.' My voice sounded way steadier than I felt, but one look at his face told me he wasn't buying a word of my story.

'I believe I made my position on liars abundantly clear just moments ago. And yet you continue to lie to me, Mr Quinn. I know you've found the girl.'

I stilled, working hard to betray nothing in my reaction. Blood thundered in my ears, and I glared at him, refusing to look away.

'Tell me where she is and this will be over before you know it,' Devlin said, waving a dismissive hand in my direction.

I exhaled as slowly as I could, relief flooding through my veins as I tried to maintain a poker face. I shrugged, and Devlin flashed me a wolfish grin. It wasn't the reaction I expected, and my relief was quickly replaced by a loosening in my gut.

Sliding off the stool, Devlin placed his hat on the bar, then shrugged out of his jacket, his movements slow and deliberate. He stood for a moment, holding his jacket, looking around for somewhere to hang it. When he strode off towards the front door, I thrashed in my seat, desperately yanking back my arms to loosen the ropes at my wrists, but it only tightened them. When Devlin reappeared, he was carefully rolling up his shirt sleeves to the elbow.

He slipped his gold cufflinks into his waistcoat pocket

and set about rolling up his remaining shirtsleeve. He glanced at his watch as he did so, and his expression clouded.

'My pet witch is running late, so I'm afraid we will have to entertain ourselves for a while,' he said, taking a step towards me. On my chest, the tattoo flared, and it felt like both fire and ice were competing for my attention. I set my jaw against the pain. I needed to play for time.

'I heard you're your own witch now,' I said levelly.

Devlin froze, his body half turned away from me and only a narrow sliver of his face visible. A vein pulsed in his temple. His stillness was unnerving, like the moment before a dog bites or a snake strikes. I braced, but the attack didn't come.

'You are ignorant, so I will overlook the insult just this once,' he said, popping the locks on his briefcase.

'I didn't mean to offend,' I said. 'This magic stuff is new to me, you know.'

He turned around, a long wooden box cradled in his hands. He smiled his condescending smile, his eyes narrowing.

'Witches,' he said quietly, 'are commoners born with a mutation that predisposes them to magical ability, although most lack the intellect to wield it properly. I am something entirely unique. Electus inter mortales.' He bowed his head as if that were explanation enough.

When I didn't reply, he rolled his eyes like a disappointed professor. 'It's Latin, Mr Quinn. It means "chosen among mortals". I am the first pure-born human to harness and claim magic in all of history.'

'Does that mean you get to choose what to call yourself?' I said, hoping flattery might buy me a few more seconds.

He smiled. 'It does. I am deciding between Arch-Magus or Ætheric Monarch. The latter will annoy Her Majesty, of course, but once I conclude my business with your witch, none of that will matter anyway.'

The reference to Gwen felt like a twisting knife in my gut, but I didn't rise to it.

'How will it annoy the Queen?' I asked. I had to keep him talking.

Devlin's eyebrow lifted, but he answered anyway. 'I will be volunteering my unique services to run the country, and when that happens, we will have no need of the royals or the buffoons who sit in parliament.'

'Sounds like a coup,' I said as levelly as I could.

'A coup involves the army. I won't have need of them either,' Devlin said. 'Really, Mr Quinn, you are a disappointment. Did you not think to ask your witch about the scale of the magic she hoards? Too busy bedding her to enquire about the power she's keeping from me?'

That slow smile spread across his lips. 'I am correct then. You are lovers,' Devlin crowed.

So much for my poker face. I gritted my teeth and tried to think of something else to keep him talking. I needed more time, although for what? For the cavalry to arrive? For Jackson to show up like he did in Nam and carry me out of this hell-hole?

There was nobody coming to my rescue this time. The thought landed so hard I caught my breath. Devlin cocked his head, and I wondered for a moment whether he could read my mind. That slow, satisfied smile still played on his lips, but this time his eyes joined in, lighting with a zeal I'd not seen before. He was enjoying my agony. A predator watching its prey concede to the inevitable.

Devlin tapped the flat of his hand on the old wooden box. 'Some of the spells in here are thought to be even older than your witch,' he said. 'It's an interesting story, actually. One I rarely get to share, but as we're killing time …' He glanced at his watch before perching back on his stool.

'Like me, my father was a collector of rare spells, and he acquired one of these from an old spell book. They're sentient, you know, the books. Darndest things I've ever seen.' His eyes drifted to the window, and for a moment, he seemed to lose his flow.

'Our German friends had to torture the thing for years before it yielded. It eventually escaped, God knows how, but by then they had already extracted one of the most important spells known to magic. They called it the Zerreißzauber.' Devlin's tone was almost wistful now, as if he were recounting some noble battle.

'Where's the book now?' I asked.

Devlin looked at me like I was an imbecile. 'Not the right question, Mr Quinn. What you should be concerned about is what I'm about to do with those spells.'

I opened my mouth, desperate to keep him talking, but Devlin was already on his feet. He placed the box reverently on the table next to him before pressing his hands together as if in prayer.

My tattoo flared, searing hot, just as the pressure in the room shifted. I heard tyres on gravel outside and snapped my head towards the window, hope flaring pitifully in my gut. Devlin laughed, and I looked back just in time to see a thin ribbon of blue light crackle between his palms. He laughed again as he stared at his hands, delighted.

My whole body reacted, trying and failing to rock the chair I was tied to. I heard Devlin mutter something, and I didn't need my tattoo to tell me he had started reciting a spell. I thrust myself forward, scanning the ground – and that's when I saw the bolts securing the chair to the floor. This was it. I thought of Gwen. I closed my eyes and took a breath. If this fucker was about to kill me, then he'd need to look me in the eye as he did it.

I lifted my head. More strands of blue light arced between Devlin's palms, building and coalescing into a glowing, writhing ball that looked like some strange planet caught in an electrical storm.

When he opened his eyes, they were the same colour as the ball in his hands. Frowning in concentration, he pinched off a thread of light and twisted it between his finger and thumb until it took on a lance-like form. Then, with a quick flick of his wrist, he shot it at me. I froze, my body braced for impact, but the lance veered off to the right, hitting the bar with an almighty crack.

Devlin ducked for cover as splinters of wood flew into the air like a hail of bullets. When he straightened, he had a hand pressed to his cheek. He pulled it away and stared at the blood staining his fingers.

'What did you do?' Devlin asked tightly. His lips barely moved, as if every muscle and sinew in his body were being employed to reign in his fury.

'Nothing but pray,' I said between heaving breaths.

Devlin squared his shoulders and strode past me. The door squeaked as he opened it, and I caught snatches of a conversation drifting in on the breeze. When he returned, a fresh square of handkerchief pressed to his face, I did a double take. He looked, of all things, hurt. Like a spoiled child bested in a game he was always allowed to win.

Quiff and the guy who looked like Bluto hurried into the room and untied me. The blood rushed back into my wrists, but seconds later, the handcuffs were back, biting into my skin and delivering a fresh wave of nausea as my body reacted to the memories unspooling in my mind.

They hauled me to my feet and shoved me towards the

back of the pub. As we passed the open front door, I saw a small woman with frizzy blonde curls in a thin summer dress march up to the pub. I tasted bile in my throat at the sight of Dr Clement's murderer. Devlin's witch had arrived.

CHAPTER 59

GWEN, AUGUST 1976

The drive east felt unbearable, the traffic slow and ponderous as if the heat were a blanket weighing down the world. I kept the windows open when I could, rolled them up when everything slowed again and the exhaust fumes threatened to choke me.

Jackson's rebuke still rang in my ears.

'This line isn't secure. You shouldn't have given your name.'

He was right. I'd blurted it all out the moment he picked up the phone and identified himself. 'Jackson, it's Gwen. They've taken him. Devlin's men have taken Dan!'

I cringed at the memory. Everything Walt had taught me. Every precaution I'd lived by for centuries, cast to the wind in my blind panic. Jackson had insisted on calling me back from a secure line, but the wait had been close to unbearable. It was only later, as I drove to the address Jackson had finally given me only after I flat out begged him, that I realised that for the first time in my life, I'd not even thought about running.

It wasn't a surprise to see the Unit's ominous black jeeps

parked haphazardly in front of Devlin's country house. Sonning, an exclusive riverside village in Berkshire, was far closer to London than Tetbury, and I somehow doubted they'd be held up in traffic like normal people.

I watched through binoculars from the trees that ringed the acres of pristine green lawn. People all over the country were collecting drinking water from standpipes in the street, and yet Devlin's sprinklers appeared to be working overtime.

Jackson was bent over a map on the bonnet of a car, two dozen armed operatives standing around him. I couldn't hear him, but even from this distance I could tell he was pissed off. Dan clearly wasn't here, and he was now desperately trying to find him.

I slunk back into the trees, hurrying towards the front gate. Jackson had warned me on the phone that the Unit was compromised, so showing myself wasn't an option, but I had no idea what to do next. Dan could be anywhere. What if they'd already—

A figure seemed to materialise from nowhere. I stopped in my tracks.

'You okay, miss?'

The light shifted, and I let out a long breath, letting my hand fall from my chest. The person in front of me was an elderly gardener, his shirtsleeves rolled high on thin, darkly tanned arms, a pair of braces keeping his long trousers in place. He'd not appeared from thin air, merely stepped from behind a large rhododendron.

'Fine. Yes,' I said breathlessly.

'You with them up there?' the gardener asked, pointing a finger in the direction of the house.

I smiled and nodded.

'I could have told them Mr Reginald was down at that pub he's having done up, but nobody asks me, do they?' he grumbled.

'That's why I came to find you. To ask. You said he was at a pub? Whereabouts, exactly?'

Five minutes later, after sprinting all the way back to the car, I was speeding through country lanes, praying I'd make it on time and hoping the gardener would make good on his promise of delivering my message to Jackson.

CHAPTER 60

DAN, AUGUST 1976

Quiff and Bluto stopped in front of a padlocked door. I heard Devlin greet Angie, his voice low and measured, her reply loud and shrill, as if she were used to having to shout at the world.

'Well?' Quiff growled under his breath.

'You said you had them,' Bluto replied.

Quiff muttered a string of curses. 'I said I had the handcuff keys. I told you to fetch the cellar keys!' he snarled, jabbing his finger at the big guy.

'Hey, watch it!' Bluto replied, making no effort to lower his voice.

'Keep it down!' Quiff hissed, ducking his head around the wall to make sure Devlin hadn't heard. 'You want to end up like Billy?'

Whoever Billy was, the mention of his name drained the colour from the big guy's jowly face.

Quiff pulled the handcuff key from his pocket and undid the bracelets swiftly. Any thoughts I had of trying to make a break for it were quashed as Bluto's meaty hands bit into my biceps. Quiff attached one of the cuffs to the radiator, and with a final warning to keep me quiet, he shot out of the back door like a man on his way to put out a fire.

The big guy checked the cuffs, then pulled a tobacco tin from his back pocket and shuffled to the open back door to smoke. I quickly rejected the idea of calling out to Devlin – making fools out of his henchmen didn't feel like the brightest of moves.

I leaned against the door, trying to make sense of what had just happened. It hadn't taken a genius to figure out that my tattoo warned me about magic, but until today, I had no idea it could protect me from it too. It had felt like a shield popping right out of my chest. If only Linh was still alive to thank.

'You're a bloody fool!'

Angie spat the words in a tone that could have stripped paint.

If Devlin replied, he spoke too quietly for me to hear him.

'Taking magic is one thing, knowing how to control it is another. How many times have I told you that? You ain't ready to do it yourself. You just ain't!'

Bluto stubbed out his cigarette, wafting the air like a schoolboy about to get caught behind the bleachers. Seconds later, Quiff hurried back into the pub, throwing the big guy a loaded look as he undid the handcuff from the radiator and snapped it back over my wrist. I gritted my teeth and sucked in a long breath.

I caught a snatch of Devlin's raised voice – '… think you need to remember who you work for, lady …' – before the cellar door swung open and my captors marched me down the rickety wooden steps, the sour, yeasty smell of spilled beer and pungent line cleaners rising to meet me.

Quiff was just attaching my handcuffed wrist to a sturdy pipe when Weasel Guy appeared on the stairs. 'Boss wants the handcuffs,' he said, before disappearing again.

'Fuck's sake,' muttered Quiff.

Something heavy crashed above us, the old floorboards sending a cloud of dust falling into the cellar.

'Get up there, quick!' Quiff yelled to the big guy.

'I thought they were friends,' I said, pushing my luck.

Quiff said nothing as he bound my hands to the pipe with rope, but his expression spoke volumes.

As he took the stairs two at a time, I heard something explode overhead.

CHAPTER 61

GWEN, AUGUST 1976

I parked the car on a quiet residential street, grabbed my knapsack from the boot and jogged to the lane the gardener had told me about. It looked like it led nowhere, narrowing to a single track after just a few hundred yards. A thick hedgerow to the left separated the lane from the stubbled field beyond. To the right sat a small copse of trees, their leaves browning in the drought.

The pub was set back from the road, half hidden behind an overgrown evergreen hedge. Scaffolding clung to the front of the long, crooked old building, its newly thatched roof a fresh crown above the ghostly outline of absent ivy imprinted on the gable end.

Save for a concrete mixer and a pile of sand in the car park, there was no sign of work. I watched from the lane, my ears straining for signs of life but hearing only the thick sound of silence, punctuated here and there with the rustle of parched leaves or the engine of a passing car in the distance.

The butterflies stirred as I crept closer. Then, without warning, an explosion cracked the air, and a blinding blue light, like summer sun on a mirror, burst from the pub window.

Stumbling backwards, I caught my foot and fell on my behind, cursing.

Before I could stand, I heard muffled shouts from inside the pub.

Dan! The butterflies tried to take flight, frenzied now as the air cracked with magic even I could feel. As I crept around the hedge, I saw four men bolt from the pub and race towards the black Cortina in the car park.

I pressed myself into the hedge, its straggly limbs embracing me like I was a long-lost friend. The car screeched out of the car park, and I caught a glimpse of the men inside, all screaming at the driver to step on it.

I ran towards the pub, keeping myself as low to the ground as possible, and flattened myself against the wall. How many times had I written scenes like this for Walt's Gideon Lockhart novels? I pushed the thought away as more shouts came from the pub. The people inside were arguing fiercely. I ducked under the window and crept closer. The voices got louder.

'You're an arrogant bastard, you know that?' a woman shrieked.

The barked laugh had to be Devlin's. I strained my ears, but I couldn't make out his reply, just the ringing condescension in his tone.

'I should never have trusted you,' she spat.

But what if Dan was in there too? I glanced up at the frosted windows and cursed. I'd need something to stand on to get to the clear glass, and there was no way of doing that without being seen.

The meadow brown appeared an inch from my nose. *Not now!* I thought, assuming she was here to petition for the butterflies' release as usual, but she simply fluttered up to the window and beat her wings against the clear glass. The vision appeared in my mind as surely as if I'd peered through the window myself.

A silver-haired man in a white shirt, blue light snapping between his fingers. A small woman with tightly permed blonde hair glaring at him as a vivid violet light sparked and crackled in her palms. Long scorch marks, some still smoking, scarred the whitewashed walls; the bar looked like snapped pencil, its polished wood lying splintered on the floor next to a smouldering cream hat. There was no sign of Dan.

The meadow brown fluttered down and disappeared over my shoulder. I followed in a crouch, creeping past the front porch and its open inner door.

I heard Devlin then, his voice unnervingly quiet. 'Your sacrifice will be for the greater good, Angie.'

'I'd rather die than let you take my magic, you piece of shit!'

The sky darkened and the air thickened. If magic was an amplifier, someone had just dialled it up to ten. A slow roll of thunder rumbled overhead, and the butterflies swooped in my chest as if fear and excitement were imprinted on each side of their wings.

I dropped to the ground as another burst of magic blew out the window I'd been sitting under just moments ago. If Dan was in the building, I needed to get him out before one of them brought the whole pub crashing down.

The meadow brown hovered above the old cellar hatch. I swung my backpack to the ground, but my hand stilled on the fastening when I saw the padlock was closed but not locked. Sending up a silent prayer to the Goddess, I heaved open the heavy wooden door just as the first fat drops of rain fell and a crack of lightning lit up the sky.

The building shook, although whether from a direct

strike or the magical battle happening inside, I didn't know. I raced down the stairs and almost cried out when I saw Dan, his right eye blackening and swollen closed, desperately trying to fray the rope that bound him to an old pipe as dust and plaster fell from the quaking ceiling.

Wide-eyed and grinning, he kissed my neck as I sliced through the rope with my knife. We scrambled up the cellar steps, already slick with rain, just as a bolt of lightning hit the mound of sand in the car park. We flattened ourselves against the side of the pub, our fingers laced together and our clothes already soaked by what felt like a biblical downpour. I'd only ever seen rain like this on the day I fled Pont Nefoedd.

A woman's high-pitched scream split the air. I peered around the corner just as Angie stumbled out into the car park. She made to run, but an arc of blue light slammed into her back and she lurched forward, her arms windmilling in the air. Devlin strode from the pub, firing another blast of energy at her before she'd even hit the ground.

A clap of thunder shook the air as if the gods themselves had roared in fury. I sensed movement beside me and grabbed Dan's wrist before he could move, shaking my head urgently when he met my eyes.

'There's nothing we can do,' I whispered, gripping his wrist ever tighter, but eased off when I saw him wince. I glanced down to see livid red welts mingled with the old scars on his forearms. 'Sorry,' I mouthed, but he responded with a shrug and a lopsided smile.

'That all you've got?' Angie shrieked.

Startled, I risked a glance and saw the small blonde back on her feet, her hands a writhing mass of violet energy and her mouth twisted into a snarl.

'You always did overestimate yourself!' she laughed.

'We need to get the spells!' Dan hissed, pointing at the pub.

'They're here?' I mouthed, wide-eyed.

Dan nodded and grabbed my hand, pulling me towards the back of the building. The thunder boomed again seconds before a bolt of lightning hit the pub, making the old walls quake.

'Stay here,' Dan whispered as we stepped inside.

I grabbed his hand and lifted my chin. I'd remind him of who had saved who if we got out of this alive. A flash of violet energy hit the side of the pub, and we fell to our knees as the bay window exploded, showering us with glass and wood. As we crawled, the scaffolding gave way with a shriek before clattering to the ground, a cacophony of steel on stone.

Dan reached the front door first and stood up, chest heaving. He motioned for me to wait, then peered around the frame. I saw him shift his weight forward, readying to move. I held my breath. If Devlin had his back to the pub, it meant Angie was likely facing it. Our only chance was to move when she was distracted. My heart thundered in my chest, and I couldn't tell if the pounding in my ears was my own blood or the tempest howling outside.

The butterflies surged forward just as the pressure shifted. A flash of blue light split the air, and I tasted iron on my tongue. When I opened my eyes, Dan was already at the other side of the door, crawling on his hands and knees towards a small wooden box on a table.

I let out a shaky breath and, holding on to the door frame, inched around it to see what had become of Angie. She lay, unmoving, on the ground, Devlin standing over her, his hands on his hips. As I watched, he threw back his head and laughed.

I snapped back to Dan. He had the box. If Devlin turned

now, we'd be done for. I beckoned to Dan, hurrying him on, but mouthed 'Stop!' as I heard Devlin's feet crunching across the gravel, getting louder with every step. Either he'd seen us or he planned to retrieve the spells and flee.

I cast around, but there was nowhere to hide. The only back door was behind me, and as soon as Devlin was inside, it would take him seconds to find Dan crouched beneath the blown-out window.

Devlin's footsteps slapped against the first flagstone, and I held my breath. I heard the squelch of leather against wet stone, followed by a gasp and a frantic clamouring, fingers desperately seeking purchase against smooth panelling. He fell hard, and I heard the air leave his lungs in one almighty humph.

Opposite, Dan crept slowly to his feet, readying himself to run towards me. The butterflies surged in my chest as Devlin rose to his feet in a move that had more in common with a rising trap door than anything remotely human. Before I could even blink, he was standing a foot away from me, his lips drawn into a delighted smile as his eyes raked over my soaking wet body.

The blue light sparked like a struck flint in Devlin's hands before erupting into a ball of spitting energy. He turned towards Dan and threw back his head and laughed, just as a bolt of violet energy struck him square in the back, lifting him off his feet and hurling him into the remnants of the splintered bar.

I peered around the door to see Angie staggering towards the pub, her dress in tatters, her hair badly singed on one side, but a broad, satisfied smile on her face. I shook my head frantically at Dan and pointed towards the door.

Just then, the sound of vehicles came roaring up the quiet country lane. They burst into the car park, sending the gravel flying like bullets. Dan took his chance and ran towards me, the old wooden box clamped under his arm. We bolted for the back door, feet slipping on glass and sodden wood. Outside, I pulled him towards the hedge, praying to find a thin enough spot for us to push through it to the lane.

I risked a glance at the car park and saw Jackson leap from the passenger side of a car that was technically still moving.

'Here!' Dan called, grabbing my hand and pulling.

We pushed through the hedge and out into the bright, airless summer's day. As I glanced back, I saw the thick black storm cloud hanging over the pub, flashes of lightning still arcing from within its depths, and for a second, I was a terrified young girl again, watching a tempest rage around the place I'd once called home.

Panting, I motioned for Dan to hand me the box.

My hands trembled as I lifted the lid, but I knew without looking that the release spell wasn't inside. I pulled the sheets out, two of parchment and the third a modern copy on paper. I handed the box to Dan and unfolded each sheet carefully.

'Is it there?'

I shook my head as I tried to wrestle down my disappointment.

'Just a copy of the safe harbour spell plus one for ripping and one for claiming another's magic. Maybe Devlin doesn't have it after all.'

'I'm so sorry, babe,' Dan said, wrapping his arms around me.

I closed my eyes and focused on the feel of him. He was safe, and that's what mattered right now.

'Quinn!'

We turned as one to see Jackson sprinting towards us.

'Shit, man. Are you okay?' he asked, peering at Dan's eye.

'I am now,' he said, holding up our joined hands and smiling at me.

'You're going to need this,' Jackson said, pulling a long cream envelope from his inside pocket and handing it to me.

I glanced down to see my full name inked in a copperplate script. The butterflies looped in giddy circles in my chest as I slid my finger under the wax seal.

'It's from a friend,' Jackson said, sounding as if he were choosing his words carefully.

My eyes swam with tears as I read.

'What?' Dan asked.

'It's the release spell,' I said, choking back my tears.

CHAPTER 62

GWEN, AUGUST 1976

Clementine, squashed into the passenger footwell by my feet, sat up as we pulled onto the track that led to the cottage. I tapped my knees, and she hopped into my lap, burying me beneath a mound of silky copper fur. Precious loved grooming her, and judging from the faint smell of strawberries, she'd recently bathed her too.

'Nearly home, girl,' Dan said, stretching over to tickle her ears.

As we emerged from the trees, the cottage appeared like a bright beacon in the moonlight. It looked like the most beautiful place on Earth.

'Home,' I whispered.

'Home,' Dan echoed as he pulled the handbrake, then cupped his palm against my face and traced his thumb across my cheek. I turned and gently kissed his wrist, which might have been romantic if Clem hadn't done the same, making us both laugh.

Once inside, I made hot chocolate while Dan made copies of the release spell. I didn't have the heart to tell him there was no need, so I left him to his work, enjoying the silence, broken only by the lap of the waves.

He sat back and dropped the pen onto the table. 'Done,' he said, looking pleased with himself. 'I was kinda expecting something longer. More, I dunno, fancy,' he said, rubbing the back of his neck.

I shrugged. So was I. That the key to my prison cell was so simple felt at odds with the enormity of my situation. I should have been able to work this out for myself, shouldn't I? The butterflies beat slow, deliberate wings against my ribs, and I got the sense that they didn't agree.

Dan had wanted me to recite the spell as soon as we got back to the car, but I'd told him I needed to say goodbye properly. It wasn't a lie, but my heart pinched at the half-truth. He was so happy, I couldn't bring myself to tell him, not yet. He thought we'd won. Good had triumphed over evil, Devlin was contained, justice would be done, and we'd get to live out our days in a cottage on a clifftop watching the sun rise and fall over a tranquil, gilded sea. We both needed at least a day to enjoy that dream.

'Are you ready now?' he asked, holding up a copy.

I shook my head. 'How about we rid the world of Devlin's spells, though? Make sure he can never do this again,' I suggested.

I burned the ripping spell first, sending my prayers to all those Devlin had killed while using it.

Next, I touched the flame to the claiming spell, swallowing around the lump in my throat as I thought of Owain, our coven's gentle scribe whose innocent mistake had compounded Nain's to make this whole nightmare possible.

My hands shook as I lifted the match to the safe harbour spell, unable to bring myself to destroy it. I knew it was just a copy; the original was still in the Pont Nefoedd archive, according to Dan's librarian friend, but it was a shock to see my grandmother's small, precise lettering after so many years.

The match guttered and the air filled with the scent of sun-warmed lavender. I swallowed past the pebble in my throat as I sniffed back my tears.

'You okay?' Dan asked.

'Just saying my other goodbyes,' I replied as I let the flames do their work.

Later, as I sipped my second hot chocolate, Dan stalked around the tiny cottage, finding hiding spots for the copies of the release spell.

One behind the coffee jar on the shelf above the stove, one tucked into the frame of the oil painting above the mantlepiece, and the last copy stowed beneath the base of the lamp in our bedroom.

I smiled at the thought of 'our' anything and wondered what it might be like to persuade his friend to sell us the cottage. I shoved the thought away. No. There was only one way this would end, and I'd have to do it soon or else I'd lose my nerve – and my mind.

Jackson couldn't protect us forever. It would be only a matter of time before the Unit found us, and while their methods might differ to Devlin's, their intention would be the same – to control magic that didn't belong to them. I couldn't, wouldn't, let that happen. The butterflies deserved their freedom, and the world needed their magic, perhaps now more than ever.

I swallowed the lump in my throat and smiled at Dan as he held out the long cream envelope containing the original spell. I hid it in my cello case and walked back into the living area to see Dan crouching next to the sofa, whispering to Clementine, who lay stretched the length of it.

'... and in the morning, we'll go for a nice long walk on the beach before it gets too hot.'

Clementine yawned and wagged her tail sleepily.

'Time for us all to go to bed,' I purred, standing so close to him that my thighs pressed into his back.

He turned as he rose to his feet, wrapping his arms around me and pulling me close as a smile that felt like heaven spread across his beautiful face. Standing on tiptoes, I brushed my lips against his swollen eye and wished it had been me who had taken the beating instead.

We made love until dawn, catching what felt to be only a few minutes of sleep before waking and starting over. I tried to savour every moment, every touch, every look, every sensation. I felt like I was storing them in a locket, tucking them away so that when the moment came, they'd give me the strength to do what was right.

I'd spent centuries believing that I hadn't really lived, but was that even true? I had loved and been loved, and wasn't that all that mattered in the end? And now that my time was ending, I wanted to focus on everything I had – not everything I'd lost or forgone.

I'd finally found my place in the world, and I was looking right at him. I could give him my whole heart without worrying that I'd one day need to bury him as an old man. That alone should have felt like a gift.

'Hey, what's wrong?' Dan said, breaking off from kissing my neck. He thumbed a tear from my cheek, and I squeezed my legs around his waist, desperate to get even closer, if that was even possible.

'I am the happiest I have ever been in my life,' I whispered, working hard to contain my emotion. I would not ruin the time we had with self-pity and tears. Grief was inevitable, but first there needed to be more of this. More love. More joy and laughter. More life.

'Shall we get married then?' Dan asked.

I threw back my head and laughed. 'And I thought you were a modern man!' I teased.

A grief-sized boulder lodged in my throat as I saw the hope in his eyes.

'Nothing would make me happier,' I murmured, which was the truth.

Dan grinned and then kissed me, and I lost myself in the tangle of our bodies and the knowledge that while I didn't have tomorrow, I had now.

We spent the day as I imagined a normal couple might. Dan made me a paper engagement ring out of a beer bottle label and made a big fuss about getting down on one knee to propose properly after a breakfast of coffee and tinned peaches. Clem made the moment even more memorable by knocking him over on the first attempt.

We walked on the beach, playing ball and paddling in the sea. After a long bath together, we drove to the village pub and had lunch. I saw Dan puff with pride as the landlord declared Clem to be the prettiest dog he'd ever seen – the lady herself making short work of the biscuits he slipped her every time he passed.

Dan and I fell back into bed when we returned to the cottage, emerging a few hours later to see Clem flat out on the sofa, her paws paddling in the air and her lip twitching as she dreamt. The sight of her, so blissfully lost in her dreams, brought fresh tears to my eyes. How many years had I longed for a dog?

Later, as Dan threw together a simple salad for dinner, I sat in the garden and played my cello. Clem sat at my side, tracking the butterflies as they danced over the sea, their wings burnished by the dying light. They flared brilliant against the fading sky as violet tones replaced the powder blue of the day. The sun streaked the sky with rose-gold clouds, casting her dimming fire like glitter onto the gently rolling waves.

The world had never looked so perfect, the butterflies never more magical, dancing together as if the Goddess herself were conducting them. Their joy reverberated down the bond, but this time, it was woven with other emotions too: love, gratitude and a heart-wrenching sadness that only comes with farewells. I bit my lip and smiled through my tears, pushing every ounce of love I had through my bow as I played their favourite piece last, 'Hiraeth'.

How many times had I played this? Seeing in my mind's eye the valley from the top meadow shrouded in dragon's breath, hearing the cry of the white-tailed eagles as they rode the wind like they alone commanded it, and the creak of Tân's old saddle shifting beneath me. How I'd longed to return to those simpler times, when the world felt like my playground and I slept soundly each night not knowing the horrors that awaited me.

All these years I'd thought my lament for was my home-land, and yet, playing it now, I realised that maybe my longing was misplaced. I was yearning for a halcyon past that had never really existed at all. So, what was I lamenting now? The answer came so swiftly it stole my breath. Myself.

'Oh my—' Dan gasped from somewhere behind me, leaving the rest of the sentence unfinished. I swallowed my self-pity as I played on.

I heard him set down the plates on the table, and then, without another word, he sat next to Clem, their eyes on the sky as the butterflies danced, and the sun slowly set on what I knew would be my last full day.

CHAPTER 63

DAN, AUGUST 1976

Gwen wasn't beside me when I woke, but I could still smell her perfume mingling with the distant smell of the sea. The first shafts of light spilled through the warped glass of the bedroom window, lending the whitewashed walls a golden hue. I rubbed at the fresh sweat on my neck. Despite the open window, the room was already hot, yesterday's heat still locked into the thick stone walls.

I lay still, listening for the flush of the toilet or the clink of mugs for a clue as to where she might be. She must have let Clem out, or else I'd be buried under a dog right now.

Long minutes passed, the silence pressing in against me as the air grew heavy in the small room. A sudden gust of wind rattled the window on its latch, and my skin goose-fleshed as the cold air planed across my bare skin. I jumped out of bed, pulling on a pair of shorts and hopping towards the bedroom door as I pulled them up.

I yanked open the door, my eyes falling at once on a small white envelope propped against the coffee pot on the kitchen counter. Next to it lay Gwen's old, battered satchel. I crossed the space in a couple of strides and tore open the letter. My blood pounded in my ears as I read.

Dan,

Please forgive me for lacking the courage to say goodbye in person. I love you so much that a letter feels like the only way I can do what's right.

I would give everything to be able to spend my life with you, but I wasn't entirely truthful about the spell. Once I release the butterflies, my unnaturally long life will come to an end. Please don't try to stop me. This is my duty and my destiny ...

The letter slipped from my fingers, and I bolted for the back door, launching myself through it and scanning left and right.

Gwen was standing up on the headland, her face tilted towards the rising sun and her arms open wide as if embracing the sky. She was wearing the white nightgown I'd seen thrown over the chair in our room, her hair flying in tendrils around her face.

I moved on instinct, vaulting over the low garden wall, my legs pumping in time with my hammering heart as I sprinted towards her, screaming her name. Clem, sitting serenely at her side, turned her head, but didn't run to me.

Frantic, I screamed Gwen's name again, my voice raw and breaking. I called again, and again, and at last, her shoulders sagged as she let her arms fall limply at her sides, her chin sinking to her chest.

She was already crying when I opened my arms to her. She barrelled into me, wrapping her arms around my back and holding on as if I'd just plucked her half drowned from the sea. I felt her body shaking as I walked us away from the edge of the cliff, whispering, 'I've got you. I've got you. We'll find another way,' repeatedly until we were back in the garden.

Gwen slumped down onto the bench and held her head in her hands until Clem pressed a cold nose to her cheek. She made a sound that was something between a sob and a laugh, lowered herself onto the grass and crossed her legs, making a hollow for the dog to climb into.

I sat next to her and wrapped my arm around her. 'It can't be true. This can't be your reward. It can't. It just can't.'

She choked back a sob, already shaking her head. 'The butterflies' magic is the only thing keeping me alive. I should be nothing but dust by now,' she said, looking up into my face.

I felt my breath catch at the sight of her. She was so beautiful, so strong, and yet the weariness – the sadness in her eyes – broke me.

'I have lived far beyond the boundaries of what's natural, and when I release the magic, Time will find me again. The Goddess will call in my debt. It is just the way of the world, don't you see?' she murmured, her eyes on the dog.

I touched my finger to her chin and waited until she met my eye.

'No. I don't see. Nature, magic, Time, the Goddess, call it whatever the hell you want, but I don't think it's that cruel. Why would it bring us together just to take you away now? No.' I sounded a lot more certain than I felt, but there was no way on Earth I was going to let her do this.

'You don't understand,' she said, her voice cracking. 'There is always a price for magic.'

'Says who?'

'Nain. It's one of the first things I learned.'

'Your grandmother sounded like a wonderful woman,

Gwen, but have you ever stopped to wonder if she wasn't half the witch you are?'

Gwen stared at me, her body stiffening against my touch. 'I don't even have magic of my own,' she said coolly.

I wasn't giving up. I shrugged, not yielding when Gwen made to lean away from me.

'What if real magic isn't all floating chairs and thwarting enemies with energy bolts? What if it's wisdom and knowledge and love and compassion and doing what's right? Maybe it's time to take your grandmother off that pedestal and start trusting your own knowing,' I said, touching my palm to the top of her chest.

Her expression softened a fraction, so I pressed on.

'Even if your grandmother was right and there is a price to be paid, maybe you've already paid it. Maybe you paid by sacrificing your chance of a normal life, or maybe you're right and—' My voice caught, and I cleared my throat. 'Maybe your life will end the moment you release the butterflies, so before you take that risk, let's find out. Together.'

Her lip trembled as she looked up at me, and I cupped her face, stroking my thumb across her tear-stained cheek.

'At least give yourself a chance. We can speak to Seren, or Maggie, or Jackson,' I said. 'And if we can't find help, or if we get an answer we don't want, then we'll run. Abroad this time. We'll find a tiny house on an island and live off coconuts, and you can do the spell and release the magic when you're old and grey.'

I tried to laugh, but the truth caught in my throat and smothered the sound. So long as she carried the orphaned magic, she wouldn't age a day, while I'd become just another in a long line of people who died and abandoned her to a lonely eternity.

'Can we take Clem?' Gwen whispered, leaning into my side and resting her head on my shoulder.

I squeezed her close, trying to steady my voice long enough to reply. 'Of course we can. We're a family now,' I said, and planted a kiss on the top of her head.

The growl, low and guttural in the dog's throat, caught us both by surprise. I glanced down at Clem to see her staring, hard-eyed, towards the side of the cottage and the track beyond. Just then, Gwen lurched forward, a marionette yanked on invisible strings.

We all jumped to our feet, but by then we could hear the vehicles, tyres crunching over the hard-baked track. With Devlin out of the picture, it had to be the Unit. I tasted bile in my throat as I looked at Gwen and for a fleeting moment saw a reflection of my horror mirrored in her eyes.

'Get Clem inside and hide the copies of the spell,' she instructed.

'But—'

'Do it. It might just be Jackson, but best be safe,' she said, looking away.

I opened my mouth to argue, but Gwen shouted, 'Dan! Grab her!'

I whirled around to see Clem, teeth bared and hackles raised, stalking towards the wall. I caught her collar a heartbeat before she launched herself over it and marched her into the cottage, just in time to see the front door fly off its hinges.

It was all I could do to hold Clem back as four black-clad operatives, one still holding the battering ram, stormed into the tiny space, Perkins following in their wake.

'What the fuck do you think you're doing!' I bellowed.

Perkins, already sweating in his ill-fitting suit, smiled. 'We have reason to believe that items belonging to Sir Reginald Devlin are concealed on these premises. We plan to make a thorough search.'

'Care to show me your search warrant?' I snarled.

'Don't need one, son. We operate outside of normal laws,' he said smugly.

'Bullshit. That's a bare-faced lie, so get the fuck out of my house.' I knew they'd be going nowhere, but I needed to buy Gwen some time to get away.

Clem snarled, and I tightened the grip on her collar.

'Control that animal or I'll have it shot,' Perkins snapped, taking a step back.

I felt a white-hot fury twist in my gut, and had I not been holding the dog, I would have knocked him out where he stood.

'Sir! Subject spotted!' one of the operatives called from outside the cottage.

'Move!' Perkins yelled, already turning on his heel.

I wrestled Clem to the bedroom, apologising as I shut the door and sprinted after the men in black, dimly registering the four SUVs parked outside and the dozen or more operatives running towards the headland – and Gwen.

The realisation landed like a punch to my gut. No. This couldn't be happening. For the second time that morning, I raced towards her, screaming her name. She turned then, and although she was still too far away for me to see her expression, I knew she was saying goodbye. She turned back to the sea.

The tackle blindsided me. One minute I was running, the next I was slamming into the ground, the air wrenched from my lungs as an operative the size of a quarterback drove my face down to the dirt.

He dragged me to my feet and pinned my arms behind my back before I could even swing a punch. I watched in horror as the other operatives raced towards Gwen.

'Run! Gwen! Run!' I screamed the words, but she didn't turn. They'd be on her in seconds.

'Please!' I begged, my voice breaking. 'Just run!'

I watched as she lifted her chin to the heavens and threw her arms wide, arching her back like a dancer about to perform. On my chest, my tattoo fizzed like a hive full of bees.

I felt the air pressure shift just as the butterflies exploded from her chest, shooting high into the waking sky then arrowing straight back to her.

My legs buckled and the operative let me fall, presumably too mesmerised by the spectacle to do anything else. I fell to my knees as I watched the woman who might have one day been my wife dissolve into butterflies, their bright wings reflecting the morning light in a mockery of my hope. I could still see Gwen's outline, but she was all wings now.

I heard distant barking but didn't register Clem's presence until she barrelled into me, panting hard. I pulled her close and slid my hands into her silky fur.

The butterflies suddenly shifted as one, a tornado of colour spinning so fast and so brightly I screwed up my eyes and flung my hand across Clem's.

On my chest, my tattoo thrummed like plucked strings as the air pressure once again built around us. Someone called my name, but I couldn't find the strength to move, pinned to the spot by my grief and the horror unfolding before my eyes.

'Quinn!'

Jackson skidded to a stop beside me, breathing hard.

'Get up, man.'

Hope flared in my gut. Maybe he had a plan. Maybe he could stop this. I jumped to my feet, but all at once, the sky filled with a blinding white light. We fell backwards, knocked off our feet by a pulse of energy that could have taken down an army.

I lay there, trying to catch my breath. Above me, the pastel wash of delicate blue sky was a riot of untethered colour. She'd done it. The butterflies were free. The magic could return to their familial lines or do whatever the hell orphaned magic did in the world. It was free from the likes of Devlin, free from the Unit. But Gwen had lost everything. I choked back a sob. Why hadn't I gone with her? Made her run?

'Trust me. You're gonna want to see this, man,' Jackson said, leaning over me and holding out a hand.

I shook my head, screwing up my eyes as another wave of grief slammed into me. He sighed and toed my thigh.

'Seriously. Get your mother-fucking ass up now, Captain!'

I ignored him, too lost in my misery, until I heard Clem barking. Perkins's threat ricocheted around my mind like a stray bullet, and I leapt to my feet.

'Cl—' Her name died on my lips as I looked up to see Gwen sprinting towards me.

CHAPTER 64

GWEN, AUGUST 1976

*J*t wasn't until I leapt into Dan's waiting arms, wrapping my legs tight around his waist, that I allowed myself to believe that I was still here.

I'd fixed my eyes on my hands as I ran, terrified that I might see them age and wither away to old bones like something from an old horror film. I'd held my breath as I sprinted, praying that I wouldn't dissolve into dust on the wind before I reached him and begging the Goddess to honour the promise the butterflies left me with.

I was so sure the spell would be the end of me, so sure that the moment I uttered those words, Time would claim me. A year ago, I would have welcomed death as a gift. My duty done, the orphaned magic returned and a natural, welcome end to my long, lonely existence. But that was before a man and a dog saved my life and reminded me what a miracle it is just to be alive.

I'd felt the butterflies surge in my chest as I ran to the clifftop. Sensing my intention, they'd beat gentle, excited wings against my ribs, and for a moment, my courage left me. I had to let them go. Had to free them, or I'd damn them to whatever vile purpose the Unit might have planned. And yet, I'd hesitated. Wanting to take one more look at the sunrise.

When I'd turned to see a dozen or more black-clad operatives racing towards me, I knew I was out of time.

I'd felt the tether of the old spell stretch in my chest even before I'd spoken the first word, the spell unspooling like a ball of string within me. I'd smiled as I finally realised what Nain had tried so hard to teach me when I was a girl. Magic isn't just spoken; it's felt.

I'd known at once that the spell was in motion, but I'd said the words aloud anyway, wanting to leave at least my last breaths on the wind as some ephemeral reminder that I'd existed. That I had lived and loved and mattered in some small way.

My heart filled as the butterflies sent their love and gratitude careering down the bond, their energy building and reminding me of Tân as he trotted, high on his toes, readying himself for the long gallop.

As the last word fell from my lips, I felt each tether burst like a bubble in my chest, and then they were free. No mental bolt to slide away this time, just an explosion of joyful wings.

I'd expected them to flee, but a heartbeat later they'd surrounded me, their gossamer wings coating every inch of my body like a second skin. I'd gasped, but then they shifted as one, whirling around me in a kaleidoscope of jewels. I'd smelled wildflowers, tasted lightning, and knew what it was to soar amongst the clouds, push my roots deep into the earth and power through the oceans of the world. I was fire and air, water and earth, love and fear and life itself.

The light exploded out of me without warning, and I staggered backwards, barely keeping my balance. I scanned the skies, hoping to see the butterflies in the distance, but saw only a reflection of myself, hovering just beyond the cliff edge. I took a tentative step forward and realised it wasn't me but the Goddess herself. And she was smiling.

Dan staggered under my weight but held me. I squeezed hard, needing to obliterate any space between us.

'I thought I'd lost you,' he said, his voice raw.

'Never,' I said, leaning back to take in his beautiful face. I touched my fingers to his swollen eye and wriggled free as I remembered his sore ribs and bruised stomach.

'I'm sorry. I'm sorry,' I said, leaning up to plant feather-like kisses on his face.

Someone cleared their throat, and we looked up.

'Look, I hate to ruin the moment,' Jackson said, sounding awkward, 'but I need to deal with this, and then I need to do a whole load of apologising.'

I had no idea what he was talking about – in fact, I was only now registering his presence – but I smiled and said, 'Okay.'

Jackson strode across the headland to where Perkins was jabbing his pointed finger into the faces of the assembled operatives.

'Come on,' I said, pulling Dan's hand. 'I think we need to hear this.'

'... and if you'd done what you'd been ordered to do, then we'd have her in custody by now! How am I going to explain to the guvnor that his magic is now free and flying to the four fucking winds, eh?' Perkins's face was so red it looked almost purple.

'First up, you need to explain this second unauthorised operation,' Jackson said, stopping within a foot of the smaller man.

'Fuck off, yank,' Perkins spat. 'I don't answer to you.'

A slow, easy smile spread across Jackson's face. He waited a beat before pulling an envelope from his back pocket and handing it to Perkins.

The other man sucked in his cheeks as he glared at Jackson for a long moment before snatching it and yanking out the letter.

'Oh, and I'm Canadian, actually. But you knew that already,' Jackson said lightly.

Perkins ignored him, his eyes scanning the letter. I felt Dan stifle a laugh as Perkins lost some of his colour. He snapped his head up to look at Jackson, his mouth gaping like a barn door.

'But we applied for the director of operations,' Perkins mumbled, his eyes still fixed on the letter.

'Oh, you might have applied for that, but I was invited to step in as director-general the moment our current leader was removed,' Jackson said, plucking the letter back. 'So, you absolutely do answer to me, Agent Perkins.'

Perkins ran a hand over his now ashen face and cleared his throat. 'What do you mean, "removed"?'

'Arrested.' Jackson made a show of checking his watch. 'About an hour ago by our colleagues in counterintelligence for colluding with Devlin and planning a coup, would you believe. Seems he also had the Unit's agents working off the books.'

Perkins swayed, as if the ground had shifted beneath him.

'Arrest him,' Jackson said to the nearest operative, pointing at Perkins.

Two men stepped forward, both looking keen to oblige.

'What charge, sir?'

'Start with treason and we'll work backwards from there.'

We were sitting on the bench in the back garden, cradling mugs of coffee, when Jackson found us.

Dan jumped up to hug his friend. 'Director frickin' general?' he said, slapping him on the back. 'Do they even know you fart like a buffalo in your sleep?'

'Weird, but it didn't come up at the interview,' Jackson said with a grin.

'Wait, you have a security detail now?' Dan asked, looking past Jackson to where two men in sunglasses and plain clothes stood just beyond the garden wall. 'Course you do. Top brass now, my friend!'

'Congratulations, and thank you. Thank you for everything,' I said, leaning up to plant a kiss on Jackson's cheek.

Jackson nodded and gave me an 'It was nothing' shrug.

'What happened to Devlin and Angie?' Dan asked, his expression serious again.

'Devlin was pronounced dead at the scene, although we've not released that information yet – I want the results of the autopsy just to be sure,' he replied with a look that said he was only half joking. 'Angie Tanner surrendered. She claims Devlin was blackmailing her, threatening her kids.'

Dan snorted and kicked out at the ground. 'She still killed a man. I saw her do it, and believe me, she didn't seem to be under any kind of duress.'

Jackson put a hand on Dan's shoulder. 'I won't let her get away with it, I promise. We'll get justice for Doctor Clement and all their other victims.'

Dan nodded, and I slipped my arm around his waist.

'And look, I'm sorry we put you both through all this just now. It's not how I planned it, but as the chief's lapdog, that bastard Perkins always seemed to be one step ahead. Trust me, though, you'll not be hearing from the Unit again.' Jackson turned to me and grinned. 'Not now that you're just a regular magical mortal.'

I laughed. 'Just a regular mortal, thanks,' I said with a dismissive wave. 'I've never had magic.'

Jackson raised his eyebrows. 'You sure about that?'

I frowned. I was about to ask him what he meant when one of the security detail coughed loudly.

'Look, I gotta run, but let's catch up soon, okay,' Jackson said, folding us both into a tight hug then bending down to ruffle Clem's ears.

As we watched him jog to the gate, I sighed and hugged Dan tighter.

'He's a good man,' Dan said. 'Maybe with him in charge, there's a chance of ending this feud with the magical community.'

I thought back to that day in Wiltshire in 1942. Walt's unbridled fury as he screamed down the phone. The sound of him weeping quietly afterwards.

'I don't know the whole story of what happened back during the war, but if you make breakfast, I'll tell you what I know.'

Dan planted a kiss on my lips. 'Done!' he said, pulling me towards the cottage.

I let my fingers slip from his.

'I'll be with you in a sec,' I said, bending to scoop up our empty mugs from the bench. As I straightened up, I felt the pressure shift around me, and the meadow brown materialised just inches from my face.

'Why didn't you go with the others, sweetheart? You're free now.'

I held up my hand and she settled on my finger, folding her wings. Clem let out a soft woof and jumped onto the bench to get a closer look. I sat back down and smiled as Clem inched closer to get a sniff of the butterfly.

Nain's voice, still so clear in my mind even after all this time, echoed in my ears. 'Your magic will come to you when you're ready, child, and not before.'

I sucked in a sharp breath.

'You've been with me all along.' The words tumbled from

my lips in a whisper. 'Since that first day on the top road to Talybont.' My voice cracked and I sniffed. 'You've always been mine, but I just couldn't see it.'

The butterfly opened her wings and rose into the air, dancing in slow circles in the bright August sunshine. She vanished without warning, and my hand flew instinctively to my chest. It took a second to feel it, but when I did, I relaxed at the familiar weight of wings beneath my ribs and the soft, rhythmic pulse of magic against my heart. But this time, the magic was all mine.

EPILOGUE
GWEN, JULY 1983

I twitched the reins, asking Eira to stand so that I could take a moment to just enjoy the view from the top meadow. She planted her feet, careful as always not to step on Clem.

My meadow brown fluttered near my left cheek, and I smiled at her. How I loved this valley, with its patchwork of forests and fields and the Black Mountains cradling it all like a secret. There were more houses now, of course, nestled together in small villages connected by twisting country lanes, but it was still my valley. Still my home.

I leaned forward in my stirrups and wrapped my arms around Eira's thick, warm neck. A dappled grey mare, she was the polar opposite of the coal-black horse of my childhood, but she shared Tân's gentle nature and his uncanny way of always knowing what I was thinking.

I sighed as I heard them approach.

'I hope you two enjoyed our thirty seconds of peace,' I said, patting Eira and directing my words at Clem.

'But why can't I just ride him by myself?' My daughter's voice cut through the quiet.

'Well, honey, for one, your legs are a little short for the stirrups, don't you think?' Dan said levelly.

'We can shorten them though. I'll show you how to do it if you like. It's not difficult, Dad.'

I turned to see Dan stifling a laugh, our daughter swaying in the saddle in front of him. Though he claimed to have cowboy genes, it was clear who the natural horsewoman was. Derwen, Dan's surefooted tri-coloured Welsh Cob, let out a long snort as if he agreed.

I raised an eyebrow at my husband, and he grinned. We'd agreed to tell her here – it was her favourite place as well as ours – but we'd not decided who would deliver the news.

I pointed at Dan, but he shook his head and nodded to me, mouthing, 'You do it.'

When they drew level, I leaned over to gaze at our little miracle, her dark curls poking out from under her riding hat. She'd taken us all by surprise, including everyone attending my very first book signing.

Clem woofed, and I glanced down to see her prancing on her back legs, mesmerised by a ball of flowers bobbing in mid-air and apparently defying the laws of gravity.

I tried to hide my laugh under a sigh. 'Margot Llewellyn-Quinn, what have we told you about doing magic in public?'

My daughter turned those sooty-amber eyes on me and bit her lip, trying to look contrite but failing miserably.

'But poor Clemmy was bored,' she said with a mischievous shrug as she sent the ball flying across the meadow, an ecstatic dog in hot pursuit.

Dan wrapped his arms around her and made her giggle. It was such a rich, throaty belly laugh that I didn't want to spoil the moment.

I'd tell her about the pony we'd chosen for her in a minute. For now, I let myself sink into the moment. The music of my husband's and daughter's laughter, the wind sighing through the trees and the scent of sun-warmed horses and meadow flowers drifting on a gentle breeze. We had all the time we needed.

The End

AUTHOR'S NOTE

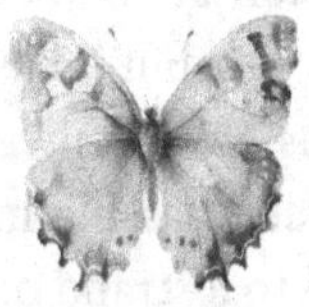

Back in January 2022, the ballroom scene from chapter sixteen, where we see the butterflies dance as Gwen plays her cello, unspooled in my mind like a film.

I knew right away that the butterflies weren't corporeal but the orphaned magic of murdered witches. I also knew that Gwen was playing a lament for her homeland. I remember racing to grab my phone, my skin tingling, as I jotted down the note, though I had no idea when I'd get a chance to write the story itself.

Life was manic. I was finishing my second book, *The Blessing of Crows*, caring for our poorly pup Bear, juggling a frenetic freelance schedule, and grappling with serious health issues that led to major surgery that spring.

I didn't return to the idea until February 2023, but even then, I only managed a third of a very messy first draft before *The Magic Keepers* elbowed *The Butterfly Witch* out of the way as it grew from a short story into a full-blown novel of its own.

I've long since surrendered to the will of stories to find their own perfect time, so I went with it. *The Magic*

Keepers launched on 18th July 2024. I returned to *The Butterfly Witch* on 24th July, and just six weeks later, the first very messy draft was done.

By then, I knew the reason for the delay. *Hiraeth*, the Welsh word that means a deep, often untranslatable longing for home, had always been at the heart of this story. I left Wales nearly thirty years ago, but it has never left me.

While my mother was alive, I always had a reason to 'go home'. But after her sudden passing in 2018, my connection to my homeland thinned to a strand of spider silk. I'd bought a holiday let near my childhood home back when times were good and bricks and mortar felt like the safest retirement plan. Ty Hiraeth was a big hit with visitors, but the pandemic and increasingly aggressive legislation turned something that had once brought me joy into something that kept me awake at night.

Selling 'the house that called me home' was gut-wrenching. But as I drove back to Berkshire in November 2024 – my tiny car packed to the roof, my heart breaking as that last silk thread snapped – I finally understood why this book had waited. I needed to feel that final piece of loss before I could do Gwen's story justice. Writing about her disconnection from her homeland helped me make peace with my own.

This book has been cathartic in other ways too. I set the final act in 1976 not only because it suited Margot's storyline (if you've not read *The First Ethereal* yet, you'll soon see what became of the sweet little witch we met in the epilogue) but because that year was catastrophic for my family. My father lost his battle with leukaemia in August 1976, just a week after his twenty-seventh birthday, and then, in October, my maternal grandfather passed away. Setting a happily-ever-after love story in the year that nearly broke us felt like my way of reclaiming it.

This book has taught me so much – not least that I can be

patient and methodical when I need to be. I have binders full of hand-edited drafts which, if you know me (squirrel!), speaks volumes about how much I wanted this book to be the best it could be. It also inspired me to start learning the cello – thirty-seven years after my first attempt was vetoed by my mother within hours.

I've taken liberties with locations. All the houses, including Gwen and Dan's cottage in the Gower, are inventions. The cottage itself was inspired by an old oil painting I have at home (which I love, and my husband hates!) and the lonesome-looking white farmhouse visible from Rhossili. When I was writing the Gower scenes, it was Broughton Bay I 'saw' in my mind's eye.

Thank you for reading *The Butterfly Witch*. Every book I write is a book of my heart, but this one is especially close to it. If you enjoyed it, please leave a review to help others find it.

If you have any questions, I'd love to hear from you. You can reach me on social media @elwilliamsauthor or via my website, www.elwilliamsauthor.com.

THE MAGIC KEEPERS

A STANDALONE ETHEREAL WORLD NOVEL

When it comes to rewriting history, some books have plans of
their own.

READ ON FOR YOUR FREE SAMPLE

CHAPTER 1

ABERYSTWYTH, JULY 1960

*L*ydia eyed the book on the top shelf and sighed. She wasn't keen on heights, and she wondered whether the book knew it. This was the third time she'd had to reposition the library ladder and her patience was wearing thin. Not wanting to climb down again, she took a deep breath and hooked her left arm through the nearest rung, anchoring herself so that she could stretch far enough to reach the little green book. Just as her fingers brushed against the spine, it shuffled another inch out of her reach.

'Oh, you stubborn little sod,' she growled through gritted teeth.

The book jumped backwards, and Lydia cursed herself. The poor thing was clearly nervous, bless it, but they had enough to do already without new arrivals giving them the runaround.

'Okay,' she said, using her best librarian's voice and softening her tone. She smiled at the book. 'Come on now, lovely, you don't have to be read if you're not ready, but we need to catalogue you, which means I at least need to read your title. Would that be alright?'

The book seemed to consider it for a moment, and then slowly shuffled forward.

Lydia smiled encouragingly. She squinted, cursing herself again, this time for leaving her reading glasses somewhere. She could almost make out the title, but the gold lettering on its dark teal-green cover was too faint.

'That's a good book,' she cooed, leaning closer.

'Still giving you the runaround?' a voice from below asked.

Startled, Lydia lost her footing and let out a cry as, for a few vertigo-inducing seconds, the arm she'd looped around the ladder was the only thing holding her up.

The little book shot backwards in alarm, hit the wall and ricocheted into a row of books on the next shelf down. Like a flock of angry geese, they took to the air in panic, rousing other books in their page-flapping wake.

Clinging to the ladder, Lydia found her footing just in time to duck as a hefty old tome, clearly late to the panic, hauled itself into the air mere inches from her face. She screwed up her eyes to avoid the cloud of ancient dust it left in its wake. It was no use. Lydia felt it settle on her face and tried not to breathe in until the worst had passed.

With both feet blessedly back on the ladder and both arms wrapped around it, Lydia opened her eyes and sighed as she watched the flock of books hurtle around the grand old library. She loved this place, with its polished wood, decorative carvings and panelled walls. Granted, it didn't have the ceiling height of her own precious library in Pont Nefoedd. That was often the trouble with basements, but of all the other magical libraries, this was her favourite. Leaving it would be a wrench for everyone concerned, but as the saying went, 'needs must when the devil rides', and in this case, the saying wasn't far from the truth. At least the new library would be more secure than a crumbling old manor house in the middle of nowhere.

With a sigh, Lydia climbed slowly down, her left shoulder throbbing and her upper arm sore. She'd no doubt have a bruise there by the morning. She was also unbearably hot. Her blouse felt pasted to her back and the elasticated waistband of her trousers was digging into her sides. Her stomach rumbled, reminding her to add hungry to the list of complaints too.

They had been re-cataloguing for days, but they were almost out of time. Powerful magical wards protected the library, but at this rate, they would need to be done again before they were ready. While they would have help from a small army of witches and members of the magical community on moving day, they were way behind schedule. If books just refrained from renaming themselves when the fancy took them, there'd be no need for re-cataloguing in the first place, Lydia thought for the umpteenth time in her long career.

'I'm getting too old for this,' she grumbled as her left knee shot her a needle of complaint when she stepped off the last rung of the ladder. The air was still thick with flapping books.

'Ow!' she yelled as a small blue book caught her a glancing blow on the back of her head. It shot off, leaving Lydia to rub the spot, although on reflection, it hadn't actually hurt. She could tell without the aid of a mirror that the heat had undone her efforts to set her hair. She ran her fingers through it as she checked for a lump anyway and thought of her late aunt's honey-coloured standard poodle. Any more grey hairs and she'd look more like a bichon soon, she thought irritably.

It looked like half the books in the library were now on

the wing, but it was far from an ordered affair. This was no murmuration to marvel at. Books, unlike birds, were too independent, some might say pig-headed, to be followers, and so each one was going freestyle. Some were darting above the stacks, pages flattened to fit themselves between shelf and ceiling, while others were swooping in great arcs from shelf top to library floor, looking like gulls diving for fish. The rest, save for a few of the smaller books that were fluttering around ankle height, seemingly confused by the commotion, just bombed around. Lydia sighed. The breeze from their flapping pages was quite refreshing, if you didn't breathe in the dust.

'Nonsense,' Frances said, reappearing, apparently unperturbed by the chaos in her usually ordered library. Lydia jumped.

'You're about half my age and as fit as a flea,' Frances said, peering over her glasses to pin Lydia with a steely look.

Lydia laughed ruefully. 'Unless you're ninety, then no, not quite half,' she said, collapsing into a chair at the reading table just in time to avoid another collision.

'Oh, alright then, you win,' Frances said amiably. 'But I maintain my point about your fitness. You've always been very robust.'

What you really mean is chunky, Lydia thought, but she knew her old friend, who despite her best efforts had the physique of a greyhound, meant it as a compliment.

Frances was a tall, fine-boned woman with poker-straight long silver-grey hair she wore pulled into a tight bun at the back of her head. Her hair had been ash blonde when she was younger, but the style had never changed. Lydia couldn't remember the point when her friend had tipped from blonde to grey, but knowing Frances, she'd barely have noticed either.

The older woman's only nod to fashion were her

bubblegum-pink winged reading glasses. Otherwise, it was a uniform of twinset and a tweed skirt in the winter and twinset and a cotton skirt in the summer months. No matter the weather, the shoes were always the same – a pair of sensible black lace-ups – always polished, but never to the point of being showy.

Without looking up from the book she was examining or raising her voice, Frances said sternly, 'Back to your places, please. Silly time is over.'

Had Frances not been a librarian and keeper of the Aberystwyth Library of Magical Texts, she would have made a brilliant headmistress at some posh girls' school, Lydia thought, smiling as she watched the careering books freeze in mid-air before dutifully gliding back into their places. Who said keepers couldn't do magic?

Lydia remembered coming here as a child when her aunt, the previous keeper at the Pont Nefoedd library, made the trip from their home in the Brecon Beacons to the little seaside town perched on the western coast of Wales. Even as a young woman, Frances didn't hold with the idea of entertaining children, so she'd put Lydia to work, finding or re-shelving books and later, when she was older, doing bits of research for her. No doubt from carefully vetted books known for their good manners. When Lydia's apprenticeship to her aunt Philippa began, Frances had become her third-year mentor, and then later, her colleague and friend.

'Treat them as you would a horse. Kindly, but suffering no nonsense,' Lydia's aunt used to tell her. 'Give them an inch and they will, mark my words, dear girl, take more than a country mile.'

Her aunt would usually follow with the story of the apprentice who had died while trying to manage a difficult book. Lydia had later discovered that the poor girl had tripped and knocked her head on the flagstones, but the story was still being used to instil a sense of wariness and respect for the books into all apprentices.

Lydia looked up just in time to see the new arrival return to its hiding place on top of the shelf. She sighed and massaged her temples to ward off the start of a headache. If only grumpy books were the worst of a keeper's lot.

CHAPTER 2

PONT NEFOEDD, JULY 1960

Maggie hopped off the library ladder five rungs from the bottom and sighed as she surveyed the cavernous room. Her mother really should think about smartening up the place. They were forever sweeping up the flakes of paint that seemed to enjoy throwing themselves off the whitewashed walls, the furniture was positively ancient, and the rugs were so drab it was hard to believe they'd even heard of the word 'colour'. Her requests to add a few posters, just for cheeriness, had elicited Lydia's infamous raised eyebrow. Well, infamous in the family, anyway. Maggie knew better than to push it, but it still irked her that her place of work felt like a mausoleum.

According to her mother, their time was better spent looking after the magical books in their care and doing the research required of them. She could hear her mother's voice in her head. 'But Mags, love, it's only us here most of the time. What's the point?'

Maggie huffed as she thought of the well-trodden argument, but stopped herself before she could fall into her familiar list of grumbles. Complaining didn't do anyone any good. That was one piece of her mother's advice that she could agree with – not that she'd admit it to her.

'Doesn't this place get you down?' Maggie said to the Siamese cat lounging on the reading table.

Boudicca blinked slowly in response and then stretched theatrically before rolling over and turning her back on Maggie.

'I'll take that as a no then, shall I, Bodie?' Maggie said, drawing out the cat's nickname and over-emphasising the 'Bo'. She knew Boudicca despised being addressed by anything other than her full moniker. Maggie supposed that if she'd had to suffer the indignity of being called Mr Tiddles for the first year of her life, she might be prickly about names too.

Boudicca flipped around, pinning Maggie with her now worryingly narrowed bright blue eyes. Her whip-like tail slashed back and forth across the table, sending loose sheets of paper sailing to the floor.

Maggie rolled her eyes at the cat and tutted loudly, but she already felt a settling weight in her stomach. She bit her lip, annoyed with herself for being spiteful, because, call it like it is, that's what she'd been. For once, it hadn't been Boudicca who had been in a bad mood – it was her.

'I'm sorry, Boudicca. Really, I am,' Maggie said with a sigh. She already knew it was too late to be sorry. Boudicca hissed, showing off her impressive canines, and turned her back. While she still appeared to be lounging, from her still flicking tail, Maggie knew she'd need to give her a wide berth for the rest of the day unless she wanted to get swiped for her trouble. *Nobody holds a grudge like a Siamese*, Maggie thought. *And I need to learn not to antagonise her*, she chided herself.

Any gratitude Boudicca had felt at being rescued from her father's slightly nutty aunt Deidre all those years ago she reserved for Maggie's mother. With Lydia, Boudicca was still an enraptured kitten – with everyone else, she veered between tetchy alley cat and wannabe velociraptor. *So much for her being my cat*, Maggie thought, the sting of disappointment still real after seven long years.

Glancing at the clock, Maggie felt her spirits lift. Just an hour more and she could go out to lunch with Keith. She smiled, picturing him waiting for her in the pub. Maybe walking her home if there was time. First, she had an essay to finish. She hesitated, considering how missing a deadline would factor in the bigger scheme of things now that she'd made her decision. Or, she corrected herself, had almost certainly decided.

The uncomfortable weight in her stomach returned. Her mother was going to be heartbroken when she told her. The mere thought of it had given her sleepless nights for weeks. But it was her life, wasn't it? She was twenty-one. A proper grown-up, so she didn't need anyone's permission anymore.

Pushing the tangle of thoughts aside, she pulled up a chair as far away from Boudicca as possible. It wasn't unheard of for the cat to exact her revenge with a well-aimed swipe, hours, sometimes days after a perceived offence. Maggie opened her notepad. She'd never submitted a piece of homework late in her life, and so decided that, regardless of the other thing, now was not the time to start.

Alongside her notepad and the books she'd be using for the essay sat a thin manila folder with the words 'Highly Confidential' stamped on the front in fresh red ink. Just looking at the folder made Maggie's stomach churn.

The memory of her mother handing it to her on the morning she left for Aber popped into her head. 'I know it's not the first crime scene report you've seen, but fair warning, love, this one was particularly nasty. The raid on the library was brutal,' her mother had said as she'd held the folder out to her.

Maggie had rolled her eyes and said something snarky that she couldn't remember now. She'd folded her arms and only let them drop back to her sides when she saw her mother's expression change. Not wanting to put a name to the look, Maggie had snatched the folder with an exaggerated sigh before putting it straight back down on the reading table.

'You know that Yolande was—'

Maggie interrupted, her tone sharper and more sarcastic than she'd intended. 'Decapitated by the magic hunters during the attack? Funnily enough, Mother, yes I do remember that little detail from the briefing.'

Lydia hadn't looked angry, even though Maggie knew she was being a brat about it all. Her mother had just looked so incredibly sad, although whether for their fallen colleague in Barcelona or her daughter who was duty bound to read the report, view the crime scene photographs and write up a report on it all, she couldn't tell. Unable to bear it, Maggie had said something flippant and made an excuse about needing the loo.

The truth was that the raids terrified her. The magic hunters raided libraries, looking for a book that could give ordinary people magical power. Some men sought the Holy Grail as they believed it could grant them eternal life and forgive their sins, while others sought power they didn't deserve.

Ironically, none of the scholars in the magical community could agree on whether such a book even existed, but so long as these men believed it did, they would stop at nothing in their quest for it.

Maggie turned her attention back to the notebook. The essay was on the infamous 'Tortured Text'. Discovered in

1945, it had provided a new and terrifying insight into the depravity of the magic hunters. Not content with stealing magical texts and murdering those who got in their way, when the sentient books refused to allow their captors to read them, the hunters tried to force their secrets from their pages.

The Tortured Text had somehow found its way back to the Elders, battered, burned and with a shattered spine that bore the hallmarks of being not just broken but wrung. It had never recovered from its ordeal.

Contained within a velvet-padded rosewood case which protected it and those who cared for it from its uncontrollable rages, a rotation of senior witches tended it around the clock, soothing it with spells and playing it classical music. It liked cello pieces the best, apparently, and somehow that always made Maggie's heart ache. Writing the essay had been a miserable undertaking, and she would be glad to finish it.

Maggie took a deep breath and picked up her pen, but her eye snagged again on the folder she'd not so much as touched in a week. She'd even dusted around it on cleaning day. If her mother came home to find that she'd not written up her report, there'd be hell to pay. Then again, she reasoned, there was going to be hell to pay anyway.

CHAPTER 3

ABERYSTWYTH, JULY 1960

The rattle of china brought Lydia back to the present. Rose, Frances's apprentice, crept into the room carrying a tray in the way one might carry an unexploded bomb. She was a similar build to Frances, although possibly not as tall. It was hard to tell because she was always so hunched, as if she was trying to curl herself into a little ball and disappear. She wore her long brown hair plaited neatly down her back. Lydia winced, and not for the first time, at the thinness of the girl's twiggy, milk-coloured arms. They would not be missing their meal tonight, no matter what, she thought.

Rose was one of the best apprentices they had, although Lydia would never admit as much to Maggie, but her lack of confidence was a serious worry. Some of the old tomes in the collection ran rings around her. They had had to move one of the grumpiest to Pont Nefoedd the previous summer after it cornered poor Rose for hours, snapping at her like an attack dog every time she tried to make a run for it.

Lydia wondered whether the story of the fallen keeper had served not to empower Rose but to frighten her into submission. Like Maggie, she was a full three years into her apprenticeship, but unlike her daughter, Rose still seemed like a fish out of water. Technically and academically brilliant, but still so painfully shy.

Lydia knew it worried Frances. They'd exchanged enough letters on the subject over the previous months, but she just didn't know what to suggest next. Rose didn't fit the mould of a keeper, but maybe that was the fault of the mould and not the young woman, Lydia pondered.

Rose slid the tray gingerly onto the table, the relief clear on her face. Lydia was pleased to see a plate of biscuits amongst the tea things. Her stomach grumbled in anticipation.

'Thanks, Rose,' Lydia said, smiling up at her. Rose flashed a brief smile and then looked at her feet.

Lydia thought of her daughter, Maggie, and felt a familiar squeeze around her heart. She had the confidence to handle even the most obnoxious of books, but Lydia secretly wished she'd chosen not to follow in her footsteps. Theirs was a dangerous world, and she'd rest so much easier if her daughter had been an accountant. Hell, even a trapeze artist would be a less risky profession.

'Stop frowning, Lydia, dear. You will get wrinkles,' Frances instructed as she stood to pour the tea. Almost forty years in this quiet corner of West Wales and her friend still sounded like the Oxford scholar she had once been.

'Oh, now that ship sailed a long time ago,' Lydia said with a laugh. 'Anyway, I prefer the term "laughter lines",' she added pointedly, her gaze straying to the dark corner near the old cargo lift.

Frances snorted and gave a wry laugh as she handed Lydia a cup of tea.

'We still need to change that lightbulb,' Lydia said with a sigh as she took it.

'We do,' Frances said with her own. 'It was a new bulb too. I only put it in a couple of weeks ago. Blasted thing. Typical that it's the one over the lift.'

'This is new,' Lydia said, inspecting the delicate porcelain cup, which was covered in dainty blue forget-me-knots.

'It is actually very old. Wedding present to my parents from the well-heeled side of the family. I decided it was no use to man nor beast sitting in a cupboard,' Frances explained. She took a sip of tea and smiled. 'It's worth quite a bit, apparently. Some collector chap made me a ridiculous offer, but I said no. What do I need money for at my age,' she added with a derisive wave of her hand.

Rose made a noise that was somewhere between a cough and a gulp. Lydia looked up to see her lower her cup to the saucer with trembling hands. Lydia gripped the handle of her own cup more firmly, too.

Frances rolled her eyes but pursed her lips, clearly deciding to keep her thoughts to herself. After a moment, she turned to Lydia and said, 'I think we will all rest a little easier once this move is out of the way.'

'We've just had a bad run of it lately,' Lydia said, regretting the words as soon as they were out of her mouth. They'd lost three libraries and their keepers in the last eight years, and the attack at Winchester a few years ago had left the apprentice and a visiting Elder dead too. And that was just the UK. The Barcelona attack had been only weeks ago. It had come just hours after the relocation. The keeper, Yolande, had returned to search for a book missing from the inventory and walked straight into the enraged hunters. Everyone was on edge, which was why the decision to move the Aberystwyth library was expedited.

The crime scene images flashed unbidden into Lydia's mind, and she took a gulp of her tea. She understood why the Elders felt it necessary to share them with the other keepers.

The Elders were resolute in their commitment to make sure that all keepers and apprentices knew the risks they were facing, but Lydia knew those pictures would haunt her for the rest of her life. That Maggie had to read those reports too made her sick to her stomach. God knows what it had done to Rose's already delicate disposition.

As if reading her mind, Frances said solemnly, 'What has been seen can never be unseen.'

After a moment's silence, Frances spoke again. 'But that we stand as witnesses to our fallen colleagues is no small thing. I find some comfort in that. And who knows, maybe in some other version of what we call reality they are still alive and well.'

Lydia frowned, the question forming in her mind, but before she could ask it, Frances pressed on.

'And we must always count our blessings,' she said. 'Our intelligence people helped to foil the attack on York, and we moved every book in that collection before they tried again. The Barcelona library survives, even if poor Yolande does not.'

Lydia nodded, remembering the week she'd spent in the York library last year, helping with the re-cataloguing. It had been a far more sombre affair, as unlike the Aberystwyth library, which was simply being moved to a more secure location, the removal of the books from York had closed the library for good, ending an institution that had given refuge to magical texts for over two hundred years. Helena, the keeper, had taken early retirement. Nobody could blame her. They'd all thought about it, hadn't they? The risks seemed to be escalating, and without enough experienced keepers to go around or apprentices ready to step up, there had been no other choice.

'Are you going to ask the Elders to top up the wards?' Lydia asked, shifting in her seat.

Frances considered for a moment, 'In theory, they should hold for another couple of days, but yes, I was planning on calling Seren in the morning. I didn't take to the witch they sent last time. There was something about her that didn't sit well at the time, and now—' Frances took a deep breath and turned her head to scan the vast space. She stopped when her gaze fell on Rose and changed tack. 'I'll call her in the morning,' she said, with a lightness in her tone that didn't quite match the tension around her eyes.

Lydia took another gulp of her tea, her mouth suddenly dry. It wasn't like Frances to get spooked by anything.

'While we're on the subject of York,' Frances said, now clearly on a mission to lighten the mood, 'the whole incident led to the discovery of the anomaly, and that is something we can all be thankful for, especially you, Lydia dear. Tell Rose about it.'

All keepers and apprentices knew about the anomaly. Aside from the raids, it had been the biggest news in their tiny, secret community for decades, but Lydia obliged, sensing Frances's need to move the subject away from the wards protecting them.

'Apparently, my library doesn't show up when people use magic to locate the libraries, even though we have records that clearly show that it has been a site of significant magical activity for hundreds, if not thousands of years.'

Rose smiled and nodded politely.

'For once, the boffins and magical folk are all united in their bemusement. Hence the anomaly.' Lydia mimed air quotes around the last word, pressing on just because talking about the phenomenon that kept her family and library safe was a comfort.

'Can you remind me how they search?' Rose asked, clearly playing along with the distraction.

'Excellent question, Rose,' Frances replied, a little too heartily.

Ceding the floor to Frances with a wave, Lydia reached for a biscuit.

'Dowsing, scrying, et cetera, on the magical side of things, and on the science side, we've heard rumours that those government boffins have gadgets that detect energy fluctuations which I suppose might be a bit like radar. Don't ask me for the frequencies, as I don't have time to look it up, but for some reason, Lydia's library is hidden. We're hoping that this anomaly means it's safe from the magic hunters,' Frances said.

'Ah, yes, I remember the story now,' Rose mumbled. 'Wasn't it an—'

Frances blustered on and Rose sank back in her chair. Maybe Rose's lack of gumption was just an inability to compete with the excessive quantities that Frances seemed to possess, Lydia thought. The notion cheered her.

'Moving York was a massive undertaking, and we were a few keepers down. What's-her-name from the Harrow library had flu, and the one from St Ives, I can never remember her name, well she was still on crutches or something similar. We were in a pickle, so the Elders asked Sylvie from the Toulouse library to help. She came over with her witch friend – what was her name, Lydia?'

'Camille?' Lydia offered, feeling almost sure that hadn't been the witch's name.

Frances shrugged. 'Anyway, the important part was that this witch, let's call her Camille for the sake of argument, brought her apprentice. Before they arrived, Valérie, the apprentice witch – we all remember *her* name – was tasked with scrying for and then drawing a map of the magical libraries of the UK. All very basic, first-degree stuff for a witch.'

Rose smiled patiently. Lydia wondered how many times she'd sat through this story. Bless her heart, she was such a pretty young thing when she smiled, and yet something told Lydia that Rose had had little reason to over the years.

'When Valérie presented her list, Camille, who had been to the UK many times, told her she'd missed one. They got other witches to check, and they couldn't find it either. She reported it to the Elders, and, well, the rest is history.'

'So, we have an apprentice to thank for finding the anomaly,' Frances said, tapping the table with her finger to emphasise her point.

'But an apprentice witch, not just a keeper,' Rose said with a shrug.

'Did I hear Frances mention earlier that you made the biscuits yourself, Rose?' Lydia asked, not wanting to get drawn into a discussion about the role of keepers. It was natural to look at witches and envy them their magic. She'd been through it herself when she was a girl and she'd seen the signs in Maggie, too, even though her daughter thought she was hiding it well.

Lydia had learned that magic was both a blessing and a curse and had decided at an early age that she was happy with the lot she'd drawn. Rose would learn that in time, as would Maggie.

Rose's head snapped up.

'I did, yes. Not really my forte, cooking, but they don't taste too bad. They're quite dry, maybe, but okay with a cup of tea,' she said, colour creeping into her cheeks.

'Nonsense. They're delicious, Rose,' Frances said, reaching for a second. 'Have some faith in yourself, dear girl.'

While Lydia thought Frances was being generous about the biscuits, Rose was right in that they were fine dunked in tea, and seeing as they'd all missed their lunch again, any food was better than none. Glancing at her watch, she realised it was already gone seven o'clock. They had promised each other they'd call it a day by six at the very latest, so that they had a fighting chance of getting a meal somewhere this evening, so they were way behind schedule. They'd resigned themselves to a bag of chips each last night, arriving at the chippy too late even for a portion of fish. After the conversation about the wards, however, Lydia could do with getting out of here sooner. She'd give it another half an hour and then suggest that they pack up by eight.

'So, tell me, Rose, have you uncovered anything new in the archives?' Frances asked.

'Well, actually, yes,' Rose said, her expression visibly brightening as it always did when the conversation moved on to matters of magical research. 'I found a very interesting spell. The date's hard to decipher, but I'd say we're looking at the sixteen hundreds, based on the paper and overall condition. It's a safe harbour spell and allows a witch to send her magic to another witch for safekeeping. They're used only when witches are in mortal danger.'

'Gosh. You don't see those often,' Frances said, leaning forward in her chair, her interest clearly piqued. 'Rare as hen's teeth. I don't think I've ever seen one. And it was here, in the archive?'

Rose nodded. Frances scowled, clearly annoyed with herself for missing it.

'From what I've read, they're very tricky to get right. Plus, it appears that this one had a whopper of a mistake in it,' Rose said, her eyes wide and the hint of a smile at the corners of her lips.

'Oh?' Lydia said, intrigued. 'What sort of mistake?'

'Well, it looks like a mistake to me. I mean, I'm no expert, but it's probably easiest for me to show you.'

Rose jumped up and, after mumbling something Lydia

didn't catch, disappeared towards the stacks. Lydia bit her lip. If this was going to be a lengthy explanation, their chances of getting out of here anytime soon were dwindling. That said, a new find in an archive was like catnip to a keeper.

When Lydia looked at Frances, the faint smile on her lips was rueful. 'It's nice to see the light in her eyes, and nothing lights her up like research,' Frances said quietly.

Lydia nodded. 'You're doing a good job with her, you know,' she whispered. 'I have a feeling she'll do great things.'

'I hope so,' Frances replied softly, but her expression suggested that she was far from certain.

CONTINUE READING THE **THE MAGIC KEEPERS**

AVAILABLE FROM

WWW.ELWILLIAMSAUTHOR.COM

AND ALL GOOD BOOK RETAILERS

ABOUT THE AUTHOR

E. L. Williams grew up in the Welsh Valleys in a tiny house overflowing with books and stories of magic.

Emma is the author of the *Ethereal World* fantasy series — a duology (**The First Ethereal** and **The Blessing of Crows**) and two standalone novels set in the same magical world hidden within our own: **The Magic Keepers** and **The Butterfly Witch.**

When she's not writing, she's usually reading, gardening, torturing her cello, or sneaking yet another houseplant into the home she shares with her endlessly patient husband.

Thank you for reading The Butterfly Witch.
If you enjoyed it, please help other readers find it by leaving a review.

ARE YOU READY FOR MORE MAGIC IN YOUR LIFE?

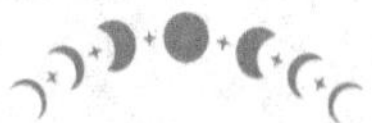

If you enjoyed stepping into the Ethereal World, there's so much more waiting for you.

Head to **www.elwilliamsauthor.com** to join my free **Readers' Club** and receive an Ethereal World short story as a thank you. You'll be first to hear about new releases, get behind-the-scenes updates and enjoy exclusive content.

LET'S STAY CONNECTED

Find me **@elwilliamsauthor** on Instagram, TikTok, and Facebook for daily bookish chat, writing adventures, and the occasional dog photo. I love a natter so please drop by and say hello.

ACKNOWLEDGMENTS

My first and biggest thank you is to everyone who's joined me so far in the Ethereal World. Whether you've bought or borrowed a book, left a rating or review, joined the Reader's Club, chatted with me at an event, or said something kind on social media – your support is the magic that keeps these stories alive.

Had someone told me five years ago, as I nervously prepared to publish my first book, that I'd go on to write three more, I'd have laughed like a drain. But here I am, hopelessly addicted to making up stories, and it's all thanks to lovely readers like you.

Heartfelt thanks to my brilliant editor, Toby Selwyn, whose sharp eye and kind heart continue to help me grow as a writer, and to the ever-talented Faera Lane for the stunning cover design. And, of course, to my wonderful husband, Stuart: thank you for being my sounding board, alpha reader, beta reader, tea-bringer, and number-one cheerleader. I truly couldn't do this without you.

With all my love and gratitude,

Emma x